THE LAST
OUTLAW

ROSANNE
BITTNER

sourcebooks
casablanca

Published by Sourcebooks Casablanca, an imprint of Sourcebooks, Inc.
P.O. Box 4410, Naperville, Illinois 60567-4410
(630) 961-3900
Fax: (630) 961-2168
www.sourcebooks.com

Printed and bound in Canada.
MBP 10 9 8 7 6 5 4 3 2 1

*Dedicated to the best, most supportive writers'
group around—Mid-Michigan Romance Writers
of America. Check out their website.*

*Wonderful writers—good friends—sponsors
of a wonderful "Retreat from Harsh Reality"
every spring here in Michigan.*

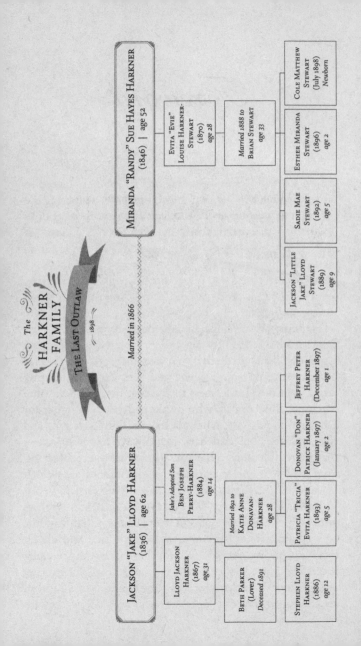

The
HARKNER
FAMILY

THE LAST OUTLAW
1898

Married in 1866

JACKSON "JAKE" LLOYD HARKNER
(1836) | age 62

MIRANDA "RANDY" SUE HAYES HARKNER
(1846) | age 52

Jake's Adopted Son
BEN JOSEPH PERRY-HARKNER
(1884)
age 14

LLOYD JACKSON HARKNER
(1867)
age 31

EVITA "EVIE" LOUISE HARKNER-STEWART
(1870)
age 28

Married 1888 to BRIAN STEWART
age 33

BETH PARKER
(Lover)
Deceased 1891

Married 1892 to KATIE ANNE DONAVAN-HARKNER
age 28

STEPHEN LLOYD HARKNER
(1886)
age 12

PATRICIA "TRICIA" EVITA HARKNER
(1893)
age 5

DONOVAN "DON" PATRICK HARKNER
(January 1897)
age 2

JEFFREY PETER HARKNER
(December 1897)
age 1

JACKSON "LITTLE JAKE" LLOYD STEWART
(1889)
age 9

SADIE MAE STEWART
(1892)
age 5

ESTHER MIRANDA STEWART
(1896)
age 2

COLE MATTHEW STEWART
(July 1898)
Newborn

Foreword

When *Outlaw Hearts* was published in 1993, I wanted to write a sequel, but because of circumstances involving the publishing industry, it just didn't happen. Sourcebooks finally gave me the opportunity, and *Do Not Forsake Me* came pouring out of my heart where it had rested for all those twenty-plus years. When I finished that book, I knew I wasn't ready to leave my beloved Jake Harkner, outlaw, lawman, and (in the third book, *Love's Sweet Revenge*) rancher.

His story wasn't finished. Jake needed closure over the fact that he'd killed his own father, the driving emotional force that had affected every decision and reaction in his life—the powerful event that sent him floundering into a world of lawlessness in the first book. Then came Miranda, the woman who awakened Jake's longing for a normal family life. Miranda handed him that gift, and two children, but that dark past always haunted Jake— that incredible abuse that caused him to overprotect his own children and eventually his grandchildren, which led to a near-hanging in *Love's Sweet Revenge*.

In this fourth book, *The Last Outlaw*, Jake still wrestles with his past. The trauma still keeps him on that thin line between sanity and insanity, between peace and chaos, between his incredible love for his family and equally incredible hatred for the man who murdered his mother and brother. I knew Jake had to come to some kind of reckoning to live out his elder years in true peace with the woman he loves beyond words—his rock, his salvation, his hope.

To Jake, Miranda is forever twenty years old, forever beautiful, forever gracious and sophisticated. He will feel forever that she's too good for him. She is the antithesis of all he's been and has stuck by him in spite of all the heartache, all the reckless living, all the running, years in prison, and all the times he tried to leave her because he thought she'd be better off without him.

If this is the first book you pick up in this series, you can certainly read it on its own. But you will want to read Jake's story from book one, *Outlaw Hearts*, through *Do Not Forsake Me* and *Love's Sweet Revenge*. I hope you enjoy the entire series, and I suspect you will have trouble forgetting these characters. They will always live in your heart, representing all the emotions humankind can both suffer—and celebrate.

—Rosanne Bittner

PART ONE

Prologue

THERE WERE NINE OF THEM THAT DAY. ALL HARD MEN, all on a mission. They were dead set on getting rich off of someone else's money—money they would steal from the City Bank in Boulder, Colorado. Their horses panted and snorted from the hard ride, and a mixture of dust and sod rolled from under the horses' hooves.

The riders wore long canvas coats over shirts and jackets in the cool spring weather, and under it all they wore gun belts packed with cartridges. Some held one gun, some two, and everyone carried rifles on their saddles. Some were clean shaven, others were nothing but filth and beards and unwashed hair. All wore wide-brimmed hats against the bright, spring Colorado sun, and all were filled with anticipation for the ways they would spend the money they were going to take today. Women and whiskey—those two came first.

They rode up toward the foothills of the Rockies and right over farmers' fields, avoiding the main roads. They were coming from the Santa Fe Trail in New Mexico, leaving behind robbed stagecoaches and freight wagons. Trains were their specialty, and always they were trying to avoid the Pinkertons, the relentless railroad detectives who hunted them.

Their leader, George Callahan, figured Boulder to be a peaceful, unsuspecting, little-guarded mountain town. They wouldn't be ready for nine men to ride in and take over a bank. They wouldn't be ready for men who didn't care who might get killed in the process. Tomorrow they would ride out of Boulder with a fortune in railroad and mining money, and head for Mexico.

There was only one problem with Callahan's plan. He'd picked the wrong day to rob a bank in Boulder. Neither he nor any of his men knew Jake Harkner happened to be in Boulder, and he would still be there…tomorrow.

One

JAKE TRAILED HIS TONGUE OVER HIS WIFE'S SKIN, trying to ignore his fear that she could be dying. Her belly was too caved-in, her hip bones too prominent.

She'll get better, he told himself. The taste of her most secret place lingered on his lips as he moved to her breasts, still surprisingly full, considering, but not the same breasts he'd always loved and teased her about, with the enticing cleavage that stirred his desire for her.

He would *always* desire her. This was his Randy. She was his breath. Her spirit ran in his veins, and she was his reason for being. God knew his worthless hide had no business even still being on this earth.

He ran a hand over her ribs, which were too damn easy to count. Sometimes he thought he'd go mad with the memory of last winter, the reason she'd become more withdrawn and had nearly stopped eating.

He met her mouth, and she responded. Thank God she still wanted this, but something was missing, and he couldn't put his finger on it. He thought he'd made it all better, thought he'd taken away the ugly. He'd feared at first she might blame him for what had happened, but it had been quite the opposite. She'd become almost too clingy, constantly asking if he loved her, asking him not to let go of her and not to go far away.

He pushed himself inside of her, wanting nothing more than to please her, to find a way to break down the invisible wall he felt between them, to erase the past and assure her he was right here, that he still loved her.

How in hell could he not love this woman, the one who'd loved him when he was anything but lovable...all those years ago. She'd put up with his past and his bouts of insanity and all the trouble and heartache he'd put her through...this woman who'd given him a son and daughter, who couldn't make a man prouder, and who loved him beyond what he was worth. She'd given him six grandchildren who climbed all over him, full of such innocent love for a man who'd robbed and killed, and worst of all...killed his own father.

He moved his hands under her bottom, pushing himself deep inside her, relishing the way she returned his deep kisses and pressed her fingers into his upper arms in an almost desperate neediness.

That was what bothered him. This had always been good between them, a true mating of souls, teasing remarks back and forth as they made love. But now it was as though she feared losing him if she didn't make love often, and that wasn't the sort of man he was. It had always been pure pleasure between them. He'd taught her things she would never have thought of, helped her relax and release every sexual inhibition. He knew every inch of her body intimately, and she'd loved it.

This was different. And it was harder now, because not only did he hate the idea of feeling like he was forcing her, but he was also terrified he would break something. She was so thin and small now. He outweighed her by a good hundred and fifty pounds by now; she couldn't weigh more than eighty or ninety.

He surged deep in a desperate attempt to convince himself he wasn't losing her. And through it all, he was screaming inside. Sometimes he wanted to shake her and make her tell him what else he could do to bring back the woman he'd known and loved for nearly thirty-two years. He missed that feisty, bossy woman, the only person on this earth who could bring him to his knees.

He'd faced the worst of men as a lawman in Oklahoma, and run with the worst of men the first thirty years of his life. He'd spent four years in prison under horrible conditions. He'd been in too many gunfights to count, taken enough bullets that he had no right still being alive. He'd ridden the Outlaw Trail and defied all the odds. His reputation followed him everywhere, and a reporter had even written a book about him—*Jake Harkner: The Legend and the Myth. Myth* was more like it. And the legend wasn't one he was proud of.

And this woman beneath him…this woman he poured his life into this very moment…she'd been there for most of it.

He relaxed and moved to her side.

"Don't let go yet, Jake."

He pulled her against him. "Randy, I can't put my weight on you anymore. You're too damn thin. You've got to gain some weight back or we'll have to stop."

"No!" She shimmied closer, pulling one of his arms around her. "I like being right here in your arms. Don't stop making love to me, Jake. You might turn to someone else. You're still my handsome, strong Jake. Women look at you and want you."

Jake sighed, the stress of her condition making him want to tear the room apart. "You have to stop talking that way."

"That you're handsome and strong?" She turned slightly. "Since when does the magnificent Jake Harkner hate compliments?"

There it was—a tiny spark of the old Randy in her teasing. Every time he saw that spark it gave him hope. "I've always hated compliments. You know that. The only thing magnificent about me is my sordid reputation. I'd like to wring Treena Brown's neck for putting that label on me in her letter."

Randy traced her fingers over his lips. "Peter's wife

was totally taken by you when they visited the ranch last summer."

"She's a city woman full of wrong ideas about what she considers western heroes. God knows I'm sure as hell *not* one, and right now your magnificent Jake needs a cigarette." Jake pulled away and sat up. "You okay?"

"Of course I'm okay. You just made love to me. How could a woman not be okay after that?"

Jake took a Lone Jack from a tin on the hotel's bedside table. "You know what I mean." She didn't answer as he lit the cigarette. He took a long drag. "Did I hurt you?"

"Of course not."

Jake ran a hand through his hair. "Randy, I mean it about your weight. If you don't start eating, I'm not making love to you anymore. Sometimes when I'm on top of you I envision every rib breaking. We made this trip to Boulder because it was time you started getting away from the ranch, doing a few things amid strangers without being glued to me."

Be patient. Don't yell at her. She might go to pieces.

He heard a sniffle, and it felt like his heart was breaking. He took another long drag before setting the cigarette in an ashtray and turned, moving back in beside her. "Baby, I've done everything I can to help you. When you're like this, it makes me sick with guilt. I should have realized what was happening when that barn caught on fire…the way it burned so rapidly. Lloyd suffers with the same guilt. We shouldn't have left the house unguarded."

"No! No! No!" Randy threw her arms around him. "Don't ever blame yourself. You blame yourself for *everything* bad that happens to this family, but you never asked for any of it, Jake."

He held her close, being careful not to use too much strength. "Randy, I want my wife back. The woman I'm holding right now isn't her."

"I will be. I promise. Tomorrow, Teresa and little Tricia and I will go shopping. I won't be quite so terrified without you at my side if I at least have Teresa with me. Thank you for bringing her along."

Jake was grateful for the Mexican woman who was such a help with the cooking as well as cleaning the big log home he'd built for Randy. It was still filled with noise at meals, some of the grandchildren or all of the family gathering, especially for Sunday meals. Before last winter, Randy had been a vital part of those gatherings—the one most in control, who loved all the cooking, who loved teaching and reading with Evie and the grandchildren. Living on a remote ranch meant no schools nearby, after all.

Randy now left it all to Evie. She was no longer her joyful self at the dinner table, although she put on a good show. He knew her every mood, and he could tell she was still suffering inside.

"Tell me what you need, Randy. How else can I help? You aren't here with me when we make love anymore. I can sense it in your kisses, in the way you respond when I'm inside you. I won't make love to a woman who's doing it out of duty."

She buried her face in his neck. "Jake, I still love it when you make love to me. It's just…" She hesitated again. How many times had he come close to getting out of her what was really bothering her?

"Just what? *Talk* to me, Randy."

She curled into a little ball against him. "That…ugly thing they did. That ugly thing. I can't…get past it. I'm so sorry, Jake."

Jake struggled against insane rage every time he thought about it. His precious Randy. Of all the intimate things he and his wife had done, asking her to perform oral sex on him had never been one of them. She'd never suggested such a thing or made an attempt, and he'd never asked. What they had together was enough for him. His first desire was always to give her pleasure, and that alone gave him pleasure in return. It would be disrespectful to ask this beautiful woman to do something he knew in his gut she wouldn't want to do. He still had the blazing memory of his father forcing himself on his mother that way right in front of her sons while she resisted. Sometimes, such childhood memories still made him wake up with screaming nightmares.

It all came down to his father…his ruthless, brutal, drunken father…the man he hated worse than all the dredges of humankind, more than the filth he used to run with when he believed he was the worthless sonofabitch his father had always told him he was.

"Don't be sorry." *God help keep me sane.* "We'll work it out."

"Don't stop making love to me."

"I won't stop."

"You do still love me, don't you?"

"Stop asking me that. You know better." He wiped at her tears with his fingers. "Get some sleep, Randy. Tomorrow is a big day."

"You won't ever be too far away, will you, even when I leave you to shop?"

"I won't be too far away."

"You'll watch for me?"

"You know I will." He'd never felt so alone. Ever since he'd found and fallen in love with this woman, he'd always had her to lean on, to keep him from the abyss of blackness that beckoned. Tough and able as he seemed to others, *she* was his strength. And now that strength was gone. The tables had turned, and he had to be strong for her. He secretly begged God to help him remember that. He wasn't sure he had it in him to last much longer this way. "Randy, when you figure out what more I can do, or what it is that will help you get

better, you tell me. Don't ever be afraid to tell me—
anything—all right? You know I've seen it all and done
it all and nothing surprises me. And I love you. I'll do
whatever it takes. Understand?"

"Yes."

"I can tell right now you're keeping something from
me—something more than what happened last winter.
You tell me when you're ready."

She clung closer, kissing his chest. "I will."

He kept his arms around her because she demanded it,
every night until she fell asleep. He closed his eyes against
his own silent tears. Without that closeness they'd always
shared, it was as though he didn't even exist. Without
this woman, who was Jake Harkner?

Two

"*Buenos días, señor!*"

"*Buenos días*, Sonoma!"

"And what is *Señor* Harkner having today?"

Jake stepped up to the long, varnished oak bar in the Silver Saddle Saloon. "Just a beer. You know I never go much further than that, Sonoma."

"*Sí.*" The young Mexican waitress began filling a mug for Jake, eyeing him as she did so and wondering if men came any more handsome than Harkner. He commanded attention when he walked inside a room, his six-foot-four frame and dark reputation making others turn and look without saying a word. He was Jake Harkner, after all, and everyone knew about his past…and the way he could use those guns he wore.

It always excited Sonoma on the rare occasions Harkner came into the saloon. She liked to fantasize about him taking her upstairs, but rumor had it that, unlike some of the other married men who came in here, he was totally devoted to his wife. Jake was half Mexican himself, and she liked that she could speak to him in Spanish. And those eyes—he had a way of making a woman feel beautiful just by the way he looked and smiled at her. His son was even more handsome, but equally unavailable. "And how is the handsome outlaw today?"

Jake dropped enough money on the bar to pay for the beer and leave a generous tip. "Sonoma, I haven't been an outlaw for years, and I'm getting too old to be called handsome."

"Ah, *señor*, some men get better with age, and you are one of them." She set a mug of beer in front of him and smiled her best smile. "I am guessing your wife is still very pleased with you." She came from behind the bar and sauntered closer, leaning over enough to expose ample cleavage. "I know I would be."

Jake took a swallow of the beer. "Sonoma, you're a beautiful young woman, but no thanks."

Sonoma smiled with pride and pleasure.

Jake turned away to take a seat at an empty table. He noticed the saloon was more crowded than usual due to businesses being closed for a spring flower show. It was part of the reason Randy had chosen today to come to Boulder and shop for a few needed items. They didn't come into town often, because of the nearly three days it took to get here, let alone the fact that Randy no longer cared for being out and about among strangers. Even so, he resolved to bring her more often this year. She needed the diversion, something exciting to help keep her from sitting around thinking about her ordeal.

A few local businessmen and a couple of ranchers sat at a nearby table, all of them eyeing Jake. Some looked with curiosity, some in genuine friendship, and a couple of them with outright animosity—including Brady Fillmore. Fillmore was a big bully of a man whose ranch was located at the southwest corner of the J&L, the sprawling, nearly eighty-thousand-acre ranch Jake shared with his son Lloyd.

Jake suspected Brady of stealing calves during spring roundup time, and once he and a couple of the other ranch hands had caught the man with a rope around a J&L steer. Brady had claimed it had wandered onto his farm and he was just returning it, but Jake hadn't believed a word.

Brady eyed him now, and Jake could tell from his look he was already drunk. "Just one beer?" Brady asked with a grin. "Doesn't the famous outlaw get drunk once in a while?"

Jake didn't answer right away, reminding himself to keep his temper. He was still under scrutiny by a judge in Denver, thanks to nearly getting himself hanged last summer. Trouble was, Jake had no respect for Brady Fillmore. The man had done a little less every year and had taken to gambling, even losing some of his horses and cattle to others to pay gambling debts. And now he was going broke and obviously wanted to "borrow" more than a tool or a wagon from his "friendly neighbors."

"The little wife give you orders not to get drunk, Jake?" Brady goaded. "What's wrong with her, anyway? She acted awful strange at the big spring cookout at the Holmeses' farm. Acts like she's scared of everybody. You beat her or somethin'? Tell her she couldn't look at other men?"

Jake took another swallow of beer, putting his foot up on a nearby chair and eyeing Fillmore with disgust. "What my 'little wife' says or does is none of your god-damn business, Brady. And what are you doing drinking and gambling in town? Shouldn't you be tending your ranch? It's time for roundup and branding. Your family has to eat, and you're sitting here losing more money."

"The wife and kid can handle things."

"Branding *cattle*? That's hardly a woman's job," Jake sneered. "Or have you already lost most of your herd to gambling debts? Maybe you aren't man enough to take care of what needs taking care of."

Some of the men at the table scooted their chairs back, eyeing Jake warily.

"And how come *you* ain't helpin' out at your own ranch?" Brady asked.

"My son runs the J&L now. It's more his than mine anyway. And we have plenty of good men, who we can afford because we do our job right. And we sure as hell don't leave it to *women*."

Brady threw in three cards and faced Jake squarely. "*Your* woman wouldn't be any good for it anyway. My wife says she's gotten so thin a good windstorm would blow her away. What happened to her, Jake? She all wore out from puttin' up with her sonofabitch husband all these years? Ain't she ten years younger than you? You makin' an old woman out of her?"

"Shut up, Brady!" The local barber sitting at the card table grumbled the words. "A man's wife ain't none of your business."

Other men inside the saloon stopped their drinking and cards to watch, all of them not sure what would happen. No man in his right mind goaded Jake Harkner. If looks could kill, Brady would be long dead.

Brady feigned an unafraid grin and turned away. Jake stood up, and the room quieted even more.

"Somebody go get the sheriff," one man muttered.

"Leave it be," another named Till Medley answered.

Jake walked over to Brady and braced his hand on the card table at the man's side, leaning close behind him. "One more word about my wife, and I'll shove those cards up your asshole, Brady. And I'll use the barrel of one of my guns to make sure they're in there nice and *tight*. These guns have hair triggers. I'd hate to see what would happen if the damn thing went off while it was shoved up inside you. I've put a gun in a man's mouth and fired it, but up his ass would be something new for me."

"You cocky sonofabitch," Brady grumbled, still feigning bravery. He didn't make a move.

"And don't be coming around my ranch again, begging for tools or any other supplies. I've got no respect for a man who doesn't take care of his own. And I'd better never catch you stealing J&L cattle again either, or my son and I will *hang* you! Understood?"

Brady glanced at the other men. "You hear that? This

sonofabitch ain't no *reformed* outlaw. He *is* an outlaw. The real man inside don't never change."

"Another word about my saint of a wife, and you'll find out how right you are," Jake told him, straightening.

Brady slowly rose from his chair and turned to face Jake. He was a big, burly man, but not quite as tall as Jake. "*Saint?* She married an *outlaw*!"

In an instant, Jake grabbed the man around the neck and shoved him back into his chair, then slammed his head down on the card table, breaking his nose. The rest of the men quickly got up and out of the way. Jake grabbed Brady's collar and jerked him back to his feet, pushing him hard against the wall. Brady's face landed sideways, revealing blood fanning from his nose.

"You have no idea how lucky you are to be *alive*!" Jake growled. "If I ever hear you saying anything more about my wife, or if I catch J&L cattle on your ranch, you'll be hanged from the nearest tree, Brady. I'll find ways to make you suffer *before* I put a noose around your neck!"

Jake let go of the man, and Brady straightened, raising his chin and wincing as he put his arm up to catch the blood pouring from his nose. "I ain't afraid of you, Harkner. I ain't armed, so you can't use them guns of yours. Besides that, you're old enough to be my father," he sneered. "I ain't worried about gettin' in a fight with you, if that's what you're after."

Jake stepped closer. "*Be* worried! Who's the one standing here with a bloody nose?"

"Jesus, Brady, are you stupid or what?" The local pharmacist, Bill Tucker, had asked the question. "Get the hell out of here and let the man drink his beer. You've already lost most of your money anyway."

Jake stepped back, fists clenched. Brady took a stance as though to fight him, then backed off. Jake could see the fear in his eyes. He dearly wanted to beat the man into the floor cracks for what he'd said about Randy.

God, how he hated all the new laws that kept a man from dealing his own justice.

"Go on. Get out," the bar owner, Clete Russell, told Brady.

After glaring at Jake a moment longer, Brady suddenly looked almost ready to cry. "I'll leave," he finally said, "but only because I don't want to break up your saloon, Clete."

"This place will be just *fine*, Clete," Jake roared. "Nothing gets broken when all you have to do is pick a man up and throw him out into the street, except maybe a few of that man's *bones*!"

Brady looked at Jake. "I'm complaining to the Cattlemen's Association about the J&L," he warned. "Us ranchers ought to help one another out, and you won't even share a little meat."

"You're no goddamn rancher, and by sharing meat, you mean rustling my cattle! You go right ahead and *complain*, Brady! The Cattlemen's Association has asked me more than once to be range detective. Maybe I'll take the job. I could keep a lot better eye on *your* place and make sure you don't steal some of our grassland or water. If they found out I'd already caught you leading one of my steers to your place, I wouldn't have to hang you myself. They would do it *for* me!"

"Haven't you heard what happened to seven cattle thieves on Harkner land last year?" Sonoma asked Fillmore, swaying her hips as she stepped from behind the bar. "You don't mess with the Harkners, especially not this one." She looked Jake over seductively, but his attention was fully on Fillmore.

"They tried to steal Harkner cattle and soon regretted it," Bill Tucker explained. "If I was you, I'd get the hell out of here. The last man that messed with Jake got his head blown off last summer in Denver."

Brady Fillmore gave Jake one more dark look, feigning a brave challenge. "You're a fucking murderer, that's what you are! You killed your own pa!" He quickly left after his last remark.

The room hung quiet for several seconds before Jake finally glanced at the men who still stood around the card table. "You know, boys, I just came in here to have a beer while my wife does some shopping. Damned if I don't always run into trouble without asking for it."

A few laughed nervously.

"No problem, Jake." Till Medley pushed Brady's chair away from the table with his foot. "Have a seat. We're all proud to know you—and to take your money in a card game."

More men laughed, and most returned to their chairs as Jake sat down. "I don't have time to get into a game, but thanks for the offer." He leaned back and took his beer from where he'd set it on another table. "And that thing in Denver...that was a bad situation. My son had been shot point-blank, and I thought he was dead. The man I killed deserved what he got. My son wasn't even armed."

"Oh, we all followed that story closely. Nobody at this table blames you for what you did, although it's not exactly something the average man would do."

"Yeah, well, most people say I'm not your average man."

The other men laughed again, still obviously nervous.

"There's an understatement," Bill Tucker commented.

Till Medley dealt out more cards. "Jake, before you came in here, me and some of the others were wondering if you'd be interested in a little shooting contest we're planning for the big fund-raiser in a couple of weeks. We heard you were in town, and one of us was going to look you up."

Jake glanced at the doorway where Brady had gone out. He was worried Randy might run into the man, and he'd say something hurtful to her. "No thanks." He finally faced Till Medley. "I appreciate the invite and your intentions, but I don't get into things like that. Believe me, it only brings trouble, and that statement is from experience. And I sure as hell don't need any more trouble."

"Oh, it will be well managed. Hell, you're famous now, Jake. You'd be quite an attraction. The money is for a good cause, you know—the modernization of Boulder. Bring in famous speakers, actors, singers—real culture."

Jake slugged down his beer, suddenly anxious to find Randy. "Thanks for the offer and the compliments...or at least I think that's what you meant."

The card players all laughed again. "Yes, that's what we meant," Medley told him.

Jake set down the empty beer mug. "Yeah, well, I don't think watching an ageing ex-outlaw shoot off his guns has much to do with culture. I've never been one to be linked to modernization to begin with." He rose. "I'm old school, boys. Still getting used to electricity and to seeing those damn motorized buggies running around town. Things are changing, and there's not a lot of room for men like me. I'll stick to the peaceful life on the J&L."

"Can't blame you for wanting some peace after all you've been through," Clete said from behind the bar. "It's the women who always want opera houses and schools and churches and such."

Jake thought about Randy, how she'd educated their son and daughter, insisting they know big words and history and things he didn't care much about. "I suppose."

"Jake, you can't blame us for asking," Medley offered.

"I appreciate it." He adjusted his jacket. "Sorry about that little skirmish, but Brady Fillmore rubs me the wrong way. I don't normally even drink, but there are times when a man just needs a beer."

"Ain't *that* the truth?" Clete answered.

"Yeah, well right now my wife is probably looking for

me, and I don't want her coming in here, so I'd better go." Jake tipped his hat to Clete. "Thanks for speaking up for me and chasing Brady out of here. I was about ready to get myself in hot water all over again."

"No problem, Jake," Clete answered, smiling. He walked closer and put out his hand. Jake ended up shaking hands all around the table.

"Any chance we could at least have a look at those famous guns?" Till Medley asked.

Jake grinned. "Sorry, boys. I wouldn't want someone to get hurt." He gave Sonoma a smile before he took a couple of long strides through the saloon's swinging doors and stepped onto the boardwalk and into the chilly air. It should have been warmer than this in June, but sometimes the wind swept down from the snow-capped Rockies in the wrong way and brought cold with it.

Back inside the saloon, everyone looked at one another, all thinking the same thing.

"Remind me not to rub that man the wrong way," Tucker voiced aloud.

Another round of laughter followed.

"Shit, the man is as fast with his temper as he is with his guns," Clete commented.

"Yeah, I was a little worried for a minute he'd just take those guns out and shoot the hell out of Fillmore," another joked.

"You can see it in his eyes," Clete commented. "He's an amiable man, but don't cross him. God knows what all he's done no one knows about—things that weren't in that book, and things he'll never tell."

"Any man who can hold a gun to a man's forehead and pull the trigger point-blank has to have a special darkness inside," Till said quietly.

"Killed his own father," Tucker added. "According to the book, his childhood was a nightmare. It's a wonder he's even in his right mind."

"Yeah, well, the look in his eyes when he shoved Brady Fillmore's head to the table *wasn't* sane," Clete told them. "A man would be best not to insult Jake Harkner's wife."

"I feel sorry for him," Sonoma told them as she brought them fresh beers.

"You just want to sleep with him," Clete told her. He took the beers from the tray and set them out for the card players, who all snickered.

"I don't care what you think," Sonoma told them, pouting. "He is a nice man. Maybe things just happened he couldn't help. That man in Denver, he was one of those who raped his daughter. That same man showed up at that cattlemen's ball and shot Jake's son. Jake was only defending his family that night. The judge believed him."

"Yeah, well, they say he had the man down and could have waited for the police. But he held a gun to his head and pulled the trigger anyway. That's more than defending your family."

Sonoma set the tray aside. "People say he and his son are very, very close. You have a son, Bill Tucker. What would you do if someone shot him right in front of your eyes? I think you would want to kill him, no?"

Tucker lit a cigar. "I would want to kill him—yes."

"Get back to work, Sonoma," Clete told her.

The woman sauntered away, and every man there watched her walk. They looked at one another and grinned.

"Ole Jake could have a good lay today if he wanted," one of the others joked.

They laughed again as Tucker dealt a new hand.

"He has a beautiful wife," Till commented. "Just beautiful. If I had a wife who looked like her, I wouldn't need any whore on the side."

"I think he is a bad man with a good heart," Sonoma called to them from behind the bar.

"*Is* there such a thing?" Clete quipped as he carried the tray of empty glasses back to the bar.

"*I* think so." Sonoma glanced toward the doorway. "And his name is Jake Harkner."

Three

JAKE LIT A CIGARETTE AND STEPPED FARTHER OUT INTO the street. A motorized buggy passed by, startling two nearby horses. They whinnied and pulled at the reins that held them to hitching posts. The buggy suddenly backfired, and one of the horses screamed and reared up, tearing completely away from the hitching post. The animal ran off, spooking another horse, which reared and nearly tossed its rider. The rider cursed at the driver of the motorized buggy and told him to "get that thing out of here!"

Jake just shook his head. Things had changed dramatically since his younger days. And through all the changes in a growing West, and what he and Randy had been through, the love they shared had never changed... until now.

He wished he could kill Brad Buckley over and over again for what he'd done to Randy. He'd like to see the man come back to life in screaming pain, his privates still blown off, and then he could torture and kill the man on a daily basis, just for the satisfaction of seeing him beg.

He looked around for Randy, always worried if she was all right. He'd urged her to go shopping on her own, without him by her side. Earlier, she'd gone into a hat shop a few doors down with Teresa and their precious little granddaughter, Tricia.

He watched the hat store and saw no sign of them at the moment, but when he looked farther up the street, he spotted something far in the distance that didn't look right. He squinted, adjusting his hat to keep the sun out of his eyes. What he saw was just a cloud of dust, the kind stirred up by stampeding horses or cattle. Some rancher probably bringing in a few steers to sell in town.

He turned his attention back to the hat store and finally spotted Randy coming out with a hatbox in her hand. She looked around anxiously, and it broke his heart to see her almost childish panic. *Damn it, Randy, how can I help you get over this?* People didn't understand why she'd become so skittish, or why she hated letting him out of her sight. No one knew about last winter… or the men who'd died for what they'd done. No one would *ever* know. Brad Buckley and those with him had simply disappeared from the face of the earth, and Jake took great pleasure in picturing them screaming from pain as they lived in the tortures of hell.

He stepped farther into the street so Randy could see him. Teresa had hold of Tricia's hand. When Randy spotted him, he nodded to her, and she smiled, looking relieved. She hurried down the boardwalk toward where he stood.

Jake stepped back up on the boardwalk and watched her lovingly. Did the woman ever age? Lord knew he'd put her through enough that she damn well had a right to be totally white-haired and shriveled up—yet at fifty-one, she was as pretty and well preserved as any thirty-year-old, but for being so thin. He'd always admired her blond tresses and those mysterious eyes that were sometimes green, sometimes blue, but over the last few months, he'd lived in fear she'd get sick and die. What the hell would he do without her?

"New hat?" he asked when she reached him.

"Yes. You don't care, do you?"

"'Course not."

"I'm going to the bank with Teresa. She has something to take care of there for Rodriguez. Do you care if… I mean… Can I take more money out of our account? I saw a dress I just love, and that fund-raising fair is coming up."

"Take whatever you need," he told her before she finished.

"You'll go to the fair with me, won't you? It's a fund-raiser for that new luxury resort Boulder wants to build—some kind of place for people to come and listen to concerts and readings from the great novelists and noted speakers and such."

Jake took hope in the fact that she wanted to go at all. "I'll go."

"They will even have preachers come. I'll bet Evie would love that. I'd really like to go, but I'd rather you were with me, even if Evie and Katie and everyone else goes too."

Jake smiled, sad inside at the plea in her eyes and the way she nervously rattled on. "I said I'd go, Randy." How many times had he been compelled to remind her he was right here and she was safe, especially nights when she clung to him, insisted that he never leave the house at night, and sleep with his arms around her? "Lloyd is pretty much running things on his own now," he added, "and I'm getting a little old to wrestle down steers. This is our time, remember? I'll do whatever you want to do."

Randy blinked back tears. "I'm sorry, Jake. I know you didn't even want to come into town—"

"Stop," he interrupted. "There's nothing I like more than being with you." He leaned down and kissed her cheek. "Besides, I like it when we get away from the ranch. Tricia can stay with Teresa tonight again so you and I can be alone."

Two women who were walking by had seen the quick kiss and heard his remark. They whispered and reddened as they hurried away. Randy put a hand to the side of her face. "Honestly, Jake, you shouldn't say those things in front of people."

Jake took a cigarette and match from a small pocket inside his jacket. "Hell, it gives them something to talk about." He paused to light the cigarette. "And last night wasn't bad, was it?" He smiled for her.

"Jake!"

"I enjoyed it. Didn't you?"

Randy sobered. "But you were upset with me afterward."

He drew on the cigarette and took it from his lips. "*Concerned*, baby. Not upset. I just want you to be happy." He glanced past her to keep an eye on the street.

"What's wrong, Jake?"

He met Randy's gaze again. "What do you mean?"

"How well do I know you? You look troubled."

He sighed, taking another drag on the cigarette. At the same time, there was hope in that little glimpse at the real Randy—the one who knew him like a book and read his every mood. "Nothing important. I had a few words with Brady Fillmore in the saloon, that's all. He's gone now."

"Oh, that awful man! He'll get himself hanged by the cattlemen someday, that's what."

Jake had to laugh at the flicker of her old spirit. "Wouldn't bother me any."

"What did he do? What did he say?"

Jake smiled and kissed her cheek again. "It doesn't matter. I think he's left town."

Randy handed him the hatbox. "Will you hang on to this?"

He took it from her and set it on a nearby bench. "I'll watch it, but I'm not going to be caught holding that thing."

Randy smiled, grasping his free hand. "You love me, don't you?"

"I've told you a thousand different ways." *Why does*

she always ask that? The old Randy never had to ask. She knew. He squeezed her hand. "It's good to see you walking around town without me."

She grasped his wrist and pressed his hand tighter against her cheek. "I'm trying, Jake."

"I know. Just quit asking if I love you. This is Jake Harkner you're talking to. I loved you the minute I laid eyes on you back in that dry goods store in Kansas, and I've never stopped loving you."

Randy looked around warily, still clinging to his hand. "Did you buy more peppermint? You always have peppermint. What if we decide to…in the morning…you always have peppermint."

"I already bought some. I have a whole bagful in my jacket pocket." He pulled out a brown bag to show her. "See?"

"Can I have a piece now?"

Jake smiled. "Well, we don't want to waste it for all the times we'll need it in the mornings."

"Jake! Honestly!" She smiled. "Just one piece? It makes me feel close to you."

Jake opened the bag and broke off a small piece of peppermint stick. He stuck it between her lips. "Now, go join Teresa at the bank."

Randy blinked back unwanted tears as she took the candy from her lips for a moment. "I'm sorry, Jake. I'm scared all the time, and that's not me. I hate this. And I don't like taking that sleeping potion Brian gives me."

"Our son-in-law is a good doctor, and he loves you like his own mother. He just wants you to be able to sleep, and so do I."

Randy nodded, unable to speak because of more tears that wanted to come. Jake set his cigarette on a railing and grasped her face with both hands. "Randy, you're the bravest woman I've ever known. You'll get over this. And right now you're in Boulder, and it's a peaceful, law-abiding town, which means I'd better not stay too long," he joked. "If anything goes wrong, it's bound to involve me." He kissed her forehead. "Now get going. And go buy that dress you were talking about."

Randy looked up at him with that "help me get over this" look he'd seen far too often.

"Go."

She gave him a weak smile, then put the peppermint back into her mouth and left. Jake watched her walk, hated the way her dress hung a little too loose. He decided he was going to get stricter with her about eating better. Another motorized buggy chugged by.

They had electricity at the ranch now, and in town, more and more men drove things with motors rather than rode horses. In town, people had telephones, and Randy was hoping they could get that, too, at the ranch.

The best thing about change was that finally all the ugly haunts and rotten, leftover enemies from his past were gone...all dead and buried, and that was fine with him. The sickening part was that his own wife had ended up paying some of the price. He watched her walk into the bank, then turned to take another look at the storm of dust in the distance. He squinted, still not quite able to figure out what it was. His concentration was interrupted when four women marched up to him and drew his attention away.

"Mr. Harkner, we have a request!"

Frowning, Jake turned to the women, all dressed very prim and proper, with hair pulled back so tightly he wondered if it hurt. They wore small hats of different designs, gloves on their hands, and long-sleeved dresses with necklines that looked like they might be choking them.

Jake tipped his hat. "Ladies?" He picked up his cigarette from the railing and took another drag. "What can I do for you?"

They looked a bit flustered. Jake knew women well, and he didn't doubt this bunch felt he was the worst sinner who ever walked the face of the earth. They likely saw him as nothing but a gunman who'd been raised by whores. Maybe they thought he still ran with women like that. After all, he was standing in front of a saloon, and everyone in town knew what went on upstairs. He didn't doubt they prayed for his soul in church on Sundays, so what in hell would such women want with the likes of him?

One of the oldest stepped forward, her huge bosom straining at the bodice of her black dress. "Mr. Harkner, we…we need your services."

Jake took another long drag on the cigarette and leaned against a support post, thinking of all the very embarrassing answers he could give to that poorly worded statement. He imagined they felt very nervous standing in front of the saloon, and he knew they didn't even realize the connotations of what they'd said. He forced back an urge to burst out laughing.

"My services? What kind of services would those be?"

"Well, we—"

Laughter came from inside the saloon, and the four women glanced at the doorway and seemed flustered.

Jake tossed his cigarette into the dirt street. "You ladies shouldn't be standing in front of a place like the Silver Saddle." He put his hand to the big woman's waist, and she gasped an "oh my!" as he escorted her and the others farther away to stand before a hardware store. "Now, what can I do for you?"

One of them blushed, and they twittered nervously. Jake braced himself against a wooden railing, watching the women. But now that cloud of dust in the distance was getting closer. He took a quick look and realized it was men on horseback. More of his old senses came alert, outlaw and lawman alike.

"Mr. Harkner, I am Hilda Conklin," the bigger woman told him. "My husband is the minister at the Methodist church a few blocks down. This lady beside me is Betty Stable, a banker's wife. Linda Tackas is a teacher, and Sara Baker, on the end there, is a lawyer's wife."

They smiled, Sara Baker twisting a pair of gloves in her hands. Hilda continued her speech. Jake found himself somewhat distracted by her bosom, wondering if the bodice of her dress might split open at any time. Even the upper sleeves looked stuffed and ready to burst.

"Mr. Harkner, perhaps you have heard about Chautauqua?"

Jake nodded. "I have. Sounds like a rich man's project and not something that interests me."

"Boulder is becoming quite popular for its wonderful weather, and we've become a civilized town, with an opera house and nice restaurants and churches and such. Soon all the streets will be bricked. We've realized we are the perfect place for another Chautauqua. These resorts started in New York State, but have been springing up all over the country, you know."

Jake frowned. "You chasing me out of town because a fellow like me doesn't belong in your fine community?" He leaned closer. "I promise I'm a law-abiding man."

The four women laughed and blushed again.

"Quite the contrary, Mr. Harkner!" Mrs. Conklin fanned herself, her bosom straining at her dress again.

Jake wondered if the woman was deliberately wearing a dress that used to fit her in an effort to convince herself she hadn't gained weight. He gave them one of his best smiles, the one that always undid Randy when he thought there was something to forgive. "What is it you want, ladies?"

"Well, we are having a fund-raising fair in two weeks

and are thinking of activities we could put on to raise as much money as possible. We thought perhaps… Well… Would you be willing to put on some kind of a show?" She glanced at the famous guns he wore low on his hips. "With your guns—either a shooting contest or something to show people how fast you can draw those"—she hesitated, glancing at the guns again and actually backing away, as though they might jump out of their holsters and attack her—"those guns and perhaps shoot bottles off a fence or something like that…something for the men. It's hard to find something at these things that interests the men. These fairs always turn out to be more an event for women, and we thought—"

"No." Jake glanced at the riders again, then turned back to address the women. "Ladies, I appreciate your hard work, and I hope you come up with a lot of ways to raise the money. I'll even help if I can, but I'll not use these guns like a circus act. I've taught my son and grandsons that guns are not entertainment. They're something to be taken very seriously."

"Well, we…we just thought—"

"You thought wrong." Jake tipped his hat. "Please don't be upset. I genuinely understand your intent, ladies. My wife and I will be here one more night—staying at the Gold Dust Hotel. If you come up with some other idea—"

The riders came closer. Jake watched them head toward the bank. "Jesus!" He pushed at the women.

One of them screamed, "What on earth?"

"Get inside the hardware store and stay there! I think the bank's being robbed!"

One of the women gasped and another screamed as they hustled inside.

Jake ran toward the saloon. *Randy!* She couldn't take something like this. She was still too fragile! And little Tricia was with her! He barged into the saloon. "Get the sheriff!" he ordered the card players. "*Now!* I think the bank is being robbed!"

The men looked at one another as Jake ran back outside.

"Sonofabitch!" Till Medley swore. "Harkner's out there! This should be quite a show!"

"Goddamn if we won't get the chance to see Jake Harkner in action!" Bill Tucker exclaimed.

Clete ran out the back door to find the sheriff.

Four

NINE RIDERS CHARGED RECKLESSLY THROUGH THE town, causing people in the streets to dive out of their way. One man jerked his little boy aside just before one of the horses would have trampled the child. The horses' hooves spewed clods of dirt and clouds of dust around them. Jake ran toward them, pulling off his jacket and tossing it down as he hurried to catch up with the riders. Peppermint sticks went flying.

"Everybody get inside!" Jake yelled as he ran, pulling one of his guns. A few women screamed, and several men hesitated, not sure what was happening. Jake noticed a young girl standing transfixed as the men rode by. He grabbed her up and ran with her to the boardwalk, half tossing her to her father. That one move cost him some time, and already five of the riders had dismounted and charged into the bank. The other four remained mounted and ready to ride, holding the horses.

A shot rang out. Jake felt the jolt in his lower left side. People were screaming and running as he went down.

"Shit!" he swore. He rolled behind a watering trough, then got to his knees and shot one man off his horse. He grunted against pain and forced himself to concentrate. The sheriff was running toward the bank, and Jake yelled at the man to stay down.

Another shot rang out, and the sheriff went down. Jake let go of his bleeding side and pulled his other gun out, then charged away from the trough, guns blazing. The three men waiting out front dropped before they even got a chance to fire their weapons again. Their horses scattered, one of them dragging its rider down the street with his foot caught in the stirrup.

Jake stumbled to grab one of the other horses as it ran past him and used it for cover, pulling it to the center of the street. "Come out of there or you're all dead!" he roared.

Everything quieted. Jake quickly put four bullets back in his .44, glad that he'd worn both his guns. He didn't always do so anymore, but he'd packed the second gun on this trip because of Randy and Tricia. Everywhere he went these days, trouble followed. He certainly hadn't asked for it this time. He glanced over at the sheriff, who lay still. "Damn it!" he grumbled.

"Who's out there?" someone yelled from inside.

"Someone who's going to blow your ass away if anybody in that bank gets hurt! Come on out of there!"

"Jake!"

Jake recognized Randy's voice. There followed a ruckus inside—a scream. Furious and desperate, Jake ignored his pain and shoved the horse toward the bank.

"Come out of there now or I'll come in shooting, and you'll wish you'd never picked today to rob a bank!"

Jake heard Tricia start to cry. "Grampa!" she sobbed. The front door of the bank was suddenly thrown open, but no one came out.

"Fill those bags!" a man shouted inside.

"Somebody help the sheriff!" someone yelled from another direction in the street.

"Oh my God, they're robbing the bank!"

"Dear Lord, my wife's in there!" another man shouted. "Susan!"

"Harry!" a woman shouted back, noise coming now from every direction.

One of the women Jake had shoved into the hardware store screamed, "Charlie! Are you in there?" She started to run toward the road, but the other women pulled her back.

"Everybody stay out of the street!" Jake roared.

"Shut up, all of you, or somebody in here will die!" a voice roared from inside the bank.

"Jake Harkner has them pinned down!" another person yelled.

Jake saw a sheriff's deputy running in his direction. "Go around behind the bank!" he yelled to the man.

The deputy hesitated, then ducked into an alley.

"Who's out there!" a man inside yelled.

"Jake Harkner!" Jake called back. "There are innocent people in there! Send them out!"

"Like hell! They're our way out!"

There came more shouts and another scuffle inside. Two shots were fired, and the next scream sounded like Randy.

"Jesus," Jake whispered. Was she hurt?

"Bring back our horses or the women in here are dead!" someone roared. "We already killed a teller for trying to run!"

Jake waved his gun at a young boy standing near two of the horses, motioning for him to bring them over. "A boy's collecting the horses!" he shouted. "Don't shoot! He's just a kid!"

Excited, the boy ran toward Jake with the horses' reins in his hand, and Jake grabbed them. "Get out of here!" he told the boy. "Get behind something!"

The boy ran off, and Jake holstered one gun in order to keep hold of the reins to the two horses, plus the one he'd been using for cover.

"I'm bringing the horses," he yelled again. "There's two left in front of the bank!" He walked them across the road, staying between the horses as he quickly wrapped the reins around a hitching post. He backed away then, putting a hand to the wound in his side. It was only then he realized how badly he was bleeding. There wasn't time to worry about it. His wife and granddaughter were inside that bank. He backed away, wiping blood from his hand onto his pants. He ducked behind a freight wagon sitting on the same side of the street, several feet from the bank.

"You've got your horses! Send the women and child out first and let them get out of the way. Do that and I'll let you ride out of town. But if you hurt any of them in there, you're *dead* men!"

"Jake! We're all right!" It was Randy.

"That really Jake Harkner out there?" a man inside yelled.

"It's me!"

"Sonofabitch!" another man swore. "I think he killed Matt and Billy…and the sonofabitch blew a man's head off last year for hurting his son."

"You bet your ass I did, and you'll all die, too, if you harm those women or that little girl!"

"Grampa!" Tricia cried again.

"You stay still, Button!" Jake yelled back. "You'll be okay."

"I ain't comin' out if it's Harkner out there!" one of the men shouted. "I don't believe you when you say we can ride out!"

"*Believe* it! All you have to do is send out the women and children!"

"You're a lyin' sonofabitch!" a man yelled. "Jake Harkner is a no-good outlaw who used to rob banks himself, and he don't ever leave a man alive! You can't even count the number of men you've killed!"

Jake recognized the voice as the one doing most of the talking. "Who's in there?" He stayed behind the wagon.

"George Callahan, and after today, I'll be famous for being the man who shot down Jake Harkner!"

"Come out and try it!" That was a name he

recognized. Callahan was a train robber whom the law and Pinkerton detectives had been after for a long time.

"I'm comin' out, all right, with four other men! And with your wife and her friend and the little girl and another woman! One wrong move and every one of them is dead!"

There came another scuffle. Finally, a tall, burly man with messy blond hair emerged from the bank with an arm around Randy's neck, keeping her in front of him, a six-gun pointed at her head. Jake saw the terror in her eyes. He felt sick at the sight. He'd worked so hard at helping her overcome her fears, and now this. Callahan was a huge man, and Randy was so small. A second man came out with Teresa in front of him and a third man holding a squirming little Tricia in a tight grip. A fourth man kept another woman in front of him, a frail-looking older woman.

"Susan!" her husband yelled from across the street.

A fifth man came out, carrying four canvas bags stuffed with what was obviously money.

"Let the women and little girl go, Callahan, or you won't live to see the sun set!" Jake warned.

"You can't shoot long as I have your wife in front of me," Callahan answered. "And you ain't gonna shoot Jimbo over there while he's holdin' the little girl."

"Don't *bet* on it!"

"No!" Susan's husband pleaded. "You'll kill my wife!"

"Harkner knows what he's doing," someone else answered.

The five men stood there, looking undecided for a moment.

"George," the one called Jimbo warned, "Jake Harkner ain't no ordinary man."

"He dies easy like any other. There's five of us and only one of him."

"From what I hear, those are odds in *his* favor, not

ours." Jimbo yanked little Tricia closer. "He's already killed Sam and the others we left outside." Little Tricia was shaking and sobbing. "Shut up, kid!" He jerked at her again.

"Stay calm, Button," Jake yelled to her from behind the wagon. "When Grampa starts shooting, you lay down flat and cover your ears, understand?"

The little girl nodded, unable to stop crying.

"*Promise* me, Button!"

"I...promise," the girl answered in jerking sobs. Her curly red hair was stuck to her cheeks from tears.

"What the hell are you talking about?" Jimbo growled, looking nervous now.

"*Cuando comience a disparar*, Teresa, *quiero que te tires el suelo con* Button!" Jake stayed out of sight as he shouted the words.

A trembling Teresa nodded. "*Sí, señor.*"

"What did he just tell you?" the man holding her asked, pressing his gun against her neck. That man would be the hardest to hit—Teresa was a hefty woman who made a good shield. He'd have to make his shots count. He'd hate to have to go home and tell Rodriguez his wife was dead.

"I... He just say to stay calm," Teresa lied to her abductor. Jake had told her to hit the ground with Tricia as soon as he started shooting.

It was a standoff. Jake watched Randy. "You know what to do, Randy," he called to her. "Stay calm."

"Jake, they'll kill you!"

"How well do you know me, Randy Harkner?"

Randy choked from tears, unable to reply.

"I asked you a question, Randy!"

Randy nodded. "I...know how good you are...with those guns. Jake, I love you!" Randy glanced at the other two women. "When he starts shooting, lay down flat."

"Shut up!" Callahan told Randy, ramming the barrel

of his gun hard against her cheekbone, making Randy wince with pain. "We're leavin', Harkner," Callahan practically screamed, "with the women *and* the money! And you ain't gonna stop us!" He turned to the man holding Tricia. "Let the brat go!"

"I ain't lettin' go of my only shield! Harkner will shoot me the minute I'm in the open!"

"Wrong, Mister!" Jake shouted in reply. "I'll shoot you even though you're holding her!"

"Don't do it!" Susan's husband pleaded.

Before the robbers had time to choose, Jake made his move. He darted into the open from behind the wagon, his guns booming. He shot so fast that onlookers could hardly count how many times he pulled the triggers. They'd banked on him not shooting. How many men would be so confident that their bullets would hit the right target? Townspeople watched in wide-eyed shock, a few women screaming and covering their ears, others turning and looking away.

Jimbo fell backward with a hole in his head, and Tricia went down with him. She screamed in terror as she wiggled from under her dead abductor, but just like her grandpa had told her, she stayed flat on the ground, putting her hands over her ears. At almost the same time, the man holding Teresa fell forward. Quickly, Teresa crawled to Tricia and lay over her to protect her.

The horses tied in front of the bank let out screaming whinnies at the roar of guns and managed to jerk away, pulling out the hitch post and running off, the post bouncing along with them.

By then, George Callahan was also down. Randy hit the ground as well, and by the time she did, the men who'd been holding bags of money had been shot. One of them remained squirming in pain.

It happened in a matter of seconds, so fast that onlookers remained stunned and unmoving. After the shattering boom of all the gunplay, the street grew dead quiet except for Tricia's whimpers and the trickle of water that poured from a hole in a watering trough. The stream rinsed over the face of George Callahan, washing away the blood that trickled from a hole in his forehead.

"Jesus God Almighty," Till Medley told the other men standing at the saloon door. "We wanted to see Jake Harkner in action, and we sure as hell did!"

People came out doors and from behind barrels and wagons and whatever else they'd used for cover.

Randy looked over at Tricia and Teresa as she got to her knees. "Tricia!"

"She is fine, Miranda," Teresa told her as she quickly looked the sobbing little girl over. She smoothed Tricia's red hair away from her face, then managed to get to her feet and pick the girl up in her arms. "I will look after her. Go to your husband."

"Grampa!" Tricia cried, looking over to where Jake lay in the street.

It hit Randy only then that Jake had not come running to help her up. Everything had happened so fast she'd not had time to digest it all, and her first concern had been for Tricia. After all, Jake knew what he was doing, and he always survived these things. She looked over to where he now lay in the street. "Oh my God, no!"

"Go to him, Miranda. You can do it," Teresa told her in her heavy Mexican accent. "I will take Tricia to the hotel room. She should not see her grandfather this way."

Randy looked at her helplessly. "Don't leave me alone, Teresa!"

"Your husband is there, and he needs you. You will be strong for him now, no? Go to him." In tears, Teresa hurried off with Tricia.

Randy turned her attention back to Jake. Surely

he was all right. Jake was *always* all right. He was Jake Harkner.

"Oh my God, he's dead!" someone shouted.

Randy managed to find her feet. She watched as people gathered around Jake. "No, he's not!" she said softly before screaming the words as she ran. "No, he's not dead! He's not dead!" She pushed people out of the way and crumpled beside his seemingly lifeless body. This was her worst nightmare. How many times had she imagined this happening, her husband shot down before her very eyes? He'd mentioned to her once that someday he would probably go down with guns blazing. And now, here he lay in the street, possibly dead from a gunfight.

Five

PEOPLE BEGAN POURING INTO THE STREET FROM THEIR hiding places. Randy knelt beside Jake and lifted his head, scooting close enough to rest it against her dress. Blood poured from a wound across the left side of his skull. At first, Randy thought that was the only injury he had, but then she noticed his shirt was soaked with blood. "Get a doctor!" she screamed. "Jake, don't leave me! Don't leave me!"

He groaned and turned his head slightly, then passed out again. An older man pushed his way through the crowd and knelt beside Jake, ordering people to step back and let him do what he needed to do.

"Don't let him die!" Randy begged. "I need my Jake!"

The doctor didn't seem to notice her words. He moved his hands through Jake's hair to find the head wound, studied it a moment, shook his head. He then ripped open Jake's shirt and put a stethoscope to his chest. "He's alive," he told Randy after listening for a minute. "Looks like the bullet just creased his skull, but it didn't penetrate. Taking a bullet to the skull is like being hit in the head with a hammer, and he probably has a concussion. Can't tell about brain damage till he wakes up, if he wakes up. But it's the wound in his side I'm most concerned about."

The doctor ordered men to carry Jake's body to his office just a few doors down. Six men scrambled to pick him up, forcing Randy to move out of the way. Terror filled every part of her mind. What would she do without

her Jake? He was her savior—her protector—her lover—
the man who would never again let something bad
happen to her. He'd saved her all those years ago when
she was dying at that awful trading post, back when she
thought he'd ridden out of her life forever...but then
there he was, holding her, promising her he'd not leave
her again. It had been the same last winter. In spite of
the horror, she hung on because she knew he'd come for
her. And he did come...and she was in his arms again...
and every time she asked him not to let go, he'd clung to
her and promised he would always be right there for her.

The doctor hurried away, and Randy just sat there on
the ground. She stared at the bloody dirt left behind as
well as her own bloody dress, while people mumbled and
whispered and talked behind her.

"I've never seen anything like it," one man said.

"We wanted a show of Harkner's shooting skills, and
we sure as hell got one today!"

A woman spoke up. "He grabbed my little girl and
got her out of the way of one of those men's horses."

"He saved my wife's life, but I about passed out from
fear when he started shooting," a man said. He seemed
to be standing close. "I really thought Susan would die
today." A woman broke down and wept against her
husband's chest.

Men carried some of the dead outlaws away.

"Find another doctor," someone shouted, "and have
the deputy come keep an eye on this one after we lay
him out. He's still alive. He doesn't deserve help, but
we've got no choice."

Someone groaned, "Help me! I'm shot! That sonofabitch shot me right in the gut!"

"You deserved it," a man answered.

Voices. Voices all around. Crying. Gasps of shock.
"Six dead," someone mentioned.

Was Jake in trouble again? Would her Jake go to prison?

"Never seen anything like it!"

"What a shoot-out! Goddamn I wish we had pictures of it! This will make the news all over the country! Jake Harkner, of all people, stopping a bank robbery! And shooting those bastards while they stood there, hostages right in front of them! This is the most goddamn exciting thing that's ever happened here! Boulder will be even more famous for this! It will help our fund-raiser!"

"Hey, if Harkner lives, maybe he could be our new sheriff. Ain't nobody gonna mess with our town if Jake Harkner is in charge!"

Randy couldn't tell one voice from another. People swarmed around, talking among themselves as though she didn't exist. She was alone! Alone! Who would protect her? She needed to go to Jake, but she couldn't find the strength to get up. She'd been through this too many times to count and wasn't sure she could ever go through it again. Several people followed those who carried Jake and disappeared into the doctor's office, but Randy remained on her knees, staring at the blood on her skirt. Others continued to swarm around the dead bodies of the men, and a woman rushed inside the bank, where she screamed and began weeping.

Must be the teller's wife, Randy thought absently. Yes, those awful men had shot a teller. And they'd shot Jake! Would she be weeping uncontrollably herself before this day was over?

"Ma'am, do you need help up?"

Randy looked up at an elderly man. Susan stood beside him. She leaned closer, and both she and the man put out their hands.

"Ma'am, you need a doctor, too," Susan told Randy. "Your cheek is bruised pretty bad."

Randy just stared at her. "I...I need to go to my husband, but I don't seem to be able to get up."

Susan and her husband reached down, one on each side, and helped Randy to her feet.

"I'm James Bird," the old man told her. "You already know my wife here, although it's sad how you met."

"Thank you for your help." Randy wanted to scream for Jake. She'd never been afraid of everything and everyone like this. She hated the constant panic, hated confining Jake the way she'd been doing, wanting him constantly with her. The only place she felt safe was in his arms. What if that could no longer be? Her whole life wrapped around Jake Harkner. No other man knew her like Jake did—physically, mentally, emotionally, intimately. No man loved her or ever would love her like Jake did. They were like one person. If she lost him, she, too, would be lost. She stood there a moment, trying to think straight, trying to get her bearings.

"Someone…please send a runner to the J&L. I need my son," she told James Bird. "As soon as we get to Jake, please go get a messenger—someone who can ride hard and fast and get Lloyd here in five days instead of six. I mean…" *Think!* She felt so confused. "I mean, it will take someone two or three days to get to the ranch and another two or three to get back here."

"Yes, ma'am, I'll send someone." James and Susan helped her walk to the doctor's office.

Yes, it would help having Lloyd here. Her loyal, loving son would know what to do. He would at least be someone to lean on. He'd helped her, too…last winter… when those men…

Lloyd was so much like his father…strong and dependable. And having her daddy here would help little Tricia not be afraid. Maybe Lloyd would bring Evie, who loved her father beyond measure. She would want to be with Jake. Evie was such a faithful Christian woman. Her prayers were strong. She could pray for her father. She'd helped Jake through the awful ordeal back in Denver last summer, sitting with Lloyd when they thought he was dying. It was Evie who'd help bring Jake out of that awful darkness.

"I've never seen shooting like that," James told her. "Never in all my born years."

"I don't know how he could be so accurate and fast when he was already wounded," Susan added. "I saw blood at his side when he stepped out from behind that wagon." She shook her head. "I saw those guns, and I thought my life was over. I felt that bullet whiz right over my head. It nearly parted my scalp!" She squeezed Randy's arm. "He's one heck of a man, Mrs. Harkner."

Randy wanted to smile but couldn't. "Yes, he is. He's more wonderful than anybody knows. Most only think about the bad. Few see the good."

Flash powder exploded as a man with a camera stepped in front of them and took a picture of Randy. She gasped and turned away. "Go away! Go away!" she screamed.

James and Susan glanced at each other uneasily. They didn't understand like Jake would.

"I have to get to Jake," she told them, starting to sob. "I have to get to…my husband."

"Yes, ma'am, we're almost there," James told her.

They reached the steps to the doctor's office, where people milled about outside. Randy hesitated.

"I…I left a hat box. I think it's by the Silver Saddle. That's where Jake was standing when…when…"

"I'll go look for it," Susan told her.

"Take it to the Gold Dust Hotel. Give it to my housekeeper, Teresa."

"Yes, ma'am."

Someone brought Jake's jacket to Randy. "Ma'am, he dropped this when he went runnin' to the bank," a nameless man told her. "A bunch of peppermint spilled out. I picked it all up and put it back in the bag and into the pocket of the jacket." He held it out.

Peppermint! Jake had remembered the peppermint. She took the jacket and held it close to her heart, bending her head and breathing in her husband's familiar scent. How many times had they shared a stick of peppermint in the morning, biting each end of the candy until their lips met? She raised her head and just stared at the door. "I'm afraid to go inside."

"We'll help you," James told her. "Might be your husband is awake and needs you, so you ought to go in."

Randy nodded. "Yes." She took a deep breath. "Just go find the hat box and take it to the hotel, please. And send someone to the J&L. Thank you for helping me. I'll be fine now." She had to be brave. She *had* to.

The elderly couple looked at each other, James shaking his head. They waited while Randy walked inside on her own.

James took his wife's arm. "We'd better go get a rider to head for the J&L."

Susan shook her head. "Such a little thing. Her arm felt so thin."

"I noticed," James agreed. "The woman has been through so much, married to a man like that."

Susan nodded. "I've read the book."

James took a deep breath. "Well, that's a lot for a woman to take, and think of all those headlines last summer. It looks like Harkner will make headlines again. But this time he's quite the hero, don't you think?"

"I suppose. But take it from a woman—this might be something his wife can't handle. A person can take only so much."

They headed for the train depot, where messengers for distant ranches could usually be found looking for work. Someone had to ride to the J&L.

Six

RANDY MANAGED TO MOVE HER LEGS TO WALK INSIDE the doctor's office. Jake lay on a long table with just a sheet under him. Randy's first thought was how hard and uncomfortable it had to be compared to their huge, specially built bed made of black walnut...back home on the J&L...in their loft bedroom...where she could lie in his arms at night and feel so safe...where they'd made love too many times to count. Jake always knew how to make it beautiful...knew how to make her feel beautiful. People didn't understand why he was so protective, how he could be friends with prostitutes without being untrue to the woman he loved far and above all the others. It all came from his childhood, how women of the night had risked their lives to protect him from his devil of a father.

Why did that fill her thoughts now, of all times? Two nurses and the doctor were working frantically getting Jake's clothes off. He was a big man, six feet four inches, and not easy to work with. Through it all, one of the nurses pressed gauze tight against the wound in his side.

"Oh my! What happened to his back?" one of the nurses commented.

Randy spoke up. "His father did that to him, with the buckle end of a belt."

The doctor glanced her way. "I saw you out in the street. Are you his wife?"

"Yes."

"He asked for you."

Randy held the jacket closer, taking heart in the comment. "He's conscious?"

"Randy?" It was Jake!

Randy laid the jacket aside and rushed to stand near him, touching his face. "Jake, I'm here!"

A nurse pulled a sheet up to cover him to just below the hip bones, leaving the wound in his left side exposed. The nurse who held gauze against the wound grabbed even more gauze and pressed tightly to stave the continued bleeding. Randy cringed at all the blood, noticing the skin around the outside of the gauze patch was a deep purple. Internal bleeding? The purple was spreading fast. The deep gash across the left side of Jake's head had finally stopped bleeding, but his eyes remained closed.

"Jake, I'm here. I'm here," Randy told him again. "Are you still awake? When I saw you unconscious in the street—"

Jake actually opened his eyes again and managed to reach up and grasp her hand, squinting from pain. "Button?"

"She's fine. She's with Teresa at the hotel."

"That...other lady..."

"She wasn't hurt. She and her husband are so grateful to you."

He noticed the bruise on her cheek. "You're...hurt!"

"It doesn't matter. It's just a bruise." Randy squeezed his hand. "Jake, you have to hang on. Don't you die on me! You can't leave me! You can't leave me!"

He closed his eyes again. "Lloyd always says...I'm too mean to die...remember?"

Randy smiled through tears and leaned down to kiss him lightly. "I can't do this without you, Jake," she said in a near whisper. "Don't leave me!"

He kept hold of her hand. "I'm...right here. Don't be scared."

"Mrs. Harkner, you'll have to move out of the way,"

the doctor told her. "I've got to get the bullet out and make sure there isn't some serious internal damage. I have to find out where all the bleeding is coming from."

"But I have to be with him."

"Then move around to stand at his head. If you've got the stomach for it, you can stay while I take out the bullet and sew him up."

Randy found some of her old strength at the man's remark. "I've got the stomach for it," she answered curtly. "You wouldn't believe the things I've got the stomach for, the things I've been through or the things my *husband* has been through. He's a strong, tough man—probably the toughest you've ever worked on."

"His age?"

"Almost sixty-two but going on forty—*that's* how tough he is."

"Most folks know about Jake Harkner, ma'am. You don't need to explain to me. But I need to stop this bleeding." He looked at one of the nurses. "Give him some chloroform." The doctor removed the blood-soaked wad of gauze from the wound, touching around it with his hands.

Jake grimaced and stiffened from pain. "Jesus, Doc, that hurts like hell!"

Randy ached for him, keeping her hands on either side of his face.

"You telling me where it hurts helps me know about where the bullet is," the doctor told Jake.

One of the nurses gently pulled Randy's hands away from Jake and laid a damp white cloth over Jake's nose and mouth. In moments, he went limp again.

"Don't give him too much," the doctor told her. "He's a tough man and can take some of the pain. Too much of that stuff can affect the heart, especially for an older man."

Randy's stomach tightened. Could the *chloroform* kill

him? Not Jake! How many old bullet wounds did he already have? His father's beatings didn't kill him. The awful shooting back in Guthrie, where he nearly bled to death from a leg wound, didn't kill him. The wound he'd suffered in the shoot-out back in California didn't kill him. My God, how long ago was that? Lloyd had only been a baby. Acute pneumonia in prison didn't kill him. He was the toughest man she'd ever known...and yet the gentlest...with his little granddaughters...with Evie...with her...in the night...

The doctor went to work, and at first, Jake didn't seem to feel anything. Randy thought about that first time they met...Jake barging into a dry goods store where she'd been shopping. He was a gruff, bearded, wanted man then, an outlaw who'd ended up in a shoot-out right in front of her. She'd been so afraid of him that she shot him herself with a little handgun, and he just looked at her—so surprised. He could have killed her then, but he just ran out.

He'd lived through that wound, too.

"I took a bullet out of Jake myself once," she told the doctor rather absently. "He was only thirty then. It's a long story—how it happened." *And later, he saved my life. I was hurt and he was so good to me, so gentle with me, and we knew we were in love.*

Jake groaned, and she leaned down and kissed his forehead, terrified he'd wake up too soon and feel the awful pain. "Jake, I'm here."

"*Yo te amo...*"

"I love you, too. Don't you die on me, Jake." She leaned close to his ear. "Remember that night in the wagon—that first time we made love? We didn't even know where we were, and you were so scared to love someone. A big, brave, wild outlaw, running from the law and running from love. I was the one thing you couldn't fight and you couldn't run from, Jake Harkner."

Randy felt more of her old self struggling to come back. Most of their life it had been Jake who'd needed her, Jake who drew his strength from her. She'd been his only barrier from going over the edge into darkness. But the last few months, she'd been the one who needed him to keep her from falling. She wasn't sure she could ever find the woman she used to be, but now she needed to be the strong one. She'd lost some of that strength when Lloyd was shot and she thought she'd lost her son...more when she sat through a hearing that could have resulted in her husband being hanged...and she lost the rest of it last winter...

She shook away the ugly memory. She must not think about it or she wouldn't be strong enough for Jake right now. She had to find a way to put it all behind her and find the old Randy, the one Jake loved most.

He groaned again, this time louder. Randy noticed him clenching his fists.

"Jake, I'm right here! I'm right here!"

How many times had he told her that very thing over the last few months?

The doctor ordered a little more chloroform. For nearly an hour, he probed and stitched on the inside, then stitched up the outside, dousing everything with alcohol and iodine. Finally, he wrapped the wound, ordering men to come in and carry Jake to a bed in another room. Randy felt sick at his cries of pain.

Through a fog of loneliness and fear, she heard the doctor tell her he thought Jake would be fine, that he just needed to rest now...to sleep. She could stay with him. Everything happened in a shroud of disbelief and uncertainty...strangers...all strangers. All she wanted and needed was Jake.

The doctor walked out and closed the door. Randy realized she didn't even know his name. She took off her hat, then looked down to realize she still had blood on the skirt of her dress. She should go back to the hotel, wash and change, and see about Tricia, but not yet. Not yet. She had to stay with Jake. He had to wake up and hold her first so she knew he'd be all right.

She removed her shoes, unpinned her hair, and let it fall. Jake liked it long and loose. She was beautiful, wasn't she? Jake always told her how beautiful she was. Brad Buckley couldn't change the way Jake Harkner touched her or made love to her or looked at her with those dark eyes and that melting smile.

A nurse brought his jacket into the room, as well as Randy's reticule.

Shivering from shock, Randy set her handbag aside and picked up the jacket to pull it on, right over the jacket she already wore against the morning's chill. Putting on Jake's jacket made it feel like his arms were around her.

She lay down on his good side and nestled herself against him. "Don't leave me, Jake," she said softly near his ear.

"*Mi esposa*," he muttered from somewhere in his own semi-consciousness. "*Tu eres...mi vida.*"

Seven

ATTORNEY PETER BROWN OPENED THE NEWSPAPER, settling in behind his large oak desk in his home in north Chicago. The headlines stunned him.

"I'll be goddamned," he muttered. "Jake did it again."

He smiled and shook his head as he read the stunning, bold print.

JAKE HARKNER FOILS BANK ROBBERY IN BOULDER, COLORADO!

From outlaw to lawman to hero, Jake Harkner, the notorious outlaw turned U.S. Marshal, reprised his lawman instincts on June twelfth in Boulder, Colorado, when he shot it out with nine men who intended to rob the Boulder City Bank. The robbers were led by George Callahan, the nemesis of the Pinkerton Detective Agency. The robbers killed bank teller John Drake and Boulder's Sheriff Mike Billings. Harkner himself was seriously wounded, but is expected to recover. He single-handedly killed five of the nine men and wounded the other four. Callahan was among those killed.

"Of course he was," Peter said softly. "The man seldom shoots to wound."

Witnesses claim Harkner not only foiled the robbery, but also saved four hostages, his own wife and granddaughter among them. The other two hostages were a Mexican woman named Teresa Ramon and a retired school teacher, Mrs. Susan Bird, a resident of Boulder.

The article was by Jeff Truebridge, the same reporter who had gotten famous off that book about Jake three years ago. The man had news connections everywhere. Someone must have phoned him or wired him the news for the Chicago papers as soon as it happened.

Jeff lived in Chicago now, but had remained good friends with Jake and his family, and with Peter himself, who had his own fond but sometimes painful memories of Jake Harkner…and his wife. The article went on about the incident and about highlights from Jake's past.

Peter didn't have to read most of that. He already knew it all. He'd lived the wild story of Jake Harkner, U.S. Marshal, when he'd practiced law in Guthrie, Oklahoma.

He took a moment to reminisce. "My God, what a life that man has led," he muttered. He reread the first part of the article.

…*hostages…Jake's own wife and granddaughter…*

"Randy," he said softly, "how much more will you suffer?" Peter had loved his first wife, still missed her since she'd died. And he loved Treena now. They were both getting older, he fifty-two and Treena forty-seven, and had been friends well before they married. When her husband passed, he and Treena had just seemed to fall in together as though it was only natural.

But she knew. Treena knew. He'd talked about Randy and how much he loved her before he and Treena had even thought about marriage. Truth be known, if he could have his way, Randy would be running his mansion even now, ordering the servants around, accompanying him to the opera and concerts and business gatherings. And oh, how beautiful she'd be! Not many women possessed that kind of beauty, especially as they aged. He'd met her back in Guthrie, when she worked for him during the times when Jake was off in No Man's Land chasing the worst of humanity. He'd watched her quietly worry, never knowing if her husband would make it back alive.

She'd been through so much—running from the law, gun battles, Jake spending time in prison, lonely years when Jake would leave because he thought she'd be better off without him. God only knew what he'd done during those missing years. Some of his best friends were prostitutes, for heaven's sake. But Randy took him back. She always took him back. There was no way she would ever leave her husband—no way she would ever love or give herself to another man. God knew he'd tried to reason with her. He'd offered her the world, but she'd turned him down for Jake.

How did anyone fight a man like that? He studied the article again, feeling how excited Jeff must have been when writing it. Jeff had been tracking and writing about Jake ever since meeting him and actually getting to ride with him back in Oklahoma. He was a big-time reporter now, but back then...

He picked up the telephone. "Yes, please get me the *Chicago Journal*," he told the operator. "Jeff Truebridge. I'm not sure of the number. You'll have to look it up." He glanced up when his wife walked into his office, her dark hair looking perfectly coifed and lovely, as always. As he waited on the telephone, he pointed to the newspaper. Treena picked up the paper as Jeff answered the phone.

"Jeff! This is Peter. I saw the article about Jake." Peter watched his wife as she read the article. She just smiled and shook her head. "Yeah, looks like he did it again." Peter laughed. "Trouble follows Jake like his own shadow, but looks like this time it was of someone else's doing. The man's a damn hero—I can just imagine the look on George Callahan's face when he found out who was in town when he decided to rob that bank. I'm just a little worried about Randy. The article says she was one of the hostages." He noticed the look of chagrin on his wife's face when he mentioned Randy.

"Those men picked the wrong day and the wrong town," Jeff told him on the other end of the line.

Peter could hear the clicking of several typewriters in the background. He couldn't help a good laugh at Jeff's remark…but deeper inside he felt bad for Randy. How many times had he wanted to hold her and tell her everything would be all right? This was one of them. "You know anything about Jake's wounds?"

"Head wound, but grazed, not penetrated. I guess they're more concerned about a wound in his left side, but my sources say he'll be okay. I wish I'd been there to see it all happen. There's nothing more exciting than watching Jake Harkner in action."

"Yes, well, we've both seen that, haven't we? You going out to the J&L this summer again?"

"Can't go this year. The wife is carrying again and she's having problems, so I'd better stay home. You?"

"I don't know, Jeff. Maybe I will. Randy might need some help. Hey, you take care, and I hope things go all right with your wife and the baby. Your first one is only about six or eight months old, isn't he?"

"Eight. We didn't want another one this soon, but human nature is human nature."

Both men laughed. "Keep me informed on whatever you hear about Jake, Jeff."

"I'm going to keep in touch with my connections in Boulder. Looks like I finished that book too soon. I didn't know so many more things would happen. By the way, is Randy all right? Have you heard from her?"

"Sure. She writes my wife. Why?"

"I don't know. Her last letter sounded kind of…I'm not sure…despondent, maybe. Could be my imagination. Just wondering if something happened we don't know about, or if something has changed."

"It didn't seem that way in her letters to Treena," Peter told Jeff. "I'll ask her about it. You take care, and let's go to lunch when I'm in the city."

"I'd love that. And I'll let you know when I hear how Jake is doing."

"You do that. I'll talk to you soon." Peter hung up the earpiece to the phone and just stared absently at the opposite wall for a few quiet seconds.

"Looks like the magnificent Jake Harkner has struck again," Treena told him, interrupting his thoughts.

Peter blinked and finally met her gaze. "You have to stop calling him that. You know he gets embarrassed by that description."

Treena laughed lightly. "I wish I'd been there when they got that letter from us and when they read that part. I couldn't help it." She set the paper on Peter's desk. "And that horse he gave me as a gift when we visited them is so magnificent!" Treena sat down across from him, sobering. "You're worried about Randy, aren't you?"

Peter rubbed at the back of his neck. "Have you noticed anything different about her letters? Any clue something might be wrong?"

Treena thought a moment. "Not really. Why?"

Peter sighed and leaned back in his chair again. "Jeff thought he caught something in her last letter. I'm thinking maybe we should go back to the J&L this summer. You loved it there."

"Yes, I did, but I have other plans. That's why I came in here—to talk to you about going to Paris. I'd like to visit my mother and sisters. Mother is getting on in age, and I feel I should go. I think a cruise on the ocean would do us good."

Peter shook his head. "I can't be gone for that long. I have too many clients and too many cases coming up in court. I have to stay here."

"Well, it's important that you take *some* kind of break, Peter. You work much too hard."

They exchanged a look that told her everything.

"You want to go to the J&L," Treena said gently. "You're worried about Randy, after this latest incident."

"A little." Peter rubbed at his eyes. "I'm sorry, Treena. There are just times when I feel like she might need me."

"Jake Harkner is her life. He runs right in her blood, Peter. I love watching them together. It's like every time he breathes in, she breathes out his own breath."

Jeff stared at the newspaper article. "Yeah."

Treena pushed back a tendril of her black hair. She would need to get it properly curled up for the lawyers' banquet they were attending this evening in the city. "Peter, we have an understanding. I know you love me, and you are a good, kind man. I know you also love another woman, one you can't have. If it makes you feel better, go out to the J&L this summer. I'll feel better knowing you're having a good rest while I go to Paris. I know the relationship you share with Jake and Randy. If you think either one of them might need you, as a friend, or for your services, then go to them. I'm a big girl."

Peter smiled. "Come here."

Treena rose and walked around his desk, taking him up on his offer to sit on his lap. He took hold of her hands. "You are a wondrous woman, Treena Brown. Thank you for loving me like you do. You've filled a deep void in my life. I do love you—very much."

Treena leaned in and they kissed deeply. She smoothed back his still-thick hair, studied his blue eyes. "I hope you find that everything is okay when you get to the J&L. I'm sure Jake and Randy will both be glad to see you again."

Peter pulled her to him and kissed her again. "There's that darker side to him, Treena—that part of him that still can't quite get over his childhood. He can be one ruthless sonofabitch, and it's when Randy or anyone else in his family is threatened that it comes roaring out of him. I just wonder what this particular situation was like, for both of them."

Treena touched his face. "You don't mind if I go to Paris?"

Peter smiled and took hold of her wrist, kissing her palm. "I don't mind, as long as you don't mind if I take a couple of weeks on the J&L. It's so beautiful there, and I like being with Jake's family."

"You'd better wire them first."

Peter shrugged. "I think I'll surprise them this time. It might be better for Randy. I have a feeling she does too much preparation and fussing when she knows company is coming."

Treena stood up and patted his shoulder. "You do what you need to do, and I'll go see my family. I think I'll leave in about three weeks and probably stay a couple of months. Can you live that long without me?"

"I won't like it, but I'll be busy, so hopefully it will go by fast."

Treena leaned down and kissed him yet again. "I'll miss you terribly."

Peter squeezed her hand. "And I'll miss you. I'll leave a little later than you. I have a big tax case coming up I need to take care of before I can go anywhere, so we may get home at around the same time. I don't want to rattle around in this big, twenty-room castle of a house by myself."

Treena got up and walked around the desk and back

to the door. "Well, today you have to rattle around upstairs and pick out something to wear to the lawyers' banquet. I'll be upstairs myself letting Mattie fix my hair." She gave Peter a smile and walked out.

Peter picked up the paper again, rereading the article. *What's going on with you, Randy? How did you make it through this one?* Randy had always been so strong in times of crisis, but last summer had been the kicker, seeing her son get shot, thinking Jake could go to prison...

But she still had her Jake. That's how she always put it. *As long as I have Jake, I'm fine. He thinks I'm the strong one, and that he needs me to stay sane and be strong*, she once told him. *But I'm the one who needs him. I'm the one who couldn't survive without his strength and without his arms around me.*

Could anything break the woman? Jeff's comments worried him. It was none of his damn business, and God knew no man would dare try to move in on Jake Harkner's woman, but he had to know she was okay. He thanked the Good Lord for Treena's understanding. They were the best of friends, and their lovemaking was sweet, but he suspected Treena knew that every time he made love to her, he saw someone else in his bed.

Eight

JAKE SMELLED THE SCENT OF ROSES BEFORE HE EVEN opened his eyes. He knew the hair that had fallen across his chin was Randy's. He realized she was lying by his side, an arm across his middle and her head on his upper chest, as though she wanted to make sure his heart was still beating.

He moved one hand to pet her hair. "Randy?"

She jerked awake, raising her head and looking confused at first. Then she smiled.

"Jake! You finally woke up!" She straightened, her hair a mess, her eyes puffy from crying.

"Randy, what—" He started to rise, only to be met with stinging pain deep in his left side. He groaned and put his head back down.

"Jake, you shouldn't move yet. You were shot." Randy leaned over him and kissed his cheek. "You've been out since Doctor Snow took the bullet out of your side yesterday. It's—" She glanced at a clock on the wall, its pendulum swinging to a soft, ticking sound. "It's nearly three in the afternoon now." She rubbed at her eyes. "You also have a head wound."

Jake lay there, trying to gather his senses. Out since yesterday? Had Randy been here by his side the entire time? He put a hand to his head, realizing then that he had bandages wrapped around it.

"Jake, how do you feel?" Randy took his hand. "Are you fully awake? The doctor was a little worried about concussion."

Still gathering his thoughts, Jake looked her over and realized she was wearing the same dress as yesterday. There was blood on the skirt. He bent one leg and tried to sit up more, but he grunted with pain again. "I'll tell you…how I feel. Like someone stuck a pine cone inside of me and then sewed me up." He put a hand to his head. "I hardly remember anything."

Randy pushed some of her hair behind one ear and sat up straighter. "Jake, you're the hero of Boulder. You foiled that bank robbery and killed all but four of the robbers. George Callahan was one of those who was killed." Her eyes teared. "I thought I'd lost you when I saw you down in the street." Her lips quivered, and she covered her mouth with her hand. "Jake, I was so scared."

He looked around the room, memories of the shootout flooding back to him. "Tricia!"

"She's fine." Randy jerked with a sob. "She's…at the hotel with…Teresa." She turned away and started to rise. "I'll get Doctor Snow."

Jake caught her arm. "Wait!" His faculties returning and his mind clearer, he took a good look at her. "Jesus, Randy, look at you! There's blood on your dress! You haven't washed or changed. Have you eaten?"

Randy quickly wiped at her eyes. "No. How could I? I thought you might die this time. I had to stay with you."

Jake saw the terror return to her eyes. "Randy Harkner, *you* have to live for *me*! At this rate *you're* the one who will die!" Anger at her condition brought back some of his resolve to get out of bed and help her. Again, he tried to sit up. This time, in spite of incredible pain, he managed to do so. Randy quickly propped some pillows behind him.

"Jake, you shouldn't be moving around! You'll break open your stitches!" she fussed. "Are you hungry? Should I get you something to eat?"

"No!" He grimaced again. "*You* need to eat!" He called out louder, "Nurse! Anyone out there? Get in here!"

"Jake, don't do this. Please calm down. You've just had serious surgery and you lost so much blood."

Jake grasped her wrist again, squeezing lightly. "I'm more worried about you! This has to stop, Randy! I can't believe you managed to get through this. And the doctor should have made you go take care of yourself. Look at you! He should have made you eat, made you clean up, given you a bed to sleep in beside me instead of letting you lay half-on and half-off this cot!"

"I'll…I'll be all right."

"No, you won't!" He kept hold of her wrist and laid his head back against the pillows. "I wish Lloyd were here. He wouldn't have allowed this."

"I sent for him. Please don't be angry, Jake. I can't eat. How can I eat or sleep when you might need me?"

"I do need you!"

A nurse came in, followed by Doctor Snow.

"Well, look who's awake!" the doctor exclaimed. "Let's have a look at that—"

"Why have you let my wife just lie here with hardly any sleep and nothing to eat?" Jake asked angrily.

"Well, I… She insisted."

"You're a *doctor*, aren't you?"

"Of course, Mr. Harkner, but—"

"But nothing! This woman needs nourishment and rest. She's been losing too much weight, and you should have noticed the state she's in. You should have *ordered* her to eat and given her something to help her sleep. She hasn't been well. You could have set up a bed beside mine if she didn't want to leave!"

"We were just too concerned about you, Mr. Harkner."

"And I'm a goddamned worthless sonofabitch compared to this woman! Someone go to the nearest restaurant and get her some food—something nourishing and something with *fat* in it that will stick to her bony ribs!

Bring it back here, because I intend to watch her eat it and make sure she swallows every last bite!"

Doctor Snow turned to his nurse. "Well, no more wondering when this man will wake up and regain his strength. Constance, go to the café two doors down and bring back some food for his wife."

The nurse glanced at Jake with a scowl. "Would *you* like something, Mr. Harkner?"

"I'd like my *guns*. Where are they?"

Constance glanced at Doctor Snow.

"They are in a trunk in my office," the doctor told him.

"*Get* them! People will know I'm in a weak state. You'd be surprised how many men might decide to take advantage of that." Jake turned to the nurse. "Go get that food."

"Jake, don't be rude," Randy argued. "I'm fine."

"I'll *be* rude when it comes to you being neglected. And you're not fine. In fact, I want the doctor to look you over and give you a tonic or something that might help you get your strength back. And I mean it about eating. You're wasting away to nothing." He looked at the doctor again. "And send someone to get her companion, the Mexican woman called Teresa. She's over at the Gold Dust Hotel with my little granddaughter. Have her pack some things and bring them over here so my wife can wash up and change her clothes."

Constance left, and the doctor moved to Jake's side. "I want to look at your stitches."

"Go right ahead. Are you sure you didn't leave a knife in me or something? It sure *feels* like you did."

"I assure you, it's just the bullet damage. It will get better."

"I've felt that before, too many times to count."

The doctor stood at his side and folded his arms. "You know, Jake, somewhere amid all of this someone said something about you being too mean to die. In fact, I think *you're* the one who said it. I'm beginning to agree with that comment. I'd like to think your personality has changed because of your head wound, but I have a strong suspicion that this behavior is common for you."

Jake closed his eyes and leaned back. "Jesus, I'm sorry, Doc. I just woke up and saw the state my wife is in, and that *really* woke me up! And I am too mean to die, so start helping Randy, not me. And I'm sorry about your nurse. I don't usually yell at women."

The doctor sighed, walking over to a cabinet to take out some scissors and clean gauze, along with a brown bottle. "This iodine will help stave off infection. I'll put more on those stitches as soon as I have a look at them." He pulled a chair to the side of Jake's bed and cut off the gauze. A little dried blood made the gauze stick, and Jake winced when the doctor pulled it away. "Someone named Jeff called while you were still unconscious," he told Jake. "I spoke with him and explained what happened and what kind of injuries you have."

The mention of Jeff brought a faint smile to Jake's lips. He glanced at Randy, who still sat on the edge of the bed, wiping at her eyes with her other hand.

"Oh, Jake, it's nice to know Jeff called," she told him. "Isn't that typical of him?"

The doctor gently applied iodine to Jake's stitches, and he winced with pain. "It sure is," he answered Randy. "I'll bet he's madder than hell that he wasn't here to see the shoot-out." The doctor began taping a clean patch of gauze over his stitches. "I can just imagine what Jeff is thinking right now," Jake continued. "He and Peter are probably shaking their heads over this one."

Randy smiled, but then the tears came. "Don't be angry with me for not eating, Jake. I thought you would die! I couldn't leave you."

He reached over and took her hand. "When have I ever been truly angry with you? I'm angry with others who should have seen you needed some medical help of your own." He scowled at the doctor, who finished covering the wound.

"Well, do forgive me," the man said with a hint of sarcasm. "I was a little busy trying to keep you from bleeding to death."

Jake couldn't help a faint grin. "Yeah, well, you still should have been concerned about my wife. You can see how thin she is. She barely eats."

The doctor looked Randy over. "Have you been sick, Mrs. Harkner?"

"No, I—" Randy glanced at Jake.

"It's just a woman thing, I think," Jake lied. Randy wouldn't want the doctor to know the truth. It was important that no one outside of the J&L know, and she'd be devastated to have to talk about it. "You know how things change for women when they get a little older. She's been depressed."

"Well, I have a tonic that might help that." Doctor Snow put back the scissors. "It's in the outer office. I'll see about it."

He left the room, and Jake looked at Randy. "You stay here when the nurse brings that food. I want to witness you *eating*. I love you and I need you and I'm not going to sit around and watch you dry up and blow away like the wind, Randy Harkner."

The doctor returned with a brown bottle and a spoon. "Take a teaspoon of this a couple of times a day, Mrs. Harkner. I'll check you over after you've cleaned up and eaten. And we have a bathing room behind that door over there." He turned his attention to Jake. "My nurse can help your wife clean up." He frowned. "When you wake up…you wake up in a big way! Apparently I don't need to wonder if you're better. I saw enough of those old bullet wounds on your body that by all rights you should have died a long time ago."

Jake put a hand to his head. "Well, Doc, for some reason, the Good Lord keeps me alive to keep putting this poor woman here through hell—and to keep doctors like you on their toes. I have a son-in-law who's a doctor, and between me and six grandchildren and accidents on the ranch, he hardly gets a day's rest, especially during roundup and branding."

The doctor sighed. "Mr. Harkner, I've heard plenty about you. How in God's name you could be so badly wounded and still manage to put bullets into the heads of those men holding hostages, I will never understand. I didn't see it, but witnesses say it was phenomenal, the best damn demonstration of fast and accurate shooting a man could ask for. By now it's in all the newspapers."

"They had my wife and granddaughter. I didn't have any choice."

"Still, it was quite something. The mayor and some other city officials are talking about asking you to be our new sheriff. Our own was shot dead by one of those bastards."

Jake felt Randy's hand tighten around his. "No, thanks. I have a big family back on the J&L, and I would never leave. My wife went through enough when I was a marshal back in Oklahoma."

"Well, just the same, I'll let you handle it." He nodded to Randy. "I'm sorry I didn't do something sooner, ma'am, but you seemed so bent on not leaving your husband's side that I didn't have the heart to try to force you into anything. I'll send word to the hotel. I'm sure that little girl over there wants to see her grandfather."

"I'll bet she does," Jake said with a smile. "And I want to see my Button. This whole thing must have terrified her. I wish I could give her a hug."

"If I were you, I'd just lie still, Mr. Harkner, for another couple of days anyway. Relax until your son gets here. I'll try to keep reporters and the mayor and others who've been clamoring outside my door out of here."

"Thanks. I don't want to talk to any of them." Jake looked at Randy again. "Little Jake will have a fit over not having been here to see his grandfather in a gunfight."

"Oh, he'll be beside himself," Randy told him.

The doctor took a moment to listen to Jake's heart, then felt for fever. "You're going to be fine as long as there is no infection." He looked at Randy. "Don't take that tonic until you get some food in your stomach." He straightened, turning his attention to Jake again. "You say your son-in-law is a doctor?"

"Brian Stewart," Randy answered for Jake, "and he's a very fine doctor. He travels around to other ranches to help with everything from broken bones to birthing babies and doctoring spider bites. I'm sure he'll come here with Lloyd so he can be with Jake on the way home."

"Well, if he's along, maybe Jake can leave sooner than I would normally let him go." Doctor Snow glanced at Jake on those words, an obvious expression of "I'd like you off my hands" on his face.

Jake grinned. "I know. You can't wait till I'm out of here."

The doctor chuckled and walked out for a moment, coming back with Jake's gun belt. "This damn thing is heavy with both guns in it." He hung it over the bedpost near Jake. "There you go. I have no desire to touch those things."

"I'd advise you not to."

"After all that shooting, the guns are likely empty."

"I'll load them myself once the nurse returns with that food and I see my wife eating."

"Suit yourself."

The doctor left, and Jake turned to his wife. "This whole thing of not eating has to stop. I can't stand to watch you wither away like this."

She blinked back tears. "I'll try to eat when they bring the food."

"You'll do more than try." Jake studied the circles under her eyes and reached out to touch her about the ribs. He grimaced from pain as he urged her to sit closer to him on the edge of the bed. "You're just bones," he told her. "I'm afraid to even hold you anymore."

Randy laid across his chest again. "You *have* to hold me. I *need* you to hold me."

There it was again. How many times had she asked him not to let go of her? How she'd managed to get through this current horror, he couldn't understand. He could only take hope in the fact that she did get through it. It meant some of the old, strong Randy was down in there somewhere, keeping her from completely falling apart. "I'm serious, Randy. I don't care if you eat so much you get fat. You've got to take care of yourself. Do it for me if for no other reason, but don't forget we have six grandchildren who adore you and need you."

"I'll try, Jake." She closed her eyes and leaned down to kiss his hand. "You won't take any of those jobs, will you? The range detective? Or sheriff here in Boulder?"

"And be away from you or make you worry? Hell no. You've been through enough for ten lifetimes, and I'm damn sorry for that. Why would I leave you now?"

"When you're better, can we go back up to the line shack?"

"What about the fund-raiser here in Boulder you wanted to go to?"

"Right now, all I want is to go home and then go up to the line shack. When we're there, I have you all to myself. I feel so safe when it's just you and me alone."

"What about the grizzlies and mountain lions?" Jake took heart in the way she smiled.

"*They're* afraid of *you*," she teased.

Jake grinned, squeezing her hand. "They *should* be afraid of me."

The doctor walked in. "Jake, Constance is back with a tray of food."

Jake kept his eyes on Randy. "I intend to watch you eat every bite, and after that, I want you to clean up, and I want you to sleep. Maybe the doctor can bring in an extra cot so you can stay close to me."

"I can do that," the doctor told him.

Someone loudly cleared her throat, and Jake and Randy turned to see the nurse standing in the doorway with a tray of food.

Jake smiled at her. "Constance! Thanks for the food. Just set it over here on this table by my wife so I can make sure she eats all of it."

"Yes, sir." Constance was a robust older woman, her dark hair pulled into a bun at the base of her neck. She carried in the tray and set it on the table next to the bed.

"Constance, I apologize for my outburst earlier." Jake turned his gaze to Randy again. "I love this woman here beyond words, and I'm worried about her health." He looked back at Constance. "Will you help her clean up when she's done eating and make sure she takes some of that tonic there?"

"Of course."

"Thank you." Jake reached out his hand, and Constance took it. He pressed her hand gently. "Am I forgiven?"

Constance glanced at Randy, who only smiled and shook her head.

"Something tells me, Mr. Harkner, that no woman stays angry with you for long. Yes, you are forgiven."

Constance walked out, and Jake glanced from Randy to the food and back again. "Start eating. You say you can't live without me, Randy, but it would be worse for me without you." He watched her reach over and pick up a biscuit and butter it.

"Want some?"

"I'll eat later. I want you to swallow everything on that tray."

Randy sighed. "I'll try." She bit into the biscuit.

Jake watched her eat, and with every bite, he wished he could land another blow on Brad Buckley and ram burning coals down the man's throat. All for her, this woman who was the air he breathed.

Nine

LLOYD HOISTED HIS SADDLE TO A FRESH HORSE. THE animal whinnied lightly and danced sideways.

"Calm down, Strawberry." He reached under the horse to grab the cinch when the animal skittered a little away again.

"What the hell is wrong with you, girl?"

He heard it then, that buzzing sound of one of those motor engines they'd seen in town. It sounded like it was getting closer, and he heard children shouting excitedly. He scowled as he finished cinching Strawberry. He hated those damn new vehicles as much as his dad did. He could hear horses whinnying in a corral outside, and the bawling of their prize bull, Gus, who was penned up behind the barn.

He led his horse outside to see someone riding down the hill toward the homestead on a motorized bicycle. Now that was one he'd not seen before. A couple of J&L men rode out beside the bicycle, escorting whomever it was. Ever since Randy had been taken last winter, men were posted all over the perimeter of the J&L, as well as at the three houses, rotating turns at different posts. A visitor seldom made it close to the houses or even onto J&L property without anyone knowing it. Lloyd's wife, Katie, and his sister, Evie, watched the noisy contraption in surprise and curiosity.

Lloyd hung on to Strawberry's bridle as he hurried toward the women, who stood in front of his house with the three boys. A young man wearing goggles and a leather helmet drove the odd-looking bicycle closer.

"I want one of those!" Little Jake told his mother.

Evie folded her arms, looking unsure. "I think you'd better stick to horses, Little Jake."

Lloyd tied Strawberry and walked up to his sister and wife, adjusting his wide-brimmed hat as he frowned at the sight. "Damn useless, noisy contraptions," he grumbled.

"You sound just like Daddy," Evie told him.

"Well, everybody says I'm just like him in most other ways, so I might as well add this to the list. That damn thing is scaring the livestock. If one of those ever came along while we were herding cattle to Denver, we'd have a stampede on our hands."

Katie moved closer and stood beside her husband. Lloyd slid an arm around her and bent down to the five-month-old baby boy in her arms and kissed his son on the cheek. "Hey, Donavan, how's my boy?"

"He's constantly hungry," Katie complained. "If he keeps this up, I'll run out of milk."

"Well then, we'll just have to start using cow's milk, and he'll have to learn to like it."

The chunky little boy smiled at his father, and Lloyd kissed his wife's red hair. "I'll just have to take over once he's on cow's milk," he teased.

"Lloyd Harkner! Your sister is standing right next to us!"

Evie covered her mouth and laughed. Lloyd enjoyed the sound. There was a time when he thought his sister might never recover from her ordeal. It had taken years of love and support from her whole family, and from her damn good husband, to help her heal. The fact that she, too, had another new baby, a sweet little girl named Esther, proved she'd found a way to be whole in herself again.

"Lloyd, you're just like Daddy—you do your best to embarrass women."

"Just expressing my desire for my beautiful wife."

Katie moved Donavan from one arm to the other. "Yes, well, we need to discuss that. I feel like I'm constantly pregnant, and I've gained too much weight."

Strawberry whinnied and jerked as the noisy bicycle came closer to the house. Lloyd hugged Katie close. "Don't be worrying about your weight. I'd rather have you strong and healthy." He gave Katie a squeeze.

Katie looked up at him, and because he stood a good foot taller than she was, she stood on her tiptoes when he leaned down to kiss her lightly.

The conversation ended when the loud bicycle reached the house. Lloyd's older son, Stephen, along with Evie's boy Little Jake and Lloyd's adopted brother, Ben, started asking all kinds of questions about the bike, too many and too fast for the rider to answer all at once. His eyes looked almost comical once he removed his helmet and goggles, white circles in the middle of a face covered with dust from his ride. He shook out his hair, a tangle of wild, dark-brown curls that hung past his collar. "Slow down!" he told the boys. "I'll show the bike to you and give you rides as soon as I deliver my message."

"Lloyd, Jake's been hurt!" Terrel Adams told Lloyd before the messenger could. The ranch hand dismounted, and Lloyd and Evie and the rest of them sobered.

"Grampa's hurt?" Little Jake asked, no longer interested in the bicycle. "What happened?"

"This kid on the bike here is named Connor Grace," Terrel told them. "He's from Boulder, and he came here to let you know. He saw the whole thing."

"*What* whole thing?" Lloyd asked, letting go of Katie.

Connor reached out to shake Lloyd's hand. "There was a big bank robbery in Boulder," he explained. "Are you Jake Harkner's son?"

"I am."

Connor nodded. "At first I thought you were an Indian, what with that long hair and all."

"Get to the point," Lloyd told the young man.

"Well, sir, it was something, I'll tell you! I doubt any man is as good with guns as your father is, except maybe you. I've heard—"

"Start from the beginning, Mr. Grace," Lloyd ordered. "This is my pa we're talking about! Is he hurt bad?"

"I'm really not sure." Connor sobered and stepped back a little.

"Oh no!" Evie exclaimed. "I'll go get Brian."

Lloyd kept his eyes on Connor Grace as Evie ran off to find her husband. "Details, Mr. Grace, and *fast*!" he told the young man. "I've got to get to Boulder."

"Well, sir, there was a bank robbery. Your mother and a little girl—one of Jake's granddaughters, I think, were in the bank at the time—"

"Tricia!" Katie gasped. She looked up at Lloyd.

"That's *my* little girl you're talking about," Lloyd told Connor. "Is she all right?"

"Yes, sir, thanks to your father."

"What about my mother?"

"She's okay, too, far as I know. The whole thing was quite spectacular, actually. I was right there and saw the whole thing!" Connor explained to the last detail what happened as Lloyd and the others stood there in wide-eyed shock.

"Grampa stopped all of them, didn't he?" Little Jake asked, sticking his chest out proudly.

"He sure did. The whole town watched with their mouths open." Connor looked back at Lloyd. "Your pa was already shot, but he still came out, guns blazing. Boom! Boom! Boom! Those men were holding that girl and the women right in front of them, but your pa fired anyway! It was something to see! He got all four of them that was holding the hostages, right in the head, shootin' right straight at his own loved ones like he was damn sure he could get those men without hurting the women. Them robbers didn't even have a chance to fire their guns, but two others who were standing there with bags of money did get a chance. That's when your pa took a bullet to the head, I think."

"Jesus!"

Katie broke into tears. "Oh, Lloyd!"

Lloyd looked at Terrel. "Go saddle a horse for Brian!" He turned to his son. "Stephen, Evie went for your uncle Brian. Run over to the house and tell her he'll need a change of clothes and his doctor's bag and that we'll have to leave for Boulder right away!" He looked back at Connor. "You sure my mother and daughter are okay?"

"Yes, sir. There was bedlam everywhere after it happened, your pa laying in the street and your mother…she was fine…but I sure felt sorry for her. They carried off your father to a doctor, and your mother just kind of sat there in the street for a couple of minutes, like she didn't know what to do."

"*Damn* it!" Lloyd looked at Katie. "You know how she's been. This must have been awful for her. I've got to go to her!"

"Of course you do."

"My daughter?" Lloyd asked again.

"The Mexican woman carried her off so she wouldn't have to see her grandfather bleeding and wounded. She was crying, but she was okay."

"Thank God Teresa was with them! She'll take good care of Tricia," Katie told Lloyd.

"And that's all you know?" Lloyd asked Connor. "You've no idea how bad my pa was?"

"No, sir. I'm sorry. I heard the doctor say he was still alive. That's all I know. I walked over to the tele-graph office to tell them what happened so's they could telegraph the news, and then an old man came over and said as how your mother said somebody should come and get you as fast as possible. I just got my new motorized bike, so I said I'd go. I took the train to Brighton and then rode here from there. I came fast as I could. Without having to rest a horse, I made it in two days."

There might be an advantage to motorized vehicles after all, but there wasn't time to worry about that now. Lloyd turned to Katie. "I already have Strawberry ready to ride. I was going to go out to the southeast quarter and check for more strays, but now I'll have to ride to Brighton and catch that train. Pa would have left our carriage there to store while he and Mom took the train on into Boulder, so we'll use that to bring him home...if he's even alive." His voice broke on the last word.

"Lloyd, Jake is tough as nails. You know that. You have to believe he's all right."

Lloyd looked at Connor. "Thank you for hurrying here to let us know. Rest yourself a spell. Katie has lemonade in an icebox inside. She'll give you some."

"Lloyd, what about Tricia? I should go with you," Katie argued. "She'll need her mommy."

"You're still nursing. You stay here. Evie will need your support, too. You know how she is about Pa. And if Brian and I go alone, we'll be able to travel faster. Tricia is with Teresa, and she loves that woman to death. She'll be fine."

By then Evie had come running back. "Brian is getting ready," she told Lloyd. "I missed what happened."

"Connor can explain when Brian and I leave. We've got to get to Boulder and see about this. Pa is hurt, but this young man here doesn't know for sure how bad." He saw his sister's terror. She worshipped her father, and after everything... He grasped his sister's arms. "Evie, you know Pa. Is there a tougher man on the face of the earth?"

She looked up at him, tears in her eyes. "I know, but—he's still just human, Lloyd. Mother was always so afraid she'd see him killed in a hail of bullets. Maybe—"

"Don't think that way! They thought I was dead, too, last summer in Denver, but I survived. Right?"

Evie nodded, suddenly hugging her brother. Lloyd put his arms around her. "Don't you worry. He'll be just fine."

"It was quite something!" Connor told Evie. "Your father shot those men even while they held hostages right in front of them! A person couldn't ask for a better show of gunplay than what people saw during that robbery!"

Evie put a hand to her stomach, remembering Dune Hollow…when her father shot the man holding her, using a rifle from so far away she couldn't even see him. She'd felt the bullet whiz by her cheek, and the only thing she'd seen just before that was the glint of a rifle barrel. It would be impossible to make out anything else. She knew better than most how accurate Jake Harkner could be.

"I'm sure the papers are full of stories today," Connor told them. "Jake Harkner, the famous ex-outlaw, foiling a bank robbery!"

"I wish I could have seen Grampa shoot those men!" Little Jake exclaimed.

Evie pulled away from her brother. "Go inside, Little Jake. Set out some glasses for your aunt Katie so she can pour some lemonade for all of us." She saw a glint of tears in the eight-year-old's eyes. Her son loved his grandfather beyond measure. He practically worshipped the man, and yearned to be all grown-up and able to carry his own guns. He and Stephen and Jake's adopted son, Ben, had been hurt last winter trying to defend their grandmother when men came to drag her off. They rode out with Jake and Lloyd and several ranch hands to find and rescue her. They were just boys striving to be men, and the descendants of a man whose reputation would follow them everywhere. She looked up at Lloyd. "What about mother?"

Lloyd sighed, removing his hat and shaking his long, black hair behind his shoulders. "I don't know. Connor here says when they carried Pa off to a doctor, she just sat there in the street, looking confused. You know what that means. She must be terrified. I've got to get there fast."

Evie looked away. "Poor mother."

Brian came running, carrying a small carpetbag of clothes and his doctor's bag. At almost the same time, Terrel came from the barn with a saddled horse.

"What's going on?" Brian asked Lloyd.

"We have to go to Brighton and catch a train to Boulder. I'll explain everything on the way. Pa's been hurt." He looked at Brian, deciding to make light of it, because at the moment he wanted to cry himself. "So what else is new? The man doesn't have enough scars already."

Brian sighed, adjusting his hat. "I'm running out of places to stitch him up."

"Yeah." Lloyd sobered. "I have no idea how bad he is, Brian, and it's been close to three days since it happened. I guess I'll have to give in and see if we can get a telephone out here so we can find out these things sooner. Go ahead and mount up. I'm going inside to get my rifle and some clothes." He stopped to shake Connor's hand. "Thanks for hightailing it out here. It's a long trip across the J&L, let alone between here and Brighton. My wife will see to it you get paid something for your trouble."

"Oh, no, sir. It's an honor to have seen your father in action, and to meet you, too."

Lloyd just shook his head. "Yeah, well, I've seen my father in action one too many times." He put an arm around Katie and headed for the house. "The women will give you something to eat and drink before you head back," he called to the messenger. He opened the door, and Katie hurried inside to lay Donavan on a blanket on the floor. She then quickly set a pitcher of lemonade on the table while Lloyd headed into the bedroom to grab a couple of clean shirts. He stuffed them into a small carpetbag and grabbed up his rifle from a corner of the room, then hurried back into the kitchen.

Katie looked at him with tear-filled eyes. "Oh, Lloyd, I hope your father isn't wounded really bad. The state your mother is in, she couldn't handle that."

"Yeah, well, a man can only take so much, and he's getting older—and don't tell him I said that. He hates it when I tease him about his age, but God knows he's tough as ever." He rubbed at his eyes. "I'm not so sure even I could take it if something happened to Pa. We covered each other's backs for so many years as lawmen back in Oklahoma."

"Be careful, Lloyd." Katie walked around the table and reached up.

Lloyd pulled her into his arms, then kissed her deeply when she looked up at him. "You just sit tight and take good care of our new son," he told her. "We'll get back here with Pa as fast as we can. If it's going to be a while, we'll send a runner back out to let you know how he's doing, or if…" He didn't want to finish the sentence.

"It will be okay," Katie tried to reassure him. She touched his cheek, then leaned up to kiss him once more. "You'd better get going."

"Yeah." Lloyd left her and headed for the door. He took his gun belt and six-gun from where it hung over the doorjamb, where it was always ready to grab in case of trouble. All kinds of things could happen fast on a ranch as big as the J&L.

"Give Connor Grace two or three dollars for his trouble," he told Katie. He headed out the door, hooking the bag of clothes over his saddle horn and then strapping on his gun belt.

Connor Grace watched him. "Is it true you're as good with those guns as your father, Mr. Harkner?" he asked.

Lloyd mounted up. "*Nobody* is as good with a gun as Jake Harkner," he answered. He rode off, Brian following.

Ten

"DADDY!" LITTLE TRICIA RAN OFF THE HOTEL PORCH to greet her father before he even climbed down from the buggy he'd rented when the train arrived in Boulder.

Lloyd leaned down and scooped her up, hugging her tight as she wrapped her little arms around his neck.

"How's my baby girl?" Lloyd asked, kissing her chubby cheek. "Daddy heard you and Grampa were in a big gunfight, and I was so scared for you."

Tricia kissed him back. "I'm okay, Daddy, but Grampa got hurt! I was scared!" Her eyes began to tear.

"I know, baby. I'm so sorry I wasn't here. Are Grandma and Grandpa okay?"

Tricia nodded. "Teresa took me to see them at the doctor's office. Grampa was sitting up, but Grandma was laying down on a bed beside his. She looked real tired, and Grampa said I shouldn't jump on her bed."

Lloyd felt tremendous relief at what she'd said about Jake, but he felt sick inside at what this must have done to his mother. If a child as young as Tricia actually thought her grandmother looked tired, that wasn't good. Kids usually didn't notice those things. "I'm just glad my baby girl is okay."

"Those men were shooting! Bang! Bang! Bang! It hurt my ears." Her arms flailed around as she excitedly told her story. "Grampa shot right back, and I felt a bullet whiz right by me. I know that's what it was, 'cuz the man holding me fell down and dropped me. I wiggled away, and I laid right down on the ground like Grampa said to do. And then Teresa laid on top of me. It was funny, 'cuz she said she was scared she would smash me."

Lloyd grinned and kissed her cheek again. He looked at Teresa, who stood watching near the hotel doorway. She was a hefty woman and laughed at Tricia's remark. "I did not put all my weight on the little one, *señor*."

Lloyd winked at her. "Rodriguez was glad to hear you're all right, Teresa. Thank you for helping save my daughter. I don't know what this family would do without you and Rodriguez."

"It is your father who did the saving. I am glad he is better."

Tricia kissed her father's cheek several times over as Brian greeted Teresa.

"Is Jake really doing better?" he asked her.

"*Sí, Señor* Doctor Brian, but he will be very sore for a while."

"I wanna see Mommy," Tricia said with a pout. "Is she here, too?"

"Mommy had to stay home with baby Don. I'll make sure we all get home real soon, and then you can see her and help Mommy with the baby again."

Tricia's bright smile returned, showing dimpled cheeks and tiny white teeth. She had her mother's red hair, but Tricia's was a mass of curls. Lloyd had to smile at the contrast to his own long, nearly black hair, which his father was constantly chiding him about. Too bad for Jake; Katie liked it long.

He gave Tricia another hug and buzzed her neck, making her scream and laugh. He looked at Teresa. "I didn't know what I would find here," he told her. "Thank you, Teresa, for watching over her and keeping her from being scared." He handed Tricia to her uncle Brian, who gave her big hug.

"Well, now, you don't look hurt at all, Tricia. I'm very glad."

"Yeah, you don't have to make me take any medicine," she answered.

Teresa stepped closer to Lloyd. "I think your father, he will be fine. He is such a strong man."

Lloyd removed his Stetson and wiped at sweat that had formed on his brow from the unusually warm day. "You don't need to tell me that," he told her. "It's my mother I'm worried about."

"Sí, señor. You are right to worry about her. Your father, he has been insisting that she eat. He, too, is worried. She is so thin. He says he is afraid that if he touches her wrong, she will break."

A man holding a camera ran up to Lloyd. "Are you Lloyd Harkner?"

Lloyd scowled at having his conversation interrupted. "What's it to you?"

"They say you're as good with guns as your father, and when I saw you—I could tell from looking at you that you must be the son! You look just like him except for that Indian hair! You should have seen it! That shootout is the talk of the town! I saw the whole thing, you know. Your pa was in the street, and he suddenly started telling people to get out of the way! He shot a couple of those men right off their horses, and then more came out of the bank holding your mother and that little girl there, and two more. Most men would have been too afraid to shoot in a situation like that, but your father—"

"Slow the hell down!" Lloyd interrupted. "Who are you?"

"I'm Dick Crenshaw, a reporter for the local newspaper. Can I get a picture?"

"No! I haven't even seen my father yet, and I'm a little upset and concerned at the moment, so go away. After last summer, my father and I don't need or want any more publicity."

"You mean that big shooting in Denver? You look

pretty good for being shot point-blank. Boy, I wish I'd been there to see what your father did to—"

"Shut up, Crenshaw!" Lloyd barked. "I said we don't need any more publicity, and if you think my father has a temper, keep pushing me, and you'll find out what *my* temper is like!"

Crenshaw, a small man wearing a tweed suit and a white shirt with a collar that looked too tight, backed away at the look in Lloyd's dark eyes. "Sir, I just thought—"

"You thought wrong. The last thing this family needs is newspaper headlines all over the country again, which I'm sure has already happened. My father has enough trouble with men who are out to make a name for themselves. This kind of news just brings that much more attention."

The reporter backed away more, and Lloyd turned to Brian. "Let's go see my dad. Something tells me my mother needs you worse than Jake does. You know how he is. He gets meaner than a skunk when these things happen, and he's probably worried about my mom."

Brian handed Tricia to Teresa. "I'm worried, too."

Still irritated over the nosy reporter, Lloyd turned to him, scowling. "Where is the doctor's office?"

Crenshaw swallowed before answering. He turned and pointed down the street. "About a block down—that building that's painted yellow. I, uh, I hope he's doing better."

Lloyd sighed, angry with himself for being so rude. "I'm sorry, Mr. Crenshaw, but I'm worried about my father." Lloyd turned to Brian. "Let's go." He tied the horse and buggy to a post in front of the hotel. "Get us an extra room, Teresa," he told the woman. "We'll probably stay the night. I'm hoping we can take my parents home with us tomorrow. We'll have Brian with us, so if either one of them needs a doctor, we'll have one."

"*Sí, Señor* Harkner, I will get a room."

Lloyd walked toward the doctor's office, lighting a cigarette on the way. He tried to remember a time when his life hadn't been in some kind of turmoil because of his father. Leave it to Jake Harkner to walk right in on a bank robbery.

"Here we go again," he muttered.

Eleven

CONSTANCE CAME INTO JAKE'S ROOM AND LEANED close to him, speaking softly. "Your son is here, Mr. Harkner. I told him to wait outside because your wife is sleeping. Are you able to walk outside to talk with him?"

Jake moved to the edge of the bed and sat up. "Of course I can," he answered quietly. "Help me get dressed." He winced as he took a pair of denim pants from where they lay over a nearby chair. "I can't quite bend over yet enough to get my feet into these damn things."

Constance smiled, kneeling down and helping him get his feet into the pants. "I'm still not used to your cussing, Mr. Harkner, but I'm trying."

"Sorry. The words just fall out of my mouth." Jake stood up, and Constance pulled the pants up with him. She stepped away as he buttoned them. "I have to tell you that some of my friends are very jealous that I get to care for you," she told him. "They've asked some very personal questions."

Jake softly laughed. "I don't think I want to know what they were."

"I told them I've never seen a man your age in such good shape. I'm taking great pleasure in teasing them about that."

Jake shook his head as he pulled a leather belt through loops on the pants, then faced Constance. "We didn't get off to a very good start, but that was six days ago, and I was in a lot more pain." He took a shirt from the back of the chair and pulled it on. "Thanks for all you've done, and for looking after my wife."

"It's been a pleasure," Constance answered.

Jake left his shirt open and took a gun from his gun belt, which hung nearby on the bedpost. He shoved the gun into his belt on his right side, away from his still-bandaged wound. "I'll likely leave tomorrow, Constance. I'll miss you."

He walked out, and Constance glanced at Randy, who slept soundly. *What have you been through?* she wondered. *Such a beautiful man physically, and so loving, yet he shot those men the other day without hesitation.* How could any man even hope to turn out decent with a past like his? What had Mrs. Harkner seen in him all those years ago?

She began pulling covers off Jake's bed, figuring she might as well change them. She smiled at the gasps and twitters and giggles from her friends who wanted to know all about Jake. *He's one hell of a man*, she'd told them. *Hard muscle everywhere, his hair still thick but with just that little bit of white in it, his smile unnerving because it's so handsome. I envy his wife, but then again, sometimes I don't.*

⌘

Jake gingerly walked outside, where Lloyd and Brian straightened from where they'd been leaning against the railing.

"Pa!" Lloyd walked up and gave his father an embrace. "You're walking!"

"Hell yes, I'm walking." Jake slapped his son's shoulder. "It's good to see you, Lloyd."

Lloyd stepped back. "Damn it, Pa, I didn't know what the hell to expect." He quickly wiped at an embarrassing tear. "I wish I'd been here for the big shoot-out. It would have been kind of like the old days of riding together."

"Yeah, well, those old days are behind us, and good riddance." Jake turned to Brian and gave him a quick embrace. "Brian. Looks like I've proven again that this family is enough to keep a doctor busy full-time."

Brian, wearing a suit like he almost always did, grinned. "Nothing broken? No infection?"

"Not so far."

"What about that new part in your hair there?" Brian asked, nodding toward the head wound.

"One of them decided I needed to show a little more scalp. The doctor said if he leaves it like it is, some of my hair will grow back."

"And I suppose Randy is upset that someone spoiled that thick head of hair she loves."

Jake sobered. "Yeah, well, she's upset about a lot of things."

Brian sighed. "I'm sure she is. Right now, all I can say is it's damn good to see you up and about. Just don't overdo it, all right? You don't need to *prove* how tough you are. That gash on your head tells me how close you came to being dead. About a half inch over and Lloyd would have been shopping for a headstone."

"Yeah. It knocked me out for a few minutes." Jake glanced at Lloyd, who stepped up and embraced him once more.

"Damn it, Pa, this shit has to stop."

"Couldn't be helped." Jake squeezed his shoulders before letting go. How many fathers and sons were as close as he and Lloyd were? His son had turned into a hell of a man. "Give me a cigarette, will you?" he asked Lloyd. "I haven't had much chance to smoke."

Lloyd took a cigarette from a pack inside his vest while Jake buttoned his shirt.

"It's your mother that worries me," Jake told him. "She's thinner than ever, and this really knocked the life out of her." He leaned in as Lloyd held a match to the cigarette.

"Seems to me like the life was already knocked out

of her before you two came here," Lloyd answered. He folded his arms and leaned against a porch post. "What a hell of a thing to happen now." He lit his own cigarette. "She probably thought she'd watched you die, and right after being held hostage, too. That must have brought back bad memories for her."

Jake took the cigarette from his lips. "I'm glad you waited out here. The doc gave her something, and I want her to sleep. Have you seen Tricia?"

"Sure have. She about choked me to death hugging me with those little arms. She's stronger than she looks."

Jake grinned. "*All* Harkner kids are stronger than they look."

"Pa, it's chilly out here," Lloyd told him. He removed his jacket. "Put this on."

"I'm okay."

"Put it on, damn it! Why do you always have to be so stubborn?"

Jake grinned. "Why do you always have to be such a good son?" He turned and put his arms in the sleeves, and Lloyd pulled the jacket up for him.

"How did everything happen, Jake?" Brian asked. "Were you already inside the bank?"

Jake winced a little as he leaned against the wall. "Nine men rode into town like an army. I just happened to be standing nearby, and it was pretty obvious what they were up to." He filled them in quickly on the rest of the story. "I honestly wasn't sure I could shoot straight, because I was already wounded, but I had to do something or they would have ridden off with the women. I couldn't let Randy go through that. She'd rather die." He looked past Lloyd to see people beginning to gather and stare.

"How are you doing, Mr. Harkner?" a man asked.

"I'll live. Thank you."

"Hey, Jake!" Clete Russell hurried up the steps to stand

near him. "Good to see you up and about. When they carried you off, we weren't even sure you were alive."

"I appreciate your good wishes," Jake told him, glancing at Lloyd. He could tell his son wasn't happy about the extra conversations.

"Jake!" someone yelled from the street. "Looks like America might go to war with Spain over Cuba! I'll bet they could use you!"

"Which country?" Jake joked.

The man laughed. "I guess you'd be running guns to whoever pays the most money."

"If this was the old days, that's exactly what I'd do." Jake grinned and turned toward the door. "Let's go inside. It's the only way we'll get to talk. Doc Snow has some living quarters behind his office, and he's gone right now."

"Good idea," Lloyd answered. "I already had to get rid of a reporter." He shook his head. "I can just imagine how Jeff reacted to this news. He probably wishes he'd been here." They walked inside. "I think I'll call him later."

Jake put his hand up for them to be quieter. He motioned toward the door behind which Randy lay sleeping.

"You two need to talk alone," Brian told Lloyd quietly. "I'll go sit with Randy in case she wakes up. She might be upset to see Jake's not there."

Jake asked Constance if they could talk alone in the doctor's quarters. Brian quietly went to Jake's room, and Constance led Lloyd and Jake to the back of the building, then inside the doctor's kitchen. Jake grunted with pain when he tried to sit down, and Lloyd quickly grabbed his arm to help him into the chair.

"Are you really well enough to be doing this?"

"Hell yes. You know how I hate lying around."

"Yeah, well, you're not getting any younger, so be careful. I can tell you're in more pain than you're letting on."

"And you're enjoying every minute of it. You're always ribbing me about how I deserve my aches and bruises."

Lloyd sat down near him. "And you know I don't mean it." He smoked quietly. "You in any trouble over this? It hasn't even been a year since Denver."

"I shot a man's head off in front of a hundred people then. That's not quite the same as defending four innocent people against bank robbers." He took a drag on his cigarette. "No, I'm not in any trouble. The mayor and some of his friends came to see me. They told me they'd make sure that judge in Denver understands what happened. They treated me like a damn hero—want me to be their new sheriff." He sighed deeply. "Naturally, I told them no. Not only do you still need help at the ranch, but it would kill Randy if I took a lawman's job again."

He met Lloyd's gaze. "I'm worried about her, Lloyd. You know she hasn't been herself since last winter. This thing the other day—it hit her hard. I don't know what to do anymore. The doctor gave her some kind of tonic that seems to help a little. I want him to let Brian know what it is, and I want to take some home with us."

Lloyd leaned back and rubbed at his eyes, taking off his hat and setting it on the table. "I wish I knew what to tell you. She's my mom, and I love her, but you're the only one who can help her. You know her better." He sighed. "I'm proud of you, Pa. There was a time when you wouldn't have been *able* to handle something like what happened this past winter. You would have ridden right out of her life, thinking she was better off, but this time, she's never needed you more. You just have to remember that you didn't cause those men to do what they did, and with that barn fire, you couldn't have stopped them from taking her. I think as long as she has you and knows how much you love her, she'll still get better. It's just going to take a little more time."

Jake sighed deeply and took a drag on his cigarette, exhaling as he spoke. "Lloyd, there are times when I want to just ride out into the foothills and scream and smash something. Preferably Brad Buckley's head. I get that awful rage inside. I have to hide it around her, and I feel like I'll explode. You know how I am. I fight it constantly. I'm scared one of these days it will come out of me when she's around, and that would kill her."

Lloyd set his cigarette in an ashtray and rested his elbows on his knees. "Pa, if you need to take off for a couple of days once we get home, Evie and I can figure something out to make sure Mom's okay."

Jake sighed, grimacing again as he shifted in his chair. "We'll see."

Lloyd leaned back again, studying his father with bloodshot eyes. "God, I was worried sick about Tricia all the way here, let alone you and Mom. I'd like you to come back with us tomorrow if you think you can handle it. I rented a buggy, and we can take a train back to Brighton to fetch yours. You wouldn't have to ride a horse any part of the way. And Brian will be with us in case you need a doctor."

"We'll go, then. I think we can make it, and home is sounding pretty damn good right now." Jake took a last drag on his cigarette and put it out in the ashtray. "What would this family do without Brian? The man remains so steadfast and calm. I've said it before and I'll say it again. Evie couldn't have chosen better. What makes me sick is I wasn't even around when they met. I was sitting in prison, and you were—"

Lloyd turned away. "Yeah. I'll never forgive myself for running off and leaving Mom and Evie on their own."

"You've more than made up for that, Lloyd. They would both be lost without you now. Even Evie. You mean the world to her."

"Well, there's one person in this family who means more to all of us, and that's you. Evie and Katie will be so happy to know you're all right."

Jake winced as he shifted again. His side was beginning to ache. "I should tell you that before that robbery, I'd been in the Silver Saddle—had a little run-in with Brady Fillmore. He kept goading me about your mother—said she was getting thin and acting strange and that it must be my fault. That I'd put her through too much. I just about lost it, and came close to getting myself thrown back in jail."

"That man has a way of *making* you want to clobber him," Lloyd answered. "If I catch him with one more J&L steer, I'll hang him."

"It didn't help that I'm a mess. He's goddamn lucky I didn't kill him. If Randy didn't need me, I *would* have. I ran him out of the saloon and told him the same thing you just said. If we catch him rustling any of our cattle again, he'll die." He borrowed and lit yet another cigarette, a sign to Lloyd of how stressed he was. The man always chain-smoked when upset.

"Lloyd!"

The men looked up to see Randy, wearing a robe and standing in the doorway. She headed for her son, and Brian followed her into the room. Lloyd stood up and wrapped her in his arms, afraid to hug her too tight for fear she'd break.

"Mom, I wanted you to sleep as long as possible."

"Oh, I'm so glad you're here! Have you seen Tricia?"

"Of course I have. We didn't wake you up, did we?"

"No, I woke up on my own. I was so glad to see Brian sitting there!"

Randy pulled away, and Lloyd leaned down and kissed her forehead. "My God, Mom, I never realized how thin you're getting."

"Yes, well, your father has been force-feeding me.

He's like a prison warden about it. I swear if I don't eat, I'll be put into solitary confinement with nothing but lard for food." She looked at Jake with a frown. "You're a mean man, Jake Harkner."

Jake grinned. "Always have been. You knew that when you married me."

Randy smoothed back her hair self-consciously. "I must be a sight."

"A beautiful sight," Jake told her. "How would you like to go home tomorrow?"

Randy frowned, walking over to him and leaning close to feel his face for fever. "Do you think you're ready to travel? And what are you doing out of bed and walking around in the first place?"

Jake reached out and toyed with her hair. "I have to get up and around sometime. I hate lying in bed, unless it's with you. You know that."

"Jake!" She straightened and folded her arms. "You insist on always embarrassing me, don't you?"

Jake just grinned.

"I think it's too soon for you to leave, but I would love to go home," she told him.

"That bullet was more a flesh wound than anything else," Jake reminded her. "I'll be fine. We'll have Brian with us, and we can take the train part of the way."

Randy knelt in front of him. "Heaven knows I need to get you out of Boulder before you decide to take that sheriff's job. I want you home on the J&L with me."

Jake smiled for her. "Then that's where we'll go. And once there, I insist you eat like a pig."

"I might get fat."

"I couldn't care less. And Lloyd thinks we should get out of this place and sleep in our room at the hotel tonight. What do you think?"

"I think it might be too hard on you to have someone extra in your bed." The three men laughed, and Randy covered her face and put her head on Jake's knee. "All of you know what I mean!"

Jake winced as he petted her hair again. "We know what you mean, but I'll heal faster with you beside me. I'll be fine, Randy."

Randy raised her head and met his gaze, her eyes tearing. "I thought I was watching you die, Jake. I felt so alone! What would I do without you?"

Lloyd sobered. "Mom, you will always have me. And Evie and Katie and Brian and all the grandkids. You'll never be alone."

Randy shook her head. "It's not the same." She put her head on Jake's knee again. "Jake loves me in a special way," she said in an almost childish way. "He protects me. No one could ever take his place."

Lloyd met his father's eyes and saw the pain there. The man was screaming inside with sadness. The woman who had laid her head on his knee was not the proud, strong woman he'd married. The whole family had known heartache and hardship, and Jake had suffered as much or more than any of them, because he blamed himself for all of it. He'd been told a thousand times none of the tragedy was his fault, but he'd never believe that or stop blaming himself.

Jake Harkner always walked that thin line between light and darkness. No one wanted to see how ugly things could get if he fell into that abyss.

Twelve

"HEY, GIRLS, COME AND LOOK!"

Gretta MacBain held out the Denver newspaper for some of her girls to see.

CITY OF BOULDER CALLS
JAKE HARKNER A HERO

"I wonder how he's recovering," one called Tilly commented. "They say he was all shot up in that robbery." She wrapped a flimsy robe closer around her nakedness.

"The man is tough as nails," Gretta answered. "He'll be fine. It takes a lot to put down a man like that." Gretta picked up her coffee cup and took a swallow. She loved the quiet mornings here at her bordello. Last night, the Range Club had been extra busy, but mornings were quiet, with the girls waking at all different times, usually late. The last of their customers had been ordered out at nine this morning, and the girls were having breakfast and coffee.

"I don't even know him, but I still hope he'll be okay," one called Peach commented. She stretched and shook out her hair, her full breasts spilling out of her red corset. She wore only that and red panties with a garter belt and black stockings. "That hearing last year here in Denver was something, wasn't it? I don't care if he did blow a man's head off. If Jake Harkner showed up at my door, I'd welcome him with open arms."

"Open arms?" another teased.

They all squealed and laughed.

"I'd open my legs for Jake Harkner or that son of his any day." Gretta laughed. She shook her head and lit a cheroot. "And I can just imagine what Judge Carter is thinking right now. Jake really pulled a fast one on him, didn't he? Carter told Jake if he ever used those guns of his unnecessarily again, he'd send him to prison; but this thing in Boulder just made him a hero. I'll bet the judge and Prosecutor Wicks are eating crow right now, and I'm loving every minute of it."

"I wish I could have seen that shoot-out," Peach said excitedly. "There can't be anything much more entertaining."

"Tell us again what he's like," another girl named Trudy asked Gretta. "You're the one who had the pleasure of seeing him up close last summer—and in his *underwear*!"

Gretta set aside her cup and sighed, leaning back in a lounge chair. This morning, she wore only a pink, fuzzy robe and nothing more, and she couldn't help fantasizing about Jake Harkner reaching inside that robe.

"He's the most handsome man I ever saw," she said with a grin. "I mean he's rugged and a little weathered from too many years on the back of a horse in this unforgiving climate, but some men just age beautifully, and he's one of them. I wish I could tell you intimate things about him, but all I got to enjoy was the sight of him half-dressed in the men's dressing room at Porter Men's Wear. I'd looked him up to tell him I suspected Mike Holt was in town."

"And he was only half-dressed?" Peach asked, grinning.

"Nothing but the shirt and pants he was trying on for the Cattlemen's Ball." Gretta smiled. "I helped him get the shirt off, and he stepped out of those pants. His long johns fit just right, if you know what I mean. Didn't leave much to the imagination, and you don't need to ask what I was imagining!"

They all giggled again. "It didn't bother him to undress in front of you?" Tilly asked.

"Hell no. He's seen it all and done it all, and he's bold and honest—and not a bashful bone in his body." Gretta wiggled her feet in frustrated desire. "And what a man! He has a beautiful build, great arms, and a smile that practically makes you climax just looking at him."

They screeched with laughter.

"And he actually asked you if that bastard Mike Holt hurt you?"

Gretta sobered. "He actually asked. He actually cared." She drank more coffee. "He hugged me when I told him how Holt treated me. And those arms!" She let out a little whimper. "Let's just say I envy his wife."

A few of the girls snickered and some sighed.

"It's too bad the judge told him to stay out of Denver," Tilly commented.

"Well, it was only for a year, and that year is almost up," Gretta told them. "But it wouldn't matter. He'd never cheat on that wife of his." She straightened up. "And it's time you girls took your baths and started cleaning up for new customers. We'd better rake it in while we can. God only knows when Mr. Harley Wicks will show up at the door, telling us the City Council is closing us down."

Someone rang the electric buzzer at the front door. Gretta pulled her robe closer and smoothed back her hair, shooing the other girls up to their rooms. She frowned as she headed for the door. It was too early for customers, and that was usually the only kind of visitors they got. She opened the door a crack, then wider. Loretta Sellers stood there, a woman she figured she'd never see at the front door of the Range Club.

"Mrs. Sellers!" She looked around behind the woman and saw no one. "You shouldn't be seen here!"

"I know, but—Miss MacBain, we need to talk."

Gretta's heart dropped. The very Christian woman had adopted her baby daughter fifteen years ago. Gretta had seen her daughter several times from a distance, but the girl never knew Gretta was her mother, and that's how Gretta wanted it. "Go through that hedge there so no one will see you, and go around back," she told Mrs. Sellers. "You'll see a gazebo. I'll meet you there."

She closed the door, putting a hand to her chest. Her baby girl! Something was wrong! She hurried to her room and quickly put on a corset and underwear, then pulled on a house dress and buttoned it up. She stuck combs in the sides of her unbrushed hair and hurried out, not wanting to take time to put on petticoats or fix her face. She stepped into a pair of slippers and walked to the back of the house and out through the kitchen, telling her cook not to let anyone else come into the backyard for a while.

A hot wind hit her. Up until now, the weather had been quite cool for late June. The shade of the gazebo felt good when she stepped inside. Loretta was already there, sitting on a bench and sniffing into a handkerchief. Once a hefty woman, Loretta had gotten much thinner since the last time Gretta had seen her, which was at least a year ago. Gretta hurried to her side. "What's happened? Is my daughter all right?"

Loretta, now a wisp of a woman with mousy-brown hair and gray eyes just shook her head. "I'm so sorry, Miss MacBain. I've failed you!"

Gretta sat down next to her and put an arm around her, hoping Loretta wouldn't be offended at the intimacy, but the woman turned and wept against her shoulder.

"She's gone, Miss MacBain! She's run off! And I don't think anything good will come of it!"

Gretta felt sick inside. "Run off where? With whom?"

Loretta blew her nose and wiped at her eyes. "With a Mexican! He has bad intentions. I just know he does!

He'll sell her into slavery in Mexico! He'll turn my little girl into a…" She hesitated, rising. "I'm so sorry, Miss MacBain, but I fear she'll end up…"

"Like me?"

Loretta met her gaze. "Forgive me."

Gretta looked away. "What's to forgive? I gave her to you so she *wouldn't* end up like me. You don't need to apologize, Mrs. Sellers."

"But I fear it will be *worse* than your situation."

Gretta rose and faced her, frowning. "What are you talking about?"

"She's a virgin, Miss MacBain. I'm sure she's still a virgin. She's all starry-eyed over this man. He's quite handsome, but he's a lot older. She thinks he loves her. She's fifteen!"

The same age I was when I gave birth to her, and I'd already been sleeping with men for money for two years, thanks to my uncle. Gretta felt sick inside.

"She's young and foolish, and she's been a bit lost since my husband died," Loretta continued. "She truly thought of him as a father and never knew any different. She was looking for that love and protection. This man— Luis Estava—he appeared out of nowhere and started attending our church and giving her a lot of attention. Before long, they were good friends, and he was filling her with all sorts of lies about…about loving her…telling her he had a huge hacienda in Mexico and he wanted to take her there and marry her. He's a smooth talker, Miss MacBain. Nothing I told her could change her mind." Loretta turned away and stared out across the backyard.

"I told her she couldn't trust him…told her it was dangerous to go into a different country at her age. I suggested what I thought this man's motives were once he got her there, and she went into a defensive rage, furious that I would think anything bad about him. She carried on about how good he was to her and how handsome he was and how he was rich and she'd have a beautiful life on his horse ranch in Mexico and live like a high-born Mexican woman. I couldn't convince her otherwise." She turned and faced Gretta. "Then one night…a week ago…she disappeared. I'm sure he's taken her to Mexico without my permission, and God knows what's happened to her!"

Gretta tried to think straight. She'd been so sure her Annie would have a much better life raised in a Christian home. She grasped her stomach, pacing. "I…I don't understand! Annie was such a good girl, so beautiful and sweet…at least from the few times I got close enough to see her."

"She was." Loretta blew her nose again. "Ma'am, girls change at her age. They start noticing boys, and in this case…this man was so handsome and charming. Even people in church liked him."

Gretta met her gaze again. "I find it hard to believe your church actually accepted this man into their congregation, knowing nothing more about him."

Loretta stepped closer. "That's how charming Luis was, Miss MacBain."

Gretta put a hand to her head, trying to think. "Is there any chance he was sincere? That he really will make a good life for her?"

Loretta looked away, strands of hair falling from under her small straw bonnet and from the bun at the base of her neck. "I prayed for that when he first started wooing her. But when I stood up to him one night and asked him his real intentions…" She looked at Gretta again. "Ma'am, you know men, but we women… I think we all have that instinct, you know? When we're a little older, I mean. An instinct for that look in a man's eyes, when they're being honest and honorable, and when they aren't. He looked at me in a way that actually frightened me. We were standing there in my kitchen alone, and for one quick moment I feared for my life. I can't explain it, but—"

"I've seen that look!" Gretta interrupted, pacing again, her fists clenched. "Too many times!"

"I just knew…the way he looked at me…that he had bad intentions for Annie. But nothing I said to her after that would convince her. She'd become totally infatuated with Luis, and she told me I was just an old widow who was jealous she had a man in her life and I didn't. She even accused me of wanting Luis for myself because he was older!" Loretta turned away and broke into tears again. "I'm supposed to be her *mother*. That's what she believes, yet she talked so mean to me. I couldn't believe how she'd changed. I think Luis… I think he'd been giving her something…maybe some kind of drug, and she fell for his compliments about her beauty." She blew her nose again. "And she is beautiful, Miss MacBain, like you."

Gretta swallowed back tears. "I'm not so beautiful anymore, Mrs. Sellers, but thank you. At thirty-one, I'm considered a used-up whore." She noticed Loretta hold her stomach and turn away again. "I'm sorry, but those are the cold, hard facts. I've accepted my life, Mrs. Sellers, but I wanted so much better for Annie."

Loretta covered her eyes. "I've failed you."

"No, you haven't. Things happen in life we can't control, Mrs. Sellers. You didn't expect that devil to come along when he did and move in on an opportunity to woo a foolish young girl away from everything she'd known." She walked over and touched the woman's shoulder. "I'm damn sorry about your husband, and about this. I'm glad you did what you did for my baby, Mrs. Sellers. You loved her like your own. And you took good care of her." She blinked back tears. "God knows I couldn't have raised her. No innocent little girl should grow up knowing her mother is a…prostitute. I did what

I thought was best for her, and what's happened now is no one's fault."

"I just don't know what to do." The woman's shoulders shook. "The law wouldn't go after her. They won't go into Mexico. I did find a man who said he'd try to find her."

"Who? Has he left yet?"

"I gave him a picture and paid him two hundred dollars. His name is Jesse Valencia. He speaks Mexican and he used to be a sheriff in some town in Mexico. He bills himself as someone who can help people here find anyone. There have been a lot of kidnappings."

"So he figured, rather than get the rotten pay he gets in Mexico to go after these kidnappers, he'd come here to America and make a lot better money doing the same thing."

Loretta nodded. "Something like that. He has an office in Denver."

"I'm not sure I trust he'll really try to find her."

"He's all the hope I have. And I've already paid him. All we can do now is wait and pray."

Gretta paced again, feeling sick inside, hoping Mister Jessie Valencia wasn't just taking money for nothing. "And what if he comes back without her—or doesn't come back at all?"

Loretta shook her head. "I don't know. I fear it's already too late. Luis Estava has likely already…already shattered all of Annie's big dreams of living like a rich man's wife. Once she's down there long enough, there will be no changing what's happened. She could even die of disease or be murdered or…who knows? If Mister Valencia can't find her, no one will."

Gretta stared at a rose bush. "I'll pay you back the two hundred dollars and pray right along with you," she told Loretta, wanting to scream and weep. Her baby had been so beautiful. She'd grown into a sweet, loving little girl with red curls and blue eyes and fair skin. *Just the kind men consider prime flesh and worth a lot of money*, she seethed inside. "I know someone who I'm betting could find her," she told Loretta. "And he's not a lawman, at least not anymore. He's half Mexican and speaks their language; and obeying the law means nothing to him. He could ride right into Mexico and fit right in. He knows prostitutes and brothels, and best of all, he knows *outlaws*."

You didn't handle those bank robbers the way you did because you used to be a lawman, Jake Harkner. You knew how to handle them because you used to be just LIKE them! Gretta smiled at the thought.

"Who are you talking about?" Loretta asked.

Gretta shook her head. "I don't even know if he would do it. He's a family man now, and recently hurt." She faced Loretta. "But if that supposed investigator of yours doesn't bring my daughter back in a month, you let me know. This man could damn well find her, and you might say he owes me a favor. I helped keep his head out of a noose last year."

Loretta thought a moment. "Do you mean that man who made such a sensation here last summer? The one who shot a man in the head at close range at the Cattlemen's Ball?"

"That's exactly who I mean."

"But he's…he's no better than an *outlaw*!"

Gretta grinned. "I guess in some ways that's still true."

"And you would trust him with your fifteen-year-old daughter?"

Gretta felt suddenly calmer. "You *bet* I would. If Jake Harkner cared that a woman like me might be hurt, he'd sure as hell care about an innocent fifteen-year-old girl."

Thirteen

JAKE GRUNTED WITH PAIN AS RANDY HELPED HIM STEP out of his pants and shirt. "Brian said the wound looks like it's healing beautifully," she told him. She hung on to him as he sat down on the bed and managed to lay back. She looked around the room. "I'm glad we could stay in our own hotel room tonight. It's only been six days, but I can't wait to get back to the J&L, away from all the attention around here."

"And I'll be damn glad when I have all my strength back," Jake grumbled. "Get your gown on and come lie down by me, Randy. The last time you were in bed with me you were fully clothed and about to fall off the edge of the doctor's cot."

Randy pulled the covers over him. "I don't like that sleeping medicine the doctor gave me. I should be awake in case you need something."

"No, you need to *sleep*. Now come to bed. We're leaving in the morning, and we both need rest."

Randy undressed, and Jake closed his eyes against the sight of her ribs and hip bones sticking out. He wanted to rip apart everything in the room at the sight of her. He'd always loved watching her undress, drinking in the sight of her full breasts and the soft curve of her hips and the small roundness of her belly and the sweet, secret spot between her beautiful legs. She had a perfect bottom that had kept its firm roundness. All those soft curves and the roundness were gone now, and her breasts were not quite so full. He watched her brush out her hair, the beautiful blond tresses he loved to get tangled in his hands.

"Come on to bed, Randy."

Randy set the brush down and walked around the other side of the bed, away from his wounded side. She watched him warily. "You're upset."

"Yeah, you might say that. I'll be even *more* upset if you don't get into this bed."

Randy turned off the lamp beside the bed and crawled under the covers, lying still on her back and not touching him at first.

Jake sighed deeply, resting an arm over his eyes and struggled to speak calmly. "Randy, I'd like to get back together with the woman who sasses me and bosses me around and who feels good in my arms, the one who is round in all the right places—the one I can tease and laugh with and whose strength makes me stronger. That time we spent at the line shack after what happened last winter—it was beautiful and necessary. You asked me to take it all away and make you mine again, and I damn well did, or at least I thought I did. But something is different. Of all the things we've been through, none of it ever made us feel like strangers, but that's how I feel right now."

Randy just laid there a silent moment. "Jake, I'm sorry. I'm trying. You know I am. I can't stand the thought of you being angry with me."

Jake stared at moonlight on the ceiling. "Baby, I'm not angry. I'm...frustrated. I'm at a loss. When we make love, it's as though you're only doing it to prove to yourself I'm right there with you and you don't have to be afraid, but you aren't... I don't know... You aren't truly wanting me as a husband. I've never forced a woman, and I sure as hell won't start with my own wife. And since this incident here in Boulder, I've realized how awful it would have been if I'd died—or even if you'd died at the hands of those men—without us having fixed whatever has gone wrong between us."

Randy moved a hand sideways to take hold of his. "Jake, how can you possibly think I don't want you that way anymore? I can't imagine many women enjoy making love as much as I do with you. You always make it so beautiful. I just… I need to put last winter behind me…somehow. It's left me…" The tears came then. "I feel like it's wrong now…to enjoy it…like you'll think it's terrible that I still want a man after what they did."

Jake breathed deeply. *God help me.* He managed to move an arm beneath her and pull her against his shoulder.

"Randy, I'm your *husband*. It's good to enjoy it. What happened doesn't change the fact that you're my *wife*. One of the strongest things we've always had between us is practically sharing souls when we make love. Two people can't get much more intimate than you and I. There isn't one inch anywhere on your body I haven't touched or tasted and made love to. I adore every part of you, and nothing makes me happier than knowing I'm pleasing you."

Randy wiped at her tears. "But…I want to please *you.*"

Jake frowned, ignoring the pain in his side. His wife was more important. He'd gotten her to talk, and he would do whatever it took to *keep* her talking. "What are you talking about? You *do* please me. You know that."

"That's not what I mean." She put a hand over her face. "You just don't understand."

Jake was able to turn onto his good side enough to look down at her, his eyes adjusted now to the room bright with moonlight. He touched her face, reached under her chin, and pulled her head up, forcing her to meet his gaze in the soft light. "Randy, there isn't a whole lot about women I don't understand, and I'm not talking about sex. I'm talking about what I watched my mother go through, and stories from a lot of the women who raised me. So what is it about my own wife I don't understand?"

She closed her eyes. "I'm afraid to tell you."

"Since when have you *ever* been afraid of me?"

She swallowed. "Promise you won't be upset."

"You know better." Jake waited the several long seconds it took her to say what she wanted to say. He wasn't sure if he dared hope that things might be turning around, but maybe this time she would open up to him.

She squeezed his hand as though trying to hang on. "Jake, that…that thing they did…" Her body jerked in a sudden little sob, the tears punctuating her words. "Jake I can't make it…go away. Not without…doing something more to take away the ugly. Those three weeks we spent at the line shack…and you made love to me, I lied when I said that made it all better. That's why…why I—why we feel like strangers. Because we never lie to each other, and I felt the lies between us." She shivered in another sob. "You're my Jake…and I've been staying close to you to make sure you…don't leave me because I lied to you. And because you refuse to understand what I really need, and that…embarrasses me and…scares me because I don't want you angry with me or I might…lose you when I need you most."

Tears spilled down the sides of her face and into her ears. Jake pulled her closer and kissed her forehead, wiping at her tears with her fingers. "Randy, when have I ever been truly angry with you? You know what you mean to me. And you know I'm not a man who's surprised by anything. I'll do whatever it takes to make you happy again, to be close again. You don't need to lie to me just because you think it's what I want to hear. I want you better, so tell me what you need. What don't I understand?"

"Please don't get upset."

"I won't get upset."

"But you have before."

"When?"

"Every time I try to tell you."

"Tell me what?"

She hesitated again before speaking up. "I just think... if it was you...my Jake...if *you* were the last one to...do that... It would make everything better. Because...you love me and you'd...you'd find a way to make it beautiful because you've always said...you had too much respect for me as a person... I mean...you understand that would be hard for me. And yet you would be doing it for *me*."

He reminded himself not to react in a way that might scare her away and end the conversation. He realized what she was telling him, but what if it brought back memories that would send her over the edge? "Randy, you're talking about something that could have a bad effect on you, even though it's me."

"No, it won't." She sniffed back tears and put her hand over his as he held his to her face. "Jake, I can't explain why. But if it was you...that's the memory I would keep. And it would make the ugly way they did it go away because it would be you...my Jake...and it would be an act of love."

Jake didn't say anything for a few minutes, weighing what she was asking. Letting this beautiful, proper woman he adored do what she was asking didn't seem right, even though he'd been totally intimate with her body. It struck him that all he'd ever cared about was making sure she took pleasure in everything he did with her and to her. He got his deep pleasure in return just being inside her, owning her, watching her breathe deeply in utter passion and surrender. If she'd ever once said no, he would have stopped. He'd never even considered she might need to feel the same way—that she needed to please him, to touch him and taste him in her own way. "We've talked about this, Randy. Those men did something I've never asked of you because I've always felt you're too proper and—"

"I know," she interrupted. "That's just it, Jake." She sniffed in another sob. "They made it so ugly, but you can make it better, because if we…did that…it would be…beautiful and…intimate…and right. I know you've never asked that of me because you think I'm too special…but I need you to understand *why* it would help me get over what happened. You think they made it so ugly…and they did. And when brutal men…do that… it's called that ugly, ugly word. But no one can call it that…if it's between a man and wife and out of love. Then the act becomes beautiful."

Jake could hardly believe his ears. "Randy, what if it just makes things worse for you?"

She shook her head. "It won't. I just know it won't. You're my Jake. You'll make it beautiful. Don't tell me you've never done that because I know how you grew up. I need you to understand *why* I need to share that with you. It would make it beautiful for me because *everything* you do to me is beautiful. I feel the adoration in your every touch. It would erase the ugly. You refuse to do it, and I understand why…and I wouldn't want to do it often. Maybe even just once. I only know I need to do this, Jake. You have to stop insisting I shouldn't. It's what I want, and if it gives you pleasure in return, I'll feel better about all of it, and I'll feel closer to you again."

He pulled her closer. "You have to be sure, Randy. I could lose you completely."

"I am sure. I've been sure ever since we went to the line shack after that horrible attack. We were so intimate, and I kept saying maybe we should do that because it might help, and you kept refusing, thinking I would hate it."

"You still might."

She nuzzled her lips against his neck. "It would be you. How could I possibly hate it?"

"Because you aren't made that way, Randy. Something like that isn't natural for you."

"Letting you be so intimate with me wasn't natural for me either when we first became lovers. But you have a way of loving me that makes it beautiful, and makes it seem so right."

Jake struggled for the right words. If he said one thing that made her feel ashamed or embarrassed or made her think he didn't respect what she wanted, he'd lose her again. "Baby, you do whatever you need to do to get better. That's all I care about." He wrapped his hands into her hair and kissed her eyes. "And you're right. I *didn't* understand, but I was only thinking of you and trying to keep away the bad memories."

"I know."

Jake leaned in and met her mouth in a deep, delicious kiss, groaning then with the thought of what she wanted to do, something that in all their years together he'd never asked of her. "Damn," he said amid more kisses, "I wish I didn't have these stitches in my side." He felt her smiling in the midst of another kiss.

"Now you have something to think about," she teased. "Something that will give you reason to heal faster."

There it was—that attempt at the old teasing remarks they always shared when making love. "Well now, here I am in bed with the woman who makes me crazy, and I can't do anything about it. This is more painful than these damn stitches."

Randy moved her arms around his neck, and they shared an even deeper kiss. "There are times when I *like* making you suffer, Jake Harkner. There are a few things you've done during our marriage that you *deserve* to suffer for."

"I won't argue that one." More kisses. Jake gently

moved a hand over her breasts through her soft flannel gown. "Tell me again you're sure, Randy, because when I'm well—"

"I'm sure."

He ran a thumb over a taut nipple. "And here I thought I might be losing you. I was imagining you turning to another man, someone who wouldn't put you through the hell my past keeps dredging up to come between us—someone like Peter Brown."

Randy gasped and pulled away. "Jake Harkner! How could you think such a thing?"

Jake grinned. There was the spark. "Hell, the man has loved you for years. If he got the chance, he'd sweep you right away from me."

"He wouldn't get the chance. You'd shoot him first."

"You bet I would." Jake grimaced as he managed to lay back down. "Randy, you have to always tell me the truth, understand?"

Randy snuggled closer. "That's what I've been trying to do, but you wouldn't listen."

Jake sobered. "Let's get something straight, and I want to hear it from your own lips. What those men did didn't change one thing for how I feel about the most beautiful woman on the face of the earth. They never touched you. Understand? You know I'm right, so say it."

She curled tighter against him. "They never touched me."

"Say it again."

"They never touched me." Jake felt her shiver. "They never touched me." She burst into tears.

Jake held her close, refusing to let on he was in any pain. She needed this. "Let it out, Randy. You've been pretending everything is fine, but you still need me in your sights night and day. You're stronger than that."

She broke into such heavy sobs that Jake's eyes teared. "Who is holding you, baby?"

She could barely get the words out. "Jake Harkner."

"And who do you belong to?"

"Jake Harkner."

"You bet." This was the closest she'd come to her old self in months. He loved her more for being too bashful to tell him what she wanted. Thirty-one years together and she sometimes acted like they'd just met. He would have to be so damn careful. How was he going to do what she wanted without bringing back bad memories?

He ran his thumb back and forth over her lips, then leaned over and found her mouth again, invading it with a long, slow kiss that was so deep it was like making love to her with his mouth. He ached to be inside her.

"Are you all right?" he asked.

"I'm just..." She put a hand to her face. "I didn't know how to tell you."

"Randy, who the hell have you been living with all these years?"

She reached under her pillow for a handkerchief and used it to wipe at her eyes. "A man who's done it all and might laugh at me asking something like that."

"You know me better."

"You were so...adamant...about not doing that. It's okay, Jake. I'm your wife. It's not disrespect. I just... I don't know how else to make what they did go away. And I feel better...just telling you." She wiped at her eyes again. "I know you well enough to know how hard this has been for you. You've devoted practically every minute of every day to me since last winter, and I love you for it. I promise to eat better and give you some freedom."

"I don't need freedom—not from you. We'll take things a day at a time, all right? I'll leave you on your own more often, and the other—it will just happen when it happens. We won't plan it, and we won't talk about it. How's that? We'll just know when it's right."

"Okay." She snuggled even closer. "You do so much for me, Jake."

The remark pained him. *I've done so much TO you*, he thought. He would never understand why she'd stayed with him through so much hell. How many times had he thought they'd finally found peace? Yet here he lay healing from a bullet wound, and they were talking about how to help her get over an ugly, brutal attack she'd suffered…because of him…because of his enemies. It was no wonder she'd half lost her mind.

Fourteen

LLOYD DRANK IN THE SIGHT OF THE HARKNER HOME-
stead as they came over the rise. Below, the Harkners'
three homes were nestled against the foothills of the
Rocky Mountains range. There should be more snow
high in those mountains, but it had been a mild winter
for Colorado and not enough rain this spring. Now they
were headed for July, normally dry anyway.

He couldn't worry about it today. It was just good
to be home, especially good that his father was healing
fast. The whole family had been through so much hell,
and strangely, in spite of most of the trouble stemming
from Jake Harkner's past, Jake remained the hub around
which the family circled. It was as though all the spokes
that emanated from that hub would fall to pieces
without that central strength. Jake would deny that, a
man who had never accepted his worth. *You're just like
your father*, people often said to Lloyd. Some men might
not take that as a compliment, considering. But Lloyd
was proud.

He lit a cigarette and waited while everyone greeted
Jake and fussed over him. Lloyd shook his head, remembering there was a time when he'd thought he hated the
man—so many years…so many memories. Jake Harkner
had a surprising capacity to love, mostly because he'd
never known the meaning of the word as a boy growing
up with Satan for a father. Lloyd supposed that was why
Jake had been determined to be the best father a kid
could ask for. It was his way of living over his boyhood

in the way he would have liked it to be. Everything they'd been through only made the whole family stronger, knitted together in a way that they would never be pulled apart.

That's why it had hurt so much to see Randy withering away. These last few months, he and Evie had feared they were watching their parents drift apart, something they never thought could happen, but there was hope in the fact that his mother actually seemed a little stronger on their trip home. Maybe it was just because she felt safer here, in familiar surroundings. Over the last couple of days he'd noticed more joy in her eyes, and she'd fussed over Jake all the way home, giving him orders for every move he made so he wouldn't reinjure himself. They'd exchanged a few biting, teasing remarks, a rather comical exchange of barbs—something he hadn't see them do in a long time.

Something had happened, but he wasn't going to ask Jake about it. His father was a man who talked about something only when he wanted to. Better to just take comfort in what he'd observed and be glad that maybe— just maybe—his parents were finding their way back to each other. *It just takes a lot of time.* His sister had told him that once, and who knew better about things like that than Evie?

He kicked Strawberry into motion, riding at a faster gait to catch up with the entire procession of family and ranch hands as they made their way down the hill, the three boys peppering Jake and Randy with questions, Little Jake riding in circles around the buggy. Chickens squawked, and horses in an outer corral whinnied, as though even the animals were glad to see Jake return.

"You really okay, Grampa?" Little Jake asked when they finally reached the house. The boy suddenly looked ready to cry.

"I'm all right, Little Jake. Everybody come inside the

house, and we'll have the girls cook up a good meal for all of us. We'll talk about everything then."

"And no jumping all over Jake. He's not healed yet," Randy told them with an air of authority. Lloyd noticed his father move an arm around her when he climbed out of the buggy. Yes, something had certainly changed.

"Mommy! Mommy!" Tricia shouted as Katie ran down the steps to sweep her daughter into her arms and hug her tight. Lloyd thought it was a beautiful sight. Katie Donavan had come into his life when he needed her most. She was beautiful and loving, had helped him get over his first wife's death, and was a good mother to his and Beth's son Stephen. She'd given him Tricia and now another son, Donavan Patrick.

How amazing was it that the infamous Jake Harkner was responsible for this huge, loving family? And now he and Lloyd ran this ranch together, a glorious eighty-thousand acres. This spring hadn't boded well for rain, but Lloyd had planned ahead and was saving grass for emergency feed in a vast valley called Evie's Garden. Horse Creek ran through there and had never dried up, even when there had been years with little rain. Mountain snows fed it, but this year that could be a problem.

There followed two hours of sheer bedlam. The ranch hands surrounded Lloyd and Jake outside with questions about the fracas and reports on roundup and branding, while the women cooked inside the main house. Nothing felt better than the whole family being together, which was why Jake had insisted on keeping a big house with lots of bedrooms. Stephen and Little Tricia slept there practically as much as they slept at home. All the kids loved Randy's cooking and being around Jake, whom they considered the toughest, most famous man on the face of the earth. Lloyd had to shake his head over that one.

Once in the house, Jake insisted on holding the two

babies for a while, little Donavan and Evie's new baby girl, Esther Miranda. They let Tricia and her cousin, Sadie Mae, sit on his lap, while Randy constantly reminded the girls not to hug their grandfather too tightly or crawl all over him the way they usually did. Sadie Mae pulled his shirt up unexpectedly to see where Grampa had been shot, and then she started crying.

The women were all over her tears, and Lloyd wondered if there would ever be any semblance of order in the growing mob of brothers and sisters and cousins the family had become.

One thing that gave him the most joy was noticing how his parents kept glancing at each other. Things were definitely better, and Lloyd suspected they'd rather have some time alone, something they hadn't had since they left for Boulder in the first place. Randy walked to where Jake sat in his favorite big chair near the fireplace and put out her hands. "Come to the table, Jake."

Jake grasped her hands, and she helped him up, a rather comical sight with him so big and his mother so small. He watched them kiss, and his mother put an arm around Jake as he walked to the table.

They all took their seats, and Jake asked Evie to say grace. Evie looked at him in surprise. "Did I just hear my father ask me to pray?" she asked teasingly.

"Yes, you did."

"You *never* ask me to pray."

"First time for everything, baby girl. Your prayers are strong. Mine don't hold water at all, so just say grace and don't ask questions."

Lloyd grinned. *Typical Jake Harkner comment.* Jake was feeling better, and it wasn't just his side that was healing.

"And include a thank you that your mother is eating better and smiling more."

"Jake, she doesn't have to do that," Randy protested.

Lloyd studied his mother closely. Was she actually

blushing a little? He glanced at Evie, who just shrugged before offering the prayer. The whole family dived in then, and Randy filled her plate and ate as though truly hungry. Lloyd wondered if maybe the shooting had been good for his mother. It had forced her to be stronger.

As soon as they finished eating, the boys continued to insist Jake tell them the story about the bank robbery all over again. Little Jake was the most excited, using his fingers to mimic handguns as he yelled "Bang! Bang! Bang!" when Teresa retold what it was like to feel Jake's bullets whizzing over her head.

Lloyd stepped outside to have a cigarette, and Evie followed him out. "Lloyd, did you see? Mother seems better."

Lloyd drew on the cigarette and leaned against the porch railing. "Yeah, she does. I don't know for sure what happened, mind you. She was still bad when we got to Boulder, and no better after that damn shoot-out—at least from what I could tell when we got there. She looked really bad. Pa was still concerned, and I could see him sliding backward, you know? He was about to do something crazy, I think, as if that shoot-out wasn't bad enough. It's probably a good thing he was injured. It kept him from… I don't know. Something he probably would have regretted. You know how he is. He told me that before the shoot-out he got into it with Brady Fillmore over that stolen steer, but there was more to it than that. I think maybe Fillmore said something about Mom. It doesn't take much of that kind of talk to set Pa off."

"We all know how ornery he can be."

Lloyd studied his sister, never quite able to stop worrying about her since her ordeal at Dune Hollow, even though it was almost five years ago. "How are you?"

"I'm okay. It just scares me to think of something happening to Daddy. I'm so relieved he seems to be recovering." She sat down in a wicker chair. "Should I ask him about Mother?"

"Absolutely not. It's something private, or Pa would have told me. Just leave them alone. God knows they've worked their way through enough other bad times that could have pulled them apart. If they can rise above this one and find each other again, there isn't much else that could come between them. And don't ask Mom. God knows, one wrong word might embarrass her or send her back to silence. She's eating and talking, so let it be."

"I know how hard something like that is, for the man and the woman. I couldn't have survived without Brian's love. He's such a patient, caring man."

Lloyd hated thinking about it. He'd shot a man in the back the day Evie was rescued, and he damn well deserved it for running from the law. Thank God he and Jake had been the law back in those days. They'd had a right to go after those bastards and blow them away. "Your husband is a real blessing," he said aloud. "If you'd married a man who abused you or didn't give you the proper love and attention, I'd have beat the shit out of him, but then I'd have to wait for Pa to do it first."

Evie smiled shyly. "Pity the young men who come calling on Tricia or Sadie Mae."

Lloyd kept the cigarette between his lips. "I don't even want to think about that."

Evie rose, folding her arms. "Well, speaking of giving a woman the proper love and attention, dear brother, I should tell you that you need to work on your own husbandry."

Lloyd frowned, taking the cigarette from his lips. "What are you talking about?"

"Katie is hiding it, but she's been depressed about gaining weight. She thinks it bothers you."

Lloyd tossed the cigarette. "That's ridiculous! I don't care about things like that. Hell, she just had a baby five months ago, a healthy new son. I couldn't be happier about that. And Katie is beautiful no matter what. Her mother is a stout woman too, but all I ever saw was a lovely woman who had an incredibly big heart and generous nature."

Evie smiled slyly. "Honestly, Lloyd, sometimes a man just needs to be hit over the head to see straight. You do realize how handsome you are, don't you? I mean, you see yourself in the mirror when you shave."

Lloyd let out a little gasp of exasperation. "Jesus, Evie, I don't think about things like that. Who the hell cares?"

"*Katie* cares. And at that cookout a month ago at the Holmeses', you talked often with little Lori Holmes. She's sixteen and a beautiful girl, and anyone can tell she's infatuated with you."

"For crying out loud, she's close to half my age! I was just being friendly."

"And being the block-headed man you can be sometimes, you have no idea how it feels to a woman who is worn out from running after kids and from constantly nursing and feeling hard on herself to see her handsome husband being friendly with a little girl gone all starry-eyed. It hurt her, Lloyd. She finally told me just a couple of days ago. We had a long talk, and I told her I think I know you well enough that it meant nothing to you, but she needs to hear it from *you*, not me."

Lloyd grasped his long hair and pulled it behind his back. "That really bothered her?"

Evie sighed in exasperation. "Honestly, men can be so dense! Lloyd, sometimes women get depressed after having a baby, and I know it's been almost six months, but with all of you men being so busy this spring rebuilding the barn that burned, and then roundup and branding, Katie says you haven't paid her a whole lot of attention. Then came the cookout and that pretty young girl. Put it all together, big brother. Your wife needs some extra attention the next couple of weeks. And if I were you, I'd bring back something really nice for her when you come home from the Denver cattle drive. She needs to know you still fancy her."

"Of *course* I'm attracted to her! But I also love her enough to realize how hard it would be on her if she got pregnant again. I've been deliberately staying away from her, because that's the *last* thing she needs right now."

"Then you need to explain that to her. *Listen* to me, Lloyd. This is a woman who understands, so take my advice. And let *her* make the decision about more babies. If you stay away from each other because she wants it, she'll understand. But this way, she just thinks you've got your eye on someone younger and prettier."

"Evie, I had my share of women before I married Beth. When I lost her, Katie filled a void I never thought could be filled. I couldn't love her more. As far as someone younger and prettier, hell, look at Katie. Women don't get much prettier than her...present company excluded, of course."

Evie waved him off. "Don't take it for granted Katie understands that. Women have to *hear* from their husband's lips how pretty they are. And quit worrying about getting her pregnant. All children are a wonderful gift, and if God means for you to have more, you'll have more. Take my advice and give her some extra attention. I have no doubt you have plenty of charm in that department. I can take Tricia and Stephen with us tonight if you want. Tricia likes to play with Sadie Mae anyway, and it might help Tricia forget about that awful gunfight. It must have been terrifying for her."

Lloyd sighed with frustration. "I'll see what I can do. It's pretty bad when your own sister has to tell you how to handle your wife. I can't believe I didn't see this."

"You've been so busy, Lloyd, and I know you've been worried about Mother." She walked up to give him a quick kiss on the cheek. "Come back inside and have some pie. We shouldn't stay out here too long, or Katie will think I'm telling you all this, which I promised her I wouldn't."

Evie walked back inside, and Lloyd followed. He sat down and watched his wife cut up pies for everyone. She glanced at Lloyd, and it was the first time he'd realized something was wrong, other than the too-quick kiss they'd shared when he first arrived. How could he not have seen it? He smiled at her, deciding he was going to take her out of here sooner than later. He'd damn well make sure she knew how much he loved her.

Fifteen

"LLOYD HARKNER, YOU EMBARRASSED ME TO DEATH, leaving the house like that! We weren't even done visiting." Katie laughed when Lloyd picked her up and carried her into their house, kicking the door shut behind them.

"You were done nursing Donavan, and I decided I'm jealous of my own son." He raised her up and kissed her cleavage. "These are *mine*!"

"Lloyd, what's going on?" She laughed again. "Honestly, everybody back at the house will know what we're doing over here, because you made me leave the baby behind!"

"He'll sleep for a good three hours, and I intend to spend all three of them with you in our bedroom."

Katie covered her face and rested her head on his shoulder as he carried her into the bedroom. "What has gotten into you?" she asked.

"*You*." He set her on her feet and put his hands on either side of her face. "You've been a little distant, Katie Donavan Harkner. After watching what my folks have been going through, I don't want that to happen to us."

She looked back at him with eyes that suddenly teared. "You could tell?"

"I've watched my father's heart slowly break over my mother, and I've been so involved in that and in rebuilding the barn and then roundup and now this thing in Boulder… I just realized I've been neglecting the one person who means more to me than anyone else except my children. You've been cooking and sewing and nursing and putting up with being alone a lot and up nights with Donavan, and we haven't been really close in a while." He kissed her gently. "I'm taking you back before I lose you."

She grasped his wrists. "You will never lose me, Lloyd Harkner, but lately I...I thought maybe *I* was losing *you*."

He pulled her close. "Why would you think that?"

"Just...all the things you just said. It just seems like all we do is pass each other in the night. You get up before sunrise for ranch work, and then I get up to feed Donavan, and then I work all morning with the kids and keep feeding the baby, and you come in for a quick lunch and you're gone again, and then we talk at supper but don't really talk, and then you go to bed because you're so worn out from ranch work, and I go to bed later after feeding Donavan, and then the next morning, it starts all over again."

"Katie, we've made love a few times."

"That's the point. A few times. And almost always in a hurry because of the kids and your work and me nursing. I just—I'm so glad you're noticing, because I thought maybe you didn't love me as much. And last month, at that cookout, that Holmes girl flirted with you something awful, and you were nice to her—"

"And that's *all* I was doing, Katie. Being nice."

"But she's so pretty, and you're so good-looking, and I'm getting fat."

"Stop that talk right now. Don't you *ever* doubt how much I love you, understand? You brought me joy and love at a time when I was so lonely I wanted to die. I thought I'd never get over Beth, and then you came along, and you put up with her memory and understood how hard it was for me to love someone else. You understood what I was going through because you'd lost a husband at too young an age, so we've *both* been through a lot." He grasped her shoulders and guided her backward until she sat down on the edge of the bed. "And then you stood right up to those raiders back in Guthrie when they took Evie, and you used that shotgun to hold them off from taking you and Stephen. And you got pregnant and gave me that beautiful little girl and now another son, and there is no way in hell I would ever look at another woman. Not in the way you're thinking." He knelt in front of her. "And you get it straight that I don't give a damn if you're heavy or thin or anything in between. You're *beautiful*. A man can hardly avoid noticing those green eyes and this gorgeous red hair." He ran his hands into her long, thick tresses. "I've been staying away from you more because I'm scared to get you pregnant again. You lost your first, and I've always been afraid something like that could happen again, but I never considered you might think I simply didn't want you. I will *always* want my Katie-girl, understand?"

She leaned forward and threw her arms around his neck. "I love you, Lloyd. When I saw you with that girl…and there I was fat and tired and holding a baby and—"

Lloyd kissed her again, laying her back on the bed, moving on top of her. "You have to *talk* to me, Katie. I'm not going to let this grow into something that comes between us." Katie let out a startled little scream when he grabbed her up once again and scooted her farther up onto the bed. "You stay right there while I take off my boots," he told her.

He sat down in a chair and yanked off his boots, throwing them aside, then removed his socks. He stood up and took off his gun belt, tossing it into the chair, then removed his shirt and his leather belt. He unbuttoned his pants.

"What are you doing?" Katie asked, scooting farther back on the bed. "I thought we were just talking."

"There is a time for talking and a time for *doing*. And what I'm doing is called getting undressed." He yanked off his pants, then his long johns, revealing something that told her he wanted his wife.

"Lloyd!"

He crawled onto the bed, hovering over her. "Now— is there something more you should tell me that I don't know about?"

"I don't think so."

"Good. Then get this straight, Mrs. Harkner. I think of you as beautiful and delicious. You have all the colors of the earth in you, and you're *mine*! If I wanted some other woman, I'd have gone after her. She wouldn't have to come to me. I've not touched another woman since I met you back in Guthrie and knew you were what I wanted, and I never will." He ran his fingers along the bodice of her dress, brushing across her full bosom, then leaned down and kissed her cleavage. "Now get undressed, and we'll finish this discussion after I get my fill of you."

"But I—"

"Get undressed. I'll help you." He lay down beside her and finished unbuttoning the front of her dress, and then her camisole, pushing it aside and leaning in to taste a nipple, licking at lingering breast milk. "Now get up and take off these clothes. Between all those petticoats and stockings and stays, I'll never get to the good stuff."

"Honestly, Lloyd!" Katie moved to the edge of the bed, her back to him, and removed the top of her dress to the waist, then her camisole and girdle, which left little dents in her skin. She stood up and pulled off the dress and slips, then her shoes and stockings. She started to remove her pantaloons, then sat down again, hesitating. "My stomach is still soft from the baby. For some reason, it's taking longer for this weight to go away."

He moved an arm around her from behind and pulled

her back onto the bed. "I like you this way. This beautiful belly is warm and comforting, and it carried my son for nine months." He pulled her pantaloons down and off and straddled her, drinking in her beautiful, pale skin, such a contrast to his own dark color. He bent close and began kissing her belly.

He took his time, wanting her to relax. He kissed her belly, her breasts again, back to her belly, and to the folds where her legs met her belly. He kissed the hairs that hid the place he loved best, making her suck in her breath and open herself to him, wanting more. He slaked his tongue into her folds and worked it in circles that he knew made her want even more. Katie gasped, mad with pleasure, and opened herself more completely. In minutes, she was clinging to the brass bars at the head of the bed and crying out in a delicious climax. He moved over her belly again, licking it and tracing his tongue up between her very full breasts, kissing her cleavage, tasting hungrily at her nipples again, then meeting her mouth. "I love you and don't want any other woman," he told her between kisses. "Understand?"

"Yes." She threw her arms around his neck. "I love you so much, Lloyd. I just never want you to be disappointed in me. I just—"

Lloyd met her mouth in another searching kiss, cutting off the rest of her sentence. He moved his lips to her neck, brushing at it with his tongue and lips in fluttering, teasing touches. He positioned himself between her legs and she leaned up and kissed at the hard muscle of his arms and shoulders. "I'd die if you did this with another woman, Lloyd. I want to always please you this way."

"You do please me, Katie Harkner." He searched her mouth in another demanding kiss, his long, black hair shrouding her face.

His wife never could resist him. He'd always told her that all he wanted was family and love. His dream had always been just to live in peace and raise a family on his own ranch. He pressed his swollen shaft against her, then hesitated, resting on his elbows as he searched her eyes.

"Katie, I've had my share of women, and I'm done with that. I'd never hurt you or cheat on you. Never. Understand?"

"Yes," she said, blinking back more tears.

"And I don't care if you gain another fifty pounds. I'll always see you only as the beautiful woman who mothered my children. Nothing else matters, Katie. What matters is that you be proud to be the wife of Lloyd Harkner and the mother of three beautiful children and maybe more. You're part of the Harkner family and the J&L."

A tear slipped out of one eye. Lloyd kissed it, then pushed himself inside of her as he grasped her bottom from underneath. "And you're a part of me!" he added. He buried his face in her thick, red tresses as he pushed deep inside of her. "And I love every damn inch of you," he groaned next to her ear.

He felt her arch toward him, relished the fact that she cried out with pleasure. He filled her with his groaning need, loving her, wanting her. He surged into her with a desire too long neglected. It was good to be home, his father safe, his mother better, his sister happy, the children playing somewhere.

"I love you, Katie-girl," he whispered into her ear, taking her hard and fast, his life spilling into her. Evie was right. If God wanted them to have another child, then so be it.

He kissed Katie hungrily, wanting to brand into her that there was no other, wanting to prove to himself things would be good now. The J&L had become a haven for all of them, an escape from the past, a soothing balm for the soul. There was a time when the family had feared life would never be this good. Now he dared to believe it could always be this way, not just for him and Katie, but for all of them.

Still, something didn't feel right, and he couldn't figure out what it was. He relaxed beside Katie, pulling her into his arms. Maybe it had something to do with Jake's confrontation with Brady Fillmore. Soon, he and Jake should pay a visit on their cattle-stealing neighbor.

PART TWO

Sixteen

"HELLO, JEFF." PETER BROWN GREETED HIS GOOD friend at the *Journal* in downtown Chicago.

Jeff, wearing his typical round spectacles and a tweed suit, rose to shake hands with Peter, grinning broadly. "Peter! What the heck brings a wealthy Chicago lawyer into my humble little office?"

"Humble? You're a prize-winning columnist. There's nothing humble about that."

Jeff laughed, offering Peter a seat. Peter Brown always made him feel like a peasant. The always-dapper Peter still sported thick, dark-brown hair and a handsome smile. Today he wore a dark-blue twill, waist-cut suit jacket with a V-cut in the front that fell into a tail at the back. His pants matched the jacket, and his white shirt sported gold cuffs and buttons, worn with a deep-blue silk tie and set off with a lighter blue silk paisley waistcoat to which a gold watch and chain were attached. The color seemed to make Peter's eyes look even bluer. Dapper indeed! In spite of his money, Peter was never anything but friendly, and comfortable in any setting, including a visit to the J&L last summer after the hearing in Denver that made Peter almost as famous as Jeff. It seemed that anyone who had connections to Jake Harkner ended up famous.

Peter sat down in a wooden swivel chair, and Jeff took a seat behind his very messy desk stacked with news clippings. "You must be here about Jake's latest hair-raising adventure," Jeff teased. "My connections say he's doing well and has gone home, but Boulder is still talking about what happened. Some of them still want Jake to be their sheriff." He leaned back in his chair. "Of course, we know Jake would never take them up on it. Randy would have a fit."

Peter nodded. "That she would. But then, Jake Harkner has a way of landing himself in situations that upset her greatly without even trying."

"You aren't here because he's in trouble again, are you?"

Peter removed his silk top hat and set it on Jeff's desk. "No. He's obviously not in trouble, certainly nothing like that fiasco in Denver last summer."

"Randy's last letter said he's not going to Denver this year. Just Lloyd is going, although that city holds some pretty bad memories for him, too. I could kick myself for publishing that book when I did—the way Jake lives, I could have added some very exciting stories to it."

Peter smiled. "Well, the name Jeff Truebridge is well known now, thanks to the Harkners, and that column of yours has had several new installments to the Jake Harkner ongoing saga. I bet you'll never forget our adventures back in Oklahoma."

"Hell no. How does a man forget something like that? Greatest adventure of my life. I'll bet you haven't found anything that exciting since you came back to Chicago, in spite of being in the big city."

Peter leaned forward, resting his elbows on his knees. "No, I haven't, but then I represent tax matters and things like embezzlement, business ventures, things that would bore a man like Jake Harkner to death. You remember Randy used to do paperwork for me back in Guthrie, when Jake was off on one of his excursions, chasing the slime of the earth into No Man's Land. The things that woman has put up with…"

Jeff frowned. Peter was talking in circles, and he damn

well knew it. Something was up. "How's Mrs. Brown these days, Peter?" he asked, deciding to remind the man he even *had* a wife.

Peter brightened. "Treena left on an ocean voyage for Paris. She has family there and decided to spend the summer with them."

"Aha! You're a bachelor for the summer and bored to death," Jeff joked. "That's what brought you here. Are you looking for some excitement?"

Peter smiled almost sadly. "Something like that. And speaking of wives, how is yours? You said you wouldn't go out to Colorado this year because she's carrying."

"She was pretty sick the first few weeks, but she's better. I don't want to leave her, though, especially since the little one's still only nine months old."

"You work pretty fast, Jeff Truebridge. You joked once about Jake and Lloyd taking you to a brothel back in Oklahoma to teach you about women."

Jeff laughed. "My God, I was such a shavetail kid. I'll always remember the first time I met Jake. I watched him ride into Guthrie with four men in tow, one of them dead and the others looking like they wished they were. And Jake—good God, he looked mean, like a man who'd explode if anyone crossed him. And I've never seen a man wearing so many guns in my life. I was so scared to approach him about writing the book that I almost wet my pants."

Peter laughed. "He can do that to you. He wasn't exactly fond of me, knowing how I felt about Randy."

"But you ended up helping him get his prison sentence reduced, and you saved his ass from a noose last summer." Jeff sobered. "Peter, that first day he came riding into Guthrie…he was all meanness and darkness, until Randy came running up the street to greet him. He set eyes on her and completely changed. I've never seen anything like it. It was so obvious how much he loved her it was almost startling, the way he changed. Except for when Brad Buckley tried to give him a hard time. My God, Buckley was a big kid, but Jake threw him off that boardwalk like he weighed ten pounds. Beat the hell out of him. That man can turn on a dime. Don't forget that."

Peter nodded and just sat there quietly for a moment.

Jeff got up and closed his office door. "What's going on with you, Peter? I visited you at that mansion of a home last year, and we met you and Treena for dinner that once, but you've never visited me here."

Peter sighed, looking sheepishly at Jeff. "You said something to me on the phone when we talked about the robbery in Boulder that has bothered me ever since," he told Jeff. "It's none of my damn business, but I just wanted to ask. You said something in Randy's last letter to you sounded strange, like maybe she was upset about something. You said you sensed something had changed and haven't received a letter since—or have you?"

Jeff removed his jacket and loosened his tie, his office growing warm from a very hot day in the smoggy city. "No, I haven't." He frowned. "And you're right. But it shouldn't concern you, Peter. You may be wealthy and successful, able to buy and sell me, but I'm not afraid to tell you that Randy is no longer your business. You're a married man, in case you've forgotten."

Peter shook his head. "You'll always be one of my better friends, Jeff, because you're down to earth and you're a good, honest young man. And you're right. I have a wife, and I love her dearly. And yes, I have no business being concerned about Randy, but I can't help being bothered by what you said." He rubbed at his eyes. "I'll always worry about her, Jeff. And I'll never stop loving her. Treena knows that, and she understands."

"What are you after, Peter?"

Peter shook his head. "I don't even know. I'm wondering if I should pay another visit to the J&L. I have a big tax case going right now, but after that, I can take some time off. I thought I'd go out to Colorado and kind of feel things out."

Jeff got up and went to the door, asking an assistant to bring a pitcher of cold water and a couple of glasses. He returned to his desk. "Peter, Jake wouldn't be too thrilled about you going out there alone. I'm sure he didn't mind when you went out there with Treena, and he and Randy were grateful for your help at that hearing. It isn't often a man blows another man's head off and gets away with it. But you'd better be damned careful that he doesn't blow *your* head off."

Peter smiled sadly. "Jake's *family* got him off at that hearing. By the time they were through defending him as the best father and grandfather on the face of the earth, that judge couldn't help but let him off, for their sakes."

"Maybe so, but you did a good job defending him. He needed you there and was damn glad to see both of us show up, but don't take his friendship and gratitude for granted when it comes to his wife."

Peter nodded, then leaned back and waited while the assistant came in with a pitcher and two glasses. He set them down and left, and Jeff poured water for them. Peter reached for his glass and drank, appearing grateful. He stared at the glass in his hand as he spoke to Jeff. "I just need to know, Jeff, what you saw in that letter that bothered you." He met Jeff's gaze pleadingly.

Jeff took another swallow of water and set the glass on his desk. "I don't have the letter here, Peter. It's at home. But I can tell you what seemed strange about it. She wrote something to the effect that there had been some kind of family trouble. It was something along the lines of 'Jake and I have had our problems, but everything is better now. We had a barn fire, and someone from Jake's past tried to destroy us, but we love each other too much for that.'"

Peter frowned in wonder. "She didn't say who it was?"

"No."

"Did you hear any news stories about it? Anything about the fire?"

"Not a word. And she never explained in any more detail."

"Who the hell could it have been? Everybody from Jake's past is pretty much dead and buried, most of them by Jake's own hands. The only one I can think of left over from those days was Brad Buckley. He showed up at that hearing, but the judge ran him out of Denver. No one's—" He hesitated, meeting Jeff's gaze. "My God! Have you heard anything about him since? When he left that courtroom, he was damn clear about still getting revenge on Jake."

Jeff thought about it and nodded. "That's right."

The two men looked at each other, thinking the same thing.

"I think something happened that Jake isn't telling anyone about. I hope to hell it doesn't involve Randy. Anyone who would touch that woman wrong would suffer an ugly end to his life at Jake's hands," Peter commented. "Jake would *never* let something like that go—not in a million years. Even if it meant a hanging."

"There's been no word of any killings or trouble at the J&L, or anything involving Jake. If something happened and they want it buried, you have to leave it alone, Peter. Don't go out there. Whatever might have happened—and we don't even know that anything *did* happen—you have to stay out of it."

Peter sighed. "I suppose I do."

Jeff couldn't help feeling a little sorry for the man. "Peter, if you want my opinion, I think that somewhere in the back of his mind Jake appreciates how you feel about Randy. He might even have given thought to knowing that if something happened to him you'd likely do everything in your power to make sure she's okay. But as long as Jake Harkner is alive, you have to stay out of it.

"You know what he's like. He owes you, and he respects you, but you'd see that other side of him damned quick if you tried for one minute to move in on Randy. Besides that, you have to face facts: not only are you a married man now, but Randy's surrounded by her kids and grandkids, let alone a whole ranch full of damn good cowboys who would all stand in front of a cannon for that woman. She'll never hurt for protection and love or for help in her old age, and they have that big, beautiful log home settled in one of the prettiest places on the face of the earth. Be comfortable knowing Randy will never want for anything, especially not for love. Let it go, Peter. Whatever might have happened, you know good and well that Jake Harkner can fix it. I've never seen two people who loved each other more."

She could have loved me…if things had been different, Peter thought. At the least, they had been good friends. Then there had been that trip they had taken together when Randy needed surgery and Jake couldn't go with her. Jake had actually trusted him to take care of his wife, but he'd seen the warning in Jake's eyes. If he'd stepped out of line even once, he would have met the hard fist of Jake Harkner.

"You're right," he told Jeff. "And it wouldn't have mattered if I had actually tried hard to win Randy over. She loves Jake beyond measure. She would never have left that man for anyone else."

"You bet she wouldn't."

"I'm just worried."

"She has Jake. That's all that woman's ever needed. Find something else to do this summer, Peter. You can start by coming into the city more often and meeting me for lunch."

Peter smiled. "Sounds like a good idea. Actually, I took a hotel room here because of this big case I'm working on. With Treena gone, it's lonely in that big house in the suburbs. I'm staying in the city for a while." He rose and put out his hand. "You will let me know if you hear anything from Randy—anything at all, right? I'm staying at the Grand Pacific."

Jeff grinned. "Must be nice to be able to afford that place." He stood up and shook Peter's hand. "And yes, I promise to let you know if I hear from Randy or Jake."

"And as far as lunch, how about tomorrow? I'll hire a cab and pick you up in front of the *Journal*."

"You buying?"

Peter laughed. "This time. Next time it will be on you."

"Fine with me, but it can't be one of the fancy restaurants you're used to."

Peter laughed again. "I'll manage." He put on his hat and left, and Jeff watched him go. Their conversation about Brad Buckley had stirred his professional curiosity. He'd never given thought to the fact that no one had ever heard anything about the man since he was kicked out of Denver.

Jake, if anyone can kill and bury a man, never to be heard from again, it's damn well you, he thought. He grinned and shook his head. *And remembering what Buckley was like, I would like to have been there to see it happen.*

Maybe nothing at all had happened, but he knew Jake Harkner all too well. If Brad Buckley had returned to hurt anyone in Jake's family, especially Randy, Jake would have made sure the man never saw the light of another sunrise.

Seventeen

JAKE CRAWLED INTO THE BIG BED HE'D SHARED WITH his wife since having it specially built for her. After the last few days of family bedlam, their big log home was finally quiet. Tonight, he and Randy were completely alone, and Jake enjoyed the sound of only the ticking grandfather clock downstairs.

Up here in their loft bedroom, it sometimes seemed as though the rest of the world didn't even exist, and sometimes he wished it didn't. Then there wouldn't be anything or anyone left to try to steal this moment, lying here in bed with his beautiful wife in the foothills of the Rocky Mountains—all his enemies dead or in prison—and with nothing more to do than watch Randy sleep…listen to her breathe. She looked beautiful by the dim light of a small lamp they kept on in the adjoining washroom. Since last winter, she'd insisted on light in the bedroom, and again he'd obliged her in the hopes it would help take away some of her fears.

He'd slipped out of bed to wash because he'd not had the chance until now. Randy was tired and went to bed early, insisting, as always, that he come to bed too, because she couldn't go to sleep without his arms around her. Before settling in beside her again, he reached into the drawer in the small table beside the bed and pulled out a stick of peppermint, putting one end in his mouth. He moved in beside her, pulling the covers over them. She lay facing him, and he leaned close and tapped her lips with the peppermint. He forced himself to ignore the lingering pain in his side. He wanted his wife back, and she'd told him what would help. Maybe now, when she was sleepy and relaxed, was a better time.

Randy stirred and put her fingers to her lips to wipe away whatever had touched them. Jake touched her lips again, and she stirred again, this time coming fully awake. She stretched and opened her eyes.

"Jake, what are you doing?"

"Watching my wife sleep, and she's so beautiful I decided I wanted to wake her up and make love."

Randy frowned and moved back a little. "You got out the peppermint?"

"You know what that means."

She took a moment to get her bearings. "Jake, what time is it?"

"I have no idea. Midnight, maybe."

"You're still injured."

He took the peppermint from his lips and traced the other end over hers. "What I have in mind won't take much effort on my part. I'll manage."

Randy ran her fingers through her hair. "What on earth? Jake, I need a bath."

"You don't need one." He pulled her close and nuzzled her hair. "I just took my own bath. I sure love the fact that we have hot water now, right out of a faucet."

"You smell good."

"That was my intention."

She kissed his neck. "Jake, we haven't even talked about this. You're still healing."

"Since when do we schedule our lovemaking? It's always been spontaneous." He tapped the peppermint against her lips again. "And beautiful. And, little lady, we *did* talk about making love, back in Boulder before we left."

"Honestly, Jake—"

"I told you I bathed. In fact, I washed up extra good,

so it will be nice for you. Do you know what I'm telling you?"

Randy licked at the peppermint sleepily, not answering right away. She suddenly gasped. "Oh my!"

Jake took the other end of the peppermint into his mouth again, and they both bit off pieces until their lips met, a ritual they'd practiced before making love since their early years of marriage. Jake studied her eyes, watching for any sign of horror or fear. He kissed her, lightly at first, then deeper, licking her lips as he held her face between his hands. "You all right?"

Randy grasped his wrist. "I...don't know."

"Then we won't do anything at all." He kissed her eyes. "I just thought that if this is what you need, what better time than in the still of the darkness with just us here in our own bed. This is *me*, Randy. I want to do this *with* you and *for* you—but not *to* you. Not in a way that brings back anything ugly. And I didn't think it should be planned, because then you'd think about it and get all nervous—"

She put her fingers to his lips and moved closer to his ear. "What if I don't do it right?" she whispered.

He forced back a grin. This was a time when he would normally smile and tease her, but he sensed she could take it wrong. Everything he did and said now could either bring her back or chase her farther away. "You'll be fine."

"I'm scared."

"Then we won't do it. I've never asked you, Randy, and in your beautiful innocence, you've never offered, and that's part of what I've loved about you. It wasn't easy for you to let me be as intimate with you as we are now, but that's me on you. This is different, so you decide. I think I understand why you wanted to do this." He kissed her again, running a hand up under her flannel gown, massaging her back as he moved his lips to her throat. "It's okay." He felt her shiver.

"You have to help me."

"Baby, you'll figure it out."

"Keep touching me."

He moved his hand around to the front of her gown, underneath, gently caressing her breasts while he scooted farther up, staying on his right side to favor his still-bandaged wound. He refused to give any thought to his lingering pain. She needed this, and he'd damn well do what he could to bring her back.

He carefully touched her in the right places to arouse her as he kissed her over and over, moving his tongue gently into her mouth suggestively. He worked his fingers over the soft mound that he could tell was slightly swelling in response, and continued kissing her before moving his lips to her ear. "I want this, too, Randy, but only if you do. It's okay to say no."

She ran her fingers into his hair as they kissed again. "I'm just scared."

He took his hand from under her gown and wound his fingers into her hair. "Don't be. This is me, remember? We can do anything we want, anything *you* want."

He could feel her trembling as she moved her lips to his neck, his throat. He kept a tight grasp of her hair as she began kissing her way down his chest, over his abdomen. Then she hesitated.

"Jake, help me."

"Just make love to me, baby. Do what comes naturally. It can be beautiful, just like you said you wanted it to be." He kept hold of her hair as she gently took hold of his penis and stroked it into full arousal, then kissed the end of it. He'd always known if she ever did this how much he'd love it, but he'd never said it. It had to be her idea. He groaned with pleasure as she put her hand around him fully and caressed his throbbing shaft up and down while also kissing it...then licking it.

"Jake—"

"Just let it happen, baby." He felt her lips come around him, and he gently guided himself into her mouth, letting her do the rest. He struggled to dismiss the image of the filthy men who'd forced such a thing on this beautiful, delicate woman. Their cruelty had made it so painful that she had been left bruised everywhere and close to death. To think how shy and inhibited she was about it with her own husband brought fury to his blood, but he forced back any dark emotions that might spoil the moment.

Enjoy it, he told himself. *She wants you to enjoy it. She wants to be the one to give you pleasure.* He had to be careful. If he got caught up in the anger he still felt over what had happened, she'd feel it. She'd back away, and he'd lose her again.

He closed his eyes and let her take in as much of him as she chose. Even just a little was enough to bring an erotic pleasure far more intense than he'd anticipated. He couldn't help the sheer thrill of it. He clung to her hair, and she took in more of him, as deeply as she could manage. She'd said she wanted him to take his pleasure for once in something *she* did to *him*, and he damn well wasn't having any trouble doing that.

"God, Randy, it's beautiful," he groaned.

She shivered again, running her tongue over him as she pulled up and down with her lips, clinging to his free hand the entire time. The ecstasy was so intense he knew he would have to release soon.

"Randy, I can pull out before I come."

She squeezed his hand with surprising strength, as though to tell him this way was all right. She made a strange little whimpering sound, and he couldn't tell if it was from terror or pleasure, but now he was too lost in the moment to decide. He reminded her again she could stop, but she moved over him beautifully. He hung on as long as possible, but the sheer ecstasy of it brought forth a pulsating climax.

He really hadn't planned for this part, because he knew what those men had done, forcing her to swallow their filth. She let out an odd groan and kept pulling at him until he finished. Jake grabbed a small towel he'd brought to bed in case this happened and eased himself out of her, handing her the cloth.

"Spit it out, Randy."

She shook her head, saying nothing. She swallowed first, then took the towel with shaking hands and wiped at her lips. "I...wanted it this way," she said in a near whisper, shivering. "I needed it to be you I...tasted." She broke into tears.

Damn it! Jake scooted down and pulled her close, nuzzling her neck, finding her mouth, tasting his own life as he kissed her with groaning pleasure. This was the most he'd wanted her in a long time. He ran his tongue into her mouth. She'd chosen to let him take away the ugly by doing the very thing that had horrified her with those men. He held her close and kissed her hair again. "Jesus, don't cry, Randy. Don't slip away from me again. Tell me you're all right. You told me it was what you wanted."

"I know." She moved her arms around him and kissed his chest. "Thank you, Jake."

He couldn't help a smile of relief. "I think I'm the one who should be thanking you." He scooted down enough to meet her mouth again, kissing her gently. "That was the most beautiful thing we've ever done."

She used the towel to wipe at her nose and eyes. "I hoped it would be. I didn't hate it, because it was you." She kissed his neck as Jake softly caressed her breasts. "Jake, I *had* to do that. I couldn't let those awful men... be the first...and the last. This is the only way I can live with it. I couldn't let...that ugly thing...be something...I never even did...with my own husband." She leaned up and met his lips again in a heated kiss, then ran her fingers into his hair.

"Tell me it wasn't ugly this time," he groaned.

"No. I knew you would make it nice. Every way and every place you touch me is always beautiful because… I mean…Jake, sometimes you do the most sinful things with me, and yet I feel like it's because you love me so much, so it's always right." Another kiss.

"Of course it's always right. You're my *wife*. What you just did was right because I'm your husband. You remember that every time I touch you. And right now I very much want to make love to you again, but my side is killing me."

"Oh, Jake! I—it was so nice I forgot about your pain."

"It's okay." He settled onto his back, and she snuggled against him. "It was most certainly worth it," he added. "I'll live."

They lay there quietly for several seconds. "I can't tell you how much that helped," Randy finally told him. "Thank you for finally listening to me. I know you thought that was the worst thing we could do, and in those first few weeks it probably was. But the more I thought about it…the more I realized that's what I needed." She wiped at tears again. "And don't try to tell me you've never done that before, the way you used to live."

He grinned into the darkness. "I was young and wild then." He kissed her hair. "It's different with you."

She grasped his hand and kissed his fingers, still resting her head on his shoulder. "And now I own you the same way you own me. Now we've shared each other completely." She scooted up and kissed his cheek. "And you're the nicest man on the face of the earth."

Jake burst into laughter. "Oh my God, a whole lot of people would argue that one! The most common adjectives I get are 'mean sonofabitch' and 'bastard.' Probably from just about everyone but my family, and there are times when even they would disagree, including you!"

Randy laughed. "I guess I should admit there have been times…"

Jake thought how wonderful her laughter sounded.

Randy sat up slightly, leaning over him. "And you're only mean to people who deserve it." She traced a finger over his lips. "But not with me. Never with me. You're always so careful and kind and devoted and gentle with me when we make love. Other people don't know how incredibly good you can be."

He reached up and ran the back of his fingers over her cheek. What he saw now was a mixture of the childish, clingy woman he'd lived with the past several months, and a definite spark of the old Randy. "You sure you're all right? No lies and no pretending, Randy. That's what led to us feeling like strangers. And if you never want to do this again, it's okay. I never want to feel far away from you, and if you feel that happening, you have to tell me."

"I will. And I'm not saying I'll never want to do that again. It was nicer than I thought it would be because I love you and you're a beautiful man. Just promise me we'll never be far apart again, Jake. I don't mean in spirit and love. I just don't want you to take any jobs like when you were a marshal, when you left for days and weeks at a time. I waited in terror all the time that you'd not make it back. I lived for that whistle you gave when you were coming into town and I knew you were all right. My heart would just burst. When I saw you lying in the street in Boulder, I was so scared my worst nightmare had become real. You don't know how many times I've thought about it. That you would die that way, with me watching."

"Randy, don't. We're here in our own bed. It's quiet, we're safe on the J&L and I'm right here beside you and I'm just fine. And I promise I won't go far away again and leave you alone. But you have to promise me that you will keep eating right and get some meat back on those bones."

"I promise." She sat up straight. "In fact—guess what?"

"What?"

"I'm so hungry I could eat a horse."

"*Hungry? Now?*"

"Yes."

"Then let's go downstairs and eat something. There's no law that says we can't eat in the middle of the night, and some of that great bread you bake is still sitting on the table."

She leaned down and kissed him again. "I obviously need to rinse out my mouth first."

"Was it bad?"

"No. It was actually kind of sweet."

He grinned. "Considering the source, I'm surprised."

She laughed again. He'd never heard such a good sound in his life. He rolled her over and nuzzled her neck, laughing with her. "You may do that again any time you want, Mrs. Harkner."

They kissed again. "Actually, Mr. Harkner, now that I think about it, it's one way I can be completely in control of the big, bad outlaw."

"I think I'd rather be in control of you. It doesn't seem right, the woman being in charge."

"We'll see about that. But I do have to say...I love it when you're in control, and I'll be glad when you feel good enough to do things my favorite way."

"How's that?"

"You inside of me in a place that feels a lot better."

They laughed together again, and she suddenly pushed him away and got out of bed. "Let me clean up a little and we'll go eat."

"Fine with me, but this is torture. I want you so bad right now I'm willing to risk breaking open this wound to make love to you."

"Well, I don't want to be responsible for injuring my husband." Randy hurried into the washroom and closed the door.

Jake breathed a deep sigh of relief and rubbed at his eyes. She was hungry. That was a damn good sign, but he was afraid to set too much store by it. Right now, she'd never seemed closer to the old Randy he could joke with and make love to for sheer pleasure and desire and not out of duty. She'd needed all this time to heal.

He winced with renewed pain as he sat up and reached for his long johns. Maybe God did answer prayer, but this was probably an answer to Evie's prayers for her mother, not his own. In spite of all of the long talks with his very beautiful, faithful, Christian daughter, he'd never believe God would for one minute give a damn about Jake Harkner. Never had, and never would.

He stood up and buttoned his long johns, then reached for a cigarette, realizing he was damn hungry himself.

Eighteen

JAKE AWOKE TO AN EMPTY BED. HE SAT UP, SOMEWHAT alarmed. In the last few months, Randy had made a habit of not rising until he did, hardly able sometimes to even go downstairs without him coming with her. He heard pans and dishes clattering in the kitchen and detected the smell of frying bacon.

Did he dare wish her change last night had been real? He threw back the covers and rose to wash and dress and perform his daily ritual of scrubbing his teeth with baking soda. Randy loved his smile, so he did all he could to keep it decent. He shaved and dressed, combing his hair before putting on socks and hurrying down the slightly winding stairs that led from their loft bedroom to the great room below—only to find Randy in the kitchen area setting their huge oak table with enough places for the whole family.

"What are you doing up and cooking?" he asked her. "Do you want me to send for Teresa?"

"No. I can do this myself. I want a day with the family. Nothing has been normal yet since we got back. Things have settled down, and I want a family day. A *normal* family day."

Jake frowned, watching her set out plates. She looked beautiful this morning, almost radiant, although she had a long way to go to put some meat on her bones. Her dress hung a little big on her, but it almost looked as though she'd worked at making sure her breasts filled up the bodice and a bit of enticing cleavage showed. She damn well knew he loved her cleavage. Was that for him?

"This is a bit of a change—a *nice* change. You okay about last night?"

"I'm fine." She stopped stirring, leaning her head against his chest. "Thank you."

Jake grinned. "A man doesn't exactly need to be thanked for something like that."

"Jake, if you ever want that again…"

He leaned farther over and kissed her cheek. "Oh, I want you any way I can get you. Let's just take things naturally." He kissed her cleavage. "And you look especially beautiful and enticing this morning."

"Get your face off my breasts, Mr. Harkner. You know perfectly well Ben or one of the grandchildren could come barging in here any minute."

He nuzzled her breasts again, and she pulled away, smiling. "Honestly, Jake, I want to make breakfast for everybody. So before you try making love right here on the kitchen floor, go outside and ring the dinner bell twice so the family knows I want them all here."

Jake turned her and planted a long kiss on her mouth. "Yes, ma'am." He walked to the door, grabbing a cigarette first from a tin on a cabinet near the door. He glanced back at her and saw *I love you* in her eyes, along with a look of yearning…to have things normal again. "You take things a day at a time, all right? And you tell me anything that's bothering you or anything you need."

"I will. Just don't leave. Remember your promise not to go far away."

He nodded. "I'll remember."

She held his gaze. "I love you. I'm not sure I've ever loved you more."

He just nodded, knowing he didn't need to say anything. He took a long match from a box near the cigarettes and walked out onto the veranda to light up.

"Do me a favor and go gather some eggs for breakfast," Randy called to him.

Jake took a long drag on the cigarette as he walked to the screen door. "*Me?* I've never gathered eggs in my life. That's a woman's job."

"Well, this morning it's *your* job. You wanted your wife back, so she's giving you an order."

He kept the cigarette between his lips as he leaned against the wall near the door. "This is going too far, woman."

Randy smiled. "Don't wring the necks of the chickens just to get them off their nests. Be gentle. A cranky hen could peck you to death."

Jake grinned. "I'm not going to say what I'm thinking right now."

Randy laughed. "You don't *need* to. I know *exactly* what you're thinking! Now go find me some eggs."

"I'm not guaranteeing anything." Jake walked out, deciding he'd have to tread lightly for a while yet—make sure he didn't do or say something that would send her back into that place he couldn't reach. He took another long drag on his cigarette, thinking how warm it already was this morning. It was going to be a hot day. He put the cigarette to his lips again, then heard it. Crying...actually more like loud sobbing...like a little girl. The sound came from near the chicken coop several yards away near the new barn. The one the men and a few neighbors had raised to replace the one that was burned...last winter...when Brad Buckley took Randy.

He shook away the memory. He was so used to awful things happening to his family that the sound of a little girl crying brought momentary terror to his soul. He threw down his cigarette and half ran to the chicken coop to find Evie's little girl Sadie Mae standing beside it, in a place where others couldn't see her. She was crying almost uncontrollably, her face dirty, as was the nightgown she still wore. She held an empty basket, and a pile of broken eggs lay at her feet.

"Sunshine!" Jake hurried to kneel in front of her. "What happened?"

She reached out, hugging him around the neck. "Mommy will be mad at me! And so will Gramma," she sobbed.

He patted her back. "Sadie Mae, it's okay."

She pulled away, shaking her head. "I...snuck out. Mommy will be mad I snuck out...without telling her. And..." Her little chest heaved in more sobs, and tears made clean paths down her dirty cheeks. "I was getting the eggs...for Mommy...but I fell down...and they all broke!" She cried even harder.

Jake pulled her away from the mess. "Don't cry, Sunshine. Grampa will fix it."

"How?" she wept.

"Look—here comes Outlaw." He nodded toward a mangy, stray dog that the kids had adopted as their own when he'd started hanging around. The animal seemed to be a homeless loner who came and went as he pleased, pretty much like Jake himself had been at one time. Little Jake named him Outlaw because that's what his grampa was once. It seemed like every animal on the J&L was named Outlaw, including his favorite horse.

Little Jake actually acts like he's proud I was once an outlaw, Jake had complained once to Brian.

I'm afraid he is proud of it, Brian had answered facetiously.

"I'll bet Outlaw hasn't eaten yet," Jake told Sadie Mae aloud.

"Mommy says if we let the dog eat eggs...he'll start getting into the chicken coop...and steal them," Sadie Mae warned through tears.

"Well, Outlaw has to eat too, right? Let's take the chance." He whistled to the dog, and the black-and-white mutt came running. "Eat up, boy!"

The dog eagerly began licking at the eggs.

"See? Now you've fed Outlaw. That's a good thing

you did, Sadie Mae. We can't let Outlaw go hungry, can we?"

She shook her head, smearing the dirt on her face when she wiped at her tears.

"Now, let's clean you up, and you can help me gather more eggs. Your grandma sent me out here for eggs, and I don't know a damn thing about wrestling with hens for them. I'll bet you're better at it than I am."

She smiled a little and nodded. "I get eggs all the time for Mommy." She looked down at herself. "What about my nightgown? It's all dirty, and I'm all sticky. And I"— she rubbed at more tears—"I wet myself."

"We'll figure something out. Just stop crying, Sunshine, or you'll make Grampa cry."

She smiled more. "Big men like you don't cry, Grampa."

"Well, you just might be surprised." He picked her up and carried her to a watering trough, pulling off her nightgown and dipping it into the water. He wrung it out and used it to wash her face and the sticky egg residue off her hands. He took off her panties and dipped her into the trough to wash her bottom and legs. She giggled from the cold water, but as soon as he took her out and started drying her off with the nightgown, she started crying again.

"Grampa, I don't got a nightgown," she lamented. "I don't wanna be bare!"

"Sadie Mae, I said I'd fix things, remember?" Jake stood up and removed his shirt, then wrapped it around her.

"Grampa! It's awful big!"

Jake took the end of each sleeve and rolled it several times until her hands appeared. "There. Now you're all covered up until I get you another nightgown. We'll hide the dirty one, and later, I'll stick it in Grandma's laundry. She has lots of you kids' clothes. She'll never know the difference."

"But your shirt is dragging on the ground, Grampa."

Jake wrapped her in his arms and stood up. She moved her arms around his neck again, hanging her head over his shoulder. "Now my shirt can't touch the ground," Jake told her. He walked with her to one of the barns, where he found Rodriguez raking out stalls. "Rodriguez, do me a favor. Go to the house and tell Randy that my daughter asked you to get a nightgown and some underwear for Sadie Mae. Tell her Evie told you she didn't have any clean ones. But bring the clothes back here to me and don't ask questions."

Rodriguez scratched his head. "I do not understand, *señor*."

"You don't need to. Just get the nightgown and make sure Randy thinks it's for Evie."

Rodriguez shrugged and set the rake aside, heading for the main house.

Sadie Mae brushed a little hand over Jake's back. "Grampa! You have owies! Does it hurt?"

Jake closed his eyes against the memories that didn't visit him so often any more. He'd been so concerned about his granddaughter's tears that he'd forgotten she'd never seen the scars on his back. He usually never took his shirt off in front of anyone but Randy, and rarely, his son and daughter. After some long talks with Ben and his grandsons, he'd let them see his back and explained how it got that way. *Sadie Mae, my father did that to me. He beat me practically every day of my life until one day I killed him.* How did he explain something like that to an innocent little girl? "Those are old owies, Sadie Mae. They don't hurt at all."

"What happened to you?" she asked, leaning back a little and putting her hands to his cheeks, frowning in innocent concern.

Satan happened to me. "A long time ago, I got in a fight with a big, bad bear, and he scratched me really bad with his claws."

Her dark eyes grew wide with fascination. "Did you shoot the bear with your guns?"

"Yes, I did. And the scratches got better, and now they don't hurt anymore."

Her eyes teared again. "I'm sorry, Grampa."

"You don't need to be sorry. I got better, and now it's all okay." He frowned. "How did you get out of the house without anyone seeing you? Who's guarding the front door?"

"Uncle Terrel. I fooled him!"

Jake decided to have a talk with Terrel Adams. Ever since last winter's incident, the ranch hands, whom the girls referred to as "uncles," had been assigned to take turns guarding all three houses at night. Sadie Mae leaned close and whispered in his ear.

"I snuck out my window. There is a little tree growing there, and I climbed down and I went around behind a shed."

Her antics reminded him of when her brother, Little Jake, had crept out of the house once back in Guthrie and run down the main street to find his grampa, just when his grampa was in the middle of a shoot-out with wanted men. The kid had nearly gotten himself killed, and Jake had ended up with a bullet in the leg. For some reason, Evie's kids seemed to have a penchant for sneaking out of the house. "Sunshine, why on earth did you do that?"

Sadie Mae wrinkled her brow and looked at him like he was being silly. "*Because*, Grampa, I was gonna surprise Mommy with the *eggs*."

She spoke the words as though he should have understood, silly man. Jake kissed her cheek and held her close. "Don't do that again, okay? Promise Grampa. It's dangerous for you to run around by yourself."

"'Cuz of bad people, like those bad men that took Gramma?"

"Yes. So don't do that again, all right? We have lots of good men here to watch out for all of you, but they can't do that if you sneak around behind them."

"Don't be mad at me."

"I'm not." Jake saw Rodriguez returning with a nightgown.

"Your wife, she did not ask any questions, *señor*," he told Jake, "but she say you better come back soon with the eggs or she will come out here herself and take a broom to you." The Mexican grinned.

"I guess I'd better get back to the house then," Jake answered, laughing.

"*Sí, señor*."

"Rodriguez, I want you to go to Brian and Evie's house and tell them I came and got Sadie Mae from Terrel to help me gather eggs. Tell Terrel he has to go along with my story. I'll explain it to him later. I don't want Evie to know that Sadie Mae came out here by herself. Understand? This is between you and me and Terrel."

The Mexican nodded. "*Sí*, I will go and tell Terrel— and tell your daughter."

"And tell Evie that Randy wants the whole family to come over for breakfast as soon as everyone is up and dressed, which they are probably already doing. It isn't often any of us sleeps in around here. Too many chores."

The Mexican nodded.

"And I think Ben and Stephen and Little Jake are all at Evie's, too. Tell the boys to go milk the cows and bring a couple of buckets of milk to the main house, and then go to our house and ring the dinner bell twice. I was supposed to ring it and forgot."

Rodriguez scratched his head. "That is a lot of things to remember, *señor*."

"You'll manage." Rodriguez left, and Jake took his shirt off Sadie Mae and helped her step into her panties,

Lloyd studied her closely as she set a basket of biscuits on the table before taking a chair. "What's going on?" he asked her. "Mom, is something wrong that you *need* me to stay here?"

"*Nothing* is wrong. I've never been better, and that's why I want all of you to stay home today. It's going to be a nice day, so let's all take some family time."

Lloyd looked at Jake. "Is she okay?"

Jake grinned. "She's just fine."

Lloyd frowned at the scratches on Jake's cheeks. "What the hell happened to your face? It's all scratched up."

"It's a long story. We'll talk about it later. Let's just be glad your mother is back to her old self, which means I'm getting bossed around something awful. I'm going to have to figure out how to rein her in."

"Did you do something? Say something? Did Mom put those scratches on your face?" he asked teasingly.

"Hell no! And quit asking questions. Just eat."

The rest of them took their seats.

"Are you better, Grampa?" Little Jake asked.

"Much better."

Little Jake grinned and nudged his cousin Stephen. "I told you he was okay. Grampa's tough."

"Heck, I know that," Stephen answered. "How did you get those scratches on your face, Grampa?"

Jake was not pleased with the literal chicken fight he'd had earlier. He scowled at the looks of unquenchable curiosity on everyone's faces.

"I had a run-in with an angry rooster this morning."

Sadie Mae giggled, and Jake winked at her, a grin replacing the scowl. He put a finger to his lips for Sadie not to tell.

"Gramma, are you happy now?" Tricia asked, innocently blurting out the question everyone else was secretly wondering.

then pulled the nightgown over her head. He grinned as he put his shirt back on, amazed at how big the family was getting. There were kids all over the place now, plus a new baby boy at Lloyd and Katie's place and a new baby girl for Brian and Evie. Little Donavan and Esther made six grandchildren, and then there was his adopted son Ben. How in hell had he ended up with all of this?

Randy. It was all due to her and the way she loved him. He grabbed Sadie Mae around the waist with his right arm and carried her hanging sideways like a sack of potatoes. "Let's get some eggs, Sunshine."

The child laughed, her long, dark hair dangling nearly to the ground. Jake set the girl on a big rock outside the henhouse and picked up the empty egg basket. "You wait here."

Just then he heard Randy hollering from the main house. "Jake, where are those eggs?"

He waved the egg basket. "I'm getting them!"

Randy went back into the house, and Jake turned to his granddaughter. "I'd better get those eggs before your grandmother comes after me with that broom."

Sadie Mae giggled. "I can help, Grampa."

"No, I want you to stay clean. I told your grandmother I'd get the eggs, and by God, I'll do it." He walked into the henhouse. Before the door closed, the rooster also strutted inside. Everyone in the family feared that rooster, also called Outlaw. The ornery bird hated men, for some reason, and every gun-toting, brave J&L ranch hand feared the creature.

Sadie Mae then heard loud squawks and a string of bad words coming out of her grandfather's mouth—the kind of words her mother had told her she should never say. She covered her mouth and giggled at the cursing and squawking that was going on inside the henhouse, glad her grandfather wasn't wearing his guns. Maybe if he got mad enough, he would shoot some of the poor hens, and he did get really mad sometimes, but only at bad people. Still, he hated that rooster as much as all the other men did.

Jake finally emerged from the henhouse, holding up a basket of eggs. He had scratches on his face and feathers in his hair. "Let's take these to Grandma," he said. "We'll tell her I went to Evie's and got you first, and you helped me gather the eggs. No one will ever know you snuck out."

Sadie Mae stood up on the rock and clapped her hands, her dimples showing as she smiled with joy. "You won't tell?"

"I won't tell."

"Grampa, you're all scratched up!"

"Yeah, well, I've had worse injuries, but that rooster should be grateful you love him, because if you didn't, I'd be carving him up right now for dinner."

Jake kept the basket in his left hand so he could pick up Sadie Mae with his right arm, keeping her feet away from his wound. Ignoring the pain he felt carrying her and the eggs, he headed for the house, thinking how this was one of the best mornings he could remember.

Nineteen

THE FAMILY BEDLAM OF ELEVEN PEOPLE SITTING AROUND the table—and two six-month-old babies babbling gibberish and rolling around on a blanket in the nearby great room—was music to Jake's ears. He noticed Lloyd and Katie and Evie and Brian watching Randy curiously. She was as much her old self as ever, ordering Katie and Evie to set out platters of scrambled eggs, ham, bacon, and biscuits.

"Mom, you're doing too much," Evie urged.

"I am just fine. I haven't done all the cooking in a long time, and I'm enjoying this." She looked at Lloyd. "And you, young man, are staying here today and not doing chores or riding off to round up strays. Let the men take care of it."

Lloyd took a chair next to Katie and leaned over to give her a quick kiss. "Mom, you know chores can't wait around here."

"Yes, they can," Randy insisted. "You were gone six days just coming to get me and your father, and it seems like it's getting harder and harder to get the whole family together at the same time. Besides that, you'll be herding cattle to Denver soon, and that means you'll be gone again, and for a good two or three weeks. Please stay home today with Katie and the children. Maybe we can have a picnic later. Just the thought of you going back to Denver after last summer gives me the shivers, but at least we know no one will be there waiting to—" She didn't finish her sentence.

Randy looked at Jake and smiled. "I am very happy, and things are going to get back to normal around here."

Lloyd and Evie looked at their father.

"Daddy, what's happened?"

Jake dished a big piece of ham onto his plate. "None of your business." He handed the platter to Stephen, who sat on his right. "Eat up, Stephen. You're a growing boy." He noticed his son and daughter exchange a look of surprise, and he knew they were filled with questions.

Randy began loading her plate with food, and practically every person at the table quietly stared at her.

"*Mom?*" Lloyd asked. "Are you really going to eat all of that?"

"I most certainly am." Randy looked around the table. "For heaven's sake, you've all been after me to eat better, so why are you staring at me like I might die any minute? You should be happy."

"We *are*," Evie answered, "but just yesterday you—"

"That was yesterday," Randy interrupted. "And I'll have you know that I was up at two o'clock this morning eating too. I had ham and eggs and biscuits, and I'm already hungry again."

All of them looked at Jake.

"That tonic she's been taking must work wonders," Brian told Jake, smiling teasingly as he spoke.

"I guess it must," Jake answered.

"Something tells me *Pa* is the tonic," Lloyd joked.

Jake just grinned and leaned back in his chair. "Evie, we'll let you say grace, as you always do. We should have thought of that before we passed the food."

Evie looked warily at her father. This was twice he'd asked her to say grace, something that was nothing short of a miracle. She glanced at her mother again. Randy was watching Jake and smiling. "Oh my gosh," Evie muttered. "Everyone hold hands."

Jake grasped Lloyd's hand on his left and Stephen's

on his right. Evie thanked God that her mother seemed better and her parents happier, thanked Him for the beautiful day, and "we thank Sadie Mae for finding us so many eggs."

On that, Sadie Mae let go of Tricia's and her father's hands and clapped a hand over her mouth, giggling.

"Amen," Evie said quickly, frowning at Sadie Mae. "Sadie Mae, you shouldn't giggle during a prayer. It's a nice thing you did, going out this morning and collecting those eggs."

The child burst into even more giggling, watching her grandfather, her dark eyes dancing. "*Grampa* got the eggs!" she burst out.

"*Grampa?*" Lloyd exclaimed. He looked at his father. "You gathered eggs?" He laughed. "Now we know where those scratches came from! You've never even been inside that chicken coop! Did Mom order you to do that?"

Jake watched his granddaughter. "Sadie Mae, you're a tattle-tale."

The little girl couldn't stop giggling over her wonderful secret, nor could she keep from telling it. She put her hands to the sides of her face and laughed even harder. "Grampa said a whole bunch of bad words too!" she revealed. "And chickens were flying all over and squawking really loud. And Grampa threw the rooster out the door, and he came out with feathers in his hair and a whole bunch of eggs in the basket and a mean look on his face!"

Jake scowled at his granddaughter. "Sadie Mae, I should come over there and tickle you till you can't stand it."

"Pa, I'm surprised you didn't *shoot* some of those hens!"

"If I'd had my guns on, I *would* have. A couple of them are lucky I didn't wring their necks and bring them in the house for Randy to cook."

They all burst out laughing and passed around more food.

"I don't know what's going on between you and Mother, but I like it," Evie told her father. "But really, Daddy, did you have to use those bad words around Sadie Mae?"

Jake cut into a piece of ham. "You know me."

"God help us," Lloyd muttered before picking up a cup of coffee.

"Son, I will have you know that last night your mother said I was the nicest man in the world."

Lloyd literally spit out his coffee, and everyone at the table broke into laughter. The children wiggled and laughed, and Randy just smiled, but she gave Jake a warning look.

"Don't you dare say another word, Jake Harkner."

He leaned back in his chair, chewing on the ham and giving her a look that said it all. She would be in trouble later tonight. She wanted to cry at the realization that she truly did feel stronger. She didn't need her husband to be constantly at her side, because he *was* constantly at her side—in spirit. They hadn't connected that way in a long time.

"I can read off a long, long list of men who would argue against you being a nice man," Lloyd teased.

"Yeah, well, they're mostly all dead now, so it doesn't much matter."

"Well, I'm one of them, but I love you anyway," Lloyd bantered.

"Thank you for your always-kind words, son."

"And thank you for gathering the eggs," Randy told Jake.

"You're welcome. Just don't ever ask me to gather eggs again, Mrs. Harkner. I hate arguing with you, but that is never going to happen."

Sadie Mae giggled again.

"And what were you doing up so early on the porch with Terrel?" Brian asked his daughter. "Jake said he saw you and came to get you to help with the eggs."

Sadie Mae's eyes widened, and she sobered, staring at her grandfather.

Jake smiled at her. "She just happened to wake up before everybody else and decided maybe she'd gather eggs for her mother. She stayed on the porch just like she's been told to do. Terrel saw me coming out of the house, and he waved me over, so I went and got Sadie Mae, and we went to the chicken coop together. I told her to wait and let me gather the eggs, because Randy had asked me to, and I decided to prove to her I *could* do it. But I don't want to see another damn chicken for a while. I don't even want to *eat* one." He winked at Sadie Mae, who smiled but had tears in her eyes.

"Sadie Mae, what's wrong?" Evie asked.

The girl just shook her head. She climbed down from her chair and ran around the table to Jake, climbing up on his lap and throwing her arms around his neck. "Thank you, Grampa. I'm sorry the bear hurt your back." She broke into tears.

Stephen spoke up. "A bear? How did you see Grampa's back? That wasn't a bear. That's from his—"

"Stephen!" Lloyd interrupted. "If Jake told her it was a bear, then that's all your cousin needs to know. She's only five years old."

Stephen looked down.

Jake patted Sadie Mae's back. "Sadie Mae, it's all better. Don't be crying." He turned her around, facing the table but sitting on his lap. "Eat now. Grampa fought those chickens to get these eggs." He reached around to wipe at the girl's tears with his fingers, glancing at Evie as he did so. "I'll explain later. She's just a little girl with a big heart, a lot like her mother."

Evie smiled, shaking her head. "Is everyone else as

confused as I am? Mother insists on a big family breakfast, Daddy gathered the eggs, which he's never done in his life, Mother is eating like a starved horse, and Sadie Mae is talking about a bear hurting Daddy's back."

"We're talking about Jake Harkner," Lloyd quipped. "In which case, it's probably better to just be glad Mom is better this morning and not ask questions." He folded his arms, looking sidelong at Jake. "As far as the egg story and the bear story, I guess that's between Pa and Sadie Mae."

Evie sighed, glancing at her husband, who just shrugged.

"I'm with Lloyd," Brian told his wife. "I quit trying to figure out your father years ago. Understanding involves too much stress and can turn your hair white…and I personally have a lot more white hairs than I did when I first met you." He leaned over and kissed her cheek. "Everybody eat," he announced.

"I'm for that," Lloyd agreed, cutting into a piece of ham. "You all right?" he asked Jake.

Jake drank some coffee. "Other than needing a cigarette, I'm fine. I am actually a very happy man this morning, in more ways than one."

Lloyd grinned. "Good. It's always a relief when my father is in a good mood. It doesn't happen often."

"I have my good days every now and then." Jake cut off a small piece of ham and fed it to Sadie Mae, who gladly stayed on his lap. He glanced at Randy to see she was eating voraciously. He kissed Sadie Mae's hair, saying an inward prayer of thanksgiving that his wife was back to her old self. He just hoped things would stay this way.

Twenty

"You care to explain that story about being attacked by a bear?" Lloyd asked Jake as he lit a cigarette.

The men sat in chairs on the veranda, letting their big breakfast settle.

Jake stretched his long legs and leaned back in the chair. "I'm not supposed to tell. Sadie Mae wants it to be a secret." He leaned his head back and closed his eyes. "Truth be told, that kid snuck out a window and went to the chicken coop long before I got there. She fell, and I found her bawling her eyes out next to a pile of broken eggs, her nightgown a mess, and she was so upset she'd wet herself. I made her promise never to do that again, then made up a big story about the whole thing and told her Evie would never find out she'd snuck out of the house. I helped her clean up and gave her my shirt to wear for a bit. That's when I picked her up and she noticed my scars. If it wasn't so hot, I would have had an undershirt on." He paused to smoke, hating to talk about his back. "I sure as hell couldn't tell her the ugly truth."

Lloyd smoked quietly as they listened to the women talk and laugh. Jake took a cigarette from his pocket. "Your mother's laughter is a nice sound."

"Yeah." Lloyd rested his elbows on his knees, glancing at his father, who still sat with his head back and his eyes closed while he smoked. "What happened?"

"Too personal."

Lloyd nodded. "Well, then, do you think it's for real? That it will last?"

Jake sighed deeply. "Who knows? I'd like to think it will. I can feel her moods and when she's telling the truth, and I really think she's telling the truth when she says she's putting last winter behind her." He thought he heard Randy say something about "none of your business" to Katie and Evie, and he grinned. Brian came out onto the veranda. He stood at a railing and watched some of the men at a distant corral, who were observing another break a wild horse.

"May I join this conversation?" he asked Lloyd and Jake.

"Of course you can," Jake told him, "as long as you don't ask me to give away Sadie Mae's secret."

Brian grinned and faced them. "Jake, once my children become old enough to know their grandfather, I might as well give up as far as fatherly discipline. They hang on every move you make and every word you say, God help them."

Jake straightened, grinning back. "I know I'm not the best example for how to live your life, but they know Grandpa loves them. I'd jump in front of a train for any one of them."

Brian nodded, lifting a cup of coffee to his lips. "You sure would." He drank some coffee. "And I personally don't think they could ask for a better grandfather or a better example of love."

"Well, the grandsons have seen the ugly side. Let's hope none of the girls ever will. The fact that my blood runs in their veins scares me to death."

Brian folded his arms. "It's good blood—tough blood. And speaking of the ugly side, what's this thing about you cussing a blue streak in the henhouse with Sadie Mae standing right outside?"

Jake laughed. "Damn hens. Randy told me they could peck and scratch a person to death. I found that out. Reminds me of a few *women* I've known."

The three of them laughed.

"I honestly can't believe you didn't kill a couple of those hens," Lloyd told Jake.

"Hell, if Sadie Mae hadn't been around, I *would* have."

Brian grinned, studying his father-in-law. "What happened to Randy? I've never seen her more like her old self…and I've never seen her eat like she did this morning. The woman was absolutely glowing, and talk about being full of vinegar again…" He shook his head. "Do you think it's that tonic?"

Jake took another drag on his cigarette and ran a hand through his hair. "No. She hasn't even taken any the last couple of days. It made her a little sick. I told her she should eat better instead."

"And that's it?" Brian asked. "We've all been telling her that for months."

Jake smiled. "We had a good talk and came to an understanding, you might say. The rest is too personal."

"Well, leave it to you to charm a woman back to her old self. And by the way, have you checked that wound this morning? Do you need me to change the bandages?"

"It's all right. Randy fixed it up last night. There wasn't any fresh bleeding."

"Good. I'm getting a little tired of patching you up."

Jake grinned. "I'm getting tired of *being* patched up. Let's hope these are my last stitches."

"Knowing you, that will be a miracle," Lloyd answered. He got to his feet as the three men watched a motorized buggy coming down the distant hill toward the homestead.

"What the hell?" Jake muttered. He walked into the house to take down his guns from over the door. "We have company, ladies. Stay inside with the kids until we know who it is." He drew both guns from their holsters and walked outside, handing one to Lloyd. They'd learned long ago to always be wary of approaching strangers.

The noisy roadster approached, puffing dark smoke out the back end, one of the J&L men riding beside it. The vehicle backfired, and the ranch hand's horse reared, nearly throwing him off. The men laughed, and all the noise brought the entire family to a big front window to watch. The man on the horse was shouting a string of curses they could hear all the way to the house as he tried to keep the startled horse under control.

"That's Vance," Lloyd told them, "but I don't know who those three men are in that damn contraption."

"Those things are a nuisance," Jake grumbled. "Give me a horse any day."

"How did they get here so early in the day?" Brian wondered. "When Billy Porter brings the mail by horse, he doesn't get here till almost evening. Takes a long time to ride across the J&L, let alone coming from Brighton…a good two days all together. They must have camped overnight somewhere."

"I suppose it takes less time in one of those contraptions, because you don't have to stop and rest and water it," Lloyd suggested. "I guess they have their good points."

"I have no interest," Jake said, lighting another cigarette.

Some of the men who'd been at the corral walked toward the house, curious. Visitors to the remote ranch were always cause for excitement. Even the twice-a-week mail delivery was exciting.

The arrival of what people were beginning to call an automobile was too exciting for the boys to stay under control. They barged through the screen door.

"Stay behind me," Jake ordered them. "Never be too anxious to greet a visitor, but be cordial once you know who it is."

The women came out next, leaving the babies inside and telling the little girls they could watch out the window. Randy hurried over to Jake's side, and Jake moved an arm around her, sensing a hint of the old fear. "Jake, you aren't in trouble, are you?"

"No. It's okay." He kissed her hair, secretly slightly alarmed. The men looked a bit too official. He knew a lawman when he saw one, and though these men wore suits and bowler hats, they were lawmen.

"They're wearing badges, Pa," Lloyd told him.

"I see it."

"Jake!" Randy moved an arm around his back.

"Relax. Boulder citizens asked me to be their new sheriff, remember? I'm not in any trouble." *Unless by some horrible coincidence they're here to ask about Brad Buckley.*

The chugging buggy finally reached the house, Vance riding up behind it. "Jake, these are Pinkerton men, here to see you," he said with a scowl. "I ain't real happy about that damn contraption they're driving, but I had to show them in."

The ranch hands moved closer to stare at the visitors as they disembarked from the odd vehicle.

One of them spoke up. "We're here to speak with Jake Harkner."

Jake gave Randy a squeeze and left her to greet the men. "Gentlemen, what can I do for you?"

"Ah, you look exactly the way I pictured you, Mr. Harkner!" one of them told him, coming up the steps and putting out his hand. "Tall and mean-looking and, as the women put it, one handsome man!"

Jake stood there with his arms folded. "I generally don't shake a man's hand until I know who he is," he answered.

"Of course! John Carney, Pinkerton Detective Agency." The small-built man wore spectacles and a striped suit. "And I am proud to shake your hand."

Jake finally accepted a handshake.

"I have to admit I actually knew you by your picture," Carney told Jake, smiling. "It's been in all the papers, you know."

"Yeah, well, my picture used to be well known for reasons I'd rather forget," Jake told him.

Carney laughed. "Oh yes! The handsome outlaw, they once called you, and now you're a hero!" He turned to the other two men, who stood near the motorized buggy. "These are also Pinkerton men—Mr. Bob Lacey and Mr. Harvey Betts."

"That so?" Jake kept his cigarette between his lips. "What's this about being a hero? I'm not fond of that label."

Bob Lacey removed his hat and stepped forward, also coming up the steps to shake Jake's hand. He bowed lightly to the women, revealing a bald spot on the top of his head, then turned his attention back to Jake. "You caught and killed George Callahan, Mr. Harkner, when we'd been setting traps for him for months. We offered a big reward for his capture or death, and we are here to pay you that reward. And the good people of Boulder want you to come to their big fund-raiser in two weeks so they can honor you publicly. They gave me a message for you—that they hoped we would find you doing well, and that they still want you to be their new sheriff. I must say, though, that the Pinkerton Agency would much prefer you accepted our offer—to be one of our detectives."

Jake felt Randy move up behind him. She grasped his arm, and Jake turned to bring her forward. "This is my wife," he told the Pinkerton men.

The three men bowed slightly, and the two who still wore hats removed them.

"Your wife is quite beautiful," Harvey Betts told Jake.

Jake moved an arm around Randy. "Thank you. I happen to agree," Jake told them with a smile. "Everyone else on this veranda is family—my son, Lloyd, daughter, Evie." Jake indicated the family members, introducing Brian, Katie, and the grandchildren. "So, what's this about a reward?"

"Ten thousand dollars, Mr. Harkner," John Carney told him. He reached into his pocket and handed Jake an envelope. "A check, sir, from the Pinkerton Detective Agency."

Jake sobered. "I didn't even know there *was* a reward."

"There most certainly is, Mr. Harkner," Carney verified. "And it's all yours!" He still held out the envelope.

"Wow, Grampa!" Little Jake exclaimed. "Ten thousand dollars!"

"You could buy a whole herd of cattle or horses with that, Pa!" Ben spoke the words with a big grin. "And winter feed and maybe build another barn and still have money left over!"

Jake dropped his cigarette and stepped it out. "No thanks," he answered. "Take that check back to Boulder and put it in the bank accounts my sons and daughter have there. I don't want it for myself."

Randy looked up at him. "Jake? What's wrong?"

"Daddy, you *earned* that money," Evie told him.

Jake shook his head. "No, I didn't." He faced the Pinkerton men. "Mr. Carney, I spent four years of hell in prison because of a man who accepted a five-thousand-dollar reward on *my* head. I *did* earn that prison sentence. You men know my reputation. There was a time when I wasn't any better than the men who robbed that bank, and I'm no damn hero. I don't want any more jobs as a lawman. I had my fill of that in Oklahoma, and my family suffered dearly because of enemies I made there. My wife has been through enough worry in her life. I'm not interested in a sheriff's job, and I sure as hell don't plan to be a part of some kind of circus in Boulder with people lauding my skills and bravery. So take that reward and put it in the bank in Boulder. My sons and daughter already have accounts there, so the bank will have all the necessary information."

Everyone quieted.

"But you *are* a hero, Grampa," Little Jake told him.

Jake studied the excitement in the boy's eyes. "I've talked to you boys about that. You know my past and how I feel about it. That money will go into your parents' accounts, and they'll make sure you get some of it when you're older. You can start your own ranches, get married, whatever. I'll be long gone by then, and I'll be happy to know you boys will all have good lives. I didn't earn that money. This whole *family* earned it just by putting up with me. And Lloyd and Evie will make sure your grandmother is always taken care of when I'm gone. They can use the money for that if they need to."

"But, Mr. Harkner—"

"I've told you how I feel," Jake interrupted John Carney, "but I don't mean to be rude, so if the women want to offer you coffee and biscuits before you leave, you're welcome to it. I know what a long trip it is to get to this homestead from Brighton." He embraced Randy a little closer. "Thank you for your efforts. I'm going for a walk with my wife." He led Randy down the steps and walked away.

The rest of the family just stood there at first, and Little Jake's eyes teared.

"Grampa shouldn't talk about what we'll do when he's gone," he cried. "I don't never want him to be gone."

"I'm sure it will be many, many years from now, son," Brian told him, squeezing his shoulder. "Look what just happened. He's been shot so many times water could probably run through him like a strainer. Just think how tough he must be to survive all the things he's been through. That means he's bound to live a long, long time yet."

Little Jake wiped at his tears. "You'll always take good care of him, won't you, Daddy? 'Cuz you're a doctor."

"Of course I will."

"Well, we certainly didn't come out here to upset

the family," Bob Lacey told them. "We're sorry for any confusion over this."

"Don't be, Mr. Lacey," Lloyd told him. "My father is pretty touchy about his past and never feels like he deserves the good things that happen to him. I'm sure he's grateful, but it's just not his nature to take credit for anything. You three come on inside, and my wife and sister will fix you a bite to eat before you head back. There's some damn good bread, and some leftover ham and potatoes."

"Well, thank you!" John Carney held up the check. "We can discuss exactly how you want this money deposited—that is, if you trust us with all this money."

"If I can't trust Pinkerton men, who *can* I trust?" Lloyd told them.

The men laughed and Lloyd ushered them inside, then looked into the distance where his parents were walking toward the new barn. How many ways were there to tell a man he was forgiven…that he was worthy of the love and family he had now? Jake would never truly accept that.

He turned to go inside, only to see Evie also watching their parents walk away.

She looked at Lloyd with tears in her eyes. "I think it embarrassed him to get that reward," she told her brother.

"Yeah, I expect so."

Their gazes held, both of them knowing their father was actually hurting right now, fighting to stay out of the dark place that always followed him whenever something reminded him of his past.

Twenty-one

JAKE KEPT AN ARM AROUND RANDY'S SHOULDERS AS HE led her into the new horse barn. "You haven't even been in here since it was built," he told her. "I was afraid it would bring back bad memories from the night of the fire." He stopped and looked down at her. "Do you want to see it?"

I see what's in your eyes, Randy thought. *Stay out of your own bad memories, Jake.* "Yes," she answered, not really sure of her emotions. She remembered the fire, remembered the horrible orange glow of it against the night sky, remembered seeing the shadow of a man run across her veranda and thinking it was one of the ranch hands...until Brad Buckley and those with him burst in from both the back and the front of the house. She remembered fighting them, remembered Ben and her grandsons trying to stop them, only to get beaten off.

She stopped at the entrance. "I think one of the worst memories is of how the boys tried so hard to stop those men...seeing them hit the boys...seeing the awful, helpless look in the boys' eyes. I felt so sorry for them."

"That's why we let them come and help us rescue you. It helped them feel better about the whole thing." Jake paused and pulled her close. "They saw me do some pretty awful things that day. I've talked with them about it." He crushed her even closer. "Damn it, Randy, I don't want them to end up like me. I hope they understand that. Everything is different now. A man can't deal his own justice anymore."

Randy hugged him around the middle, being careful of his wounded side. "Jake, they were raised entirely different from you. They know love and they know the Christian faith and they know right from wrong. They'll be fine." She leaned back and looked up at him. "And I'm glad you're putting that money into Lloyd and Evie's accounts, and some to Ben; but you *do* deserve it, Jake. How many men survive what you have survived in your lifetime? You've come so far. Everyone has forgiven you—even the *law* has forgiven you. You just need to forgive *yourself*."

He shook his head. "Think what you want. I just can't quite accept any of it. An ex-outlaw accepting a reward for bringing down men no different than he was just doesn't seem right." He led her farther inside the barn, where Rodriguez was raking out a stall. "*Amigo*," Jake called to him. "Can you go do something else for a while?"

Rodriguez set the rake aside. "*Sí, señor*." He smiled and nodded to Randy. "*Señora*, it is good to see you out here. It is a beautiful barn, no?"

Randy looked up at the two-story-high rafters, lofts running along both sides of the barn, everything held by huge pine beams. The building was at least twice the size of the one that had burned. "Yes, it is!" She looked up at Jake. "How many stalls are there?"

"Twelve on each side," Jake told her. "We keep only the best riding and cutting horses in here, but we have some stalls to fill yet after losing so many horses in the fire. Lloyd will be looking to buy more when he drives the cattle to Denver."

Rodriguez nodded to them and left, and Randy looked up at Jake again. "Jake, you aren't going to Denver, are you? I think you should wait a year."

"Don't worry. I'm not going." He led her past his own horse's stall, and Outlaw whinnied and tossed his head.

Jake reached out and petted the horse's neck. "You're glad to see Randy in here too, aren't you, Outlaw?"

The horse nodded and shuddered.

Randy smiled and stroked the big animal's black mane. "Seems like every animal around here is called Outlaw."

"Thanks to the kids," Jake told her. "I know that damn rooster in the henhouse sure earned the name."

They laughed, and Jake took her arm and led her to another stall, one that had a name engraved on the gate. PEPPER.

"We figured we should commemorate Pepper in the new barn, so we had his name engraved on this stall. We'll never use it for a horse. We put Pepper's saddle, bedroll, and gear in the stall."

"Oh, Jake!" Randy put a hand to her mouth. "Poor Pepper! He was such a loyal hand."

"Yes, he was. I kept trying to go in and get him, but the fire was just too hot and burned too fast." He turned away for a moment, sighing deeply. "Jesus, Randy, we should have known. We should have known."

"You couldn't have. When you hear your best horses whinnying in terror because they're being burned alive, how can you think of anything else but trying to save them?" She touched his back. "It's all right, Jake. We worked things out last night, and I've made up my mind that it's over and I have to move on, just like Evie had to do. She told me once that part of the reason she managed to do that was for Brian. She had the best husband a woman could ask for, and he was so patient with her for so long. She realized she was punishing her own husband in a way, for something he didn't even do. She was letting those awful men destroy something beautiful, and Brian didn't deserve that. I thought about that after we talked, back in Boulder, and I realized I was doing the same thing to you. Our relationship was never so strained. I was missing how it used to be, just like you were. And last night…you have no idea what that meant to me."

Jake turned around and pulled her close again, running his hands into her hair, which she'd left long this morning. For him? She knew he liked her hair down. "It wasn't exactly a sacrifice on my part, Mrs. Harkner."

She laughed lightly and kissed his chest.

He pulled lightly at her hair so she had to look up at him. "My God, Randy, do I dare believe I have you back? Two or three days ago, you couldn't have joked about that."

"I know. But when you actually *listened* to me and understood…" She felt the blood coming into her cheeks then. How ridiculous was it to feel embarrassed in front of the man she'd been intimate with for over thirty years? She laughed and put her face against his chest. "My God, Jake, it was like being with you for the first time. And at the moment, I am totally embarrassed."

He kissed her hair. "Why? This is Jake—your husband—remember? And last night was beautiful. And everything we do is up to you, understand? I love you for the incredible woman you are, and I love *making* love to that woman. That's all I need or will *ever* need from you." He grasped her face and leaned down to kiss her gently. "You're the air I breathe, Randy Harkner. These last few months have been the loneliest I've ever experienced, even though I was with you night and day. I never want it to be like that between us again."

Randy searched his dark eyes. "I'm so sorry, Jake."

He put fingers to her lips. "Don't say that. Just stay with me this way. We'll take it a day at a time, and whenever you need something I don't seem to understand, you tell me, all right?"

"You have to promise to do the same."

Jake grinned. "I don't generally leave any doubt about what I need or want."

Randy laughed. "I have to agree with you there."

"Yeah? Then what if I told you I'd like to take you up in the loft and make love to you the old-fashioned way?"

"I'd say no, because those Pinkerton men are still here and we really should go visit with them."

Jake frowned. "Boring. I like my idea better. I've never felt closer to you." He nuzzled her neck. "And I've learned something new and sexy about you."

"Jake Harkner, we are *not* going into that loft. You will have to save that for tonight. Right now, we are going back to the house." She ducked from under his arms, but Jake caught her and held her gaze as he gently gripped her.

"You really okay now?" he asked her. "Tell the truth. That's what you always ask of me, Randy."

She put a hand over his. "I'm really okay."

"And who do you belong to?"

"Jake Harkner."

"Has anyone else ever touched you?"

"Just my first husband, and that was thirty-four years ago, before he went off to war never to return. And we were kids. Then along came Jake Harkner, who saved me from dying and who has loved me better than any man on earth could love me. There will never be another Jake Harkner in my life."

Jake searched her eyes. "Remember that when a bad memory tries to destroy what we have, Randy. Open your eyes and look at me and remember *I'm* the one touching you. Don't slip away from me again, baby."

"I won't." Randy studied him in a shaft of sunlight. "As long as I have you and as long as you understand, I can handle it."

He smiled sadly. "Nobody understands better than me what it's like to battle bad memories, so you talk to me when you need to talk about it. You've always told me that, so I'm telling you the same thing."

Randy's eyes teared. "All I have to do is open my eyes and see you, and it all goes away." She came closer again and leaned up to capture his mouth with her own. "You're a beautiful man, and the best lover a woman could ask for."

Jake grinned. "This isn't the way to talk me out of throwing you over my shoulder and carrying you up to that loft, Mrs. Harkner."

Randy ducked away again. "We have company, Mr. Harkner." She backed away. "We will finish this tonight."

Jake folded his arms. "Save your energy."

Randy laughed lightly and hurried out. Jake watched after her as he lit a cigarette. He had his wife back, all right, and seemingly better than ever. He thought he knew everything about her...had her all figured out. He took a deep drag on the cigarette. "*Women*," he mused, shaking his head before following her out of the barn.

PART THREE

Twenty-two

July 10, 1897

GRETTA ADJUSTED THE BODICE OF HER PURPLE RUFFLED dress as she went to the door, looking down to be sure her breasts were exposed nearly to the nipples. She opened the door and smiled at the man standing there. He was decent-looking and relatively clean but had a mop of brown hair that stuck out from under a wide-brimmed hat, and he looked like he hadn't shaved for a few days. He wore a clean shirt with its long sleeves turned up, a tie that looked like it had seen plenty of wear, denim pants that were a bit too big on him, and scuffed black boots. He nodded to her. "Ma'am? Might you be Miss Gretta MacBain?"

Gretta smiled. "I might be. Who are you?"

"Can I come inside?"

Gretta shrugged. "Sure." She stepped back and let him in, ushering him into the parlor. Two of her girls were there drinking with their own customers, one sitting on a man's lap and giggling when he reached inside her see-through negligee.

"Make yourself at home, big fella," Gretta told the stranger. "Would you like a drink?"

"No thank you, ma'am," he told her. "I ain't here for that, or for…you know…the other."

Gretta almost laughed at his shy attitude. "Have you ever been to a bordello before?"

He looked her over, his eyes showing more curiosity

than desire or bad intent. "No, ma'am. I came at some-body's request—with a message."

"Oh? Who?"

He looked around, noticing the woman in the see-through negligee was practically naked now, her customer putting his hand between her legs. The woman made a moaning noise, and the stranger looked back at Gretta. "Can we go someplace else? Where there ain't no other women?"

Gretta smiled, moving up close and touching his face. "My room?"

"No, ma'am. Maybe the kitchen or somethin' like that, as long as there ain't no other women around."

Gretta thought it an odd request, but she shrugged and indicated he should follow her. She led him to the back of the house and to the kitchen table. "Have a seat," she told him. "Sure you're not thirsty?"

"Yes, ma'am, I'm sure." The man sat down. "A Mrs. Loretta Sellers sent me."

Gretta instantly sobered. "Loretta!" She sat down across from him, suddenly self-conscious of her nearly naked breasts. She put a hand over her cleavage. "What happened? Is my daughter all right?"

"I don't rightly know, ma'am. I brought a message from Mrs. Sellers that she said would be important to you. She said you'd probably be open for business, and she was afraid to come in the evening like this. She asked me to come on account of I'm a man, actually a *single* man, so she said it would be okay."

Gretta's heart fell. She'd struggled to keep her worry over her daughter buried deep so she could continue with her business. She'd considered the fact that some-one in Mexico might ask for some kind of ransom money, so she'd been saving up as much as possible. Lord knew no decent person in Denver would help her with any of this.

"What's the message?" Gretta asked. "And where on earth did you come from? That sounds like a Texas accent."

"That's on account of I *am* from Texas, ma'am. I have a horse ranch down there, almost clear to the border in Brownsville, where right now it's doggone hot." He removed his hat and set it on the table. "It's a lot cooler here in the Rockies."

"No small talk, mister. What's your name, anyway?"

"Otis Clark, ma'am. I recently took care of a man down at my place by the name of Jessie Valencia, afore he died. He said—"

"Died!" Gretta gasped the word. "From what?"

"From a couple of bullet wounds, ma'am. It happened across the border. He made it as far as my farm, and I took him in. Afore he died, he said he'd gone to Mexico to look for a young girl that was kidnapped. Them that took her put up a big fight, and he got shot when they chased him to the border. That's all I know, except he said to tell Mrs. Sellers here in Denver that he wasn't able to get the girl but that he knew where they keep her, so if Mrs. Sellers wants to hire somebody else to go get her, that might help."

Gretta closed her eyes against tears. One of the girls came into the kitchen and told her one of her regular customers was there to see her, and she snapped at her. "Not tonight, Tillie! Maybe not ever!"

"Gretta! You okay?"

"No!" Gretta wiped at her eyes. "Have one of the other girls take care of him. I know who it is, and he won't care."

"Sure." Tillie left, and Gretta wiped at her eyes with a cloth napkin lying on the table.

"Ma'am, I'm sorry to upset you. I came all the way up here on account of there's no phones down in Brownsville and on account of it involved a young girl, so I figured this Mrs. Sellers was the mother, and I thought such news ought to be delivered in person. Took me about four days to get here. If it weren't for trains and stagecoaches, it would have taken me a lot longer, but I have to get back to my farm, you know. Anyways, when I told Mrs. Sellers, she was really bad upset, and she said as how I should come here and tell you on account of you're the girl's real mother."

Gretta nodded, swallowing back more tears. "I truly thank you for taking care of Mr. Valencia and making such a long trip, Mr. Clark. I—would you like a cold beer or something?"

Otis nodded. "Well, I said I wasn't thirsty to be polite, but a cold beer does sound good. That would be real fine."

Gretta felt removed from her own body as she got up and went to the icebox. "It's true. That girl is my daughter, Mr. Clark," she explained. "I had her at a real young age and...well, I couldn't raise her in a place like this, so I found a good Christian couple to adopt her. That was Loretta Sellers and her husband, of course. Mr. Sellers died, and my daughter took it hard. She reached those years where girls get all starry-eyed over the first handsome man who comes along, and one did." She brought a bucket of beer to the table and poured some into a mug. She breathed deeply for self-control. "Did Mr. Valencia say anything about the kind of men who came after him?"

Otis drank down some beer, then pulled a folded piece of paper from his shirt. "He wrote down the name of a...well...a brothel...just across the Rio Grande. It's wrote in Spanish, but he says it means House of Heavenly Women. He said it was a place where they... well, where they break girls in for wealthy customers. They keep the prettiest ones, and I guess your daughter was one of those. They take the rest of them someplace else. Mr. Valencia, he was mostly Mexican himself, so he fit right in, but when he tried to help the girl escape, they got found out and he had to run. He ended up gettin' shot. He got infection at my place, and there was nothin' I could do. He died in awful misery. I felt real sorry for him."

Gretta put her hands over her face, feeling like she might vomit. "I wanted so much more for my daughter," she lamented. "I can't explain how I ended up like this, Mr. Clark, and it doesn't matter now. What matters is getting my daughter out of there. I just fear too much damage has already been done, but I have to try." She wiped at her eyes again. "I'll pay you whatever it cost you to get up here. And it helps so much to have the name of that place."

"Yes, ma'am. I thank you for payin' me back. I don't know how you'll get her out of there, ma'am. It would take an army. The whole thing is actually headed by a white man, not a Mexican, name of Sidney Wayland. According to Mr. Valencia, a lot of men guard that place. Men good with guns."

I know someone who might be able to beat those odds. "I just have to…find someone…maybe several men this time."

"Mrs. Sellers, she said you knew of somebody who might be able to do it—some gunfighter, I think she said."

Gretta poured herself a beer. "He used to be a gun-fighter. Then he was a lawman. He helps his son run a big ranch now." *How can I possibly ask Jake to do this?* "I just don't know if he's even able," she told Clark. "He was hurt about a month ago stopping a bank robbery in Boulder. For all I know, he's in a bad way now."

"Well, ma'am, it don't hurt to find out. Maybe once he knows it's a young girl needin' help, he'll do it for you. Is he the type?"

Gretta smiled sadly, remembering the day she told Jake that Mike Holt had visited her brothel and was violent with her. Jake actually cared that she might have been hurt. How many men truly cared about a prostitute? And who knew brothels and prostitutes and this whole sordid life better than an ex-outlaw who'd lived in that world? And he was half Mexican and spoke the language. Besides that, Jake Harkner knew what it felt like to have a daughter in trouble.

"Oh, yes, Mr. Clark, he's the type." She picked up the folded piece of paper.

La Casa de Mujeres Celestiales.

Jake would be able to read it. She stuck the paper into her cleavage. *I'm so sorry, Jake. I don't know where else to turn.*

Twenty-three

"THE BIGGEST SECRET IS TO SQUEEZE THE TRIGGER, Ben," Jake told his adopted son. "Don't jerk it. If you squeeze it, it's less likely the gun will jerk from your target once you fire it. And don't doubt yourself. You have to see that target in your mind, not just with your eyes. And don't forget those are hair triggers, so when I say squeeze, it won't take much. Keep your trigger finger against the side of the gun until you're actually ready to shoot, or that thing might go off before you want it to."

"I'm nervous," Ben answered, sweat trickling down his temples. "This is the first time you've let me or anybody else besides Lloyd touch one of your guns."

Jake lit a cigarette. "You might as well start learning. I promised when each child and grandson turned thirteen he could fire one of these. And by the way, I told Lloyd to pick up a good .45 for you while he's in Denver. That's your birthday present."

Ben lowered the gun a moment. "Thanks, Pa!" Love moved into the young man's blue eyes, which warmed Jake's heart. Ben was eight years old and being beaten with a belt when he'd found him. His own memories of such beatings had triggered a fury that sent Jake barreling into Ben's father. He'd grabbed the belt from the man and begun using on him until Lloyd had finally managed to pull him off. After that, the sonofabitch actually agreed to give up his own son to Jake, as though the boy meant nothing to him. Jake legally adopted Ben, and the boy had been part of the family ever since. The now tall, strong young man was much bigger than his age would imply. "You deserve your own handgun, Ben, but only if you handle it the way I've taught you. And it won't be long before you'll be able to handle a lot of other things to do with running the J&L. I'm proud of you."

"What about *me*, Grampa?" Eight-year-old Little Jake looked up at him with eager anticipation, a boy straining to be a man like his father and his uncle Lloyd and Jake. Jake noted a tiny spark of jealousy in the boy's eyes.

"Little Jake, you have enough stubbornness and determination in you to outdo *all* of us some day. I have absolutely no doubt you will be one hell of a co-owner of the J&L. You know good and well where you stand with me."

"I wanna be just like you—big and strong and good with guns."

Jake smoked quietly, looking at the distant fence railing where several cans had been lined up for Ben to shoot. "No, Little Jake, I assure you that you don't want to be just like me. And I don't want you using a gun for the wrong reasons, understand?"

"Yes, sir."

"You're better off fashioning yourself after your father, Little Jake. Brian Stewart is just about the all-around best man I've ever known. Your father has an inner strength I don't possess, and he's wise and patient. Those things are important. Me, I don't have much control over my temper, and I've done things no man should be forgiven for. Like Lloyd says, the Good Lord and I will have plenty to talk about when I stand before Him, if He even gives me the chance. He just might send me straight to hell without a hearing."

Little Jake smiled. "No, he won't, Grampa."

I'm pretty sure He will, Jake wanted to answer, but Little Jake worshipped the ground he walked on, and he got upset easily whenever Jake talked about the

Hereafter. The kid didn't want to think about life without his grandfather in it, but some day he'd *have* to. "Ben, go ahead and shoot. Soon as we're done here, we'll head out to Evie's Garden and check fences. Maybe we'll even catch sight of Lloyd and Stephen and the rest of the men who went on the cattle drive. Lloyd should be coming back any day, as long as he didn't have any trouble in Denver."

The thought of Lloyd going to Denver brought pain to his heart, remembering what happened there last summer. It was only by God's miracle his son was alive now, and he'd never forget the feeling of seeing Lloyd shot down point-blank.

"He can get there and back a lot faster now 'cuz he can load cattle onto train cars, huh, Grampa?" Little Jake asked.

"Yup. Our days of long cattle drives are pretty much over, Little Jake, now that we can catch a train from Brighton to Denver. It's a little more expensive, but it saves us in extra pay and in food for all the men."

The days of old-fashioned ranching were changing, and Jake wondered how long it would be before he'd have to let some of the men go…and before the government came along and set up so many new rules about grazing that Lloyd might have trouble making money on this place. He figured he wouldn't be around to see it, but he damn well hated the thought of not always being here to help his son and the rest of the family.

Ben wiped at sweat with his shirtsleeve, then raised the gun, supporting his wrist with his left hand. "It sure is heavier than I thought," he told Jake as he took aim.

"Remember what I told you, Ben. Decide which eye you'll use and always practice with that same eye. Always. Consistency is important."

After a few seconds, the young man squeezed the trigger. Jake's gun boomed, and a can went flying.

"I hit it!" Ben exclaimed. He raised the gun again and fired, this time missing. "How in heck do you draw and fire it so fast, Pa? And you always hit your target."

"Just a lot of practice over the years." Jake took the gun from him and holstered it. "When Lloyd gets back with your own gun, you can start practicing with that. The best way to get better is to practice with the gun you will always use. Get used to the feel of it and whether it shoots high or low. These guns are adjusted to true sights."

"Show us, Grampa!" Little Jake asked. "Practice now!"

"Little Jake, you know I don't show off with these things."

"Just once, please? Draw your gun and shoot the rest of those cans."

"Those cans are pretty far away, Little Jake," Ben told his nephew.

"Not too far for Grampa, I'll bet. Come on, Grampa. Show us."

"You've seen me shoot, Little Jake, last summer when those ranch hands gave us trouble, and again last winter." *When we all went to rescue Grandma.*

"That's not the same. Those men last summer were up close, and last winter you were already shooting back and forth. We just want to see you draw and shoot down all those cans. Show us how you could shoot down those bank robbers while they were holding Grandma and Tricia right in front of them!"

"I suppose that's the only way to shut you up, isn't it?"

Little Jake giggled. "Yup."

"Step away, then." Jake switched guns so the one on his right hip would be fully loaded. "This can get expensive, Little Jake, so this is the last time. In fact, I might start making my own cartridges with the spent shells. The price of bullets keeps going up, and I don't like wasting them."

The boys stepped back, and Little Jake covered his

ears. It took all of two seconds. Jake drew and fired in such rapid succession, Little Jake couldn't count the shots. Six cans went flying almost at the same time. The boys stood there with their mouths open.

"Pa, you didn't even aim," Ben commented, shaking his head.

"I didn't have to, not with my eyes anyway. Remember what I told you about seeing your target in your mind?"

Ben shook his head. "I'll never be able to do that."

"Sure you will. But until you're sixteen, I need you to promise me that you'll never practice or mess around in any other way with your new .45 unless I'm around, got that? If I catch you using it alone or showing it by yourself to Stephen and Little Jake or anybody else, I'll take it away, and you'll be *eighteen* before you can use it again."

"Yes, sir."

"You can hunt with our 30/30. I just don't want you messing with a handgun." Jake began reloading his six gun. "Too many men have had too many accidents with handguns, and if you wear one, it tends to start fights. Take it from someone who knows." Jake noticed Randy coming toward them. It struck him then how much weight she'd gained back in just a month. She was close to her old, perfect self, round in all the right places, yet slender in the waist. Life hadn't been this good between them in a long time, and he looked forward to getting back to her after a couple of days of riding fence with the boys. Nights in that big bed they shared had become extremely pleasant, and she was beginning to enjoy being as intimate with him as he'd always been with her. He holstered his gun as she came closer.

"Are you teaching these boys how to be outlaws?" she teased.

"I'm teaching them how to *shoot* at outlaws," Jake answered.

"Well, then, you'd better be careful, or they'll be shooting at you."

The boys laughed.

"Mom, I shot Pa's own gun! He let me try it once," Ben told her. "And I hit a can with it!"

Randy folded her arms. "I'm not so sure I like that idea."

Jake tossed his cigarette, stepping it out. He walked up to Randy and moved an arm around her. "What are you doing out here so far from the house?"

"I just wanted to see you once more before you leave with the boys for a couple of days. You know I hate it when you go away."

Jake caught that whisper of the frightened woman again. "There are plenty of men left here to watch over you and Katie and Evie, and Brian is here too. He's gotten pretty good with a gun himself, thanks to plenty of lessons from me."

"Yes, well, he *isn't* you. Brian is a fine and brave man, but he's better at *fixing* gunshot wounds than *causing* them." Randy moved her arms around him and looked up at him. "You'll come back as soon as you can, right?"

"I will. And you'd better have a good supply of your famous bread ready when I get here." He leaned down and kissed her, and Little Jake giggled while Ben looked away. "I want you and Evie and Katie and the babies and little girls to stay together at the main house, all right? The men know what to do. You'll have plenty of protection." He read her thoughts, hated the fact that she'd come so far but still was afraid to be alone at night. "Cole will sleep right downstairs on the couch, and you can have Button and Sunshine sleep in bed with you. Those two little imps will do so much jabbering you won't have a chance to think about being by yourself, because you *won't* be, understand?"

Randy put her head against his chest. "I understand."

Jake wrapped her in both arms and lifted her feet off the ground. "You sure feel a lot better in my arms, Mrs. Harkner. I finally have something more to grab on to." She looked up, and he planted a long, deep kiss on her mouth.

Little Jake laughed again. "Grampa! Old people don't kiss!"

Jake laughed in the middle of the kiss and stopped, kissing Randy's eyes. "They sure as hell do, and by the way, who are you calling old?"

"*You* are!" the boy answered.

"Don't make me come over there and show you how wrong you are, Little Jake. I'll throw you all the way over to those cans if you call me old again."

"Oh, I know you're still strong, Grampa, but old people aren't supposed to kiss."

"Some old people kiss a *lot*," Jake answered before planting another kiss on Randy while the boy laughed again. He set her on her feet and Randy pulled away, also laughing. She kept hold of Jake's hand.

"Are you saying I'm old too?" she asked Little Jake.

The boy shrugged. "Yeah, but you don't look very old at all, and you're the prettiest older lady there is. You're almost as pretty as Katie and my mom."

"Almost?"

"Well, they're kinda younger."

"And you're kinda in trouble," Jake told his grandson. "Remind me to teach you the proper way to talk to a woman. You keep up this kind of talk when you get older, and there won't be a young woman in all of Colorado who will want to kiss *you*."

Little Jake wiped at his lips. "I don't care. All I care about is ridin' good and shootin' good and learnin' how to run the J&L."

"Well, those are good goals, Little Jake," Jake answered, keeping his arm around Randy. "But some day you'll be wanting to be good at a few other things."

"Will you teach me?"

Jake and Randy laughed, and Jake hugged her close. "Nope. Those are things you'll have to learn on your own. Don't worry, though. It will come to you naturally." He swung Randy around and kissed her once more. "Go on back to the house. I'll watch till you get there. We have to get going."

"All right." Randy touched his chest. "Be careful, Jake."

"Who shot those robbers down with hostages right in their arms?"

"You did."

"There you go. You know damn well I can take care of myself, and all we're doing is riding fence for a couple of days. Go on with you so we can leave."

Randy reluctantly let go of him, watching his eyes for a few seconds as she walked backward.

"Hey, woman, who do you belong to?" Last night they'd done a good job of messing up the covers of their big bed.

"Jake Harkner," she answered.

"Every beautiful inch of you. Now get going."

Randy smiled and turned away, hurrying back to the house. She'd no more reached it than Rodriguez came charging down the hill toward the homestead, riding like a maniac. The Mexican's horse actually stumbled, and Rodriguez went flying, tumbling down the hill along with the horse.

"What the hell?" Jake mounted up on Outlaw, telling the boys to stay put. He rode hard to meet up with Rodriguez, who thankfully didn't seem to be hurt. The short, stout ranch hand was getting to his feet. Jake dismounted to help him up.

"*Fuego! Hay un incendio!*"

"Slow down, Rodriguez! A fire? Where?"

"*En el Jardín de Evie! Toda la hierba, está en llamas! No lo puedo apagarlo!*"

"Evie's Garden?"

"*Sí!*" Rodriguez took a deep breath. "It is as I said. All the grass, it is on fire! Lloyd is there now, with Stephen. He and the men, they were riding home and saw it—other ranchers are there also! They say it is that farmer, Brady Fillmore, who started the fire! Someone saw him setting the fire, and they are going to hang him! Your son, he say to come and get you first to be sure you agree!"

"Jesus!" Jake climbed back onto Outlaw. He turned the horse and rode back down to the boys. "Mount up and follow me—now! There's a fire at Evie's Garden!" He turned and charged up the hill. "Go tell the women!" he shouted to Rodriguez, who was helping up his horse and checking for injuries. "Tell them not to worry, there are plenty of men there! And tell Katie that Lloyd is back!"

His voice drifted into the wind as he headed at a full gallop toward Evie's Garden. Ben and Little Jake charged behind him on their horses, already packed and saddled for their planned trip with Jake.

Jake prayed the whole damn valley hadn't burned. The spring and summer had been so hot and dry; that grass they'd been saving was all they had for an emergency.

Twenty-four

JAKE FINALLY SLOWED DOWN. OUTLAW WAS A BIG horse and fast. The boys had fallen too far behind, so Jake dismounted and waited for them to catch up. Outlaw shuddered and shook his head, sweat flying off his neck. The boys caught up, and Jake told them to rest their horses.

"We'll never make it if we ride these mounts until they drop," he told them. He looked toward the southwest. The J&L was so big that they wouldn't make it to Evie's Garden until tomorrow morning. The huge, treeless lay of the land to the south was barren except for grass—and what should have been good grazing grass—but it was so dry Jake decided not to even light a cigarette.

"Look there," he told the boys, pointing to what looked like smoke on the horizon. "That must be it."

The boys dismounted and came to stand beside him.

"I can almost smell it," Ben commented.

Jake noticed the boy's voice was dropping more to a man's voice lately. He was going to be a fine man, that was sure. "I can too," he told Ben. "It's drifting on the wind. I just hope to hell they can get it out before the whole J&L burns down. I don't know what we're going to do for feed later this summer. Good thing I got that money from the Pinkertons. Lloyd might need it to buy feed."

"I feel like cryin'," Little Jake told them. "Evie's Garden is so pretty. Now it will be all black."

Jake deliberately buried his fury over what had

happened. If it was true that Brady Fillmore had set the fire, there would be hell to pay, and it wouldn't be pretty. "Little Jake, usually after a fire, the grass comes back prettier and greener than ever. Sometimes prairie land *needs* a fire. The ashes put nutrients into the ground that make next year's grass even hardier. And the fire will burn off any insects that might do damage. I just wish it hadn't happened now. We're going to need that grass if this weather keeps up."

"Are they gonna hang Mister Fillmore?" Ben asked.

Jake sighed, looking at the smoke on the distant horizon, praying it would dwindle, because that would mean they'd been able to stop it. "I don't know, Ben, but if he did it, it's likely they will."

"You ever see a hanging, Grampa?" Little Jake asked.

"I was almost the one hanged more than once myself," Jake answered, "but that was a long time ago. But to answer your question, yes, I've see a couple of hangings, only it was outlaws doing it to men who'd crossed them."

"You've seen a lot of bad stuff, haven't you, Grampa?" Little Jake asked.

Jake mounted up again. "Yeah, Little Jake, I've seen a lot of bad stuff, a lot of things I hope you and Ben and Stephen *never* see." He turned Outlaw and urged the big black gelding into a gentle trot. "Let's go, boys, a little slower this time. No matter how hard we ride, it will still be tomorrow before we get there."

He headed toward the awful sight and smell of smoke. He hated leaving Randy so suddenly and for something so ugly. Once she heard it was a fire, she'd be scared. There had been a fire the night she was taken…the barn consumed in flames…horses dying…one of their best hands dying in the fire…and all the while, men were dragging his wife away. He wished they were alive right now so he could tie them up and throw them into the grass fire and watch them burn. Killing them hadn't been enough satisfaction. Slow, prolonged suffering would have been better.

Twenty-five

MOST OF EVIE'S GARDEN VALLEY WAS GONE. JAKE FELT sick at the sight.

"Looks like the fire is out," Ben commented. "But Lloyd lost most of his emergency grass."

"There's a whole bunch of men over there, Grampa," Little Jake said, pointing to what looked like a camp far to their right.

"You boys hang behind me, all right? I don't know what we'll find when we get there," Jake told them. He urged Outlaw forward to what appeared to be a rather quiet camp full of men from the Twisted Tree ranch, located east of the J&L. He recognized the owner, Henry Till. With them were the J&L men who'd gone to Denver with Lloyd. Jake's grandson Stephen sat on a rock, tracing in the dirt with a stick, his arms and hands filthy. Brady Fillmore was tied to a pine tree that had somehow avoided being burned. He gave Jake a pleading look. "Untie me, Jake! I didn't do anything!"

"Shut up, Fillmore!" Cole snarled. "When Jake finds out the truth, he'll agree with all of us about stringing you up!"

Jake dismounted. Cole was one of the J&L's best hands and damn near as ruthless as Jake and Lloyd could be. He walked with a limp from an old war wound, but Jake knew little else about his past—even which side he'd been on in the war. All that mattered to him was that Cole was honest and a hard worker, a hardened man who was nearly Jake's age. He liked to drink but never got mean with it. Jake had always been good at reading men, and he'd been right on Cole. If Cole thought Brady needed hanging, he probably did.

Every man there was black with soot and ash, and the ground was dug up all around the nearly mile-wide east edge of Evie's Garden. It was obvious these men had worked like demons to save as much as they could of the valley. When riding in, it looked as though part of the western end of the nearly two-mile-long valley had never burned, thanks to the wind blowing the flames eastward. Sheer rock walls on either side of the valley had kept the flames from spreading north and south.

Jake was greeted with bloodshot, tired eyes, coughing, and a few nods. About fifteen men sat around a morning campfire, drinking coffee and smoking cigarettes.

"Jake." Henry Till greeted him.

"Henry." Jake came up beside Stephen and looked around. "Where is Lloyd?"

"He's over behind that big boulder, taking a pee," Stephen answered. "He's real mad, Grampa."

"I don't blame him. I'm getting real mad myself, and I don't even know the whole story yet." Jake looked at the others. "Looks like all of you helped put this fire out. I'm grateful. This is going to be a hot, dry summer, or so it seems, so feel free to water your cattle in Horse Creek if need be. It's little enough pay for helping out. Just take it easy, though, or the creek will run dry if we don't get more rain."

"We'll be careful," Henry told Jake. "Thanks for the offer."

"It's the least we can do."

Cole spoke up. "At least no cattle were lost."

Lloyd came out from behind the rock, and Jake felt sorry for the look in his eyes. His son had worked his ass off building the J&L. The ranch had been his dream through the dangerous, trying years he'd ridden with Jake as a U.S. Marshal in one of the most dangerous, godforsaken places on the face of the earth. Jake ached inside at realizing how many enemies they'd made because of the job. His reputation had done so much damage to the family. Now this. "I'm sorry about this, Lloyd."

"Nothing to be sorry for. That sonofabitch tied to that tree over there is the one who should be sorry. He started the fire deliberately!"

"It's your pa's fault," Brady tried to explain. "He shouldn't have pushed me back in Boulder last month! He shamed me in front of a barroom full of men and accused me of being a cattle thief!"

"You *are* a cattle thief," Lloyd roared, "and now you're apparently an *arsonist*!"

"I...I was gonna make a campfire, that's all. It got out of control!"

"Does someone here want to explain this?" Jake asked. "How did all of you end up here together like this? And how do you know Brady set the fire on purpose?"

"We saw him," Henry told Jake. He sipped some coffee and looked up at Jake. "Me and the boys were coming through your property as a shortcut to Brighton. I was supposed to pick up quite a few cows and yearlings there that I bought from a rancher up in Wyoming; he shipped them down to Brighton by train. We ran into your Mexican on the way, and he was all panicky and carryin' on about Evie's Garden being on fire, so we headed there, and he rode to your homestead to let you know. That was early yesterday."

"If the fire was already going, how do you know Brady did it?" Jake crouched near the campfire and lit a cigarette.

"They caught him making off with one of our steers again!" Lloyd answered for Henry, his dark eyes on fire with anger. Jake saw himself in his son's eyes. The Harkner temper was one thing that seemed to run in the blood.

"I was rescuing that steer from the fire!" Brady argued.

"Your face was black from smoke! And when you saw Henry and his men, you turned and ran. What more proof do we need than that?"

Brady hung his head and started crying.

"Rustling, in itself, is a hanging offense, Jake," Cole told him. "You know that." He tossed a cigarette butt into the campfire. "But starting a grass fire, especially with the dry summer we've had—that's unforgiveable. I don't see where we have a choice."

"It's *your* fault, Jake Harkner!" Brady yelled between sobs. "You pushed me into it back when you broke my nose! You Harkners think you own Colorado, and neither one of you deserves what you've got! You're *outlaws*, that's what! I don't care if you *did* ride as lawmen once. You got no right hangin' a man when *you're* the ones who ought to hang, especially *you*, Jake! You've done a whole lot worse things than take one lousy steer from a man. Shit, you killed your own pa! Who are you to sit and judge?"

Lloyd walked up to Brady and backhanded him, splitting his cheek open. Brady screamed from the punch and then cried more. "You *bastard*!"

"You shut up about my father! You don't know a goddamn thing about the man! There's not a better man who ever walked, you stupid sonofabitch! I waited for him because I wanted to give you a chance to explain yourself to him so we could make the right decision! He just might have helped keep us from hanging you, but now you've lost your chance!"

Jake just smoked quietly, staring at the fire. All the men waited for his reaction with bated breath. Lloyd walked over to stand behind him, his long hair blowing in the hot wind. "Pa? You all right?"

Jake sighed deeply, putting his cigarette between his lips and rising. He looked over at Ben and Little Jake still on their horses, and his other grandson, Stephen. He could see they would drink in his every word. Little Jake's jaw was set, his eyes narrowed in fierce anger, and Jake knew it was because of Brady's words. The kid was always one of the first to defend his grandpa. "Go ahead and hang him, Grampa! He didn't have no right sayin' those things about you."

"They're all true, Little Jake." Jake turned his gaze to Lloyd. "I'm not one to judge any more than I deserved that Pinkerton money. This place is more yours than mine, so I'll leave it up to you and these other men. I think you should let him go."

"What?" Lloyd tossed his cigarette into the campfire. "Pa, he stole another steer and burned up half of Evie's Garden! We needed this extra grazing area more this year than we ever have before. We're going to run out of good grass and won't have any to store up for the winter."

"You have my ten thousand dollars," Jake told him. "With that, you can store up all the feed you'll need. The Twisted Tree can use our water and some of the grass that's left if they run out before summer is over. And you won't have a *hanging* on your conscience!" Jake turned to look at the rest of them. "Take it from me, boys. You don't want to live your whole life regretting things you've done. It makes it pretty hard to sleep at night. And when you do sleep, you'll keep waking up with nightmares." He turned back to Lloyd. "If this involved any physical abuse to you or any member of the family, I'd gladly hang the sonofabitch. But if this came up in front of the law, what actual proof would we have? Remember that the boys are watching. There's nothing much uglier than a hanging, and they already saw enough last—" He checked himself. *Last winter.* What he and Lloyd did to Brad Buckley and his men last winter had surely left an impression on Stephen and Little Jake and Ben. But it was something none of the other men here knew about, and he intended to keep it that way. "It has to end somewhere, Lloyd, or you'll end up with a lot of the same regrets I have," Jake continued, sighing deeply. "And those boys will walk right into all of it and think this is how things get solved. One of them will end up in prison, and we both know who that would likely be. I don't want to go to my grave thinking that my grandsons might end up like me. Let him go. But he has to promise to get the hell out of Colorado. He has to promise to sign his land over to the J&L, for *nothing*! It will be payment for the loss from the grass fire and for any unbranded yearlings he might have stolen and sold that we don't even know about."

Lloyd shook his head. "This sure isn't like you, Pa. And after those things he said—"

"They're all true and we both know it. I'll never live down killing my own father, in spite of the brutal, worthless, drunken rapist he was! I just got my wife back, and I need some peace. You do what you have to do." Jake walked off, and Lloyd turned to the others.

"You boys heard him. What do you want to do?"

Henry Till rose. "It's your land, Lloyd. I say he hangs, but I'm not the one who suffered the loss."

Lloyd nodded. "I can make up for that. I agree you can use my water, Henry." He pulled his hair behind his back and glanced at Brady. "The Cattlemen's Association will hear about this, Brady Fillmore!" he said louder. "And I'm requesting that if any of them sees you anywhere on my land or any other rancher's land, they have a right to hang you, understand? I'm letting you go, but you're going to sign a deed giving me your land, got that? You're going to leave Colorado, and I never want to see your face anywhere again. If I do, I'll hang you myself, law or no law!"

One of the men from the Twisted Tree walked over and cut Brady's ropes.

"You'd better never say bad stuff about my grampa again!" Little Jake shouted to him. "If I was bigger, I'd sock you a good one, you sonofabitch!"

Some of the men snickered, and Brady glowered at the boy, then turned to Lloyd. "The bad blood just trickles right down, doesn't it?" He started for his horse, when out of nowhere, Jake was there with his rifle. He bashed the butt of the gun across Brady's head, sending him flying, then walked up and planted a foot on his neck, forcing the man onto his back as he half choked him with a big boot. He swung the repeater around and pressed the end of the rifle against one of Brady's eyes.

"That was for the things you said about my *wife* back in Boulder," Jake growled, "and for what you said about Little Jake. I just let you off from a fucking hanging, you ungrateful bastard, so I'd be careful insulting my offspring. They're the only good thing that's ever come of my blood, and you're goddamn lucky I don't do a repeat of what happened last year to Mike Holt. So get your ass off this land, and don't say another word doing it. You ride your ass back home, and you write up something saying you're giving your ranch over to Lloyd. In a couple of days, some of my men will be over to your place. *You* had better be *gone*, and the right paperwork had better be there, or I'll change my mind about not hanging you. By God, I'll hunt you down and make sure it gets done!"

The three boys looked at each other and grinned. "I knew he'd get real mad before he let him go," Little Jake said quietly.

"Get up and get the hell out of my sight!" Jake roared at Brady, taking his booted foot away from the man's neck.

Brady choked and coughed, rolling to his knees and finally getting up. He stumbled to his horse and managed to climb into the saddle. He turned and faced Jake, who raised his rifle and aimed it at the man.

"Not a goddamn word," Jake warned. "I've killed enough men that it won't bother me to kill one more."

Brady sniffed and wiped at his eyes. Blood poured from cuts on both sides of his face. He glanced at Lloyd and started to say something, but Jake retracted the lever on the rifle.

"Not a word," Jake repeated. "And do as I say, or you won't live to tell how you narrowly missed being hanged. There isn't a cattleman in Colorado who would blame us for putting a noose around your neck."

Brady turned and rode off.

Jake lowered his rifle. The rest of the men sat quietly, never sure what to do or say around an angry Jake Harkner. Lloyd stood there, feeling torn, wanting to hang Brady but realizing his father was right about hanging a man in front of the boys. They'd already seen plenty of brutality. He was more concerned at the moment about Jake. He'd be fighting that dark place that always tried to pull him in whenever the subject of his father came up.

Jake walked to his horse and shoved his rifle into its boot. He mounted up and rode off.

"Grampa?" Little Jake called to him.

"Leave him be, Little Jake," Lloyd warned. "Sometimes Grampa just needs to be alone. You help us clean up this campsite, and you thank the men from the Twisted Tree for helping put out the fire. This is our land, and they didn't have to do that."

"Yes, sir."

The boys walked up to Henry Till to thank him. Lloyd ordered Cole to follow Fillmore and make sure he did what Jake told him to do. Deep inside, he was surprised Jake had refused to hang the man. He turned to watch his father ride off, headed in the direction of the homestead, which, thank God, was in the opposite direction from Brady's trail back to his house. This was the first time he'd sensed a real tiredness about Jake—tired of all the turmoil in his life. Jake wanted something better for his younger son and grandchildren. Lloyd supposed letting Brady Fillmore go was one way of doing that.

Twenty-six

RANDY WAVED LLOYD OVER TO THE VERANDA AS SOON as he rode in. He could see she was distraught as he headed Strawberry to the main house and dismounted. Evie was also there, and Katie sat on the veranda rocking Donavan. They all seemed anxious, and Lloyd hardly knew which woman to go to first. His mother was still mending emotionally, Evie was always upset over anything that affected her father, and he needed some time with Katie after being gone for nearly ten days.

"What's wrong with your father?" Randy asked Lloyd anxiously when he came up the steps. "He got home a couple of hours ago, and he just sits in that big chair by the fireplace and won't talk to me." She folded her arms. "What happened out there?" She looked around, her eyes tearing. "And where are the boys—and the rest of the men?"

A very tired Lloyd removed his hat and set it on a table. He ran a hand through his hair and then pulled it behind his back. "The boys stayed behind for some camp cleanup. They'll come back with the rest of the men. They'll probably only be a couple more hours getting here. And I need a bath and a shave. I managed to wash off most of the soot in the creek and put on a clean shirt, but I'm so damn tired I'm not real sure I can deal with Pa right now."

"You *have* to! He's deeply troubled about something, Lloyd. I'm not ready for this!"

Lloyd grasped her arms. "Mom, relax. You know he

sometimes just needs time to sort things out." He led her to a chair and made her sit down, looking at Evie, who seemed as concerned as her mother.

"What's wrong with Daddy? He's almost as distant and unreachable as he was after you were shot last summer."

Lloyd rubbed at his eyes. "I'll go talk to him. You women stay out here."

"Lloyd, what happened?" Katie asked.

He sighed deeply. "Brady Fillmore started a grass fire and tried to steal another steer."

Katie's eyes widened. "Please tell me you didn't hang him in front of the boys!"

Brian walked up behind Lloyd. "Welcome back. What the hell happened out there?"

"Brady Fillmore started a grass fire," Evie told her husband.

Brian moved beside her, turning his gaze to Lloyd. "Well, something more than that happened. Your father is in a mood, Lloyd, like he doesn't care about anything. He's in there chain-smoking and won't talk to anyone, not even Randy."

Lloyd leaned against a porch post. "Yeah, well, some ugly things were said. Brady Fillmore insulted him pretty bad in front of the boys, which normally wouldn't faze Pa. He's used to it. But—I don't know. He came close to shooting Brady, but then he said to let him go. Made him promise to sign over his land to the J&L to make up for our loss, and to get out of Colorado. But something else was wrong. He rode off before the rest of us, so I followed. I was afraid this would happen. I was just hoping it wouldn't."

Randy put her face in her hands. "I need him, Lloyd. Things have been so good the last month or so. And he was in such a good mood when I left him at the barn four days ago. He was going to take Ben and Little Jake to check the fence line, and the next thing I knew,

Rodriguez came to the house, carrying on about a fire, and Jake and the boys were gone. Jake came back a changed man."

Lloyd knelt in front of her. "I'll talk to him. You know he always perks back up after things like this, and he loves you."

"Brady Fillmore said something about him killing his father, didn't he? He talked about his outlaw days."

"Pa just didn't think we should hang Brady in front of the boys, although I dearly wanted to. Pa said he didn't feel he had the right to judge, but he really clobbered Fillmore. For a minute, I was scared he was going to shoot him point-blank, but he didn't. I think he thought about you and the boys, so he walked away."

"You can get through to him, Lloyd. You always can. You know how he thinks…as a *man* thinks. I can only speak from a woman's point of view."

"Will it help if I talk to him?" Evie asked. "After you were shot, I—"

"No." Lloyd rose. "I'll do it." He turned to Katie, walking over and kissing her cheek and kissing the baby. "Go on home and get things ready for me to take a bath," he asked her. "I'll be along."

Katie looked up at him, and he kissed her lips. "I missed you," he told her.

"I missed you too. After what happened last summer, I hated the thought of you going to Denver. I'm so glad you're home."

He smiled for her. "Me too. And things went fine in Denver. I got a good price for the cattle."

"How about Evie's Garden?" Brian asked. "What's the loss?"

"Most of our backup grass. Pa said he wants me to use that bounty money to buy feed to get us through the winter, then the neighboring ranchers can use some of our grass if they have to. And we might have to share

Horse Creek with some of them. We can only hope for the best."

"I'm sorry, Lloyd. Is Little Jake okay?" Evie asked.

Lloyd smiled sadly. "You know your son. He wanted us to hang Fillmore. He was furious that the man had insulted his grandfather."

Brian closed his eyes and shook his head. "He's going to be one tough Harkner man someday."

Lloyd touched Brian's shoulder. "He's also a Stewart. And he has a father who is a great example of how to remain calm and fair and how to settle things peacefully. And his mother is next to a saint, so those things will have their effect. I think what Pa did yesterday will stick with him. I think Jake was thinking about what those boys saw last winter and figured he'd teach them not everything needs to be handled that way. He told them this was different because no family member was hurt. But for some reason, the ugly things Brady said hit Pa harder than normal. He just rode off without saying much…and apparently we've just added another couple thousand acres or so to the J&L."

"Well, there's one good thing." Brian stepped back and studied his brother-in-law. "Go in there and see what's wrong with your father. You're a hell of a good man, Lloyd, and sometimes you can get through to him when the rest of us can't. I have a feeling he needs to talk to you, not Randy. You and Jake have a special understanding of each other, and God knows there are things about that man you'd understand far better than I would. I don't have quite a mean enough streak in me." He gave Lloyd a rather sad smile.

"Yeah, well, God knows I inherited *that* from him," Lloyd answered wryly. He rubbed at his neck wearily before going inside.

Jake sat in his favorite red-leather chair near the huge stone fireplace at the end of the room, smoking quietly.

Lloyd noticed he wore the same clothes he was wearing when he left. *Shit*. He'd never, ever looked defeated before, and that's how he looked now. That wasn't Jake.

Twenty-seven

LLOYD WALKED OVER TO SIT DOWN IN A VELVET LOUNGE across from Jake. He lit a cigarette, watching Jake's dark eyes as he did so. "Sometimes you're a hard man to read, Pa. You want to talk about whatever it is that's put you in a mood?"

Jake put a foot up on one knee and leaned back in his chair, smoking. "Not especially."

Lloyd took a deep drag on his cigarette, then leaned forward with his elbows on his knees. "Well, you *are* going to talk to me, so those women out there will quit nagging me. When you get like this, *they* get all over my shit to do something about it."

That got a faint grin out of Jake.

Lloyd rubbed at his eyes. "You know, Pa, I'm thinking you made the right decision not to hang Brady Fillmore."

Jake closed his eyes with a sigh. "I had no right asking you not to. I was acting on my own emotions, which were pretty high at the time. Normally it'd be the other way, though, and I'd have said to string the bastard up."

Lloyd stared at a braided rug on the wide-plank wood floor. "You might as well tell me what's wrong, Pa. Mom is really upset, and so is Evie—and that makes me upset. Ever since what happened last winter, you've had to be the strong one, but as brash as you are on the outside, we both know who the strong one really is. I'm proud of how you've been so damn tough for Mom, but I see you slipping backward. I saw it these last few months while you fought to be there for Mom. And now that she's better, you're going in the other direction. I haven't seen you like this in a long time."

Jake sighed, running a hand through his hair. "I'm just tired, Lloyd. I'm tired of all the bullshit. I'm tired of wrestling with bad memories and trying to forget them. And I'm tired of other people constantly reminding me of what a bastard I am and what a worthless sonofabitch I was the first thirty years of my life. I don't need to be reminded. It is what it is."

"And no one in this family cares. We've been through this before, Pa. What's different this time?"

Jake snuffed out his cigarette and stared at the fireplace. "The boys, I guess. Little Jake wanted to hang that man." He looked at Lloyd. "I know they're learning to be men, but I don't want them to think the answer to everything is violence. It comes naturally to me, because I was *raised* on violence, and you learned it because of me. I don't want it to live on in those boys."

He sighed and rose, walking to a window.

"Things are changing. The days of the outlaw are gone. We have electricity now, and probably soon a telephone. Men are running around in motorized buggies, and trains take our cattle into Denver. And we might have all gotten into trouble if we'd hanged Brady Fillmore, because now you have to have solid proof of what a man did wrong, and we didn't really have that. The boys have to learn that's how it's done now. I'm damn lucky I got away with blowing Mike Holt's brains out last summer. I could just as easily have been strung up for it. I don't want any one of those boys to do something that will turn them into outlaws or send them to prison. I've been there too, and I came close to dying in that wretched place."

"Pa, you know damn well those boys know what's right and what's wrong. You have to stop judging how they'll turn out by how you were raised. It's been nothing like that for them. They know about love and forgiveness. You never knew that till late in life." Lloyd rose and faced him. "It's hard for you to see the difference because of what your father did to you. Not many boys would have even survived that and come out of it sane."

Their gazes held on the comment until Jake turned away. "We both know your mother is the only thing that has kept me on the right side of sanity."

"And comparing your past to how those boys have been raised is like night and day, so stop worrying they'll turn out wrong. They have the lessons you've taught them, and they have me and Brian to look to. And God knows nobody could teach them love more than Katie and Evie and Mom."

Jake nodded. "Lloyd, I know you wanted to hang Brady Fillmore. I just want to make sure that from now on you remember this is a changing world. You might even have to deal with the government someday over free rangeland. I see it coming. I likely won't be here when it comes, but those boys have to be prepared to fight a new way—maybe even go to college and learn about the law, learn how to deal with it like Peter Brown does." He faced Lloyd again. "When Brady said those things about me, it hit me—I'm one of a dying breed. I'm sorry if I crossed you, but I saw those boys watching, and I knew Little Jake was kind of proud that his grampa is some kind of famous outlaw. He was expecting me to show how ruthless I can be, and I just couldn't do it with those boys around. They've seen enough already." He cleared his throat and swallowed, as though the words didn't come easy. "And then there's that…your mother. If she'd married someone like Peter Brown, just think of the nice life she would have had. What the hell was I thinking, marrying a woman like that when I was still a wanted man?"

"It goes both ways, Pa. *She* wanted *you*. She made her

choice, and she loves you fiercely. She saw right through to the man inside, and that's who she fell in love with. And right now, she's out there ready to fall right back into that black hole she just climbed out of because she thinks maybe she's somehow lost you, so get out there and hold her and tell her you're okay. I'm damn tired and I need a bath and I miss my wife—and I need my father to be his old self just as much as Mom needs you in the same way."

He paused, hoping he was getting through to the man.

"You're not a dying breed, Pa. You're a *special* breed. There's nobody else out there like you. Those boys aren't proud of what you *were*. They're proud of what you *are*—one hell of a husband, a father, and a grand-father. Those boys aren't too young to understand the strength it takes to rise above the ugly parts of life. You have to take some credit for your accomplishments. You should have accepted that offer to go to Boulder and let the people there show their gratitude for what you did. There's nothing wrong in that."

Jake shook his head. "No. I'm not going to do that. As far as that money, this is your place, not mine, and I want you to have it for emergencies. It was mostly your money inherited from Beth that built this ranch, and God knows if it weren't for me, you never would have lost Beth in the first place. But that's a long time ago and can't be changed. Giving you that money kind of helps me get over that." He turned back to the window. "I'm old school, Lloyd. That run of lawlessness is in my blood way too deep for me to ever be a totally peaceful, quiet man—and there's a meanness down deep inside that comes from my father's blood. I fight it, but it's there. I've always known it, and it's why I never drink more than one shot of whiskey or more than one mug of beer. I'd be just like him if I did, and *nobody* wants to see what *that* is like, believe me. I'll be ruthless in defending myself or my own, but I wanted those boys to know it wasn't necessary this time. That's something for the law to handle."

"Well, you didn't mind landing the butt of your rifle across the side of Fillmore's head."

Jake grinned. "No. I didn't mind that at all. That was for things he'd said about your mother, not for setting that fire."

Lloyd rose and walked closer to Jake. "Pa, we'll all be okay. Quit worrying about how those boys will turn out. They're learning all the things they need to know about running a ranch. And you…" Lloyd shook his head. "You have no idea how important you are to this whole family. You're the hub of the wheel, Pa, and when you're gone from this world, we'll all have one hell of a hard time getting by. I personally hope that's way far in the future—and considering how you keep kicking death right in the face, it's bound to be a long time yet before I won't have my father to turn to. I love you. We've had each other's backs for a long time, and I hope it will stay that way for a lot more years."

Jake put his hands on his hips and smiled sadly. "Then I'll do my best to stay on top of the ground rather than under it."

"Well, it would help if you'd stay out of trouble."

"Trouble looks for me. I don't look for it."

"I know, but just try to see it coming and then duck out of the way." Lloyd smiled and was relieved to see his father return the smile. "You know how to work that smile on Mom, and right now she needs to see it, Pa. Understand?"

Jake nodded. "I just couldn't talk to her about this, not when she's just getting back to her old self. The woman knows me inside and out, and we've had our own long talks, but this time, I just—I don't know. I was just afraid I'd chase her back into that shell."

"She's okay now, Pa. But don't leave her out on things like this—she just worries more. She used to be your sounding board, and I think she'd be happy to keep that up. It will help her feel stronger. She's the kind that wants to share your hurts just as much as the good times."

"I suppose." Jake put out his hand, and Lloyd took it. The handshake led to a quick embrace.

"You know I love you, Pa," Lloyd said, pulling away.

"Yeah, well, same here. And speaking of your mother, you have your own beautiful woman waiting for you out there."

"You sure you're okay?"

"I'm okay. Go home. You've been gone a while and have some catching up to do."

Lloyd nodded and left. Jake watched him go through the door, then turned away. His eyes fell on the poker iron beside the fireplace, and a memory rushed in. His father, using one on his little brother...the boy lying lifeless on the floor, a bloody gash on the side of his head. The boy had been about little Sadie Mae's age when he was killed. He took a deep breath and closed his eyes, telling himself to put the memory back where it belonged, deep in the recesses of his mind where he was usually able to lock it away for months at a time.

"Jake?"

He turned to see Randy standing inside the doorway. "Do you know how beautiful you are?" he asked her.

Randy smiled warily. "I only know what you tell me. As long as I look beautiful to you, that's all I care about."

Jake smiled. "Do you have any fresh bread? I haven't eaten for almost two days."

She shook her head, a scolding look in her eyes. "Then get to the kitchen, and I'll feed you. And you need a bath. You smelled like smoke when you walked past me earlier—without saying a word, I might add. And you're not to leave this house the rest of the day.

You look like you also haven't *slept* for two days, so after you eat, it's straight to bed."

Jake watched her walk to the kitchen to slice some bread. He followed and walked up behind her, moving his arms around her and kissing her hair.

"Our son is quite something, isn't he?" Randy asked softly.

"That he is." He moved one hand to her throat and leaned around to kiss her cheek. "And so are you."

"Sometimes you're a hard man to handle, Jake Harkner, but you've never scared me. So you relax and accept the good life you have now, or I'll come after you with a broom." She turned her head, and he met her lips in a sweet kiss.

"Tell you what," he said, kissing her forehead, "I'm bone tired, so I'll take your advice to sleep. But how about we leave in the morning for the line shack?"

Randy turned and wrapped her arms around him. "I'd love that! We haven't gone back up there since…"

Since the three weeks we spent there after you were attacked. Jake hugged her tighter. "It will be completely different this time. We'll go there for no good reason but to just to be together and alone, and to get out of this heat. It's a lot cooler up there. We'll take Terrel and Cole with us. They can camp a bit away but be handy in case of any trouble. That should make you feel a little safer."

"All I need for that is you."

"Just the same, with all that's happened, it can't hurt to bring them with us. That's grizzly country, and I'm not taking you up there without extra protection. It was winter when we were there last, and the bears were hibernating. And if something happened to me, you'd be up there alone."

"I suppose."

"All the men are back from taking the cattle into Denver, so Lloyd can spare a couple of hands."

Randy leaned back, and he studied the tiny lines around her eyes. What had he done to this woman? There should be a lot more of those lines by now, and her hair should be completely white, but it was still the golden color that he loved, her exotic gray-green eyes still beautiful. She always said he got better looking with age, but it was the same with her. She had that kind of beauty that shone through as strength and bravery, the beauty of a mature woman who understood the world because she'd seen it all.

She reached up to trace a finger along the thin and faded scar down the left side of his face. "So many scars, Jake, inside and out. I know you. Something upset you out there, and you're going as much for yourself as for me, aren't you?"

He smiled sadly. "Probably. And speaking of scars, all those old bullet wounds are taking their toll. Some days I ache everywhere. I feel like an old warrior who needs to put down his sword for a while." He kissed her again. "And be alone with his wife."

"You're a warrior, all right. It is time you hung up that sword for good, Jake."

He glanced at his guns, hanging, as always, over the doorway. "We'll see."

Twenty-eight

IT WAS WARM ENOUGH THAT JAKE COULD CLEAN UP outside while Randy slept. He finished his ritual of washing and shaving and scrubbing his teeth with baking soda. He intended to go inside and make love to his wife. Randy loved that; she was always more relaxed in the mornings.

For once, not every bone in his body ached—just his hip, where he'd taken that bullet in a shoot-out all those years ago in California. Randy was hurt that day, and he could have lost his son. It had been one of those times when he was sure his wife was better off without him and should divorce him.

He'd left her… He'd left her. He'd spent nearly two years on the Outlaw Trail, trying to forget her, but those had been the most miserable two years of his life. And when he finally found a way for them to be together again and came back, he'd found her faithfully waiting for him. And with their daughter.

"Shit," he grumbled, dumping the used pan of water.

He hadn't been there for either child's birth. He'd walked out on Randy just before she'd had Lloyd, scared to death at the idea of being a father. And when she had Evie, he was getting drunk and gambling on the Outlaw Trail, trying to forget her, while she nearly bled to death. The doctor'd removed all the parts needed to bear more children, and that broke her heart. And there she'd been, going through that alone.

He kicked the empty pan in his guilt and frustration,

sending it flying several feet away. He couldn't count all the ways he'd failed her, the best woman he knew. There she lay in the cabin, almost thirty-two years since that first day, and after all he'd put her through, she still lay there sleeping, happy as a lark.

He'd never taken Miranda Hayes Harkner for granted and never would. If she'd ever chosen to leave him, he would have let her go. He had no right trying to stop her. Then again, how in hell could he have gone on with life without her in it? At times he felt he had no right to go to her bed, though nothing gave him more satisfaction. All the whores in the country couldn't come close to what he'd found with Randy...because she loved him, and that made all the difference. He had to be one of the most *un*lovable men who ever walked. And when they were together, it was more than physical pleasure. That's what made it all so beautiful and fulfilling.

He breathed deeply of the cool mountain air, the sweet smell of pine filling his nostrils. This was where he found the most peace, and Randy was a part of it. As he headed for the door, he heard a wolf howl somewhere in the distance.

He hesitated. The last time he'd heard wolves howl in daylight, it ended up being an omen. Disaster had struck the family—twice. He'd nearly lost his son in Denver... and nearly lost his wife last winter. How much more was anyone supposed to take?

He shook away thoughts of the bad times and forced himself to consider only the good, the best of which lay inside on a feather mattress on a homemade log bed with solidly linked pine slats under the mattress for support. Inside the door, a mantle clock ticked off the time, and he looked at a sleeping Randy. Years. So many years together. Where had they all gone? Time was marching right past him and leaving him in the dust.

He quietly closed the door and stripped down, pulling back the quilts and grabbing a piece of peppermint from a table beside the bed. He crawled into bed with his wife, who lay with her back to him. He reached around her and traced the end of the peppermint stick along her lips.

Randy opened her eyes, licking at the peppermint stick. "I've been awake," she told Jake.

"Could have fooled me."

She smiled and turned to face him. "I saw the peppermint stick on the table, so I was pretending to sleep." She bit off a piece. "And truth be told, I snuck out of bed and washed while you were outside doing the same. And I used some of that rosewater you got for me in Boulder. Which reminds me, I haven't even checked that wound the last couple of days."

"Oh, it's healed. See?" Jake raised the blanket to reveal that the gauze patch was gone.

Randy saw he was naked and laughed, pushing at him. "That's not the only thing that's healed and doing well."

Jake saw that she was naked too. He moved on top of her. "I guess we thought alike."

Randy smiled. "It's called reading each other's minds," she told him. "I was pretty sure what you'd want this morning." She sobered. "The trouble is, I also can tell you've been troubled ever since coming back from the fire."

He stuck the peppermint back into her mouth. "Right now, I don't want to talk about that. I just want to know I'm not getting too old for this and that I can still satisfy my beautiful wife."

"You're Jake Harkner. You'll be satisfying me for a long time to come."

He bit off his end of the peppermint. "I'm afraid that's starting to depend on what hurts and what *doesn't* hurt. Right now, the only thing that hurts is this thing pressed against your thigh, because it's aching to be inside of you."

Randy chewed on the peppermint, running her hands

over the hard muscle of his upper arms and over his shoulders. "Well, I don't want you to hurt anywhere, Mr. Harkner. Let me help you feel better."

She reached down to caress his shaft, but he grasped her wrist. "Not so fast."

He met her mouth in a deep kiss, then moved his lips to the side of her neck, just behind her ear, in that way he had of making her feel wanton. "You first, *mi querida*." His light kisses moved to her throat, her lips, back to her throat, then down to her cleavage. He tasted her breasts as though they were ripe fruit.

"Far be it from me to argue how we should do this," she said softly. She wound her fingers into his hair as his kisses wandered farther down her body, while his strong but gentle hands felt her breasts. He caressed her taut nipples as he licked at her belly and meandered to the crevices hiding that which belonged only to Jake Harkner.

She closed her eyes, never tiring of the way he had of making her want to open herself to him, using licks and kisses to bring out sweet juices. Always, always he made sure to do everything he could to make lovemaking pleasant for her, as though he knew this was a little harder for her now that she was older. It was all part of his determination to never hurt her, even when they were doing something beautiful.

She wondered how many men knew how to work this magic. She remembered one woman at the spring cookout who laughed and covered her mouth when she joked about the fact that she and her husband never made love anymore because it "hurt too much." They'd all been standing and gossiping about the men, and when they looked at Randy, she just smiled and said nothing. Jake Harkner had a way of bringing her the most exotic climaxes, even at times when she really wasn't in the mood. He always found a way to change her mind.

"Jake." She groaned his name when she felt the

pulsating explosion, and she grasped his hair tighter. He ran his hands and lips up over her belly, back to her breasts, to her throat, to her lips. He consumed her mouth and gave her a taste of her own juices and slid his hands under her, grasping her bottom while he moved inside her. He left her mouth and licked at her ear, whispering to her in Spanish.

"*Tu eres mi vida, mi querida esposa.*"

She'd been with him long enough to know what the words meant...*you are my life*. She sensed a kind of desperation in the way he said them. Something was wrong. She found his mouth again, kissing him hungrily, promising him through the kiss that everything was all right. She arched her hips to meet his thrusts. They came fast and hard, as though he needed to brand her, as though he needed to know he was deep inside of her and that she wasn't going away.

She felt lost under his big frame, grasped his strong arms again, and leaned up to kiss his chest, loving the fact that there was still nothing soft about this man. That there remained a wildness about him, an untamed spirit that made him do things like take on all those men back in Boulder.

You know what to do, Randy, he'd told her during the standoff with the bank robbers. Yes, she knew what to do, because *he* knew what to do, and she had complete confidence in his abilities. It wasn't the first time he'd taken on several men, but she prayed hard that it was the *last* time. How many times could he do something like that and still come out on the winning end? Even when he did, he'd been wounded too many times.

The thought made her give back even more wildly. He got to his knees and grasped her hips so he could bury himself deeper. She met his fiery, dark eyes, and there was that message. He owned her. He'd always owned her, and she'd put up with so much, because what woman *wouldn't* want to belong to this man? He knew everything about her and knew how to handle her every mood. The trouble was, she wasn't always sure how to handle *his* moods. She still saw something there, something amiss.

He came closer, wrapping her in strong arms as his life spilled into her. She could feel the forceful surges deep inside.

"Who do you belong to?" he asked in the same ritual he always asked.

"Jake Harkner," she moaned.

"Every beautiful inch of you."

She felt the same way. She'd done the one thing with her husband they'd never done in all the years they'd been married. She'd tasted him, swallowed his life. She owned him too.

He remained inside of her as he settled on top of her. "Am I hurting you?" he asked.

"No. Just stay on your elbows a little."

"I don't want to pull out." He kissed her eyes, her mouth. "I could stay like this forever."

She put her hands to either side of his face. "Jake, what's wrong?" She actually thought she detected tears.

He closed his eyes and buried his lips against her neck. "I'm what's wrong. Why in God's name have you stayed with me for so long, and through so much?"

She wrapped her arms around his neck. "You're my Jake. Plain and simple. I've never doubted how much you love me. You're always considerate of my every mood, and I know how hard the last few months have been on you." She caressed his hair. "I'm sure you've wanted to scream at me at times or wanted to just let someone else take care of me, but you didn't. *You* took care of me, and you've been so patient—which is not exactly one of your strongest skills, Jake Harkner."

He smiled through tears. "No, ma'am." He pushed

her hair away from her face. "But I'll always be patient with you. And you have no idea how happy it makes me to see you gaining weight, and to see you smile and to hear your sharp orders sometimes. No man tells me what to do, but, woman, you have me completely hog-tied."

"And I so enjoy jerking that rope at times and tying you to my saddle horn."

"I'll just bet you do." He laughed lightly, kissing her eyes, her mouth.

Randy sensed he was still holding something back, but she knew him far too well to press the issue. It might be better at the moment to get his mind off of whatever was lurking inside, instead of spoiling the moment.

"Mr. Harkner, I'm not over that beautiful climax yet. Can you help me?"

Jake grinned. "As much and as often as you want, *mi querida*."

He searched her lips, and they made love all over again, and before the day was over, she claimed him for herself again, caressing and tasting him in a desire to give him pleasure the way he gave her such sweet climaxes in return. By nightfall, they made love yet again, a slow and beautiful dance of tasting and touching and uniting in the physical sharing of a love that could not be broken.

By dark, they were spent, and Randy fell asleep in his arms, that strong, safe place that she so loved. She heard a wolf howl somewhere in the mountains. Jake drew her closer.

Twenty-Nine

"JAKE, AREN'T YOU COLD?"

"No. And you look ridiculous."

Randy stood near him, wearing a sheepskin jacket Jake had left at the line shack last winter. "Well, I am cold, and now I'm wrapped up in your arms."

Jake looked her over and shook his head. "More like completely buried. That damn thing comes to your knees, and your hands have disappeared somewhere up under those sleeves."

Randy stepped farther down the steps to the ground. Under the jacket, she wore a dress but no petticoats or camisole, and she wore leather button shoes. "Isn't it beautiful? You can see for miles up here. That's why I love it so much. It's like this is our own special little world."

Jake sipped on a cup of coffee. He sat in an old wooden chair on the sagging front porch of the sun-weathered line shack, wearing just his denim pants and a blue shirt.

"I know the homestead is out there somewhere to the east, but I can't make it out," Randy told him.

Jake rose and walked up behind her. He pointed. "It's way out over there. If you study it for a minute, you'll see it. That dark spot in the middle of open land is that island of pine trees beyond the outer corral."

Randy squinted, trying to find the spot he was talking about. "Oh, my gosh! I think I see it!"

"It's a good eight hours away, but that's it."

"How far do you think we're seeing?"

"Well, the homestead is about fifteen miles, and we're seeing well beyond that, so maybe thirty miles—maybe even more than that."

Randy leaned her head against his chest. "That seems impossible. It's all God's country, isn't it?"

"He made it all."

Randy smiled. "Jake, let's go for a walk."

"Hell, there's mountain lions and grizzlies and all kinds of creatures out there."

"And they're all afraid of *you*," Randy teased. She met his gaze. "Do you realize that in all the years we've been married we've never just walked together? We've ridden together plenty of times, but not just gone for a simple walk."

"That's what old people do."

"And what are we?"

Jake smiled. "Old people."

"So let's go for a walk."

Jake just shook his head. "If that's what you want. Let me get my rifle first. I'm not going for a walk in grizzly country without a gun. And in case you haven't noticed, I don't even have my boots on." He walked on stockinged feet into the cabin and came back out wearing boots and a wool plaid shirt over his blue shirt. He checked his Winchester repeater for cartridges.

"No handguns?" Randy asked.

"Those six-shooters are fine for men, but a grizzly would just swallow the bullets and get madder." Jake came down the steps and looked her over. "You really going to wear that thing?"

"The one I brought isn't warm enough. It was so hot down at the homestead that I forgot how cold it can be up here in the mornings."

"Well, just don't trip over the damn thing and go rolling down the mountain."

Randy laughed as Jake held his rifle in his right hand and put his free arm around her. He pointed with the rifle.

"Over to the left. We'll walk in those pines. The road going back down to home is too steep. We'll save all that dangerous slipping and sliding for when we head home."

Randy leaned into him as they walked slowly into the nearby pine forest, the trees creating an almost soundless haven from the outside world. She breathed deeply of the rich scent. "Sometimes I never want to go home. If it weren't for those beautiful grandchildren, I'd stay up here with you forever. I like having you all to myself."

Jake squeezed her shoulders. "I don't mind that myself."

Their voices seemed lost and muffled against a bed of pine needles.

"Oh, look!" Randy left him and hurried over to pick some deep-blue wildflowers. "Jake, they're so pretty." She rose, sniffing them. "I hope Rodriguez is taking good care of all my roses."

"He always does." Jake studied her. Five days here together had been good for both of them. Randy looked healthier than she'd looked in a long time, and he loved how her hair shone thick and golden in the light of the sun that streamed through the pine branches. She spotted more flowers and ran over to pick them, having trouble keeping the sleeves of his jacket pushed far enough back. "Don't go too far from me, Randy. Grizzlies are good at hiding and surprising you." He studied the woods around them.

"I remember another encounter with a grizzly just about a year ago on our way to Denver," Randy told him, "and I've never been so humiliated in my entire life!"

Jake laughed. "Oh, I remember that one, all right. That thing caught us in a very compromising position."

Randy walked closer to him again. "Yes, well, you've always enjoyed my utter mortification, haven't you?

Thank God I had time to make myself presentable before Lloyd came charging up to see if we were okay." She stood on her tiptoes for a kiss, and Jake obliged her. "And I will never let you drag me into the woods to get under my skirts again," she chided, "not when we're traveling with the entire family and half the J&L ranch hands."

"We'll see."

"No, we won't see, Mr. Harkner. You have embarrassed me one too many times."

"You love it, especially the disrespectful stuff."

"And you can be *most* disrespectful."

"You don't do too bad a job yourself," Jake quipped. "I love it when you're disrespectful."

Randy laughed. "I'm sure you do." She stopped and picked more flowers, and suddenly, Jake was beside her, pressing on her shoulder to stay down.

"Want some fresh venison?" he asked in a near whisper.

Randy looked into the direction where he was watching a large buck.

"Sure."

Jake slowly raised his rifle, and Randy covered her ears.

One loud shot. The deer collapsed. Jake kept the rifle steady. "Don't get up yet," he told Randy. "More than once I've had a deer suddenly bounce right back up and run off. I hate the thought of a wounded deer running around in pain."

"Oh, but not a wounded man?"

"Hell no. I can think of a few I'd prefer were stumbling around the rest of their lives in great, unbearable pain." Jake lowered the rifle and slowly rose, helping Randy to her feet.

"This has been so nice, Jake. It's like we're the only two people in the world when we're up here. That's why I want us to be buried up here."

"Well, let's hope that cabin has completely fallen in by then. In the meantime, we have a big family plus a lot of ranch hands to feed, and the meat in that big buck will help. Trouble is now, we have to get it home."

"Then we'll have to clean it ourselves and salt the meat down good."

"It means leaving when we're done. That carcass is going to be a big attraction to grizzlies and mountain lions until it's rotted dry, and I'm not keeping you up here in that kind of situation."

"Terrel and Cole are camped not that far away."

"Same for them. They only have a tent, which is even more dangerous."

"Jake!" Cole was somewhere in the distance yelling for him. "You all right?"

Jake turned and fired his rifle into the air, making Randy jump. "Over here!" He whistled a few times until Cole came riding toward them on his horse.

"You two okay?"

"Got a big buck. We've got to hog-tie it and drag it up to the cabin and clean it while it's fresh. Randy will salt down the meat, and we'll wrap it in a sheet or something. With plenty of salt, it should keep for the few hours it takes to get home."

"Terrel and I can take it for you."

"Doesn't matter. The smell of that carcass is going to attract mountain lions and bears for miles around. Randy and I will have to go on home. That line shack is getting so sun rotted that a big grizzly could push the walls right in if it got mad enough."

"Gotta agree with you there."

"You and I both know how far a grizzly can go even if it's wounded. I don't want Randy in that kind of danger." Jake set his rifle against a tree and surprised Randy when he grabbed her around the waist and lifted her onto Cole's horse in front of him.

"Jake, what on earth—"

"Take her back to the cabin and come back here with a couple of good knives and a sheet," he told Cole. "She looks pretty silly in that big jacket, doesn't she?"

Cole moved an arm around her middle to hang on to her. "Pretty silly." He turned his horse and headed for the line shack. "Shoot your gun twice more," he yelled to Jake. "Terrel will know it's a signal to come to the line shack."

"Cole, I could have walked back," Randy told the man.

"Not when there could be a grizzly around." He charged his horse back to the cabin. "You go inside and stay there. Terrel will meet us here in a minute flat, and we'll both go help Jake clean that buck. One of us will have to watch for anything that smells that blood."

"But Jake is out there alone."

"He's not that far away, and he has a rifle. If any man can take care of himself, it's Jake."

"I suppose."

Randy thought how Cole knew Jake just about as well as Jake knew Cole. The medium-built man had all the signs that he'd once been handsome, maybe even happy. Something had changed all that, maybe the same time he'd gotten that limp, and no one knew what it was. Most of the J&L cowboys kept their backgrounds quiet. They were a wild lot who didn't always bathe and shave like they should, unless they were going into town to have a good time with whores. Yet Jake and Lloyd trusted every one of them, and so did she.

Cole dismounted and lifted her down. "Ma'am, all the men are glad to see you lookin' so much happier," he told her.

Randy clung to the flowers, suddenly self-conscious. They'd all been there that terrible day. They all knew. They'd all seen.

She turned toward the line shack. "Thank you, Cole. Come in, and I'll find some knives and give you a sheet." She hurried inside to quickly pull a sheet off the bed before he could come in and see the wild array of messy bedcovers. She and Jake had stayed here before, but this time…this time…it had never been more beautiful. Their lovemaking had seemed to somehow gone up a level, to something more meaningful than it had ever been before.

Cole came inside, and she handed him the sheet, then hurried over to a cabinet to find the sharpest knives she could.

A horse galloped up close to the cabin. "Cole!" Terrel shouted. "What's wrong?"

Cole smiled and nodded to Randy as she handed him the knives. "You stay inside like I told you, ma'am. And you'd best pack up. We'll have to hightail it home, because we'll be grizzly bait the whole way." He turned and walked out, explaining to Terrel about the deer.

The men rode off, and Randy was relieved that they would both be with Jake while he cleaned the buck. She hated the thought of leaving, but they had been here for five days, and everyone at home would be happy for the fresh venison. Besides that, she missed the grandchildren, especially the babies. It was time to go home.

Only what if this was the last time? A wave of despair suddenly swept over her, so much so that she gasped. She felt like crying. She told herself it was just that she was growing older, but she couldn't help the awful thought that maybe she and Jake would never come back here. She walked to the bed, crawling onto it and curling up. She used Jake's pillow because it smelled like him. She wrapped her arms around it and broke into tears, wondering if they would ever have another beautiful morning like this one had been—rising late, eating breakfast alone, drinking their coffee, and enjoying the morning air and the incredibly beautiful scenery outside, even walking together in the pines. It seemed that life moved past much too quickly. Things had never been better. The sad part was that it had taken so many years to reach this peace…if indeed they could hang on to moments like these and she could keep her husband close from now on.

PART FOUR

Thirty

THE FAMILY GATHERED AROUND JAKE, STRIKINGLY handsome this morning in a black silk suit and white shirt with a black string tie. The women fussed over who was standing where, while Dennis Rivers, a traveling photographer, waited for them to finally choose the perfect pose. The men had moved Jake's favorite big, red-leather chair out onto the wide veranda for the picture because of the more natural light, and to keep the messy, white flash-powder residue out of the house.

Little Tricia and Sadie Mae, wearing identical flowered dresses—one green and one blue—sat on their grandfather's knees. Randy, wearing a ruffled dress in yellow, Jake's favorite color on her, sat on the left arm of his chair, her hair pulled back at the sides and pinned with real flowers. Katie, Lloyd, and Donovan were on Randy's other side, dressed to the nines, Lloyd's long hair pulled straight back and tied into a tail at the base of his neck.

To Jake's right sat Evie, her hair down and dark against her dark-blue dress, little Esther in her arms and dapper Brian standing behind. And there beside him was Little Jake, who'd suddenly shot up a couple more inches over the summer, and next to him and behind Jake stood Ben, only thirteen but looking much older, his thick shock of blond hair combed into place and his face ruddy from too much sun. His blue eyes sparkled with happiness.

Stephen also stood behind Jake, between Ben and

Lloyd, taller as well, and his chin held high in an effort to look more like a man than a boy. The three boys wore woolen suits and were anxious to get this picture over with so they could change into something cooler.

Rivers had shown up just two days after Jake and Randy returned from the line shack, and the women were more than thrilled to have a family picture taken.

Finally, everyone settled into their proper places, and Rivers told everyone to sit still and "smile pretty" so he wouldn't have to take too many poses. He excitedly talked about his camera as he prepared his own position. He was using the latest box camera by Kodak and tried to explain how it worked, but Jake finally told him to "just take the damn picture." Being on wanted posters had made it a lot less pleasant having his picture taken.

The nervous photographer stopped talking and studied the big family under a black cloth behind the camera lens. When the flash powder exploded, the little girls screamed and the boys laughed. Tricia started to cry, remembering all the gunfire the day of the bank robbery in Boulder. Jake kissed her cheek and assured her everything was fine, and the photographer tried again. Anxious, wiggling granddaughters and snickering grandsons forced him to take two more photos until he was finally satisfied.

"I'm afraid some of the powder coated your roses, Mrs. Harkner," he told Randy.

"They'll be fine," Randy answered. "It's worth it to finally get a family portrait. We've never done this before."

Everyone scattered about their own business after that, the children to play and Katie into another room to nurse Donavan.

"Let me see now," the excited photographer noted as he came into the kitchen with his notes. "I want to get this right. I'll write everything down for you to keep with the picture so you remember the year it was taken." He studied the list. "Tell me if I get any of this wrong. From left to right first row—Brian Stewart and wife Evie Harkner Stewart, holding seven-month-old daughter Esther Miranda. Next to her is Jake, holding granddaughter Sadie Mae Stewart on his right knee, five; and Patricia Evita Harkner on his left knee, also five. Sitting on the arm of the chair is Miranda Sue Harkner, Jake's wife, and to Jake's left is Katie Donavan Harkner, age twenty-eight, holding her son Donavan Patrick Harkner, six months old; and just behind her is Lloyd Jackson Harkner, age thirty-one, and to his right behind Jake is his son Stephen Lloyd, twelve. Next to Stephen is Jake's adopted son, Benjamin, thirteen, and between Ben and Brian Stewart is Brian and Evie's son Jackson Lloyd Stewart, better known as Little Jake, and he is almost nine."

He finished writing, then looked at those left around the table—Lloyd, Evie, Jake, Brian, and Randy. "Do I have everyone?"

Jake took a cigarette from a tin on the table. "Sounds like it."

Randy rubbed his shoulders. "We've grown quite a brood, haven't we?" she told Jake.

"From what I've read about you, Mr. Harkner, you've had quite an adventurous life," the photographer stated. "You are an amazing man."

Jake shook his head. "There's not a damn thing amazing about me, Mr. Rivers. I'm just blessed."

The photographer took a few more notes. "Can I ask about—"

"No!" Jake interrupted before he could finish. "You know all you need to know from Jeff Truebridge's book. This is just a picture, not a story. Any more personal questions, and your camera will be lying out in one of the corrals for the horses to stomp on."

"Daddy, don't be rude," Evie scolded.

"Pa gets a little testy talking about his past," Lloyd told Rivers, scowling at Jake as he spoke. "Don't take it too personally."

Rivers cleared his throat, looking intimidated. "Yes... well...I'm sorry." He studied his notes a moment longer. "Well, then. I'll go out to my wagon and develop the pictures for you. You can have your choice of which is best, and we can do a larger print, but you can keep all of them."

The man left, and Randy went to the stove to pour Jake some coffee. She carried it over and set it in front of him.

"Your mother looks extra beautiful today, doesn't she?" Jake commented. "I've always loved her in yellow."

"She *always* looks beautiful," Evie answered. "And I swear she looks younger than she did when you two left to go up to the line shack."

Jake grinned, and Randy blushed as she sat down beside him. Lloyd and Evie exchanged a look that told Randy they were bothered by something. There came an awkward silence. Jake sensed it too. "What's going on?" he asked Evie.

She glanced at her mother, then back at Jake. "Daddy, while you and mother were gone, we got a letter from Jeff," she told them.

"We did?" Randy moved around to sit at the table. "Why on earth didn't you tell us sooner?"

Evie looked at Lloyd, who sighed. "Because he wondered if we'd seen or heard anything about...Brad Buckley."

Randy's smile faded, and she glanced at Jake, who reached over and pressed her arm. "The answer is simple. No, we haven't. As far as anyone knows, the man disappeared off the face of the earth. Maybe he went on to California. He sure wouldn't be stupid enough to show himself here on the J&L. That's all you need to tell Jeff."

"I'll answer the letter," Randy spoke up. "If one of you answers it, he'll suspect something. I'm always the one who writes to him."

"We just weren't sure if we should let you read it without warning you," Evie told her mother. "Jeff has been checking back in Guthrie and said no one there has seen Buckley since around the same time Mike Holt showed up there. Jeff said Holt was practically tarred and feathered and run out of town. Our friends back there remembered he was part of..." Evie hesitated, her bad memories coming to mind. "Dune Hollow," she finished.

Randy closed her eyes and sighed. "I know what to tell him," she told Evie. "And I can talk about it now if it comes up. Don't be worried about it." She smiled through unwanted tears. "Your father and I have had plenty of long talks. We've worked it out, and I'm a lot stronger now. Thank God you are too, Evie. It's time to move on from all of that."

Lloyd met Jake's eyes. "As long as *Pa* stays strong. I have to give him a swift kick once in a while."

"How about we change the subject, like to ole Gus?" Jake suggested, giving Randy's arm a light squeeze before letting go. He drew deeply on his cigarette. "Have you put that bull to work yet?"

Lloyd grinned. "You call that work?"

"Well, with respect to that bull's duty to produce more cattle for us, yeah, I call it work. He'd better come through, or we'll be eating lots of steaks next year that have come off his hide."

"If you had a harem like Gus, you sure as hell wouldn't consider it a job."

"I did have a harem once, until your mother came along," Jake teased. "Anything else in Jeff's letter?"

"Just that Jeff isn't coming out this summer to visit," Evie answered. "His wife is carrying again, and she's having a bit of a hard time."

Jake frowned. "That's too bad. I hope things go all right for them. Jeff is one of the finest men I know. I'll never forget that first day he approached me back in Guthrie, scared to death that I'd shoot him on the spot. The mood I was in, I considered it."

They all laughed, and Evie loved the way her mother glowed. Maybe now the Harkner clan would know some real peace.

"Did Jeff happen to mention Peter Brown?" Jake asked then, a tone of irritation in his voice.

"No," Evie answered. "He did mention that Mrs. Brown is sailing to France this summer to visit family there." She sighed. "I can't imagine what it must be like to take a ship across the ocean and visit another country."

"Yeah, well, if anyone has the money and time for that, it's those two," Jake answered, obvious sarcasm in his words. "Just think—if your mother had married Peter—"

"Stop right there, Jake Harkner!" Randy ordered. "Don't even suggest I would have been happier with some other man. And after all that Peter has done for us."

"And we all know why."

"Daddy, do you think Peter is the only man who thinks he loves mother? Half the men on this ranch are in love with her."

"Evie! That's just silly," Randy scolded. She rose to start clearing the table.

"Hell, it's true," Lloyd teased.

Jake put out his cigarette and rose, walking around to grab Randy from behind and leaning around to kiss her cheek. "Maybe I should keep this woman locked up," he joked.

"Just try it." Lloyd laughed. "She'd clobber you with a frying pan, and you'd let her. You'd do anything she asked, and you know it."

Jake kept his hands on Randy's shoulders. "No argument there. Right now, I intend to get out of these fancy duds and take care of chores that got neglected this morning."

"Daddy, you look so handsome in a suit and tie," Evie told him. "And so does Lloyd."

"I can't listen to this," Lloyd said, shaking his head as he rose. "Your husband is the one who looks natural in a suit and tie," he told Evie as he rose from his chair. "Pa and I feel more comfortable in denim pants and plain cotton shirts."

"I've gotten used to those clothes myself," Brian answered. "Ranch life does that to a man."

Lloyd grinned. "I'm going to check on Katie and then go home to change."

"You should talk to Katie about switching Donavan to cow's milk," Evie told her brother. "That boy is getting too big, and he's too hungry all the time. You need to start feeding him bread and mashed potatoes and give Katie a break."

"I agree, dear sister."

Brian rose and took the baby from Evie. "Let's go."

"Come back here for dinner," Randy told them. "Jake and I have been gone a while, and I've missed everyone. I'll cook some of that venison we brought back."

"Sounds good to me," Brian answered, following Evie out the door.

Jake watched Randy. He loved seeing her so happy. Their time at the line shack had been healing.

"I need to change too," she told him, heading for the stairs to their loft bedroom.

Jake felt strangely worried. He suddenly wished they were back at the line shack and could just stay there. And then there it was…that mournful howl from higher in the mountains. He followed her up the stairs.

Thirty-one

IT WAS LIKE A STRANGE DREAM. RANDY AWOKE TO A strong hand gently massaging her belly, moving down into her underwear and stroking that place in that special way that gave her so much pleasure. It was dark, and she had no idea what time it was, but she knew her husband's touch and realized this was more than just a pleasant dream.

"Jake?"

"I just want to be inside of you."

"I'm half-asleep."

"Sometimes it's nicer that way."

Remaining under the covers, she bent her legs, and he pulled off her underwear.

"Jake, I have to pee." She felt his smile.

"Sometimes that makes a climax even more intense."

"Says who?"

"Says some woman from somewhere in the past. I think it was you."

"Are you getting your women mixed up?"

That brought a light laugh as he pushed up her night-gown. "I'm getting too old to remember for sure."

He moved a finger into her folds again, stroking gently as he nuzzled her neck. Randy drew a deep breath when he pushed more than one finger inside of her to draw forth the needed moisture so she could enjoy this. She sensed an urgency about him, but she didn't ask questions. She just breathed deeply and arched toward his hand as he toyed with what belonged to him. He worked his thumb over her magic spot while continuing to tease with his fingers until she felt a sensuous climax that was so intense she grasped his hand and pushed, demanding more as she groaned his name.

"See what I mean, *mi querida*?" he said softly. He was on top of her then, and she realized he was naked. He moved between her legs, and she opened herself to welcome his fullness. The whole act seemed almost unreal, so much so that she wondered if she really was dreaming this. He groaned with every push, a strange anxiety to his intercourse, an odd desperation to the way he took her. He raised to his knees, taking hold of her hips and pulling her to him as he pounded into her depths for several minutes before holding himself inside her with a powerful release and a gasp of pleasure.

He lowered his body, pulling her into his arms, burying his face in her hair as she kissed his neck.

"Jake, what's wrong?"

He didn't answer right away. He pulled her closer. "I just needed to be inside of you, to feel your closeness."

He sighed deeply and rolled onto his back.

Randy fished under the blankets and found her underwear. "It's more than that, Jake. I'm going to pee, and when I come back, you are going to tell me what's wrong." She climbed out of bed and half ran to the adjoining toilet room, then cleaned up. She came back into the bedroom to find Jake standing at an open window, smoking a cigarette. He pushed the window farther aside and rested his elbows on the windowsill as she walked up behind him. "Look out there," he told her.

Randy moved up beside him to drink in the sight of the Harkner homestead bathed in the light of a huge moon.

Jake put his hand out the window and pointed to things as he spoke. "It's almost like daylight out there, the moon is so full. You can see cattle in the distance, see the horses we left in the corral, see the main bunkhouse, the new barn."

Randy kissed his bare arm, thinking how hard-muscled he still was, no big belly like most men his age, just rock hard—physically, but in other ways too. He was a hard man on the inside, and she felt that side of him trying to make an appearance. The way he'd just made love to her had been more like he was trying to prove something to himself. "Remember our promise of no secrets, Jake? Our promise to tell each other what's bothering us before it festers?"

He drew on his cigarette, exhaling before he answered. "I remember."

"Then talk to me."

He paused, taking a deep breath of fresh mountain air. "You cold? It's always cool here at night, even when the day has been miserably hot."

"No, I'm not cold, and stop avoiding the subject."

"I couldn't sleep, that's all. I'm sorry I woke you up that way."

She wrapped her hands around his arm and rested her head against his shoulder. "I can think of a lot worse ways to be woken up." She kissed his shoulder. "Talk to me, Jake. Stop dancing around whatever's bothering you."

He remained silent for a few minutes. "I look at all this, and sometimes I wonder if I fit in anymore."

"Fit in? You're as much a part of this family and this great big country as the animals out in those pine forests, and sometimes just as wild."

"That's partly my point." He waved his arm again, indicating all that lay before them in the moonlight. "All that out there, it belongs to Lloyd and Evie and the grandchildren and to Ben. It's *Lloyd's* dream. I just came along for the ride, to help him build all this because he damn well deserves it. I don't really belong here. That's part of what I talked to Lloyd about after the fire. I've never brought it up to you. In spite of my talk with Lloyd, certain things still bother me and always will. I am that dying breed. I see all this and think about Denver last summer, and I realize the way things are now, there isn't much room for men like me. One of those newspaper articles about me in Boulder called me the last real outlaw. Now they have all these new laws, which is why I couldn't let Lloyd hang Brady Fillmore. Our boys have to learn a whole new way of living. I'm in the way of that."

"In the way?" Randy turned and leaned against the windowsill, facing him. "Jake, if you're thinking you're just some has-been outlaw, or that society would be better off without you, think again. We all think you should have gone to Boulder to accept their accolades. People need to know more about that side of you. You were one of the best U.S. Marshals in Oklahoma. Maybe it was part of a prison sentence, but you got the job done."

"And Evie paid. So did Little Jake and Lloyd…and eventually you."

"I suppose you think you should just ride off into the sunset and leave the rest of the family to a new century."

He faced her. "Sometimes."

Randy folded her arms. "After what you and I have been through? After knowing what you mean to me? How much I need you?"

He reached out and pushed some of her hair behind her ear. "You're the only thing stopping me. I guess that's why I woke up wanting to prove something to myself. My reason for staying is you lying next to me in that bed."

"And not the son who worships you? Not the daughter who thinks you're an avenging angel? Not those granddaughters who climb all over you and those grandsons who hang on your every move and your every word? Not your adopted son? Ben would be terrified if you left us. You promised him no one would ever hurt him again. You promised to always love him. You've risked life and limb and even prison and a near hanging for this family. Don't ever wonder where you belong, Jake Harkner. You belong right here on the J&L, surrounded by all of us." Randy could see him clearly in the moonlight. She knew him too well—knew when he was in a mood to just ride out of their lives. She watched a sad smile cross his lips.

"Hell, I couldn't leave anyway, because you, being the determined woman you are, would damn well get on a horse and come after me. I couldn't get away from you thirty-two years ago, and it wouldn't be any easier now."

"You're exactly right." She took his hand and kissed his palm.

"Baby, I just want you to...I don't know, be prepared, I suppose. Something is nagging me lately, and I can't even explain it except that I keep hearing a wolf howl when it's too early in the day for it. The last time I heard that..." He hesitated. "It might be nothing. It's probably just from all the other things that have happened, and now, suddenly, everything is peaceful. It's hard for me to trust that peace. I know that a man like me isn't likely to die a peaceful death in bed, or that big leather chair downstairs. I don't even *want* to die that way. I don't know how or when, but it will be quick and sudden and probably violent."

"Jake, don't—"

"I just want you to know it would be okay with me. That's how it should be for a man like me, and I won't mind a bit. As long as I get my turn in front of God so I can explain a few things, because it's a sure thing you will be going up, and I want to be there with you. I'll be waiting for you, so if things work out that way, you remember that. I am always with you. Remember how

I told you that back in Oklahoma every time I rode out after the scum of the earth?"

Tears slipped down her cheeks. "And you always came back. Always." She clung to his hand. "Jake, why are you talking this way?"

He moved an arm around her and pulled her close. "I just feel old sometimes. Some days every bone in my body hurts, and I worry about the day coming when I can't even make love to you anymore."

"And you think that would matter to me?"

"It would matter to *me*. You're ten years younger than I am, and you've always needed a man to hold you."

"Hold is the word, Jake, and you're holding me right now. That's all I've ever needed. I don't need the other. God knows you've been the best lover a woman could ask for. We have some pretty wild memories in that department, wild and beautiful."

"I'll give you that one." He pulled her tight to his side and kissed her hair. "I guess it's the sound of a wolf howling that has kept me awake. I always feel like it's some kind of omen of something bad to come."

"Right now you're here and well, and I'm not sure what all hurts at the moment, but it certainly did not affect how you made love to me, so let's just take a day at a time. All your old enemies are gone, and the family is fine now. A portrait of our beautiful family hangs over the fireplace, and every person in that picture, other than me, Katie, Brian, and Ben, are the spawn of Jake Harkner, who deep inside, even in his worst years, wanted nothing more than what he has right now. God loves you beyond measure, and so do I. And right now you are still my strong and handsome Jake. Every time you touch me, you make me feel special."

"You *are* special. *Lo nuestro será eterno…tú y yo estaremos unidos eternamente*."

You and I will be united forever. She knew the words.

She reached up and put her arms around his neck, and he pulled her up, feet off the floor.

"By God, either you've gained weight, or I'm losing my strength," he teased.

"You're the one who told me to eat more," she answered.

"I guess I did, didn't I?" He moved an arm under her legs and carried her to the bed.

"Am I getting too fat?"

"Baby, you have a long way to go to be too fat. In fact, you're still too thin." He raised her higher and kissed between her breasts. "At least you haven't lost any of this cleavage."

Randy grinned. "If you had to shove these things into a corset or camisole every day, you'd wish they were smaller."

He dropped her onto the bed and crawled on top of her. "I *have* helped you shove those things into your camisole, and I enjoyed every minute of it."

"Well, I still think they're too big."

Jake started unbuttoning the front of her nightgown. "Let me be the judge of that."

She laughed and pushed his hands away. "I need to go back to sleep, Jake. Lloyd and Katie are coming for breakfast in the morning."

Jake lay down beside her. "Just so you understand, there isn't a man alive who thinks breasts can be too big."

Randy laughed and moved her arms around his neck again. "The more to please you with, my love."

"I am *very* pleased."

"And I am very tired, so go to sleep." Randy turned over, her back to him. He pulled her against him, knowing that was still the only way she could fall asleep. He kept a hand on one breast, and she smiled. "Don't even think about it, Jake."

"When I'm with you, I think about it all the time."

She grasped his hand and held it close to her heart. "Jake, everything will be fine. We have each other and the children and this big, beautiful log home on the J&L. Somehow by sharing grass and water, using the reward money carefully, we'll get through this drought."

"I know."

What was he not telling her? Was he in more pain than he let on? The man was forever strong, forever handsome, forever kind, forever protective and able. She couldn't imagine the day he could be anything else. He was such a survivor…but something was stirring that dark side.

Thirty-two

JAKE JAMMED THE POSTHOLE DIGGER INTO THE GROUND with all his strength, prying the handles apart to hold the next scoop of dirt for the pile. A few feet away, Lloyd, Ben, and Stephen were working on the same thing.

"I can't get it deep enough, Pa," Stephen called to Lloyd. "I wish I was as strong as you."

"You will be, sooner than you think, and probably stronger," Lloyd answered. He glanced at Jake and shook his head. "Don't you ever age? I was all set to outdo you, and you're digging these damn holes as fast as I am."

Jake grinned. "Believe me, I'll pay for this later. Your mother better not expect any big hugs tonight, because my arms might be dead meat."

Lloyd shoved his digger into the ground and left it there, walking over to a flatbed wagon full of posts and wire. He took a canteen from the back of it. "It's hotter than hell out here."

"Something tells me hell is a lot hotter. I'm likely to find that out some day." Jake shoved his digger into the ground and walked over to wait for Lloyd to take a long drink before he took the canteen from him and poured water over his head and shoulders. Then he put it to his lips and drank some. "You boys can take a break if you want," he told the younger ones.

They worked with their shirts off. It was hot, and no women were around, and the boys already knew about the scars on Jake's back. They drank water, and Ben sat down in the high grass and lay back in it.

"This grass stayed pretty green, Pa," Ben told Jake.

"That's why we're fencing off this area, so stray cattle from other ranches can't come and overgraze it. Eventually we'll put ole Gus out here to graze on his own, away from the females. That poor old bull shouldn't have to suffer watching the cows shake their hind ends in front of him when he can't do anything about it."

The three boys giggled, and Jake took another swallow of water, grinning as he capped the canteen. "Everything all right with you and Katie now?" he asked Lloyd, handing back the canteen. "She's looking awfully happy."

Lloyd finished retying his long hair behind his back and took the canteen. "Yeah, well, speaking of bulls…" He turned and put the canteen back in the wagon.

"Jesus, Lloyd, don't tell me."

"Yeah. She's pregnant again."

Jake shook his head, smiling. "If you two don't learn to control yourselves, you'll end up with fifteen kids."

"Easy for you to say." Lloyd put his hands on his hips. "If Mom could have kids, you'd probably have about twenty-five by now. I'd like to see you have to abstain for very long."

Jake looked around at the fencing they had already managed to put up. "Lloyd, when you get my age, abstaining gets a little easier. Pain has a way of spoiling the passion."

"Something tells me you just grin and bear it."

Jake chuckled. "Most of the time." He sobered, facing his son. "Katie okay with this?"

Lloyd nodded. "She is. I can tell the mother in her is excited. She'll just need some extra help from Teresa at first, what with Donavan still being a baby himself. At least she's weaned him onto cow's milk." He leaned down to pull up a piece of grass to chew on. It was too dry to smoke, and chewing on something was all that helped. "I love having another kid, Pa. I wanted a big family, and Katie knows it. To me, she just gets prettier with every one."

Jake walked over to his posthole digger. "You just make real sure she's rested and healthy and that she really wants more. It can't be easy on a woman to pop out a baby practically every year."

"Hell, there's four years between Tricia and Donavan. Could be after this one, we'll go another four years. We're just taking what God gives us and thanking Him for it."

Jake shoved in the posthole digger again. "That's one way to look at it. Your mother loves it when there is a new baby around to love on. Gives her another sprout to hold and rock." Jake pounded the digger a little harder, hating the fact that Randy had gone through Evie's birth and that awful surgery alone. He paused. "I should have been with her, Lloyd. Instead, I was raising hell up in Wyoming, trying to forget her." He angrily slammed the digger together and ripped out more dirt, releasing it on the pile next to the hole.

"Don't go there, Pa. That was a good twenty-seven years ago, if you go by Evie's age."

"Sometimes it seems like yesterday." Jake walked down to where Ben was starting to dig again. "That's quite a pile of dirt there, Ben. Go ahead and start another hole down past Stephen."

"Yes, sir." The kid's hair was whiter than ever because of exposure to the sun, and his ruddy complexion just made his hair look even lighter. He walked farther down to start digging another hole while Jake checked Stephen's. "You did a good job getting this one started, Stephen. Makes my job easier. Go ahead and start a new one."

"Yes, sir."

"You going to give me an order too, Pa?" Lloyd teased, walking past him with his own posthole digger.

"Yeah. Give poor Katie a rest."

Both men laughed. They walked together past the boys to start their digging again.

"You should know that from their letters, Katie and I are pretty sure her folks are going to sell their farm next year and come out here to live on the J&L," Lloyd told his father. "You know Mrs. Donavan. She'll take over the mothering to the point that Katie will have hardly anything to do. She'll be a big help."

"Good! That's real good, Lloyd, for Katie's sake. I love that beautiful woman to death, and the Donavans will be a big help in a lot of ways. Those brothers of Katie's too, if they come. If they're sure, we should start building a place for them to live in." He shook his head. "There will be enough family on the J&L to start a small town," he joked.

"Looks that way."

They both started digging again.

"You okay, Pa? Seems like you're doing a lot of thinking about the past lately," Lloyd said before ramming the digger into the earth. "You be careful about going too far back in that mind of yours."

Jake dug quietly for a few minutes. "Just a lot of things catching up with me for some reason. Maybe that's what old men do—think about the past and all their mistakes."

"Well, there is nothing old about those muscles I see you using to dig these holes. You're lean and mean."

Jake jammed the digger down again. "No doubt about the mean part." He grimaced with pain in his left shoulder, a leftover ache from a gunshot wound in Denver. The memory stabbed at him like a sword in the heart, but he'd never regret putting a hole in Mike Holt's head. He paused a moment to wait for the pain to go away. That was when he noticed it…a fancy buggy coming from the southwest range. At the moment, it was nothing more than a wavy silhouette, almost unreal, but it definitely was coming toward them. "Who the hell do you think that is?" he asked Lloyd.

Lloyd stopped digging to look. He shaded his eyes and squinted. "I don't know, but it looks like two people, and I think one of them is a woman."

The boys stopped digging as they waited for the buggy to come closer. As always, out on the open range, it took close to twenty minutes for the rig to get close enough to make out who it might be.

"Jesus," Jake muttered. "If I see who I think I see, that's Gretta MacBain."

"What the hell would the richest whore in Denver be doing coming out here?" Lloyd commented.

Jake grinned. "I guess we'll soon find out." He turned and walked to the supply wagon to grab his shirt.

Lloyd shook his head. Only Jake Harkner would respect a whore enough to go put a shirt on. "Get your shirts on, boys," he told his son and Ben. "As far as your grandfather is concerned, there's a lady coming." He smiled, walking to the wagon to get his own shirt.

Thirty-three

THE CANOPIED BUGGY FINALLY DREW CLOSE ENOUGH for Jake to be sure it was indeed Gretta MacBain, the most notorious prostitute in Denver. She was riding in the front seat beside her guard and constant companion, a man Gretta called Sam. Jake had never learned Sam's last name.

Terrel and Cole rode beside the buggy, apparently the outriders who'd first spotted it. Jake thought it a bit comical that Gretta wore a prim gray dress with no frills and a high neckline. Her red hair was pulled back at the sides and pinned under a tiny straw hat. She wore hardly any paint on her face and just one tiny pair of diamond earrings—no other jewelry. Her look was a far cry from the wanton prostitute he'd met back in Denver and who'd sat in the courtroom talking about her profession proudly, as though it was no different from teaching or owning a millinery. She actually looked prettier and younger without the paint.

"Jake!" Gretta called out. "You handsome outlaw, you! I didn't think I'd run into you clear out here! Figured we'd have to go all way to the homestead to find you!"

Jake walked up and helped her out of the buggy, sweeping Gretta into his arms and whirling her around. "Gretta MacBain! What the hell are you doing on the J&L?"

Gretta hugged him around the neck, and Ben and Stephen just stared, grinning.

"That's that lady who said nice things about Grampa at that hearing last year in Denver," Stephen told Ben.

"I know. She's one of those bad ladies Pa always said we should treat good even though they're—you know—I think they sleep with men for money."

"I like her. She was nice to Grampa."

"Oh, she was nice to Grampa, all right," Lloyd put in, smiling.

"Jesus, Gretta, you look like a schoolmarm," Jake told her. "Have you changed professions?"

Gretta threw back her head and laughed. "Well, I can't go traveling around in the general public with my breasts hanging out and a face full of paint, can I? I have to look respectable when I travel."

They laughed, and Lloyd walked closer when Jake let go of Gretta. She stepped back to eye both of them.

"My God, is it you, Lloyd? I can't believe it! After seeing you lying in blood on the floor at that cattlemen's ball…" She put her hands over her mouth, and her eyes teared. "I know you were starting to get around at that hearing, but I never really thought I'd see you standing so tall and strong again." She put out her arms. "Give me a hug, you gorgeous hunk of man."

Lloyd took her up on the offer. "Just a light one. We've been working out in the heat, and we're all sweaty. Hugging us can't be that enjoyable right now."

Gretta laughed. "Harkner men? I'll take a hug from you two any time and any way I can get it. Hell, it's not like I've never been around sweaty men before, and you two smell good even when you need a bath." She patted Lloyd's back and kissed his cheek, then turned to Jake. "And you! Last I heard you got yourself all shot up in Boulder. You just keep coming right back for more, don't you?"

"I learned by the time I was eight years old that you have to be tough, Gretta." Jake put an arm around her and turned her to face the boys. "Meet my adopted son, Ben—the big one there with blond hair. Can you believe he's only thirteen?"

"By gosh, he looks eighteen! I saw all these kids at the hearing in Denver last year, but I wasn't sure which one is which, except for that Little Jake of yours. He stood right up to that prosecutor, didn't he? I thought he was going to sock the man. He's all Harkner, that one!"

Jake grinned. "I'm afraid he's the biggest trouble-maker. He belongs to my daughter, Evie, who is the gentlest, kindest, most gracious Christian woman who ever walked. Trouble is, she has Harkner blood, and some of the orneriest came out of her in the form of Little Jake." He pointed to Stephen. "That handsome kid there who is too tall for his age is Lloyd's son, Stephen."

Gretta walked up and gave the boy a once-over. "Of course he is. He has his father's and grandfather's dark good looks. And this one—" She tousled Ben's wild, thick mane of white-blond hair. "He's going to be a big man someday. He'll be one of your best workers, I'll bet." She looked at Jake. "How'd you come upon an adopted boy?"

"Back in Oklahoma. Caught his father beating the hell out of him. I took the belt out of his hand and used it on the man himself so he'd know how it feels." He walked up and crooked an arm around Ben's neck, giving him a hug. "The sonofabitch decided he didn't even want his son anymore, and even if he did, I wouldn't have let him leave. I took Ben home with me, and that was that."

"Well, now, I keep learning things about you that just don't fit that reputation of yours. You're a complicated man, Jake Harkner."

"My wife keeps telling me that."

Gretta shook her head, studying his still-fine build with great appreciation for what she saw. "Too bad about that wife. Do you know how hard it is on a woman like me to be around men like you and your son and know you're unavailable?"

Jake grinned. "There are plenty of men about two hours from here who can help you out."

Cole spoke up from his horse. "There's two of them sittin' right here."

"Careful, boys, there are young ears around." Gretta sobered. "Besides, I'm not here for that. And I wouldn't even think of coming to a man's homestead and behaving that way. Too many little ones and decent women around." She looked up at Jake. "I've got another reason for looking you up, Jake, but it's best we go to your home first. And it's probably best your wife and daughter are a part of all this."

Jake folded his arms, studying the sadness in her eyes. "All what?"

Gretta shook her head. "Not now. Let's just go to your house, unless you think I'm unfit to go inside. It's fine if you want to talk someplace else instead."

"Are you kidding?" Jake walked up and lifted her in his arms, carrying her to Outlaw and plopping her on the saddle. He mounted up behind her, taking up the reins and moving his left arm around her before turning the horse. "Get everything together and bring the wagon and the boys back," he told Lloyd. "We'll send a couple of the other men up here to keep going for the next couple of days. I'm taking Gretta to the homestead myself."

Gretta settled against him. "Well, now, I didn't plan on this at all! I get to ride in this man's arms for the next two hours? My God, how much is a woman supposed to take?"

"You be good, Pa," Lloyd joked.

"Believe me, it's no fun answering to your mother when I'm not." Jake turned the horse and kicked Outlaw into a gentle lope.

"Good God almighty," Lloyd muttered. "Mom will sure as hell have something to say about Pa riding in with Gretta MacBain in his arms." He grinned and turned to Sam. "What the hell is she doing here, Sam?"

The big, burly, bald-headed man shook his head. When he spoke, his missing front tooth was visible. "Not sure. I guard the woman, kick out the no-goods that abuse any of the women, service Gretta myself when she wants a man who actually cares about her, and we're good friends—but there's some things she never tells me. She just said she needed something from Jake Harkner and asked me to bring her out here." He looked around. "You have a beautiful place here, Lloyd. Really beautiful. I can't believe how healthy you look, considerin'."

"Yeah, well, if you were to punch me in the gut right now, I'd go down pretty hard. I'm still not totally healed on the inside. I can tell."

"Well, you look big and strong enough that I still wouldn't want to take you on." Sam grinned. "I'm real glad to see you lookin' so good. I'll never forget the look on your father's face that night. I've never seen anything that dark and vicious in a man's eyes as when he put that gun to Mike Holt's head."

"Yeah, well, we have tried to put it all behind us." Lloyd looked at Cole and Terrence. "You two take Sam on in. I'll be along pretty quick with the wagon and the boys."

"Sure, boss." Cole took off toward the homestead, and Sam followed. Lloyd glanced farther across the broad expanse of green and yellow grass to see Jake headed north toward the homestead. "This should be interesting," he said, turning to the boys.

"Will Grandma be mad?" Stephen asked.

Lloyd just grinned and shook his head. "Hard to say, boys. Hard to say. I know she appreciates the things Gretta said at that hearing last year, and your grandma knows your grandpa pretty good. Women like that were mother figures to your grandfather, so he'll always show them respect." Lloyd picked up a role of wire and a posthole digger. "Grandma understands that. I'm just not sure how she'll feel about your grandpa riding in alone with Gretta MacBain. She's beautiful and has quite a reputation."

The two boys looked at each other and giggled as they started picking up tools.

"Yeah, and we know why," Ben teased, sharing a laugh again with Stephen.

Lloyd threw the wire and digger onto the wagon. Most ranchers used barbed wire, but he hated the stuff. Too many cattle and wild animals had died slow deaths from it. He walked over to pick up another posthole digger. "You boys remember to treat Gretta with respect when we reach the homestead. She's one of those bad women with a good heart, as your grandfather would put it." He stopped and wiped at sweat on his brow, looking across the grassland again. He couldn't see his father or the horse anymore. *What the hell are you doing here, Gretta?*

Thirty-four

"JAKE, THIS IS BEAUTIFUL! JUST BEAUTIFUL! MAGNIFICENT is an even better word. Hell, Sam said we've probably been on J&L land the last day or two."

"Eighty-two thousand acres and growing," Jake told her. "This was Lloyd's dream, and he damn well deserves it after having my back for over three years in Oklahoma. He didn't have to do that, but he did...for me. He's a hell of a son. He has three kids now and another one in the oven."

"Well, that doesn't surprise me. What woman could stay out of his bed?"

Jake grinned, keeping Outlaw to a walk to rest the horse. "Sorry I'm such a mess," he told Gretta. "We've been digging postholes all morning, and it's damn hot—and you smell good, which makes me feel even worse. I like to be bathed and shaved when I'm around a beautiful lady."

"And only a man like you would call me a lady." Gretta grasped the arm around her middle. "You don't really think I care that you need a shave, do you? I take great pleasure in being this close to the handsome outlaw," she joked. "I'll never forget how nice you were to me back in Denver."

"At least you don't need to worry about Mike Holt anymore."

"Yes, well, you have quite an unusual way of making sure a man is dead."

Cole rode closer to them, and Jake looked his way.

"Ride on in and let Randy and the girls know we're coming in and who is with us," Jake told him. "Tell the girls I said to make some fresh lemonade. And it might be best that Randy has advance notice."

Cole laughed, looking Gretta over. "I'll let 'em know," he told Jake.

Jake knew damn well that half the men at the bunkhouse had visited Gretta's establishment more than once, and likely some of them had paid good money for Gretta herself. She was probably no more than thirty and still a fine-looking woman, with hair as red as Katie's and brilliant blue eyes. "You tell the men to stay at the bunkhouse, Cole. No catcalls, understand? I don't want that around Little Jake and my granddaughters—and it wouldn't set well with my wife and daughter either."

Cole grinned. "Well, you ridin' in with Gretta there on the same horse ain't gonna set well either."

"Don't you worry about that. Just get the hell on down to the homestead."

"Can the men at least *look* at her?" Cole winked at Gretta.

Jake grinned. "I don't think I'll have much control over that. They're grown men."

Cole tipped his hat to Gretta and rode off.

"Jake, I didn't come here to cause any hard feelings."

"Don't worry about it. Randy knows me better than I know myself. She won't be upset. And Evie sits at the right hand of Christ himself. She'll welcome you like a long-lost sister. Katie…well, she might be a bit intimidated. She worries about her weight, and now she's carrying again. She's a gorgeous, gorgeous woman, but she's aware of how handsome her husband is, so I wouldn't make any remarks about Lloyd around her."

"Well, it won't be easy, but I'll be good."

Jake rode up to Horse Creek, which the summer's heat had dwindled from its normal rushing force to a gentle trickle. He reined Outlaw to a halt. "I've got to wash off at least some of this sweat and water my horse." He dismounted and reached up to lift Gretta down.

"You sure you're healed enough to be throwing me around like a bag of oats?" she asked.

"A bag of oats probably weighs more." He led Outlaw to the creek to drink.

Gretta noticed his ivory-handled .44s hung in a gun belt around his horse's neck. "Word is you were awarded ten thousand dollars for killing those bank robbers," she told him. "Congratulations!"

Jake knelt beside the water and washed his hands. "None due. I wouldn't even have taken the money if it weren't for this ranch and Lloyd. This drought has depleted our grassland, and a neighboring farmer with a grudge set fire to one of our prime grazing valleys. Almost got himself hanged for his trouble." He splashed water over his face and dripped some through his hair and over the back of his neck before going to his horse and untying his bedroll. "At any rate, I took the money in case Lloyd has to buy feed for the winter, but I didn't feel right doing it since I was a wanted man myself once."

He opened his bedroll and laid it on the ground, taking out a clean shirt that was rolled up inside. "Why are you here, Gretta?" he asked, removing his dirty shirt and tossing it onto the bedroll. "I know I invited you to come and see the J&L, but I'm thinking this isn't a normal visit." He faced her as he quickly pulled on a clean shirt. Gretta suspected he wanted to be sure she didn't see his scarred back.

"You're right. This isn't just a visit."

Jake buttoned the shirt and walked to his horse to fish out a cigarette and light it. "And?" he asked. "What's the rest of the story?"

"I'd rather wait, Jake," Gretta answered, sobering. "I need your whole family to hear me out. And if we take too long getting to the homestead, it won't set well with your wife, so I'd best not take the time to explain just yet."

Jake took a deep drag on the cigarette and grinned. "You're probably right." He looked her over. "How are things in Denver? Your clients treating you okay?"

Gretta shook her head and smiled rather sadly. "Only *you* would ask that. And the answer is yes. And so far, the city hasn't closed me down, but I see it coming. The pious women of high society think it's time to rid Denver of its embarrassingly sinful citizens. Little do they know that I've slept with half their husbands."

Jake laughed, taking the cigarette from his lips. "You're probably worth more as a good person than all of them put together."

Gretta smiled softly. "That's a nice thing to say. That's what I love about you, Jake Harkner. You just put it right out there and say it like it is. I've never met a man quite like you."

"And saying it like it is often gets me in trouble," he joked.

Gretta shook her head. "Speaking of trouble, did you ever run into that Brad Buckley again after Denver? He seemed to have a real big grudge against—" Gretta nearly gasped at the change in his entire countenance. He turned and walked a few feet away. "Jake?"

"Shit." He said the word under his breath, but Gretta heard it.

"Jake, what's wrong? I've obviously hit a raw nerve. I'm sorry." She walked closer, and when he turned, the darkness in his eyes was almost as bad as the night of the cattlemen's ball. He tossed the cigarette into the creek and took her arm, leading her to the shade of a lone pine tree several yards away. He towered over her as he spoke.

"You need to know something, Gretta, and you need to know because I don't want you saying Brad Buckley's name in front of Randy or the rest of the family." He kept hold of her arm. "I'm trusting you on this."

Gretta slowly nodded. "How well do you know women like me? We keep men's secrets all the time. I could destroy half the marriages in Denver if I wanted to, so if I'm told not to say anything, then I don't. It's that simple."

He held her gaze for several long seconds, then let go of her and turned away. "The story is that Brad Buckley has disappeared from the face of the earth. None of us ever saw him again after the judge sent him off." He nervously lit a second cigarette.

"And the truth?"

He didn't answer right away.

"Jake, I helped keep your neck out of a noose last summer, and that judge said if you took the law into your own hands one more time, you would hang. What did you do?"

He sighed deeply before continuing. "We had a barn fire—a big one—last winter. It distracted me and Lloyd and all the help. We lost several prime horses and one of our best hands in the fire."

"Which one? I knew a lot of them."

"Pepper. Big belly. Old and kind of grizzly but a big heart. He liked to chew tobacco."

"I remember him! He had an index finger missing from a roping accident."

Jake turned to her, the remark making him smile a little. "You do remember your clients."

Gretta grinned, hoping she'd helped allay his dark mood. "I keep a ledger."

Jake grinned. "That could be pretty incriminating for some men."

"Oh, believe me, it helps me get my way in what you might call the political arena of prostitution."

Jake looked her over, his smile fading. "Brad Buckley

and some other men set the fire to distract us"—he turned away—"while they dragged my wife off with them in the middle of the night."

Gretta gasped. "Oh no! Oh, Jake, I'm so sorry!"

He said nothing for several long seconds. "We couldn't go after them until morning because it was too dark to track them," he finally continued. "They were men who'd worked for us, men we'd injured and kicked off the J&L, so they knew their way around the ranch. Long story short—we caught up to them at a line shack south of here. I won't go into details, but we trapped them there and killed every last fucking one of them."

"You killed Buckley, after that judge said to stay away from him?"

He didn't answer right away. "Do you remember last year in Denver, when we left that jewelry store where I picked out my wife's ring? On our way back, we talked a little more about Mike Holt and Brad Buckley. You said Brad was…a strange sort. That he only liked sex one way."

Gretta put a hand over her eyes and walked a few feet away. "Jesus in Heaven," she said softly.

"He forced oral sex on my wife. Him and one of the others. That's something I never asked of Randy." He growled the words through gritted teeth. "There are some things you just don't ask of a woman like her. On top of that, they beat her pretty bad. It's amazing she lived."

Gretta noticed tears in his eyes before he turned away.

"I won't even go into detail about what I did to him," Jake continued, "except that I was ready to shove red-hot coals down his throat when Randy came out of that line shack with only a blanket over herself. She'd taken away one of the men's guns, and she walked up and shot Brad Buckley herself. First in the chest, and then…in his face."

Gretta shook her head. "Dear God," she said softly.

"She looked at me and said that now no one could

accuse me of killing Brad Buckley." Jake's voice wavered on the words. "Several of the men were there," he continued, "and Lloyd, and the boys." He threw his head back and drew a deep breath. "We have a pact. We burned that line shack and buried the bodies, and no one is ever to talk about it. As far as the outside world knows, Brad Buckley just up and vanished. And to be honest with you, I'm not even sure Randy remembers killing him. The whole thing affected her mind, and she wasn't herself for quite a while. She never talks about shooting Brad, and I'm afraid to bring it up. She was so…horribly bruised and sick. And mentally…she was a mess for quite a few months. I lost her for a while there, but things are a lot better now. She's gotten a lot stronger. Happier."

"Jake, I don't know what to say."

"You don't need to say anything. I just wanted you to understand why you can't mention his name. They beat her so bad, but it was the other thing that just about destroyed her. We've finally…worked things out, so to speak. She's eating better now and has gained a little weight, but she's still too thin. Mentally, she's pretty much back to her old self."

"I have a feeling that if any man can cure a woman of that kind of horror, you can. Me, I'm not offended by something like that, but being beaten and forced, that's another matter—and having met that beautiful, gracious wife of yours, I can't imagine how awful that had to be for her." Gretta walked up and touched his arm. "I'm glad you told me." *What am I doing here?* she thought. *This family has been through so much.* "Jake, maybe I'd better just go back to Denver. You and your family need some peace."

He turned and took her arm, leading her back to Outlaw. "No. You're here now, and you're welcome. We're all grateful for your help after Lloyd was shot, and how you stood up for me. So you won't be shunned by one person on the J&L. Randy understands."

Gretta let out a little scream when he suddenly lifted her onto Outlaw again.

"But if we don't get our asses to the house, all that understanding and forgiveness might not mean a thing. We've stayed here too long."

Gretta grinned as he mounted up behind her and moved an arm around her again.

"My son will be coming along soon with the boys, and he's going to wonder why this is all the 'farther' we've gotten."

Gretta patted his arm. "Well, I'm just sorry for the *reason* we took a little too long. You okay?"

"No, but I'm used to being beat up and dragged around. I've grown a little numb to tragedy. I just hate it when it happens to others in my family, because it's usually my fault. That's something I live with day and night."

"You're a good man, Jake. It's not your fault. There are simply evil people in this world, and we can't do much about it."

Jake urged Outlaw into motion. "Randy is a goddamn tough woman, Gretta, little and delicate, educated and sophisticated, kind and gracious—all the things I'm not. But she's tough as nails. Inside, she's a lot stronger than I am."

He headed through the huge valley, kicking Outlaw into a faster lope. Gretta could see how he and Lloyd fit this endless expanse called the J&L—big and tough and rugged. How was she going to tell this family why she'd come? They needed some peace. If her reason for being here was for her alone, she'd go right back to Denver. But she had to think of her daughter. She had to think about her Annie.

Thirty-five

RANDY STOOD ON THE VERANDA, ARMS FOLDED, AS SHE watched Jake ride in with Gretta MacBain on his horse in front of him. She smiled and shook her head when she saw that just about every man who'd been working at the homestead was lined up to greet Gretta, all of them nodding and smiling, but respectfully, not whooping and whistling, which Randy knew they very much wanted to do. How often did a notorious, big-city prostitute come onto the J&L? She suspected Jake had told someone to forewarn them about making a fuss.

"Honestly, Daddy can be the most brazen man," Evie said, stepping up beside her. She put an arm around her mother.

"Jake is just being Jake," Randy answered. "And I have a feeling he ordered the men to mind their manners. As far as he's concerned, he's riding in with a lady."

"At least it's Jake she's with and not Lloyd," Katie commented.

"Oh, Katie, my brother would never do you wrong, and you know it."

Both Katie and Evie held their babies in their arms. Brian joined them on the veranda, shaking his head at the sight. "Randy, you have the patience of a saint," he joked.

"I just know my husband, that's all."

Little Jake rode his spotted Appaloosa out from the new barn, charging up to Jake. "Hi, Grampa!"

"You're getting pretty good at riding that big horse," Jake told him.

"I'm good as any man," the boy answered proudly.

"You sure are," Gretta told him. "Kid, you've really grown the past year. Remember me? From Denver?"

"Sure I do! You're that pretty lady that said nice things about Grampa when those men wanted to put him in jail."

"Well, you have quite a memory, young man." Gretta winked at the boy.

"Where's Stephen and Ben, Grampa?"

"They'll be here soon." Jake finally made it to the house.

"Oh my, look at all the rose bushes!" Gretta exclaimed. "They're beautiful!"

"That's all Randy's doing. She loves roses," Jake told her as he dismounted. He lifted Gretta down, then took her arm and led her up the steps of the veranda. He leaned down and kissed Randy. "Randy, you remember Gretta."

Randy gave him a look of mock scolding. "Oh, how could I forget the woman who said such nice things about you? I particularly remember how she described encountering you in a men's dressing room."

Gretta put a hand to her chest, her eyes wide. "I was only warning him about—"

"We know, and we appreciate the things you did, Gretta." Randy smiled and reached out to embrace her. "And thank you for all your help."

Evie was next, walking up and hugging Gretta while holding little Esther on her right hip. "Welcome to the J&L, Gretta. This is my third child, Esther."

Esther pulled at the hat ribbon under Gretta's chin and managed to untie it. Everyone laughed, and Gretta gently held the child's arm and kissed the back of her hand.

"I'm Katie, Lloyd's wife," Katie offered next. "And this very heavy baby in my arms is Lloyd's newest son, Donavan."

"Well, who could doubt that, with that dark hair and those big, dark eyes," Gretta answered with a grin. She turned to Evie's husband. "Doctor Stewart! It's good to see you again."

"And you." Brian shook her hand. "I remember you often brought food to us in Lloyd's room while he lay near death. We appreciate your help, Gretta. That was a really bad time for the whole family."

"Well, *some*one had to help. Heaven knows most of the town was scared to death to even go into that room, the mood Jake was in." Gretta could hardly believe the welcome she was getting. She glanced at Jake, who still had an arm around Randy while two little girls clung to his legs. He let go of Randy and reached down to pick them up. They wrapped their legs around his middle from each side and hugged him around the neck. "Gretta, the redhead here is Tricia, Lloyd's daughter. The other little troublemaker is Evie's daughter, Sadie Mae, and we keep each other's secrets, don't we, Sadie Mae?"

Sadie Mae giggled and kissed Jake's cheek. "We got a secret about chickens!" she said, her dimples showing when she smiled.

Gretta smiled, feeling sick inside. How could she ask Jake what she needed to ask him? She scrambled to make up an excuse for coming here, something different from why she'd really come. But then she had to think of Annie. Her little girl hadn't been so different from these little girls at one time. Gretta had been so sure Annie would have had a better life than what was happening to her now.

"Come in and have some lemonade, Gretta," Randy told her. "How long will you stay? You most certainly need to stay at least one night. We have plenty of guest bedrooms. And how on earth did you get here if you had to take Jake's horse to make it all the way in?"

"Oh, I came by train and then a buggy. My

companion, Sam, brought me. You remember Sam from the cattlemen's ball, don't you? He was with me that night."

"Oh my, after all that happened, I'm afraid I don't remember Sam," Randy answered, leading Gretta through the door. "Where is he now?"

"He's on his way in with Lloyd, Ben, and Stephen. They stayed behind to pick up their fencing tools."

"I didn't want her sitting around in the hot sun," Jake told Randy, "so I brought her on in."

Randy just grinned. "How nice of you. And didn't the buggy have a canopy?" she teased.

Jake winked. "Of course it did, but that's not the same as being in a big, cool house like this and drinking cold lemonade."

"I accept your explanation, Mr. Harkner."

Jake leaned down and kissed her again, and Gretta couldn't get over how beautiful Randy was, but just as Jake had warned, she was too thin. It made her sick to realize what had happened to the woman. She could only imagine how Jake had reacted when he'd realized Randy had been taken. The rage she'd seen on his face when Lloyd was shot was bad enough.

There followed complete bedlam, as always when the entire Harkner family was together. Gretta just watched. Little Jake came inside and hurried over to hug his grandfather, asking to go along the next time to help dig postholes. Lloyd finally arrived with Ben and Stephen, and after taking time to wash off the sweat and put on clean shirts, they all came inside, along with Sam, who was also royally welcomed. Sam greeted everyone and then bowed out, insisting he would stay at the bunkhouse, and Evie sent him off with a glass of lemonade.

Gretta was amazed at the family's open friendliness. She felt nothing fake about any of it as they sat her down to the table and served lemonade and pie.

"You must be tired and dying to cool down with a bath," Randy told Gretta. "The guest bedroom down the hall has a toilet and washroom attached. I know what a long ride it is from the train station clear across the J&L to reach the homestead."

"Oh, this ranch is so beautiful," Gretta answered. "Jake pointed out a few places, but of course it would have taken days to show me all of it. But from what I saw, it's just magnificent. I'm so happy for all of you. And Lloyd, I can't get over how healthy you look."

"Yeah, well, my wife takes good care of me," he answered, winking at Katie.

"Apparently so, considering the fact that Katie is going to have another baby," Gretta joked. "At least that's what Jake said."

Katie blushed, and Lloyd took her hand. "A man has to have some reason to get well fast," he answered. "I mean, *look* at her. Any man would heal fast for this."

Katie covered her face. "Please change the subject!" she begged.

Esther sat in a high chair next to Jake, eating pieces of a biscuit. She suddenly got squirmy and made a face, wanting out of the chair. She reached for Jake, who pulled her out and hugged her close. She put her head on his shoulder and sucked her thumb, looking sleepy.

"Well, I was just about to have a cigarette. I guess that's not going to happen," Jake said, patting the girl's back.

"I can take her and put her down, Daddy," Evie offered.

"No. Let her fall asleep this way first, or she might fuss."

Gretta didn't know whether to laugh or cry at the sight. She'd watched Jake Harkner put a gun to a man's head last summer and pull the trigger. She'd seen a terrible darkness in his eyes, and even the Denver police had been afraid of him. He'd locked himself in Lloyd's room and was determined to be the one to nurse his son back to health, and warned the authorities that anyone who tried to stop him would die.

Yet there he sat, refusing a cigarette because he held a little granddaughter in his arms and insisted he would hold her until she fell asleep. She'd never known a man of such contrasts, or such a close-knit family.

"I'll show you to your room now, if you like," Randy told her when they finished eating. "You can rest and freshen up before supper. We'll make it a family dinner, and then one of the men can show you around the homestead. I have no doubt the hired hands will fight each other over who gets to give you the grand tour."

Ben and Stephen giggled at that one.

"You gotta see our new barn!" Little Jake added. "I can show it to you."

Gretta smiled. "I'd like that just fine, Little Jake. Do I need to wear boots?"

"Yeah, you better. Grandma has boots. There's horses in there, and horses go to the bathroom a lot," he added with a giggle.

More talk. More laughter. More warmth. Randy showed Gretta to the guest room, a large, pleasant room with pine-board walls and floor, checkered curtains, and a lovely quilt on the bed.

"We have electricity now but no phone yet," she told Gretta. "We do have running water. Jake insisted on that. He's done so much to help relieve me of extra work, and we have Teresa, a Mexican woman who does so much around here. Jake refuses to allow me to do the cleaning, and he insists Teresa help me with the bigger family meals, though I really don't mind doing it myself. I love to cook." She walked over and fussed with one of the curtains.

"That man loves you to death, doesn't he?" Gretta said, watching her.

"He is incredibly good to me, and loyal, which is why I've stayed with him for nearly thirty-two years." She held Gretta's gaze. "You and I never really talked much back in Denver, what with Jake and me sitting by Lloyd's side day after day, both of us in so much grief. I just thought I'd explain that I understand why he gravitates to women like you. You understand the kind of life he once led, and when he was little, he sometimes lived with prostitutes, and they protected him from his brutal father." Randy folded her arms. "So if you wonder why I don't get upset when I see something like my husband riding in with you on his horse, that's why. He has this deep-down eternal gratitude for what your kind did for him, how they protected him. I trust him implicitly. And please, when I say 'your kind,' don't think I'm looking down on you or insulting—"

"I understand, Mrs. Harkner. And you have to be the luckiest woman alive having a husband like Jake."

Randy smiled sadly. "Jake would say quite the opposite. He's never appreciated his own worthiness. He blames himself for everything bad that happens to this family."

Including what happened to you last winter. Gretta watched her eyes. This woman who loved and protected Jake Harkner like a fierce mother grizzly was wondering why she was here. Her defenses were up, not because she didn't trust Jake, but because she'd lived too long worrying she'd lose him in a different way...to violence. She felt as though someone was stabbing her in the gut, because what she wanted might indeed bring violence to the man. "He's a good man," she said aloud. "One of the best I've ever met. And you're wondering why I'm here."

"I am, Gretta. I have this terrible feeling it has nothing to do with your profession. That doesn't worry me at all. Women like you are no novelty to Jake, and you're too smart and respectful to have come here to flaunt yourself to the men. You wouldn't do that in front of the family, but you also aren't here just to visit, or you would have written first. Does Jake already know why you're really here?"

Gretta turned away. "No. But I'm sure he realizes it can't be just for a visit." She faced Randy again. "I'll have to tell all of you together. This evening after supper, if that's all right. And…maybe you should send the children off somewhere to play and look out for one another then. I have to talk about something that maybe they shouldn't hear."

Randy sighed, rubbing at her eyes. "All right." She walked past Gretta to the door.

"I'm sorry, Mrs. Harkner," Gretta told her. "This is something that can't be helped."

Randy stood at the doorway. "Please call me Randy. I know you're a good twenty years younger than I am, but Mrs. Harkner just makes me feel even older."

Gretta met her gaze and shook her head. "You are an incredibly beautiful woman, Randy. And in more ways than I will ever be." She smiled nervously. "And like you suspect, I'm not here just for a visit, and it has nothing to do with my profession, at least not directly."

Randy closed her eyes against a growing terror. "You're going to take Jake away from here, aren't you?"

Gretta rubbed her forehead. "I honestly don't know. It will be up to him."

Randy turned. "I need him, Gretta. I can't live without Jake."

Gretta folded her arms over her middle and turned away. "I'm so sorry," she repeated. "I have no choice."

Randy fought back tears. "I'll have Sam bring your things. And if you want Sam to stay in here with you, it's all right. It won't shock any of us." She walked out.

Gretta watched after her. Jake was right. There went

one tough woman. "You'd fight tooth and nail and more for that man if you thought you had to, Randy Harkner," she said softly, smiling. "And here I am, about to ask you to let him risk his life…for the daughter of a whore."

Thirty-six

"YOU ALL RIGHT?" JAKE SAT IN A PORCELAIN BATHTUB in the washroom. He wasn't about to go to dinner without getting rid of the rest of the sweat and dirt from earlier in the day.

Randy poured a half bucket of water over his hair after just shampooing it. "I'm just worried about Gretta's real reason for coming." She handed Jake a small towel for his face, then walked to a sink to fold some other towels.

"Why don't you get in this tub with me?" Jake teased.

Randy smiled. "Because when I do, we end up having some very unusual lovemaking, the kind I call disrespectful, which is the kind you enjoy the most. And, Mr. Harkner, that water is extra dirty this time, although there is someone downstairs who would probably gladly climb in there with you anyway."

Jake grinned. "She's not you." He finished washing and rose to grab a bigger towel from a stand near the tub.

"She certainly isn't. She's twenty years younger than I am, which makes her half *your* age, and she loves big, strong, handsome, brave men. Who can blame her for that? I happen to love one myself."

Jake finished toweling off, then opened the towel and wrapped her close. "And I love *you*. And you're right about the age thing. I'm a little too old to keep up with the likes of Gretta MacBain."

"Oh, please!" Randy kissed his bare chest. "As you age, Jake Harkner, sex is the *last* thing you'll cross off your list of things you're still able to do. And how should I take that remark? Do you mean an *older* woman like me is easier to keep up with?"

Jake shook his head. "Hell, you're ten years younger than I am, and since you've become your old self again, you aren't so easy to keep up with either, speaking of which, since I'm already naked—"

Randy ducked away from him. "We have company in the bedroom right below us, and she wouldn't have any trouble discerning what's going on up here if we romped in that bed." She hurried into the bedroom and threw some long underwear at him, as well as a shirt. "Get dressed, Mr. Harkner. Cover that thing up before it's too big to cram into that underwear."

Jake laughed and tossed his towel aside. He picked up the underwear and pulled it on. Randy watched, admiring her husband's beautiful build, which belied his age. She wished beyond hope they could stay in this playful mood, but a dark cloud hung in the room.

Jake's smile faded. "I'm a little worried too," he told her. "You've been through enough the last few months. I hate the thought of you having any more pressure on you, especially right now."

Randy folded her arms in front of her. "It all depends on what Gretta wants. When I showed her to her room, she said it's possible that what she needs will mean you leaving the ranch. You know how I feel about that, but I'll try to understand, Jake. In the end, it's your decision, but I know you all too well. Someone must be in trouble, and you're Mister Good Samaritan when it comes to things like that."

He finished buttoning his shirt, the blue one Randy liked best. He walked closer, leaning down to kiss her lightly. "It can't be all that bad, Randy."

"Can't it? Our luck has never held up too well when it comes to living a peaceful life."

He pulled her close and tugged the pins from her hair, gathering a fistful of her golden tresses into his hand and burying his nose in it. "You smell good—like roses, as always."

"Don't change the subject, Jake."

He kissed her hair, her forehead, her eyes, then took her face in his hands. "Baby, Gretta is decent enough that she'd never deliberately make trouble. She wouldn't be here if it wasn't for something important. She knows what Denver did to all of us."

Randy studied his eyes. "Well, then, I will have only one main objection to whatever it is she wants."

"What's that?"

"That if you have to go away, you won't be traveling alone with Miss Gretta MacBain."

Jake grinned. "You saying you don't trust me, after all these years together?"

"I'm saying I don't trust *Gretta*."

His grin grew wider. "You damn well know me better than that, woman."

Randy let out a little scream when Jake suddenly picked her up and tossed her onto the bed. He crawled onto it with her and lay on top of her. "I'm not dressed yet, Mrs. Harkner. How about if we—"

"Absolutely not!" Randy objected. "Not this time of day with company right below us!"

Jake sobered, studying her eyes. "Please tell me you aren't serious about Gretta, Randy. We've been through way too much for you to even give thought to such a thing."

She traced a finger over his lips. "Like you, Jake, I'm just trying to think of something to avoid the obvious. You're going to have to leave. I feel it in my bones, and it will be something dangerous." Her eyes teared. "I'm not ready for this. I still need you beside me. I need you in this bed every night. I need to feel your arms around me. I'll never get over the fear that each time you go away you won't make it back, not when there is danger and gunplay involved. And if Gretta is here, it's going to involve danger and guns. Why else would she come to you for help? She has half the men in Denver wrapped around her little finger, or blackmailed, and she knows you aren't impressed by beautiful prostitutes. She wants you for something those men can't do, something besides sex that she knows you're good at—better than any other man she knows. And that's guns."

Jake didn't answer right away. He searched her eyes. The last thing he wanted was to see that look of fear again—fear of being without him. "Randy, if I have to leave, I'll damn well come back just as fast as I can. I need you in my arms at night just as much as you need to *be* in my arms. Who do you belong to?"

"Jake Harkner."

"Every damn inch of you, plus your heart and your soul. I have you back, and I don't want to lose you again. *Yo te amo, mi quiero. Tu eres mi vida.*"

"You know how much I love you, Jake. And I'm stronger now, but I'm still afraid without you. And the only reason I'm worried about you coming back is because you've been a little different ever since the fire in the valley. I know you all too well, and you're seeing a changing world that doesn't have room for men like you any longer. But *I* have a need for you. They don't make men like you anymore. The only one who comes close is Lloyd, and this new world will be a struggle for him too, but it will be easier because he doesn't have the ugly past that drives you."

He smiled sadly. "I promise to hang around, for your sake. Whatever Gretta needs, we'll find a way to face it together. You just remember that we are always together in spirit...*always*. Wherever I am, I'll be right here in this bed with you every night. Promise me you will remember that."

Tears filled her eyes. "I'll try. But you're my Jake. You keep me safe."

"Every man on this ranch will keep you safe, most of all your son and your grandsons and Ben. You'll be protected and loved, and I'll be with you. We don't even know yet that I'll have to go anywhere at all, so let's be strong, *mi vida*. If I have to leave you, it will be just as hard on me as on you."

He kissed her and started to move off the bed when the front corner that held most of their weight suddenly crashed to the floor. Randy screamed as it went down, and Jake hung on to her as they rolled off the bed.

The broken bed helped relieve their worries as they broke into almost uncontrollable laughter. Jake kept hold of Randy and rolled her away from the bed. They ended up lying on a braided rug.

"Mother?" They heard Evie call out the word.

"Oh Lord, Jake, can you imagine how this sounded downstairs? And you're in your underwear!"

Jake reached up and pulled a quilt off the bed, both of them still laughing as he covered himself. By then Evie was knocking at the door. "Mother, are you all right?"

"Yes!" Randy yelled the word amid laughter. "Go away!"

"What's wrong?" Evie yelled through the door.

"Something came loose on the bed," Jake yelled. "Go help Teresa with dinner, and make sure the boys have that side of beef roasting."

"Oh dear Lord," Evie said through the door. "Mother, you will never live this one down! We have company right downstairs!"

"Evie, just go!" Randy called to her. She broke into laughter again as Jake held her close inside the quilt.

It took both of them a few minutes to stop laughing.

"Oh, Jake, Evie was right. I'll never live this one down! You always find a way to humiliate me."

"That's because it's so much fun watching you blush when we're around other people." Jake kissed her several times over until they sobered.

"Jake, I'm scared," she told him. She threw her arms around his neck. "Everything has been so good between us lately. Why this, now?"

"Let's wait and see. Maybe this isn't nearly as bad as we think it might be." He rose and pulled her up with him. "You should see yourself. Your hair is a mess, and your dress all wrinkled. You'll have to change."

Randy ran her fingers through her hair. "And I'll have to repin this, thanks to you." She shook her hair out. "Honestly, Jake. How many times have you done this to me? People will think we were doing more in that bed than we were."

"You know me. I don't care *what* they think."

"You don't get embarrassed as easily as I do." Randy laughed. "The worst part is we'll need to send someone up here to fix the bed."

Jake left her and pulled on his denim pants. "It's probably just a couple of loose screws where the frame fits into the headboard. I'll take a look at it and fix it myself. Will that make you feel better?"

"Much better."

He buttoned his pants and studied her lovingly. "Randy, thank you for being so nice to Gretta. Not many wives would understand."

"And not many men grew up like you did." She gave him a chiding look. "However, I can't forget that she once said you reek of sex. I'm quite sure she didn't mind having your arm around her all the way from that fence line to the house."

Jake grinned. "Hell, I was just being polite."

"Mmm-hmm. And women like that can walk all over you."

"Hell, *you* walk all over me." He walked closer and wrapped her in his arms.

"I'm not so sure it isn't the other way around," she told him, breathing in his familiar scent. "And you smell so good I *would* like to go to bed with you right now, if the circumstances were right. And now the bed is broken."

"We can always use the floor."

She wiggled away from him. "We *have* to get back downstairs!"

Jake began tucking in his shirt. "Yes, ma'am. And don't be worrying about Gretta and whatever it is she needs. My whole worthless life depends on you being well and happy. This is the most we've laughed in a long time."

"It is, isn't it?" She rushed up to him and stood on her tiptoes to give him a quick kiss. "Go ahead downstairs. I am going to make up the bed so it isn't a mess, in case Lloyd decides to come up here and fix it." She left him and closed the washroom door, then covered her face at her embarrassment. "Oh, dear Lord." The only good thing about the bed collapse was it had helped relieve their worry over why Gretta MacBain had paid them a visit in the first place. "God help us," she said quietly as she repinned her hair.

Thirty-seven

JAKE LIT A CIGARETTE AS HE WATCHED GRETTA STROLL toward where he sat in his favorite leather chair in front of the fireplace. She wore a soft-green high-necked dress, and her hair was pulled back and tied into a tail at the back of her neck. Again, she wore no makeup and no jewelry. He couldn't help respecting her attempt to look the part for the sake of the women and children.

The house was already getting noisy with family again, and the smell of fresh bread filled the air. Stephen was sent out to check with the ranch hands and find out if the side of beef they were roasting was ready yet. Lloyd came inside toting Donavan on one arm. He came over to sit down across from Jake just as Gretta sat in a rocker near them. She grinned at Jake.

"A little problem upstairs?" she asked. "That was quite a crash I heard, and the laughter was infectious. You had me laughing into my pillow."

Jake smiled back at her as he drew on his cigarette. "Apparently, we've worn out our bed."

Lloyd set Donavan on a braided rug and gave him a rattle. "What the hell is she talking about, Pa?"

Jake kept the cigarette between his lips and leaned back in the chair, putting his long legs up on a footstool in front of him. "The damn bed broke. It was funny as hell at the time, but your mother is so embarrassed, I'm not sure she'll come down and join us. And we were *not* doing what you're thinking. We were just messing around."

"Jesus, Pa, when are you two going to get old enough to stop behaving like kids?"

"Never, if I can help it."

Gretta laughed, looking him over with womanly appreciation. "I have a feeling your wife feels the same way."

"Just don't kid her about it," Jake told her. He looked at Lloyd. "Evie was here, and she came pounding on the door like she thought somebody had died. You know Evie. I told her just now not to say anything to your mother. I'm still not sure what she'll take as funny or what will hurt her, and I'm sure I can fix the bed myself. And don't be thinking we were romping around like teenagers. We were doing no such thing."

"Oh, so she really believes no one knows you two still act like damn newlyweds half the time?" Lloyd asked.

Jake took a drag on his cigarette. "Don't talk to me about behaving like newlyweds. You're the one who has a pregnant wife who just stopped nursing a baby not even a year old yet."

Gretta laughed again, raising a foot and shoving Lloyd's leg with it. "He's got you there, you handsome devil."

Jake drew on the cigarette again. "For once, we don't have someone or something to worry about as far as danger or being hunted. It's nice to be healed and finally have some peace." He noticed Gretta's smile fade at his remark. "Lloyd, I told Gretta about Brad Buckley. I *had* to. I was afraid she'd bring up his name in front of your mother. We can trust her not to tell anyone."

Lloyd glanced at Gretta. "That's damn important, Gretta. We aren't even sure Mom remembers killing Brad, but he was dying anyway because of things my father did to him." He looked away. "...things he deserved."

Gretta glanced at Jake, seeing that hint of revenge in his dark eyes. "I'm sure he *did* deserve them. I couldn't have a lower opinion of the bastard if I tried."

Randy finally came down the stairs, looking radiant

in Jake's favorite yellow dress. Her hair was pulled back at the sides, and she'd pinned some tiny flowers into it from a bouquet in the vase on the bedroom dresser. She walked up to Jake and leaned down to kiss him. "Say one embarrassing word, and I will divorce you," she told him.

Jake glanced at her cleavage, very tempted to do exactly what she'd ordered him not to do. "Yes, dear," he replied with a grin.

Randy held her chin proudly and glanced at Gretta. "I'm sorry if we…woke you."

Gretta couldn't help laughing. "And here I thought it would be nice and peaceful on the ranch."

Randy smiled and turned to walk to the kitchen area of the great room. Jake rose, tossing his cigarette into the fireplace. He hurried up behind her to slip his arms around her waist.

Gretta looked at Lloyd. "How old are those two?"

Lloyd shook his head as he, too, got up. "Sixteen," he answered.

Gretta laughed lightly as she followed Lloyd into the kitchen.

"That food ready yet?" Jake asked Evie as he kissed Randy's hair, then her cheek.

"Yes," Evie answered, giving her parents a knowing smile. "I'm sure you two have worked up an appetite."

Teresa giggled, and in the next moment, every adult was laughing.

"Evie, I told you we weren't doing what it seemed like we were doing," Jake scolded.

"Daddy, I can't help it. And besides, it's nice to see you and mother so happy."

There followed more teasing, lots of eating, talk of other things, and through it all, Gretta was accepted at the table as though she was part of the family. A meal of huge steaks from the side of beef Rodriguez had cooked was served, so much food that not even the men could finish it.

"Outlaw can have the bones, can't he, Grampa?" Sadie Mae asked Jake.

"That's better than feeding him chicken eggs," Jake answered with a wink.

Sadie Mae covered her mouth and laughed. "Don't tell our secret, Grampa."

"Oh, I won't. I promise."

"Who is Outlaw?" Gretta asked. "I know that's what you call your horse, but horses don't eat steak bones and chicken eggs."

"Outlaw is our dog!" Tricia said proudly.

"Your dog?" She looked at Jake. "Is every animal on this ranch called Outlaw?"

"Seems that way," Jake answered. "The horse I rode when I met Randy was also called Outlaw. Kind of fitting for me, don't you think? To be surrounded by outlaws?"

Everyone chuckled, but Jake could feel the tension building. Why was Gretta here?

Coffee and pie followed the meal, but Gretta set her fork down early. "I can't imagine how you women stay so slim, the way everyone eats here on the J&L," she commented.

And through it all, Gretta looked like she'd been fighting back tears. Jake wanted to believe it was because she was being so kindly treated, but he feared it was much more than that. He exchanged a look with Randy and knew she'd noticed the same thing.

Finally, Jake ordered the boys to take Tricia and Sadie Mae to Lloyd's house and watch them and let them play.

"Grampa, we want to stay here," Little Jake complained.

"We have some important things to talk about," he answered. "Just mind what I say, Little Jake."

The boys seldom argued with their grandfather's orders. They left with the girls, Teresa following them.

Evie turned to Gretta once the children had left. "It's time you told us what's going on. We all can tell there is something wrong, Gretta. You helped us once, so tell us how we can help you now."

They remained around the kitchen table. Gretta glanced at the doorway, where Jake's guns hung high over the door frame. She closed her eyes and just sat there a moment, putting a hand over her eyes.

"I don't know how to say this. You're all so happy now." She looked at Jake with tears in her eyes. "I don't know where else to turn."

Jake sighed, lighting a cigarette. "I'm pretty sure this involves me, so just say it, Gretta."

Gretta swallowed, scanning every face around the table. Good people. People who'd been through enough. "I...have a daughter."

Katie took a quick, deep breath, and they all looked surprised. Jake glanced at Randy, who seemed to wither a little at the remark. Already she suspected where this was heading, as did everyone else in the room.

Jake frowned. "How old is she?"

Gretta met his gaze, deciding she might as well get this over with. "Fifteen—the same age I was when I had her."

Jake took the cigarette from his lips and sighed deeply. "And she's in trouble," he said, as though to speak Gretta's very next words.

Gretta quickly wiped at a tear that slipped down her cheek. "Yes. She's... I..." She sniffed and swallowed. "You all should first know how I ended up...doing what I do."

"Gretta, you don't need to—"

"Yes, I do," Gretta interrupted Evie. "I'm not just some man-hungry, loose woman. I was like any other happy young girl, till my parents were killed in a fire when I was ten. An uncle took me in." She covered her eyes. "I don't think I need to explain beyond that.

Within six months he was…using his strength to make me do things I didn't want to do."

"Dear God," Katie whispered.

"By the time I was twelve, he was selling me to other men, and my career, if you want to call it that, was born. By fifteen, I had a baby, and I had no idea which man was the father. I gave her away to a decent, Christian couple who couldn't have children. From then on, I figured I didn't deserve a decent man, so I did what I knew best…to survive." She put on a pretend smile. "After a while, you don't think about the bad parts anymore. I decided that if this was going to be my way of life, I'd make damn good money from it, and I have. But all these fifteen years, I've kept an eye on my daughter. I named her Annette Marie—my mother's name. She's beautiful, and she has no idea I'm her mother."

She took a deep breath and wiped at another tear and stared at her coffee cup as she explained about Luis Estava and Annie's disappearance. "Fifteen-year-old girls who've never seen the bad side of life are easy to fool. Loretta, the woman who adopted her, said she didn't trust this man at all. Her suspicions proved right. She hired a man by the name of Jesse Valencia to go look for Annie. He was something like a private investigator mixed with a bounty hunter." She glanced at Jake, then at Randy. "I don't know how to tell you this."

"He didn't make it back alive," Jake said, already sure what Gretta was after.

Gretta nodded her head. "A man from Texas came all the way to Denver to tell me. He was a simple farmer, a kind, sweet man. Valencia made it as far as his place… all shot up. This farmer—Otis Clark—he nursed him. Valencia wrote down some information before he finally died of infection, and Mr. Clark brought me his notes. He was afraid I wouldn't get them if he didn't bring them himself." She broke into tears. "I wanted my daughter to have a normal life and marry a decent man and never go through what I did," she sobbed. "Now I fear the worst! Valencia wrote down the name of the brothel where he'd found her…where they take the prettiest girls. They send the rest someplace else. I'm sure Annie would be…one of the prettiest ones. She's a beautiful girl, but so damn innocent. She knew nothing about men. God knows what they have done to her."

Evie shivered, and Brian reached over and took her hand.

"I'm sorry, Evie," Gretta sniffed. "I should have been more sensitive, after what you've been through."

"You have no choice but to tell us all of it," Evie replied. "We can't help you if we don't know everything."

"But none of you should have to be involved in this. I saw in that courtroom last summer what a close family you are. It's all the love that judge saw that made him let Jake go. And now I'm taking your father away from you in a different way." She looked pleadingly at Jake. "I can't hire lawmen to go there, because they aren't allowed to cross into Mexico. Besides that, they aren't about to help the likes of me, not even for my daughter. You're the only man I could think of who actually understands and cares about women like me. And you'd fit right in down in Mexico. Those men down there are vicious. If I sent some other man, they'd know in a minute who the gringo was and why he was there. You could… I mean, you're part Mexican, and you know the language, and you know how to behave like—"

"Like one of them?"

Gretta saw a darkness already moving into his eyes. "Yes. You know that world, Jake. You'd find ways to fit right in." She looked down at her lap. "I'm so sorry to come here and interrupt all of your lives, but I didn't know where else to turn. When I read that article about what you did in Boulder…it reminded me how good you are with guns, and that you were once a U.S. Marshal. And I remembered how concerned you were that Mike Holt might have hurt me." She shook her head. "Me. A *whore*. And then I realized you might do this—not for me—but for a fifteen-year-old girl who doesn't deserve the terror she must be living in right now." She met his gaze again. "You were the only person I could think of who might be willing to help."

Everyone remained silent for a few minutes. Jake looked from Gretta to Randy and saw the devastation in his wife's eyes. She knew he couldn't turn Gretta down, but he'd promised her he'd never ride off into danger again. He'd promised never to leave her for anything but a night of work on the J&L. He leaned back and rubbed at his eyes. "Did Valencia write down the name of the brothel?"

Already, Randy knew there would be no arguing. There was nothing Jake hated worse than a woman being mistreated, especially when she was an innocent young girl. Jake's father had raped Jake's sweetheart, after all, and she'd been only twelve. Fifteen-year-old Jake had killed him for that, and lived with a constant need to make up for his inability to help Santana. He'd been only a boy.

Randy felt her heart breaking. She would lose her Jake again. She'd watch him ride away and straight into hell for a young girl he didn't even know. All the fun and laughter they'd shared earlier was gone now. Already, she could see Jake falling backward…spiraling into the depths of a past that had never let him go. Rage and revenge and his outlaw spirit were fast welling up in his soul. Soon, he would be unreachable.

Thirty-eight

THE ROOM HUNG QUIET. EVERY PERSON PRESENT WAS lost in thought and despair while Gretta took a moment to regain her composure. "The note is in Spanish," she told Jake, "but Otis asked someone to interpret it for him, and in English it means…House of Heavenly Women." She picked up a cloth napkin to wipe at her eyes. "My God, I feel so awful about this. All of you have to understand this was the hardest decision of my life. You don't owe me anything, but I have nowhere else to turn." She wiped at more tears and faced Jake, her stomach tightening at the look on his face. He hardly looked like Jake Harkner, the affable, handsome family man. He was someone else, and the darkness in his eyes was overwhelming.

"Otis said he was told that the place is heavily guarded," she told Jake. "There are lots of men there who know how to use guns. And it's run by a white man named Sidney Wayland. The brothel is just across the Rio Grande from Brownsville, Texas, so if she's still there, you wouldn't have to go far."

Randy noticed Jake stiffened at the mention of Brownsville. He put a hand to his chest as though he felt pain. "She's still there, all right," Jake said. "If she's as pretty as you say, she's still there. Do you have a picture?"

"Yes." She took a photograph from a pocket on her dress and handed it to Jake with a shaking hand. He studied it a moment.

"Jesus, she looks twelve."

The rage in his soul was palpable. Gretta had never seen nor felt such darkness. Jake handed the picture to Lloyd, and from him it passed around to the whole family.

"Where is this uncle of yours now?" he asked Gretta.

"Dead."

"Good, because if he wasn't, I'd hunt him down, and he'd *be* dead when I got through with him." He snuffed out his cigarette in the remains of a piece of pie. "Any idea what tactic this man Valencia used? Maybe they saw him right away as some kind of lawman, or maybe he just grabbed your daughter and tried to run off with her."

"I have no idea," Gretta admitted. "Loretta is the one who hired him. I never even met the man, but I repaid her the two hundred dollars she spent, and I will pay you well if you do this."

"I don't want any pay. I don't need it, and I wouldn't do something like this for money."

"Nevertheless, I'll feel much better if you let me pay you. I brought almost four thousand dollars with me. Take it with you. It's easy to bribe men like the ones who have my Annie, and one dollar American goes twice as far in Mexico. You might even be able to buy my daughter back. That would be the easiest way to get her out of there."

Jake stared at the picture again when it came back to him. "Buying her won't stop what's going on down there. Someone needs to kill Sidney Wayland."

Randy gasped. "Jake, no!"

"Pa, you're not a lawman anymore," Lloyd reminded him, "and even if you were, American lawmen can't go into Mexico."

"Jake, going there to kill a man could land you in a Mexican prison the rest of your life…or worse!" Gretta reminded him. "I'm not asking you to do something like that. I just want my daughter back."

The look in his eyes actually frightened her.

"This will keep happening if the man in charge isn't gotten rid of. It's that simple." Jake rose and walked across the room to the fireplace at the other end. "I'll have to pose as a customer, maybe even a buyer, like you said." He ran a hand through his hair, turning and packing back and forth in an odd frustration.

"Jake, what aren't you telling us?" Randy asked.

He braced his arm against the fireplace mantel and rested his head on his arm. "I grew up in Brownsville." The words came out as though he was in pain.

Randy quickly got up and walked closer to him. "Jake?"

He straightened, putting his hands on his hips and taking a deep breath. "That's where I spent those first ugly years," he said through gritted teeth. "Once I left, I never went back. Never! Not to Brownsville and not even back to Texas. I haven't even thought about Brownsville in years."

"Jesus," Lloyd said under his breath. "Pa, you know what going there will do to you," he said louder. He left the table and joined Jake and Randy at the fireplace. "I don't like any of this!"

"She's *fifteen*!" Jake roared. "And she's Gretta's *daughter*!"

"And I'm not letting you go down there alone!"

"Yes, you *will* let me go alone! You have a wife and three kids, another one on the way, and you still aren't healed after a whole year of pain and hell. Not to mention you have an eighty-thousand-acre ranch to run and a bunkhouse full of men out there who depend on you for their *jobs*. And if something happens to me, you've got your mother to think about. She can't lose us both, Lloyd! She can't lose us *both*!"

"I can't lose *you*!" Randy pleaded. "Not now, Jake!"

Gretta broke into renewed tears. "I'm so sorry."

Evie stared at her father, grief written all over her face. "Daddy, I know you. You'll go after her because that's what you do, but I have an awful feeling about this. And if something happens that sets your temper off…you know what that will do to you. You could end up in a Mexican prison, or worse."

"Jake, you'd better think this one over really good," Brian warned. "One man has already died. I know he probably didn't compare to you when it comes to using a gun, but you should still take someone with you. If not Lloyd, then a couple of the ranch hands. Cole and Terrel are good shots."

"*I* should go!" Lloyd argued in a near rage. "We've had each other's backs since we rode together in Oklahoma. I'm not letting you do this alone, Pa!"

"Lloyd, you *can't*!" Katie protested, breaking into tears. "I'm going to have another baby. And you have the ranch to run. My God, Lloyd, don't leave all this. You know Jake is right. You can't go with him."

Jake faced them with determination. "Katie's right. Of every member of this family, I'm the one who's needed the least," he told them.

Evie gasped. "Daddy, don't say that!"

"I didn't mean it that way," Katie told him, tears starting to come.

"I know that."

Jake began to pace. Randy knew the signs. No one would be able to argue with him, not even Lloyd. In minutes he'd turned from a gentle, loving husband and affable grandfather to someone else…to the man she'd first met and feared. And she knew deep inside that the possibility of bringing his past right in front of his eyes again was what had him the most upset.

"Every person in this room is a keeper of the J&L," Jake told the family, finally standing still to face them. "You all represent the future of this place. I'll never truly fit into that future. I'm part of a past that will never be again."

There it was! Lloyd realized why his father had been so restless the last few weeks. It was as though he'd known something like this was coming. He wanted to grab Jake and beg him not to go, but he knew better. "Pa, you have to let me and a couple other men go with you."

Jake shook his head. "No. Not you. Not my son. I already watched you die, or close enough as to make no difference. You're too important to this whole family, and I'll not let anyone else risk his life over this. I'll talk to the men. Maybe Cole can go with me, but only him."

Randy turned away. "Jake, you promised not to leave me again."

"I know what I promised, but I can't let this go, Randy. You have to trust in me. We both knew when we talked upstairs that I might end up having to go away."

Gretta spoke up. "Jake, I could go too. I could claim I'm looking for new girls."

Evie broke into tears, covering her face as Brian put an arm around her and drew her close.

"I won't take the risk of you ending up in their hands any more than I'd risk my own wife or daughter," Jake told Gretta. "It doesn't matter what you are. You're a *woman*, and I won't risk any woman's life. I can do this alone. The only reason I'm taking Cole is for backup to get Annie out of there if I'm..." He hesitated. "If I don't make it out."

"Damn it, Pa, I know we can do this together!"

Jake faced Lloyd, his countenance like a rolling thunderstorm. He looked ready to explode with a mixture of determined anger and undying love. "You've followed me to hell and back too many times," he told his son. "You're the most decent and most loyal son a man could ask for, but you're also a *father*, and young enough to learn how to live with all the new laws and new ways. It won't be long before you'll have to defend this ranch against the changes that are coming. If you don't stay here and stay healthy, the ranch could be broken up and parceled out. You're smart and educated, and you'll know how to handle things without violence. And violence is all I know, son."

Lloyd held his gaze, his eyes teary, his jaw flexing in horrible indecision. "What if you get shot? I can't let you die alone, Pa. No man should die alone, especially not my…" His voice choked. "Not my father."

Randy covered her face and wept. Jake looked at her, pain ripping through his heart. He could lose her again. She was still so fragile. He turned away. "In spite of your mother and this family, in a way I've been alone my whole life, Lloyd. You know what I'm talking about. It's a different kind of alone."

"You aren't going down there just to find Gretta's daughter, are you? You're going down there to prove something to yourself. You grew up by the gun, and you think you should *die* by the gun. I saw it in your eyes when we had that talk after that deal with Brady. Some little part of you gave up right then. I heard it in your voice. You saw the future, and you think you don't belong in it, but you do, Pa! You do belong in it—for Stephen and Ben and Little Jake and the girls…for me and Evie…and for that woman standing beside you—the woman you just pulled back from hell and made whole again. That's what you do, Pa. You pull people back from hell because you know what hell is like.

"So you go ahead and go to Mexico and take that girl out of *her* hell, because I know not one person here is going to be able to stop you, including Mom. But you, by God, had better not give up. You've survived a hell of a lot, so don't be using this as your excuse to finally give it all up, Jake Harkner!"

It struck Gretta that there was far more going on here than Jake rescuing her daughter. Did the man have a death wish? He was surely a tortured soul, in spite of the big, loving family that surrounded him…in spite of the woman who'd given up so much for him. She realized she probably didn't know half of what Randy Harkner had been through in her married life, over and above what happened to her last winter. "I'm so sorry," she told them again. "I wish I wasn't the one asking this. I'll leave, and I will find someone else—"

"No!" Jake answered. "Once you mentioned Brownsville, I knew it had to be me."

Randy wiped at her eyes and faced him with determination. "You've left me before, and I was always sure you would do everything in your power to make it back. But something about you is different this time. I'm looking at Jake, the outlaw who thinks he's worthless. But he's worth a hell of a lot to a lot of people, and he's my life. So you come back, damn you! You come back, because when I die, I'm not going to be *buried* up at that line shack alone. Do you understand me, Jake? We're going to live and love together for a lot more years, and one day we'll be buried *together* up on that mountain. Don't you take that away from me, Jake Harkner! Don't you *dare* consider yourself dispensable to this family—and not ever dispensable to me! You know damn well how much I need you!"

Jake studied her a long, silent moment, a spark of the abused little boy flickering in his dark eyes. "I have something to do besides going after Gretta's daughter, Randy. You know what I'm talking about." He walked past her. "I'm going out to talk to Cole, and I need to find Rodriguez. He knows the right things to pack in my gear for me." He paused at the doorway. "And all of you understand something. I don't want one person in this family blaming Gretta for this. It is what it is, whether her daughter or someone else's. And, Gretta, none of this is your fault. If anything, it's your uncle's. If he was here right now, I'd make him a sorry man for what he did to you." He reached up and took down his guns from where they hung over the door, then faced Gretta. "Pack some underclothes and a dress and give them to Rodriguez. Your daughter might need something decent to wear when I find her." He started out again.

"Daddy!" Evie shouted before he could get out the door.

Jake hesitated. "Don't say it, Evie. You won't change my mind."

"I don't intend to try. All I want is your promise that you won't go riding off in the morning without all of us being there to pray for you first."

Jake sighed and leaned against the doorjamb. "You don't give up, do you?" He faced her, his brows lowered.

"No, I don't. I'm a *Harkner*. I didn't give up on myself or my marriage after Dune Hollow, and you aren't going to give up just because you're getting older and you think you don't belong on this earth any longer. You forget how well we all know you and how you think. The Good Lord knows we've all had our share of time talking you out of these moods. But once you're gone from here, we'll have to leave what happens up to God Himself. He will be the one who chooses when you leave this world, Jake Harkner, not you. I prefer to ask Him to bring you back here, and with that girl. So don't you dare leave without letting us pray for you!"

Jake shook his head and turned. "Lloyd, go upstairs and fix that goddamn bed." He walked out.

Not one of them could help smiling through their tears. Only Jake would say such a thing at such a serious time.

Randy looked at Gretta.

"I'm sorry, Randy," Gretta told her. "But Annie is the only good thing I've ever accomplished in my life. I can't leave her down there with those animals."

"Of course you can't. And you couldn't have picked a better man to go after her." *Jake! You promised not to leave me again! You promised!*

Gretta looked at her lap, Jake's remark about packing clothes for Annie playing over again in her mind and giving her hope. He'd said "*when* I find her"…not "*if* I find her."

Thirty-nine

RANDY SAT ON A QUILTED BENCH BESIDE A BEDROOM window, listening to the bellow of cattle, the occasional whinny of a horse, the hoot of an owl…and in the distant mountains the howl of wolves, the sound Jake hated.

She felt empty and alone. Jake hadn't returned since leaving the house earlier. Wouldn't he even come back to hold her one more night? Maybe he thought it was better to stay away, to just leave without making love to her one more time—maybe that would make the leaving easier.

Her heart raced faster when she heard a noise downstairs, some rustling sounds, the squeak of one of the stairs as someone came up. She rose from the bench and waited. The door opened, and there was no mistaking his big frame in the moonlight. "Jake—"

He walked up to her, and in a breath, she was in his arms, her feet off the floor. He held her against him with one arm and wrapped his other hand in her hair.

"I'm so sorry, Randy, but I have to do this," he told her.

"I understand."

"Don't be scared. It's like we talked about. We're always together in spirit, even when I'm gone. It was like that back in Oklahoma, and it will be the same this time."

She kept her arms tightly wrapped around his neck, deliberately breathing deeply of his familiar scent. She was used to the smell of tobacco, and it didn't bother

her. His scent was all man…all leather and sage and just Jake.

"I left my boots and all my gear downstairs. Is it safe to leave my guns out? Are all the kids gone?"

"Yes. It's just us. Gretta went to sleep at Evie's house. She knew we'd want to be alone."

"Is the bed fixed?"

Randy jerked in a sob. "Yes. Oh, Jake, I was afraid you wouldn't come up here. I was afraid you'd think it was best we didn't do this before you leave."

He carried her to the bed and laid her on it. "I considered it, but just like all the other times, I couldn't stay away." He met her lips in a desperate kiss. "I want to remember every inch of you," he told her. "Every move you make, every curve, the way you taste, your breath, your voice." He pulled up on her gown as he spoke.

Randy sat up, and he pulled the gown over her head and tossed it aside. She wore no underwear, hoping for this moment.

"Don't move," he told her. By the moonlight, she watched him remove his shirt, his denim pants, his long johns. He climbed back onto the bed. There was nothing more to say. He met her mouth again as he moved on top of her, kissing her almost violently. When they found themselves in this kind of situation, his lovemaking was always more deliberate, wilder, more demanding, as though he needed to see and taste and touch her as thoroughly as possible so he wouldn't forget, so he could take her with him in his mind and heart.

His hands were everywhere, caressing, massaging, exploring. She let him do what he needed to do, wanting the memory as much as he did. He kissed and licked and spoke to her in Spanish, moving over her eyes, her lips, her throat, massaged her breasts as he suckled them hungrily, as though tasting a delicious meal. His hands and lips worked their way over her belly, her hip bones, down her thighs. He gently pushed her legs apart and tasted and licked every secret place until she groaned from the ecstasy of his touch.

When he was in this mood, she always just let him ravage her in that strange way he had of making her completely helpless under his spell. It was so much like that first night…in the middle of nowhere…in the back of a wagon. Back then, Jake Harkner had guarded her on the way west and ended up saving her life. Then he'd taken that life and bent it to his will, claiming her in a way that had left her branded.

This was the reason she trusted him, the reason she always waited for him…always. The man was like a drug she couldn't resist. Her only fear was that this time he could be saying goodbye for more than just one trip. This could be his way of remembering her as he prepared to die.

No! He'd come back to her! He'd come back!

He licked his way back over her body to her lips. Randy grasped the slats of the headboard as first he entered her teasingly, knowing she was close to an intense climax. He wanted to be inside her when it happened, for her ultimate pleasure. His tantalizing thrusts took her to that place where utter, desperate ecstasy surged through her loins. As her insides pulled at him in her climax, he pushed deep with an erection that felt bigger than normal, and normal had always been all she could handle. She literally gritted her teeth as he grasped her bottom and grunted with every thrust. He buried his face in her hair as she grimaced from the power of the man.

"Do you know how much I love your perfect bottom?" he asked.

She didn't reply. She just enjoyed the way he plied her bottom while pushing hard. It helped the pain a little. She wanted to tell him it hurt, but she was not about to spoil this very necessary mating of souls. It could be the last time they did this. Climaxing while he entered her made the pain more bearable, an erotic experience of agony and pleasure.

"Who do you belong to?" he groaned.

"Jake Harkner," she moaned, still clinging to the headboard.

"Every inch of you. No one else will ever own your soul, Randy Harkner."

Why did he say that? Of course no other man would ever own her. She let go of the headboard and raised up enough to wrap her arms around his neck. "Don't talk that way."

"*Yo te amo, mi quiero. Siempre recuerdes cuanto te amo.*"

Always remember how much I love you. When he spoke to her in Spanish, it only heightened her desire and her love for him.

His life spilled into her in hard pulses. Their lovemaking had always been like this back in Oklahoma, each time before he rode away into No Man's Land. It was a feeling Randy always hoped she'd never have to experience again. Yet here he was, riding away again, after promising he wouldn't. The only way she could stand it was knowing he truly didn't have a choice. How could he say no to Gretta, when a child's life was on the line?

That was the one thing Jake Harkner couldn't stand. Every abused woman was young Santana, or his mother. His whole life he'd tried to make up for being too little to help her when his father killed her. The horror of what it must have been like, of having to help bury his own mother and hide the murder was unimaginable. It was a miracle he'd managed to stay halfway sane, and she knew deep inside that the only way he did that was to believe that every man he'd killed was his father—over and over again.

He met her mouth in a deep, demanding kiss. She

could taste herself on his lips. He moved his mouth to her throat.

"Jake, I want to taste you. I want to remember."

"You don't have to."

"I want to."

He rolled to his side with a groan. His countenance was not that of the man who'd been gently making love to her these past many months. He was Jake the outlaw, and that made it easier to let her do this. He grasped her hair tightly as she kissed her way down his powerful chest and flat stomach. She realized she didn't care that he'd just been inside her, that he tasted of a mixture of their sweet juices. He grew hard again in moments from her gentle kisses and licks, to the point where she could take him fully into her mouth and remind herself that this could be beautiful. This was Jake. This was Jake.

"My God, Randy." He gripped her hair tighter.

She kissed her way back up and over his powerful arms, straddling him as she met his mouth, her hair shrouding his face. He reached down and guided himself into her, grasping her thighs then pushing up to fill her. She rocked herself over him for several minutes, until he turned her onto her back and began his own powerful thrusts all over again, this time taking longer—both because he'd just climaxed, and because they both wanted this to last forever and forever.

When his life spilled into her a second time, she felt him tremble. "I'm so goddamn sorry, Randy," he told her yet again, moving to his side and keeping her close. "If I make it back, I want you to be just like this. Don't be scared anymore. I'm always with you. Always."

"How will I sleep at night without you?"

He kissed her hair. "Back in Oklahoma, when Evie was missing and I wanted to die—when you were far away, having that surgery, and we couldn't be together in the worst time of our lives—I walked into our house after those men had ransacked it," he told her. "But when I went into the bedroom, it was untouched. God didn't let them destroy that place where we shared each other in the best way there is. I took up your pillow and put it to my face, and I could smell your rose scent, and it made me feel like I was with you. Hold my pillow, baby, and just pretend it's me in your arms, because I will be, understand? I will be right here with you. Nothing can change that. You've kept me sane all these years. I'd have no life without you."

She curled into him, her back against his chest. She grasped the powerful arms he'd wrapped around her. "Don't give up, Jake. If you find where you used to live, remember I'm right there with you too. Okay? I'm right there with you. Don't let it take you into that dark place. Stay in the light."

He sighed and hugged her even closer. "It's been forty-five years since I rode away from there for the last time, but it's still all so vivid." He nestled his face into her hair, drinking in her scent, wanting to remember it. "I doubt I'll even remember where to look for that shack of a house. It's not likely it's even still there. The main thing I remember is a hackberry tree high on a hill behind the house. It wasn't very big then, but big enough to produce those little dark berries. I remember it because"—he hesitated, his grip around her tightening—"that's where my father…dug the hole and threw my mother and Tommy into it. Some of those berries fell into the hole." He made an odd groaning sound. "I wanted to jump in there with them."

Randy kissed his arm. It was as rigid as a rock. "Jake, remember you have a big family who loves you. You aren't that scared little boy anymore."

Jake swallowed. "I should have gone back years ago and at least tried to find where my mother and brother are buried…maybe put some kind of marker there."

Randy closed her eyes. "You shouldn't do that alone, Jake."

"I can do it because I've *needed* to do it all these years. I would feel like I've done something to make up for not being able to help them."

Randy rubbed his arms. "If you manage to find anything left of where you grew up, I'll be standing right beside you, Jake. You remember that."

He moved one arm away and let out a short gasp. Randy knew he was wiping at tears. "I'll remember."

"You come back, Jake. Come back to the life you have here and now—the life God has blessed you with. To the son and daughter who worship the ground you walk on, and those grandsons who desperately need your guidance, and those little granddaughters who will need you to watch out for them. Even more when they're old enough for young men to notice them. Heaven knows anyone interested in your granddaughters will play hell getting anywhere near them."

He put his arm back around her. "You bet they will. And first they'll have to get past Brian and Lloyd. That will be bad enough. When they get to me they'll be shaking in their boots."

Randy smiled, glad to get his mind on something else.

He sighed deeply, taking hold of her left hand and holding it up. "What is that thing on your fourth finger that's sparkling in the moonlight?"

"It's the incredibly beautiful new wedding ring you bought me last summer in Denver."

"That's right. Every time you look at that ring, you remember who loves you beyond life itself. I promise to do all in my power to come back, all right?" He ran a hand over her breasts and turned her toward him, meeting her mouth in another searching kiss. "You have loved me through so many bad times, when you shouldn't have loved me at all. How does a man thank a woman for something like that?"

Randy kissed his chest. "He never leaves her without

coming back, that's how. And he makes her feel like the most beautiful woman on the face of the earth by the way he makes love to her." She kissed his chin. "So make me feel beautiful again, Jake."

She could see his smile in the soft moonlight. "I haven't ravaged you enough?"

"Not when I know you're going away."

"You know, it would be awfully embarrassing if we have to send Lloyd back up here to fix the bed again. I hope he got those screws back in good and tight."

"Oh my! I didn't think of that."

He pressed a hand to her belly and moved his fingers inside her to reignite the fires of desire that licked at her depths. "Too late." He moved over her again, and all talking stopped.

Forty

SOMETIME IN THE NIGHT THEY MADE LOVE AGAIN, gently, desperately, adoringly, deeply. But all too soon, morning brought reality. Jake was up first, after kissing Randy and handing her a peppermint stick.

"Oh, Jake! I don't want it to be morning."

"Thank you for last night. I hurt you, didn't I?"

"It's all right. I wanted it that way." She rolled onto her back. "I want to always remember."

He put the peppermint stick into her hand. "Do you know how beautiful you are in the morning?"

"Oh my goodness, after what we did last night, I must be a complete mess."

He kissed her eyes. "A mess with big, gray-green eyes and long, golden hair." He squeezed her hand around the peppermint stick. "Lay this on the stand beside the bed. I want to see it still there when I get back. I'm okay, Randy. I know what I have to do when I get to Brownsville, and after that, I'll get that girl out of Mexico."

Randy took the candy and leaned up to kiss him. "Jake, what will you do? I'm scared for you."

He got up from the bed. "I have to do this on my own." He walked into the washroom. "You rest right there while I clean up. I have to hurry up and get downstairs before any of the kids get here. If I know Evie and Lloyd, they'll be up early, wanting to see me off, and every kid on this ranch will come with them. I have guns lying on the kitchen table, and I need to load some of them."

He went into the washroom and closed the door. Randy sat up, kissing the peppermint stick and laying it on the night stand. It would be like all the times he'd ridden into danger when he was a marshal, only this time, Lloyd wouldn't be with him, and he would be so far, far away.

Everything went fast after that. Too fast. Jake washed and dressed and Randy hurried behind. She brushed her shoulder-length hair and pinned it back at the sides, then hurriedly dressed, leaving off most of her petticoats. She chose a yellow-checkered dress because Jake loved the color and loved the neckline. It was a simple dress but fit well. He loved dresses that showed off her shape.

Be strong, Randy, she told herself. *Be strong for him so it won't be so hard for him to leave.* She hurried down the stairs and put a kettle of coffee on the coal cooking stove and lit a fire under it. She didn't want to look, but she had to. She'd deliberately avoided seeing what she didn't want to see when she first came down the stairs, keeping herself busy with the coffee and setting out some bread.

Finally, she had no choice. Already her husband was strapping on his famous .44s. He wore denim pants, the blue shirt she loved, and a brown leather vest, looking both incredibly handsome and incredibly dangerous at the same time.

He shoved another handgun into the back of his gun belt. Every loop in that belt had a cartridge in it. Another belt of cartridges lay on the kitchen table. He would take that along and likely wear it over his shoulder when he reached Mexico. A repeating rifle and a shotgun lay on the kitchen table. He packed more cartridges and some shotgun slugs into a saddlebag and set everything, including a duffel bag of clothes, near the door. Then he took his black Stetson down from where it hung on the wall and set it with his gear.

"Tricia and Sadie Mae will be afraid of you, looking

like you do right now," Randy told him. "They've never seen you quite so decked out with guns, and they've certainly never seen your dark side."

"They won't be afraid. They know their grandpa."

Someone knocked. "Mother, are you decent?"

Randy looked at Jake and smiled. "Am I?"

He walked up to her and leaned down to plant a long kiss on her mouth. "No. You're the most indecent woman I've ever known."

"You did that to me. I used to be decent."

He kissed her once more and went to the door, opening it to see Evie, Brian, Little Jake, and Sadie Mae standing there, Evie holding the baby. Her eyes widened.

"Daddy, you look mean and angry, just like you used to look before leaving on another mission back in Oklahoma. You'd better smile for Sadie Mae, or she might run away."

Sadie Mae stood there, staring. "Are you Grampa?"

Jake smiled sadly, reaching down and picking her up in his arms. "Yes, I'm Grampa." He looked past Evie to see Katie and Lloyd coming with Stephen, Ben, Tricia, and Donavan. Gretta and Sam walked behind them. He turned with Sadie Mae still in his arms. "Here comes the gang," he told Randy. He turned and handed Sadie Mae to Brian. "Take good care of my girls," he told his son-in-law. "The little ones and the big one standing beside you."

Brian moved an arm around Evie. "You bet I will." He held Jake's gaze. "You just make sure you make it back here, Jake. I'm not sure how I'll handle this woman if her father doesn't come back home. You're the light of her life. You remember that."

Jake looked past them at Lloyd, whose eyes betrayed his devastation. They all came inside, Katie looking radiant.

Jake leaned down and kissed her cheek. "Katie, I

swear you're more beautiful when you're carrying than when you're not. Trouble is, I can hardly remember when you weren't carrying." He cast Lloyd a chiding look as most of the others laughed at the remark. "If you weren't so damn busy making babies, you'd be able to go with me."

"Well, that's what she gets for being so beautiful."

More laughter…all nervous…all thinking the same thing. Was this the last time they would see their father and grandfather alive?

"For someone who's trying to get away from his outlaw past, you sure look like one right now," Lloyd told Jake. "You going to war?"

Jake limped a little as he walked back to the table. "Could be."

"That hip giving you problems again?" Lloyd asked.

"Off and on."

"Too much activity last night?"

Jake grinned as he took a cigarette from a tin on the table. "Possibly."

"Don't you say another word," Randy warned. She set a basket of warm biscuits on the table. Evie had brought them from home. "Sit down and eat something, Jake. And you shouldn't be riding a horse at all today. You're obviously in pain. You didn't seem to be sore earlier this morning."

"I try to hide it, but right now I can't." Jake took a long drag on the cigarette and did not sit down. "Don't worry about it. It'll go away again. And just give me coffee."

"You have a long ride ahead of you, Jake Harkner," Randy scolded. "Eat something."

Jake kept the cigarette between his lips as he grabbed a biscuit and coffee and walked over to the fireplace. Little Jake followed.

"Mom told me what you're doin', Grampa. You could take me and Ben and Stephen with you. We know how to use guns now, and we helped you get Grandma back last winter."

Jake set the biscuit and cup of coffee on the fireplace mantel and took the cigarette from his lips. He put a hand on Little Jake's shoulder. "Little Jake, I am grateful for your offer, and by God, I don't doubt all three of you would be a big help. But this is something I have to do alone, for reasons no one in this room understands. And I'll feel a whole lot better knowing you three are right here watching after your grandmother, Evie, and Katie while I'm gone, especially the times when Lloyd and the men have to leave for other things. I know the ladies and your little sister and Sadie Mae and the babies will be in good hands."

Little Jake straightened, puffing out his chest a little. Jake scrutinized him closer. He was growing fast, and the boy was exceedingly handsome. He'd be a lady-killer someday. "Little Jake, I believe you'll soon be so big we'll have to stop calling you Little Jake. You're clear up past my elbow. I swear you've grown a good three inches just since last winter."

"Sure I have! I'm gonna be tall like you and Uncle Lloyd!"

Jake reached over and drank some coffee. "I think you will be." He glanced at Gretta as she walked closer, looking him over.

"If I didn't know you, you'd scare the hell out of me right now. I'm thinking maybe you really can take on all those men down there." She shook her head, lowering her voice. "If you weren't so happily married, by God, I'd give you a hell of a send-off."

Jake grinned. "My wife already did, which is why my hip is giving me a time this morning."

Gretta let out a bawdy laugh. "You're something else, Jake Harkner. A person is damn lucky when they can call you a friend." She sobered then, her eyes tearing.

"I don't know what to say, except if God listens to somebody like me, you'll be okay, because I'll be praying for you. And something tells me he does listen to that beautiful daughter of yours."

Jake drank some more coffee and took his cigarette from where he'd left it on the fireplace mantel. "I'm sure He does, Gretta."

Gretta wiped at a tear. "Damn it! I don't usually cry so damn easy."

Jake reached out and squeezed her shoulder. "I'll get your daughter back or die trying, Gretta. That's a promise."

Gretta moved her arms around his middle for a quick hug. "Don't talk about dying, Jake. Just get my Annie out of there."

Jake hugged her in return, then left her and limped over to the door, where his rifle and shotgun sat propped. "I'm going to get Cole," he announced. "There's no time to waste."

"Jake, give us a little more time!" Randy chided. "We should all eat something first."

Jake shook his head. "It's hard enough leaving all of you. There's no sense dragging this out."

He put on his Stetson and picked up the long guns and his duffel, then grabbed a sheepskin-lined corduroy jacket from a nearby coat stand and walked outside.

"Damn him," Lloyd swore under his breath. He hurried out, and the whole family followed as Rodriguez helped Jake tie everything onto Outlaw. The horse and packhorse were ready to go, and Cole was already mounted and waiting. He nodded to Jake. "I'm ready if you are, boss."

"Daddy, you promised to wait and let me pray first," Evie told him.

Jake shoved the shotgun and rifle into leather straps on Outlaw. "You've done enough praying for me, Evie.

I imagine the Good Lord is getting tired of hearing it. He's probably up there somewhere shaking His head and telling you to give it up, because there is no hope for your father."

"Daddy!"

Jake turned, taking the cigarette from his mouth and stepping it out. He sighed and walked up to his daughter, wrapping her in his arms. "A man couldn't be more blessed with children than I am with you and Lloyd, Evie. I'm sorry when I get like this. It's just how I am."

Evie leaned up and kissed his cheek. "You let all the kids hug you before you go. They deserve that much. And maybe it will remind you of all the reasons you have to come back home."

Jake pressed his hands to either side of her face and kissed her forehead. "You have no idea how many times I've thanked God for that husband of yours, Evie." He glanced at Brian and reached out to shake his hand. "It's a good feeling to know my daughter is so loved, Brian. Not many men could handle what you've been through. And thanks for Little Jake and Sadie Mae and my sweet baby girl, Esther."

There came a round of hugs from every last one of them, Ben looking devastated for fear the man he'd called Father for the last five years wouldn't make it back home.

"You're the man of the house now, Ben. I know you're up for it."

Ben struggled to hide his tears. "I'll take good care of Mom."

"I know you will." Jake looked at Lloyd. "And so will this guy."

"Pa, this is killing me," Lloyd protested. "I don't feel good about any of it. I should be with you."

"You should be right here with a great big family that needs you." Father and son embraced. "After last summer, I just thank God you're even alive," Jake told him. "You've had my back long enough, Lloyd. This one's on me, and don't you feel bad about it. No man could be more proud of his son than I am of you."

Randy came last. He pulled her into his arms and held her close while the rest of them held hands. Evie reached out for Gretta. Surprised, Gretta took her hand. Jake kept holding Randy, rocking her in his arms while Evie prayed.

"Heavenly Father, we don't always understand Your choices, but we believe everything happens by Your will and Your will alone. So please keep my father and Cole safe, and let them bring Gretta's daughter back unharmed. Bless my father in whatever he might face from his past, and please help him understand that his ability with his guns is a blessing, not a curse. Help him understand that what he has is a gift from You, and that he is Your instrument—sometimes Your Avenging Angel—and that's okay."

Randy broke down and wept.

"We are all leaving Him in Your hands," Evie continued. "Whatever happens is Your decision, Lord. But we hope Your plans are to bring Jake Harkner back home, with Cole and Annie in tow. You've brought him through things no man should suffer and most wouldn't survive. We beg You to do so again. Amen."

Randy clung to Jake, not wanting to let go.

"Baby, the sooner I go, the sooner I'll be back." Jake kissed her hair and grasped her arms, gently pulling them from around him. "Look up here, woman."

Tears ran down her cheeks as Randy met his gaze.

"Of all the reasons to come back, you're the most important one, understand?" Jake told her. "You keep that peppermint stick right where you put it. We'll damn well need it when I get back. And don't forget the pillow."

Randy couldn't speak.

Jake leaned down and kissed her hair, her eyes, her lips, her tears. He turned to Rodriguez. "Did you pack everything I told you to pack?"

"*Sí, amigo*. And your daughter, she gave me a Bible to give to the girl if you find her. She say it will comfort the girl and help her to trust you."

Jake glanced at Evie, who just smiled and nodded. Only Evie would have thought to give Annie a Bible. It was a good idea. He nodded a thanks to his daughter before turning back to Rodriguez.

"*¿Te recordaré de las cosas que le pedí a Gretta que te diera?*"

"*Sí, jefe, estan empacadas,*" Rodriguez replied, assuring Jake everything was properly packed and nothing left out.

"*Gracias, amigo.*" Jake walked up to Outlaw and grimaced as he mounted up.

Cole took the reins to the packhorse and turned his horse, walking the horse slowly as he left and waited for Jake to catch up.

"One of you take Annie straight to Loretta," Gretta told him. "Her full name and address are packed with the clothes I gave you. I don't want that girl to know anything about me."

Jake nodded. "I understand, but your daughter ought to know how much she's loved by her real mother."

Gretta shook her head. "It's better this way. Just bring her home, Jake." She met his gaze. "God go with you."

Jake adjusted his hat. "That's up to Him. It's your daughter who needs His blessings, not me."

Outlaw snorted and tossed his head, a big, strong, black horse that seemed made just for a man like Jake Harkner. The horse turned nervously in a circle. Jake scanned his family. He would never get over the fact that they all came from his blood. How could that be possible?

He looked at Randy. She'd made it all possible. "*Lo nuestro será eterno, Randy... Esta tierra es eterno... Tu y yo estaremos unidos eternamente. Tu eres mi vida, mi querida esposa.*"

He turned Outlaw and kicked the horse into a gentle lope.

Randy watched him ride off, as she'd done too many times before. "*Que Dios te acompane, mi amor,*" she whispered. She'd learned enough of the beautiful words of love he'd taught her to know how to tell him *God be with you, my beloved*. She turned and hurried into the house. She couldn't watch him disappear over the distant rise. She made right for his chair, which was where she knew she'd sleep with his pillow until he returned. She couldn't bear lying alone in their big bed upstairs. She curled up into the chair and studied the family picture above the fireplace. There sat Jake, in the center of it all, surrounded by his beautiful children and grandchildren. There was the man she'd met all those years ago in a supply store—bearded, angry, wild, dangerous, notorious...a wanted man who never once in his life had known love. She thought about his remark to Lloyd, the one that worried her most of all. *In a way, I've always been alone.*

It was then she noticed it on the fireplace mantel...a half-finished cup of coffee...and his uneaten biscuit.

PART FIVE

Forty-one

JAKE WATCHED OUT THE WINDOW AS THE SOUTHERN Pacific steamed into Brownsville. Nothing looked the same. Considering the fact that he'd been only fifteen years old when he left, that was no surprise. A few motorbikes and motorized buggies chugged about, and electric poles and wiring were strung up and down the streets and alleys. It was no longer the lawless little settlement where he grew up…where a man could beat his wife and child almost daily and get away with it. That same man had even gotten away with murdering his wife and youngest son and secretly burying them, telling others they'd run off.

Didn't anyone wonder why the man's older son had stayed? No. No one asked questions. No one knew he'd stayed because the couple of times he did try running off, his father had made him regret it in some of the worst ways.

He'd missed Randy since the day he'd left, and right now, here in this place, he dearly wished she was beside him. "It's been a long trip, Cole."

"Yup." A man of few words, Cole Decker took his dusty boots down from the back of the seat in front of him and made ready to get off the train. He'd cleaned up before leaving the ranch, and again two nights ago at a whorehouse in northern Texas, and Jake had done the same. Cole stayed all night with one of the women, but in spite of plenty of offers from the other whores, Jake had gone back to his hotel room and ached for Randy.

They'd either camped out or stayed in hotels the rest of the way, talking about ranching and cattle and women, pretty much in that order. Cole had finally admitted he'd been married...a long time ago. "It was after the war and my injury. She couldn't handle the bum leg, and she ran off with another man. I hunted them down, and I killed him," he admitted. "Came west, and that was the end of it."

Both of them had a lot in common—an outlaw past that included some ugly events. Both were once wanted men. Jake knew if it weren't for Randy, he'd be a lot like Cole. Wandering, no family, no real purpose to life other than survival, bedding a whore once in a while, getting drunk and into an occasional fight. One brave little slip of a woman had kept him from all of that. He'd tried to go back to it when he left her in California, but once a man had a woman like Randy in his bed and in his mind and heart and blood, there was no turning away from her. And no going back.

He shook away the thought. "Let's get our horses off this train," he told Cole.

The men got up, attracting stares. Both were well armed, both intimidating. Cole was average height, but broad-shouldered. He'd accepted Jake's request to ride with him because he knew the mission, and Jake knew he could trust Cole with Annie if he didn't make it out of Mexico alive. Cole was the type who'd lay with a whore every night if he could, but he'd never touch an unwilling woman or an innocent young girl. He was simply a man who'd had his heart torn from his chest by a woman whose love wasn't strong enough to handle what war had done to him. Deep hurt sometimes made a man do things he would never ordinarily do. He'd killed his wife's lover and had ended up a drifter, a cowboy, a man who'd given up on living any other way. And other than Pepper, who'd died in that barn fire last year, Cole was their best ranch hand. He'd been with them since they first came to Colorado to build the ranch.

They disembarked the train and walked to the cattle cars where their horses were kept, most of their gear still packed on them. It took several minutes to get them off the train.

"I have something to take care of," Jake told Cole once they left the depot. "I'm tired as hell, but this can't wait."

"I understand. You want me to go with you? I know all about what you're lookin' for, Jake. Lloyd said he wished you wouldn't go alone."

Jake mounted Outlaw. "Lloyd's a good son who worries too much." He lit a cigarette. "I'll be okay. You get us a room. While you're at it, you might want to ask around about a whorehouse across the border where they keep the best girls. People need to think we're down here looking to buy horses and cattle—might as well make it look like we're wanting a good time on the side, so no one suspects the real reason we're asking. And see if you can find out anything about Sidney Wayland. Tomorrow morning we'll head into Mexico. If we're lucky, the man will be at that whorehouse when we get there." He held Cole's gaze. "I meant what I said when I told you to just get the hell out of there with that girl if things work out the way I plan, Cole. Me—I'm not leaving there without killing Wayland. If he's not there, I'll hunt him down, but I'm not going home until he's dead. You have no obligation to do one damn thing but get that girl back to Denver."

Cole nodded. "I understand, but I'm used to havin' your back, Jake. And huntin' down Wayland could land you in a Mexican prison, which I hear is worse than death."

"You just go home and protect Lloyd's back. I'll feel better knowing men like you and Terrel and Vance are at the ranch, looking out for my family. As far as I know, my past is done catching up with me, Cole. Maybe my family can have some peace from now on." He took a long drag on his cigarette. "And after today, maybe I can have some peace too. There's one more thing left for me to do to get rid of my past." He turned Outlaw and headed away from the train depot.

Forty-two

JAKE WAS A BIT OVERWHELMED BY HOW MUCH Brownsville had grown. When he'd fled this area at fifteen, the city had been an infant, barely two years officially a town. Before that, it was nothing more than a dusty, lawless, unorganized hodgepodge of farmers, ranchers, outlaws, saloons, and whorehouses, as well as an almost evenly mixed population of whites and Mexicans. He had a vague memory of his father being good-looking, tall and strong…brutally strong. And his personality when drunk had made him an ugly, ugly man. Someone had once said his own toughness came from his father's beatings…and maybe it did.

He searched the business signs, riding up and down every street until he found what he was looking for…a mortuary. It was set back off the road, several headstones of various shapes in front. He trotted Outlaw up to a hitching post at the front door and dismounted, aware that a couple of women outside, looking at headstones, now stared at him instead. He tipped his hat to them. "Ladies."

They looked him over, appearing wary of the guns he wore, yet curious. The younger one smiled at him. Jake smiled back and went inside, surprised at how calm he felt. Maybe it was knowing that, if he was lucky, he could finally do something to honor his mother. Or maybe his brain was fooling him. At times like this, he didn't trust his own emotions.

Inside, he found a tall, bony man dressing out a corpse.

He looked up at Jake and nodded, stepping aside. "Doesn't he look nice?" he asked, indicating the dead man. He smiled through yellowing teeth, and the black-silk suit he wore appeared to have seen better days. "I think the blue suit is best on Mister Clay, don't you?" the man asked Jake. "Are you a relative?"

"I'm a possible customer," Jake told him. "I want a headstone made. I just don't know where it will go yet." He took a piece of paper from a shirt pocket and handed it to the mortician. "That's what goes on the headstone." He lit another cigarette as the man read the note, frowning.

"'Evita Ramona Consuella de Jimenez,'" he read. "And"—he squinted—"'Thomas.'" He looked up at Jake. "Just Thomas?"

"I don't remember his middle name," Jake answered. "He was my…" There it came. The rage! He had to keep it at bay! He wished Randy were with him. She could always calm him in moments like this. "…my little brother. The woman was my mother."

"Thomas doesn't have a last name?"

Harkner. It was my mother's last name too. "I don't want the last name shown. It would memorialize my father, and I don't want to honor the sonofabitch in any way! Just put 'Beloved Mother and Brother' after the names and don't ask questions."

The mortician scrutinized him, noticing the guns, the size of the man. "I'm Orlando Bruce, and I own this place. And you don't look like any ordinary man. Who the hell are you?"

"I'm Jake Harkner, and I have to get across the border tomorrow, so I need this settled today. How much will the stone cost?"

"Jake Harkner?" The man stepped back a little. "The *outlaw*? The *gunfighter*?"

"Once upon a time, mister. I'm just a rancher now.

Promise me that stone will get engraved and properly set. My problem is to decide where."

"Sure, but Mister Harkner, I'm considered the official historian for Brownsville, and you're a part of the history down here. Nobody ever thought you'd come back, and you never did. Then some of us saw that book about you and learned the truth. I mean, for a while you were wanted for murder, you know. Over your father's murder, and the young girl he was found with."

Jake turned away. *My God, Randy, I need you.* He hadn't expected this...hadn't expected to run into someone who knew so much about it. "I figured that story faded years and years ago," he said, struggling to find his voice. *Fifty-four years since I helped bury my brutally beaten mother and brother! How could it possibly suddenly be so clear in my mind? How could it feel like it had been only a few days ago?* It wasn't supposed to happen this way. He'd had it all figured out. It would be easy. He'd just find where his mother and brother were buried and put a headstone there and feel better about it all.

"No, sir," Bruce told him. "Everyone knows the story, and of course, every town has its old ghost tales or sensational stories about its beginnings. The famous Jake Harkner being raised right here in Brownsville, that's one of the draws here. You know—like the birthplace of Billy the Kid or Wild Bill Hickok, or the Coles and the Youngers. Nobody ever figured you'd actually show up here. The little stone-and-cement house you lived in... where your pa was found with that girl...it still stands. Once in a while, a traveler goes to see it."

A blackness enveloped Jake's heart and mind so heavily he thought he might pass out. He grabbed hold of a support post inside the mortuary and bent over.

"Mister Harkner?"

"Where?" Jake groaned the words. "Where is the house?"

"Out of town a little ways. If you stay on the main street and head east, you'll see it on a little hill. There isn't much left of it—no roof or anything, and no interior but one wall—otherwise, just the outside walls. The city took over the property and kept it for storytelling, an attraction, so to speak."

The man's eyes widened at the look on Jake's face when he turned toward him. "An attraction? An *attraction*?" Jake roared.

"Mister, you asked, I told. Don't take it out on me if it upsets you."

"Do you own a maul? Some kind of sledgehammer?"

"Yes, sir…out back, standing against the wall."

Jake headed into the back of the business.

"Hey! That's where I live back there!"

Jake ignored him and charged through the man's living quarters, ignoring a woman peeling potatoes in the kitchen. She gasped and watched him, then looked at her husband. "Who is that?"

"Jake Harkner, that's who!"

"The famous one?"

Her husband didn't answer. He followed Jake through the back door, where Jake tore through tools in the backyard until he found the sledgehammer.

"Mister Harkner, what the hell are you doing? That stuff belongs to me!" He stepped well away when Jake whirled, sledgehammer raised.

"Mister, I'm borrowing this. I'll bring it back." He reached into his pocket and pulled out some bills, not even counting them. "There's your pay for the headstone. I'll tell you where to put it when I get back, and then I'm leaving for a few days. When I come through here again, that headstone had better be where I tell you to put it, or I'll use this goddamn sledgehammer on *you*, understand?"

Orlando swallowed. "Yes, sir."

"And is my father buried somewhere around here? And the girl?"

Orlando stepped even farther away. "The parents came and got the girl, or at least that's what the historians tell us. They took her to Mexico and buried her there somewhere."

Santana! I'm so sorry.

"Your father was buried in an old graveyard that doesn't exist anymore. It got flooded out bad in a hurricane a long time ago, thirty years or more. A lot of the graves got washed away, and the old, decayed bodies mixed up together. They had to be reburied in a mass grave in the new cemetery. There aren't even any headstones."

"*Good!* That's how John Harkner *should* have been buried, with no kind of acknowledgment." Jake struggled not to throw up...not to scream...not to cry out in anguish. It was all here. It was all right here, not the past any longer.

The little boy in him wanted to go to his knees and weep. *Randy! My God, Randy! You said you'd be with me if this happened.*

He had to think of that...only that...Randy. He charged away, walking around the building and still carrying the sledgehammer. He headed for Outlaw and mounted up, then noticed Cole a few yards away. "I told you to get a hotel room!" he shouted.

"Sorry, Jake. Lloyd told me that no matter what you said, I should stay with you when we got here, maybe lag behind but keep an eye on you. And from the way you look right now, I'm guessin' he was right."

"This is *personal!*" The words were growled from somewhere deep inside.

"I know, Jake. I know."

Jake turned Outlaw in a circle, wielding the sledgehammer. "Follow me if you want. We might have to get out of Brownsville tonight after all." He charged away on Outlaw. People stared as he tore through the main street and headed out of town. Some had to jump out of the way, and one woman screamed. Cole followed, bringing the packhorse along. After several minutes of riding, Jake finally pulled up, staring at a huge hackberry tree on a hill. Partway up the hill sat a completely deteriorated stone house and nothing else. It looked naked and lonely.

Naked and lonely, like I felt at eight years old when you made me help bury my mother! John Harkner might as well have been standing right in front of him, and Jake *wished* he were. Because then he could beat him until he broke every bone in his body, then bash his head in with the sledge hammer. He dismounted and walked up the hill, walked around the house. He removed his hat and tossed it aside, then unbuckled his gun belt and tossed it aside also. He removed his vest, his shirt, leaving on only a sleeveless T-shirt as he let out a roar unlike Cole had ever heard, like a wild animal. He started wielding the sledgehammer against the crumbling stone walls still standing, battering them with a mighty strength Cole didn't think the man could possibly still have in him. He slugged and pounded and hammered and battered for what must have been two hours, growling with each hit, demolishing every stone and the cement that held them until there was nothing left but a pile of rubble. He went to his knees then, tossing the sledgehammer aside. He put his hands to his head and sobbed.

Cole dismounted and slowly walked up the hill, not sure what to do or say. He picked up Jake's gun belt and hat and clothes, then dared to step closer. "Tell me what to do, Jake."

Jake bent over, keeping his hands behind his head as he pressed his face against the ground. "God forgive me," he sobbed. "I had to do it. I had to do it. I didn't mean to kill Santana. It was an accident! The bullet went right through my father and into her. I didn't know anything about guns then!"

Cole realized Jake probably hadn't even heard him. He sighed and stepped back, feeling like crying himself. Everybody knew the story. Everybody knew killing his father had been a weight around Jake Harkner's neck his whole life, and the source of all his lawlessness. He wished Randy were here. She'd know what to do, what to say to him. This was the dark, ugly side of Jake Harkner that no one but his closest kin could handle.

Cole walked back to the horses and took the reins, leading them up to the big hackberry tree to give them some shade. He sat down there and waited, letting the horses graze on some soft, green grass.

Their train had arrived that morning, and it was deep into the afternoon before Jake finally got to his feet and came up the hill. He dropped to his knees in the cool grass.

"This is where he made me help bury my mother," he told Cole in a gruff voice, "after he beat her to death and then killed my little brother. They're buried here together. I remember this tree. I was only eight then, but I remember it." He breathed deeply, obviously still highly distraught. "I was forced to throw dirt on their faces. He didn't even put a blanket over them first!" He brushed his hand over the grass. "I wanted so badly to be in there with them." He wiped at tears on his face with his fingers. "I can't believe this. I can't believe I found them. God, I need my family, Cole."

"I know." He'd seen Jake do some incredibly ruthless things to those who'd threatened or hurt his family. Now he understood why. Jake Harkner had lost all that was dear to him as a little boy, and he wasn't about to lose what he'd found in his new family. This was the source of his fierce protection of those he loved. It was why he'd killed most of the men who'd so horribly abused Evie, why he'd blown Mike Holt's head off in Denver after

Holt shot Lloyd, why he'd gone after those who'd taken Randy and tortured Brad Buckley. Every time he did those things, in his mind he was probably defending his mother and brother and killing his father all over again. Pity the man who harmed any of them.

A few people had gathered at the bottom of the hill. They were pointing and staring. A man started up the hill. He looked like a lawman. "Hey, what's going on up here?" he called.

Cole jumped up and headed down the hill to intercept him. "Don't go up there, mister."

"I'm the chief of police here in Brownsville, and someone said a man was destroying one of our landmarks. That's destruction of public property! This is the house where Jake Harkner grew up."

"That *is* Jake Harkner up there, mister, and the mood he's in right now, you'd best leave and take those people with you. He's in a killin' set of mind, if you know what I mean. That man suffered mightily in that house as a child, and right now it's best to leave him alone."

The man frowned and backed away. "You get him out of here by morning."

"I will. But he claims his ma and little brother are layin' under the ground up there under that tree, and he was forced to bury them after his pa murdered them. I believe him. A man don't forget somethin' like that. Jake's already been to see a mortician. I suspect he asked for a gravestone he'll be wantin' to put up there, so I suggest the city let the mortician put it there and *leave* it there. If I know Jake Harkner, he'll come back to make sure it is, and he won't be a happy man if it's not there. When he gets in a killin' mood, there's not much anybody can do about it."

The policeman scowled. "I'll see what I can do." He turned and walked back down the hill. Minutes later, he'd cleared out most of the onlookers.

Cole went back up the hill and poured some water from a canteen into his hat to water the horses, then led them to a grove of small trees on the other side of the hill, away from where people could see them. He took down his bedroll, made camp, and waited. Jake needed to be alone.

Sometime in the night, Jake came to the campsite and took down his own bedroll. He opened it and stretched out on it, then lit a cigarette.

"Coffee's still hot," Cole told him.

"Thanks." Jake took a deep drag on the cigarette. "In the morning, I'll have you return that sledgehammer to the mortician and tell him where to put the headstone I ordered. I'll leave town the back way and wait for you. I've drawn enough attention. We'll head on into Mexico. There's a man down there who needs killing."

The mood Jake was in, Cole had no doubt Sidney Wayland didn't have long to live. "I'll be ready."

Jake smoked quietly, laying his head back on his saddle. "I'm trusting you with that girl, Cole. I'm staying behind to kill Sidney Wayland after we get Annie out of there, so it's possible I won't be going back with you."

"Don't be talkin' like that, Jake. I ain't leavin' without you."

"You do what you have to do to make sure Annie is safe. That's all that matters." Jake took a deep breath. "What happened here today *needed* to happen."

"It's okay."

"I just want my mother and brother to be remembered. Someone should know they existed."

"I can't blame you there." Cole wasn't sure what else to say. "Your mother produced a fine son, Jake. I'm guessin' she's watchin' and she's happy you found her again and you're honorin' her this way. She's happy for all the joy you've found in that family of yours. She's probably with those grandbabies right now, thinkin' how proud she is that they came from her blood. You remember it's *her* blood in you and those young ones too—not just your pa's."

Jake felt for his mother's crucifix under his shirt, something of hers he'd kept ever since she died. He'd hidden it from his father because he knew the man would try to sell it for whiskey money. He'd worn the cross next to his heart through all his outlaw years and all his married years, those awful years in prison, all of it. *Lo siento, mi mater. Favor perdoname. Que Dios te acompane.* He rolled to his side and fell asleep with his hand wrapped around the crucifix. He wished the town hadn't buried his father all those years ago. He should have been stripped and left for the buzzards to feast on.

Forty-three

AFTER DESTROYING ONE OF BROWNSVILLE'S "FAMOUS" landmarks, Jake figured he'd better get out of town a different way than using the main crossing point. He headed west first, keeping Outlaw at a slow walk along the Rio Grande as he waited for Cole to catch up.

By midmorning, the two of them headed across the Rio Grande in a more nondescript area. One Mexican soldier stopped them, asking their business.

"*Venimos aquí para las hermosas mexicanas,*" Jake told him, expressing his desire to find beautiful Mexican women.

The soldier grinned broadly. "*Sí, aquí tenemos las mujeres más bellas!*"

Jake smiled and nodded. "*Entiendo que hay un sitio por estas partes que se llama La Casa de Mujeres Celestiales. Queremos encontrar el sitio.*"

"*Ah, sí!*" The soldier pointed to the east. "*Sur de Matamoros. Es una hacienda Hermosa.*" The man grabbed his privates and laughed. "*Te va costar mucha lana para una de esas mujeres!*"

"*Pagaré lo que sea.*" Jake tipped his hat and rode off.

"What was that all about?" Cole asked when he caught up.

"I told him we were looking for beautiful women and would pay whatever it cost for the best. The place we're looking for is just south of Matamoros." Jake removed his hat and wiped at sweat on his brow. "I've been living in the Colorado foothills so long I've forgotten how hot it can get down here. I miss the J&L already."

"You aren't the only one."

"Did you take care of the tombstone?"

"Yes, sir."

"If I don't make it back, you make sure it's there before you go home. Will you do that?"

"'Course I will."

They rode silently for a good hour. "Sorry I went a little crazy yesterday," Jake finally said.

"No apologies necessary. You did what you had to do."

Jake halted Outlaw and lit a cigarette. "We'll get to that brothel late afternoon. Best way to gain their confidence is to act like real customers, so you, my friend, get to roll in the hay with one of them, as long as she looks like an experienced whore. If they bring you some young thing shaking in her shoes, you ask for somebody else. Tell them you like a woman with experience. I won't tolerate some unwilling young girl, even from you."

"Shit, Jake, I'd never do that, and you know it. And just what the hell are you gonna do?"

Jake drew on the cigarette. "I'm going to ask for a virgin. If we're real, real lucky, Annie's still there and for some reason still untouched. They save girls like her for the highest-paying customer, and I'll pay plenty. We'll lay low for the night and take her out of there in the morning. Staying a while will help us gain their confidence, and making a run for it in the morning is better timing as far as the guards being alert. If we're real lucky, we won't have any trouble at all."

"You're gonna spend the night with her?"

Jake frowned. "Jesus, Cole, how else can I make this look real? It's just for show—but first I have to talk them into it. I'm not touching her one way or the other, but for now I have to play the part, understand? Don't pay any attention to anything I say. There's no sense going into that fort of a hacienda like a lawman, which is probably what Jessie Valencia did. I'll win their confidence as just a customer. And it's going to take a lot of money to convince them to let me have her." He looked at Cole and smiled. "Does this look friendly enough?"

Cole shook his head. "Jake, when you get in that dark way you have, no smile is gonna help. That's the meanest, most murderous smile I've ever seen."

A more genuine smile crossed Jake's lips. "It's the best I can do."

"Well, you'd better use that special smile that makes women faint. That will work better."

Jake actually laughed lightly and shook his head. "You just be ready tomorrow morning. Get up and get your pants on before sunup and leave with the packhorse. Wait a ways away from the place. I'm hoping they'll let me flat-out buy her, but if I have to steal her, I'll steal her. When I come charging out, it'll be fast. If she comes out on her own, you grab her up and ride like hell straight for the border."

"And you?"

"With any luck, I'll be right behind you. Either way, it's me they'll be after."

Cole turned away. "Shit." His horse snorted and shook its mane. "Jake, if we get out of there with the girl, that's all that matters. Why risk your life by killing Wayland?"

"Because he'll keep doing this if I don't. And I'll kill Luis Estava if he's there too. He won't be charming any more innocent young girls into a brothel."

"Damn it, Jake, you're in such a bad way that you're not thinking straight. You're taking a big risk. You're in *Mexico*, damn it! They aren't real kind to their criminals and murderers down here, especially Americans."

"Just do what I said and get the girl into the United States and keep going, no matter what, understand? No matter what! If they get hold of you and her, you'll be dead, and she'll be right back where she was. I promised Gretta I'd get her out of there."

"And you promised your family you'd come back."

Jake smoked quietly. "I'll find a way."

Cole shook his head. Jake Harkner was not in a family-man frame of mind right now. He was still hung over from his rage at his father, and he was using it to build himself up for getting Annie out of that whorehouse. He was Jake Harkner the outlaw, and no argument against anything he wanted to do would work.

Jake tossed his cigarette onto the hard ground and kicked Outlaw into a faster lope, heading east.

"Here we go, boy," Cole said to his horse. He held on to the pack animal and jabbed spurs into his roan gelding, riding hard again to catch up.

Forty-four

LATE AFTERNOON BROUGHT A THUNDERSTORM, WELCOME rain for parched ground and browning grass. Lloyd walked out of the new barn and looked up at dark skies. He'd felt uneasy ever since yesterday. *What are you up to, Pa?* He ached to be with his father, worried if Jake had found anything from his past, and what it would do to him if he had. Once in an outlaw frame of mind, there was no stopping him, and Jake Harkner didn't always think straight when he was like that.

He saw another fancy buggy coming over the rise toward the homestead. It couldn't be Gretta. She'd gone back to Denver only six days ago...to wait. And there couldn't be news about Jake yet. He would only have arrived in south Texas a day or two ago.

He closed the bottom half of the barn doors and walked farther out into the rain, not caring that he was getting wet. The cool rain felt good, and he thanked God for it. He took off his hat and shook his long hair behind his shoulders and let the rain pour through it before walking to his still-saddled horse. He hooked his hat over the pommel of his saddle and mounted up, riding out to greet whoever was coming.

Terrel rode beside the buggy, and as it drew closer, Lloyd realized who it was. Peter Brown. "What the hell?" Where was Treena? He rode at a faster gait to intercept the buggy before it reached the houses.

"Peter!" he called out. He'd never known how to feel about the man. Peter was the lawyer responsible for getting his father's prison sentence reduced—the sentence that had sent Jake to ride as a U.S. Marshal in the most dangerous, godforsaken part of the country. Peter was also the reason the family had been able to move to Colorado for a better life, and last summer he'd come to Denver to help keep Jake's neck out of a noose.

What he hated about the man was that he'd done none of it for *Jake*. It was because he was in love with Randy Harkner. Even though the man was married, Lloyd wasn't fond of him visiting. Last summer he'd come with his wife, and she'd been greatly impressed by the J&L and wanted to come back. So why wasn't she here with him now?

Peter waved with one hand, then drew the horse pulling what was likely a rented buggy to a halt. "Lloyd!" he shouted. "By God, you're looking good!" he added when Lloyd rode closer. "When I left here last summer, you were still pretty weak. I didn't think you'd be looking this strong and robust." He climbed out of the buggy and reached up to shake Lloyd's hand.

Lloyd reached down and grasped Peter's hand, squeezing lightly. "It's been a long road, Peter." He dismounted. "I still don't think I could hold my own yet in a fist fight."

Peter looked up at the strapping younger man. "Well, now, I wouldn't want to bank on that if I was on the other side of your fist." His grin faded. "What's this Terrel tells me about Jake being gone? I didn't expect that. He's in Mexico? Going after Gretta MacBain's daughter? For God's sake, who knew that woman even *had* a daughter?"

Lloyd looked toward the main house, wondering if his mother had already seen the visitor arrive. "Peter, this isn't a good time for you to be here. This is really hard on my mother. And where is Treena?"

Peter read the jealousy in Lloyd's eyes, realizing he might as well be standing in front of Jake himself. Lloyd had never liked the idea that any other man loved his mother, and with Jake gone, Lloyd was going to make damn sure Jake Harkner's wife was shielded from any man who would even consider getting anywhere close to the woman. Even Terrel, on the way in, had seemed a bit defensive.

The rain suddenly stopped, and it seemed almost too quiet, their voices softened by air that hung heavy with humidity.

"Lloyd, I swear I had no idea Jake was gone. How in hell could I know that? Treena is in France visiting relatives. She'll be gone at least another month. I was caught up on my work, and this place is so beautiful and cool and such a tremendous relief from the heat and smoke and noise of the city—I just thought I'd take a couple of weeks and get away from it all instead of rambling around in that castle of a house we have in Chicago. Believe me, if I'd known Jake was gone, I wouldn't have come, but I'm here now. At least let me talk to your mother. Maybe now is a good time for her to have a friend."

Lloyd walked a few feet away, removing his hat and pushing some wet strands of his hair behind his ears. "Peter, she's not totally herself. She's scared to death my father won't make it back this time, and frankly, so am I. I should be with him. It's driving me crazy." He faced Peter. "After riding with him over three years in No Man's Land and both of us protecting each other's asses…he took Cole with him, but that's not the same. It should be me, but I have this place to run and three kids and another one on the way. And it would be even harder on my mother if both of us were gone." He stepped closer. "This is fucking killing me! On top of going into danger down there to rescue that girl, Pa went to Brownsville. He grew up in Brownsville and hasn't been back there since he left after killing his father. I don't have to tell you what that means. One way or another I'm worried he'll end up in a Mexican prison."

Peter sighed and grabbed hold of the harness of the

small, painted mare attached to the buggy. "Jesus," he muttered. "Lloyd, I should go talk to your mother."

Lloyd scowled. "Just go home, Peter. Go before she sees you."

Peter looked up to him, unafraid in spite of the warning look in Lloyd's dark eyes. This man and his father could be the most intimidating men on the face of the earth, but one thing he knew about them was they would never hurt a friend of Randy's, and he'd damn well been that.

"I'm not going anywhere, Lloyd. Part of the reason I came is because Jeff Truebridge is worried. He told me Randy's last letter sounded strange, and that was months ago. It's not like Randy to not be herself, as you put it, even when Jake goes riding off. She's always been strong and independent and confident in Jake's abilities to take care of himself. What's really going on?" He saw a flash of distrust and near guilt in Lloyd's eyes.

Lloyd turned to Terrel, who still sat on his horse nearby. "Go on down to the bunkhouse, Terrel. I'll handle this."

"Sure, boss." Terrel rode off, and Peter watched after him. He got the feeling the entire ranch was on some kind of alert, everyone on edge. Was it just over Jake? He noticed a woman come out onto the porch of the main house. With that long, dark hair, it had to be Evie. He looked back up at Lloyd.

"Tell me what the hell I'm dealing with here, Lloyd, because I am going to go down there and talk to Randy whether you like it or not. Help me know what to say to her. It might help her. Sometimes talking to a friend is a relief from family, because family is *too* close."

Lloyd's horse whinnied and turned in a circle, ending up between them. Lloyd smacked its rump and shoved the steed out of the way. "Get going, Strawberry!" He smacked the horse's rump again, and it ran off, charging down the hill toward the barn.

Lloyd faced Peter. "They always head for home, no matter how far away." He took a cigarette from his pocket and lit it, his dark eyes telegraphing a warning as he took a deep drag.

"My God, Lloyd, from what I'm looking at, Jake Harkner will never die because he's standing right in front of me. If looks could kill, I'd probably be dead, but thank God I trust you not to act on what you're thinking right now."

Lloyd sighed, taking hold of the buggy horse and turning it, leading it up and over the hill far enough that they were out of sight of the house. Peter followed, not quite sure if Lloyd wanted to talk or meant to beat him into the ground.

"Get into the goddamn buggy," Lloyd told Peter.

Peter did as he was told, and Lloyd climbed into the front seat beside him, resting his elbows on his long legs. He took the reins and tied them around a hook to keep the horse still, then kept the cigarette between his lips as he spoke, a gesture Peter had often seen from Jake.

"Peter, between thinking I could be dying and her husband could be hanged, last summer was hard enough on my mother." He smoked quietly for a moment, staring at the floor of the buggy, then finally took the cigarette from his lips. "What I'm going to tell you is in complete confidence. The whole family knows it has to be, even the boys and the ranch hands. As far as anyone knows, Brad Buckley has disappeared off the face of the earth, and good riddance."

"Oh my God...don't tell me." Peter removed his hat and hung his head. "That judge told Jake if he took the law into his own hands one more time he'd go to prison. He—" He hesitated. "Please don't tell me this has something to do with *Randy*."

"It does." Lloyd's jaw flexed in repressed anger. "We had a barn fire. While we all fought that, Buckley and some other men made off with my mother."

Peter covered his face. "Oh my God! God, no," he groaned.

"You can imagine the rage my father was in. Him and me both. We went after them and…found her. Needless to say, they're all dead and buried. We burned the line shack we found her in to the ground. My mother totally changed after that. It was like she was twelve years old. She clung to Pa like a scared kid clinging to her father… wouldn't let him out of her sight. It took months for Pa to get her back to her normal self, or at least close to it. He loves the hell out of that woman." He cast Peter another warning look. "As you well know."

"You damn well don't need to tell me that."

Lloyd sighed and drew on the cigarette again, holding it between his fingers as he continued. "I never thought Pa could be so strong and stay sane after something like that, but he did it, for her. Mom was finally pretty much back to her old self, until Gretta came along. Gretta was desperate to help her daughter, and Jake was her last resort. She couldn't get the law to help her, and the first man that went down there to rescue the girl never made it back."

"But that didn't stop Jake from going next," Peter said with a hint of sarcasm. "God knows there isn't an ounce of fear in that man."

"You know Pa. Heaven forbid an innocent girl should be in trouble. He can't stand the thought of a woman abused."

"He had to know this would kill your mother, especially when she's not long recovered from…" Peter stopped and rubbed at his eyes. "Goddamn it," he muttered. "What did Buckley and his men do to her?"

Lloyd remained quiet for several long seconds. "Not what you think."

"Did they beat her?"

"Yeah—pretty bad—but they didn't break any bones. And let's just say they humiliated her in the worst way. If I went into any more detail, I'd feel like I was betraying her. She'd die of shame if she thought you knew any of it. If she pretends everything is fine, you have to go along with it."

Peter held his head in his hands. "Jesus God Almighty." His voice broke as he spoke the words. "Damn it, Randy."

Lloyd knew in that moment how much the man loved his mother. He spoke her name as lovingly and with as much agony as Jake would have. "She can't know I told you," he reiterated, "and I'm only telling you because, much as I resent your feelings for my mother, I know you care about her and about this whole family. And as Pa's lawyer, you know there are some things you can't talk about."

"Of course not." Peter raised his head, and a tear slipped down his cheek. "Lloyd, I have to talk to her. Just as a friend come to visit." He sniffed and wiped his cheeks. "Maybe it will help get her mind off of Jake. It might be good for her to have a visitor." He took a deep breath. "Is she really doing better?"

"She was till Pa left for Mexico. I see the desperate fear in her eyes that he won't make it back this time. What he's doing is really dangerous, and one man has already died. The place where they took the girl is pretty heavily guarded. It's just that Pa is determined to kill the man who owns the brothel—figures it's the only way to stop the abduction of more young girls."

Peter shook his head. "The man is determined to get himself shot or hanged, isn't he? Heaven forbid he should die of old age—not a man like Jake."

"That's what scares us the most. I know how he thinks, and he's thinking it's his time. He belongs to another world, Peter, one we can only partly understand. Pa understands it best. If he makes it back, it will be for Mom, but I know what's in his heart. He doesn't want to be in this world anymore." The gravity of it hit Lloyd suddenly, and he choked on the words. "None of us... can picture life without Jake Harkner in it. If he does come back, it won't be because he's fought for his life. I can tell there are times when he *does* want to die.

"But he'll come back for my *mother*, because he promised her he would, like he's done so many times in the past. It's just that this time… I don't know. I'm scared if he's badly injured or something like that, or if he ends up in prison, he'll give up."

They sat there for a few minutes, not talking at all. Finally, Peter took a handkerchief from his suit pocket and blew his nose and wiped at his eyes. He put the handkerchief back, ran his fingers through his still-thick hair, and put on his bowler hat. "I'm going to the house, Lloyd. Just remember I'm a married man, and I do love my wife. But you know damn well I also love your mother and have for years. And in all those years, even when I was still single and she worked for me back in Guthrie…I never once tried to move in on your father. You have to believe that. Not only was I scared to death of the man, but I also respect him. And more than that, I respect your mother. Believe me, I am well aware of how much she loves your father. No man on the face of the earth could take his place in her heart. At least afford me the satisfaction of being here for her for a while and helping keep her mind off things. I can keep a conversation going—tell her what's happening with Jeff—what my wife is doing—maybe take her for walks or a buggy ride. Anything to keep her from going crazy with the waiting."

Lloyd wiped at his eyes with his shirt sleeve. "I guess that might help, but no buggy rides without one of the men going along. I promised Pa she'd never be left unguarded. I know you carry a gun yourself, but ever since last winter, Pa's wanted extra protection for the women." He looked at Peter, his eyes red. "Besides, I'm not about to let a handsome, wealthy lawyer who's ten years younger than Pa go riding alone with my mother." He grinned a little.

Peter smiled sadly. "I don't blame you one bit." He

unwrapped the reins and whipped the horse into motion. He turned the buggy around and headed back over the hill to the three serene-looking log homes below, set against the magnificent backdrop of the Rocky Mountain foothills.

A beautiful woman with blond hair came out onto the veranda, which was bordered with three rows of rose bushes in full bloom. Randy loved roses. That much Peter knew. He also knew she kept her own secret brew of oil from rose petals and used it like a perfume. He'd smelled it on her before, even just standing beside her.

"My God, she's so thin!" he remarked.

"Yeah. I should have warned you. She's actually gained some weight. After last winter, she stopped eating. Pa was scared she'd die from malnutrition. He finally got her eating again, and she's doing pretty good in that department. But don't say anything about her weight. She might think she has to explain, and she won't want to."

"I understand." Peter pulled up in front of the house, and Randy covered her mouth with her hands.

"Peter! Oh, my goodness, you couldn't have picked a better time to visit!" Randy opened her arms as Peter stepped out of the buggy and walked up the steps to greet her. "I just took some of my bread out of the oven," Randy told him as they embraced. "I know how much you love it. I'm so glad to see you. Come in! Come in!"

Peter kissed her cheek. "This place is a wonderful relief from big-city life," he told her, "and nothing smells better than that bread you bake."

They walked inside.

"Where is Treena?" Lloyd heard his mother ask.

"She's in France, visiting family," Peter answered. "She would have loved to come back out here and probably will again next summer. And I'm sorry to hear Jake isn't here."

"I'll bet you are," Lloyd said under his breath. He turned away. "Shit." He felt like a damn jealous kid.

Forty-five

SIDNEY WAYLAND HIMSELF GREETED JAKE AND COLE IN the outer courtyard of the lovely hacienda. The appearance of the place was deceitful, looking more like the home of a wealthy don. They followed Sidney to the courtyard gardens, where they sat in the shade of beautiful, flowered greenery, including red and yellow roses. The air was filled with their aroma. Smelling the roses made Jake's heart ache for Randy. If not for what this place really was, Randy would love the amazing garden.

"Go and get the girls," Sidney ordered a maid. "We have a very special guest. This is the famous gunman from America, Jake Harkner." He turned to Jake. "Even here in Mexico we know of you," he told Jake with a wide grin. "And we greet all our special guests with wine and dancing. It gets them excited for one of our lovely women, and I am sure the handsome Jake Harkner, who was raised by whores, appreciates beautiful women."

"Sidney, I've been with the same woman for a lot of years, but she's in Colorado and I'm down here, and what she doesn't know won't hurt her. I'm ready for something different…and younger."

Sidney laughed heartily and signaled a small band to come out of an alcove and entertain his guests. The four men played a rapid-beat Mexican tune using maracas, a guiro, guitar, and violin. In the next moment, four beautiful young women emerged from a side door into the courtyard, smiling and swirling to the music. They swayed and turned in beautiful, brightly colored skirts and low-cut tops. They grabbed the ruffled hems of their skirts and lifted them in circular, shifting motions, just enough to give the men a peek at the fact that they wore nothing underneath.

One woman in particular moved in rhythmic thrusts toward Jake to indicate she could most certainly please him in bed. Her flat belly rolled in tempting lunges, her hip bones showing above the very low waistline of her skirt, just above the hairs of her privates. Her blouse threatened to burst open from her generous bosom as she shook her breasts temptingly close and cast sexy, suggestive smiles through full lips. Her dark eyes promised a very satisfying night if Jake chose her.

None of it affected Jake. His leftover rage from yesterday kept away all thoughts besides his purpose. He gave the woman a once-over look that told her he desired her, but the only desire he had was for Sidney Wayland's death.

The four women finished the dance with a quick lift of their skirts as they turned and bent over to reveal four naked and very firm young bottoms. Jake couldn't help wondering if more than one of them had been an innocent virgin not so long ago. How many were here of their own free will, and who had been forced into this by Wayland, a small-built man with a slightly upturned nose. His lips were so thin it was almost as though he had no lips at all, and his pale-blue eyes were oddly lifeless—a man with no feelings, Jake guessed, other than for sex and money. Jake could read him like a book. What Wayland was doing made him feel important…a small man aching to be famous and feared in his own way.

Jake lit a cigarette as Sidney handed him a glass of wine. "Tell me, Jake Harkner," the man asked. "Why do you bring this man with you? Might you have ulterior motives for being here, which is why you need an extra gun along?"

Jake sipped some wine, scowling. "I don't bring 'extra guns' along if I have gunplay in mind. I don't need them."

Sidney chuckled. "I have offended you?"

"Yes, you have. I came down here to buy horses, which is why I brought one of my ranch hands to help me herd them back home. Someone up in Brownsville suggested I look up the Heavenly House of Women while I'm down here, so I thought I'd take them up on their suggestion." Jake drew deeply on his cigarette and drank more wine. He could hear Lloyd scolding him for drinking, which was dangerous for him in his state of mind. He had no choice. Too much alcohol could turn him into the monster his father had been, but he had to convince Sidney Wayland he was for real. "The man I spoke with told me you specialize in young white girls from America...virgins. Hell, it's been a long, long time since I screwed a virgin, and I figure if you have one here, she's probably already a little wild."

He scanned the four beauties parading in front of him. "You are all beautiful," he told them. "*Gracias*." He turned back to Sidney. "These girls are some of the prettiest I've ever seen, and my friend Cole here can have his pick. He just wants to poke something. Me—if I'm going to come to a place like this, I'm going to take a look at the top of the line, so to speak. And at my age, a virgin would be damn exciting, and I have plenty of money with me."

Cole signaled one of the four women to come and sit on his lap. "This is all I need right here," he told Sidney. "How much?"

"Two hundred dollars American."

"Two hundred!" Cole squinted in thought. "That's a lot of *pesos*."

"And she is worth it," Sidney told him. "She will do things you have never even thought of doing, my friend. We offer only the best to wealthy American men.

That is why we are so successful." He waved his hand. "Look at this hacienda! It's big and beautiful and clean. How do you think I got all of this? And I have my pick of all these women whenever I need one. I never sleep alone, my friend, and usually with a different woman every night. I love it here in Mexico. A few U.S. dollars go a long way here." He smiled at Cole, who looked at Jake questioningly when Jake sipped on another glass of wine.

Jake knew what Cole was thinking—the same thing Lloyd would be. Cole could drink any other man right to the ground, but he knew Jake Harkner and alcohol didn't mix well, and Jake was in a bad enough mood as it was. Jake raised his glass to Cole and grinned. "I know you're itching to have at it, my friend, so you go ahead and take that pretty young thing to her room. I'll pay the man, but it's coming out of your pay when we get home."

"As long as you're willin'," Cole answered. The Mexican whore screamed as Cole picked her up in his arms and made off with her. He glanced back at Jake. "What time do you want to leave out in the morning for them horses?"

"Early. Sunrise."

"You'd best lay off the wine then, Jake," Cole told him with a warning look. He set the girl on her feet and headed down a long hallway, past the courtyard, with his arm around her.

Jake turned to Sidney. "I'm holding out for a virgin, which is why I can't drink any more wine. The Harkner blood doesn't mix well with alcohol—makes us mean. Besides, I want to remember and feel and enjoy every minute tonight, and sometimes alcohol can make a man—you know—not quite up to par. Plus, I have a long ride ahead of me in the morning." He took a last drag on his cigarette then put it out in a stone ashtray on a table beside the big wicker chair. "From the stories I hear, you always have one or two virgins that you save for special sales."

Just then, a very handsome Mexican man joined them. He wore a sleek, blue-silk suit, his smile bright, his black hair slicked back. "*Señor* Jimenez told me we have new customers of a higher class," he told Sidney. He flashed a bright smile at Jake. "I am *Señor* Wayland's right-hand man," he said, putting out his hand.

"Luis, this is the famous Jake Harkner, the gunman from America," Sidney told him. "He is in Mexico to buy horses, and he heard about this place. He is, uh, interested in a virgin."

Jake took Luis's hand and longed to squeeze it until he broke every bone. So, this was the very man who'd stolen Annie away. He was every bit the handsome, charming man Gretta had described. He could see how easy it might be for the man to lure a young girl into a fate worse than death. "I prefer blonds," he told Luis.

"What about the little blond girl from Denver?" Sidney asked Luis.

Two birds right here in my hand. Jake struggled to keep from killing both of the bastards right then; he had to be sure he had Annie first.

"I sold her to Don Jesus Ricardo de Leon just yesterday," Luis told Sidney. "How strange that *Señor* Harkner asks for just such a girl. I just got back from Don de Leon's, which is why I'm late. The don is to pick the girl up here in the morning."

Sidney frowned. "That's too bad. Mr. Harkner had his heart set on breaking in a virgin. How much did Don de Leon pay?"

"Six thousand pesos." Luis smiled at Jake as though to challenge him.

By this time tomorrow you'll be dead, Jake thought. "I'll double that offer," he told Sidney.

Sidney grinned. "That is roughly three thousand American dollars."

"That's right," Jake answered. "If she's a virgin, she's worth every cent."

"Don de Leon will be furious," Luis told Sidney, looking seriously concerned.

"He doesn't need to know," Jake told Sidney. "I'm paying twelve thousand *pesos* just to be her first. After that, you can still give her to Don de Leon. You'll make out both ways and more than double de Leon's money."

"But the don wants a virgin," Luis reminded Sidney with a frown.

"I'll try not to tear anything, and I'll clean her up," Jake answered. "She'll just go to the don wanting more of the pleasures I'll teach her. You can order her to pretend de Leon is hurting her, because that's probably what the man enjoys most. But he'll soon discover she enjoys it, and I doubt he'll know the difference. She'd just better still be a virgin like you claim, or I'll want my money back, and I'll damn well get it," he warned.

Luis smiled and rubbed at his privates. "It was not easy, but I knew she would bring very good money, so I did not touch her. But I had a good feel of her, and I showed her what a man looks like, and made her touch me with her hand. And I told her what she will have to do once someone buys her."

You fucking bastard, Jake thought. "What's the girl's name?"

"Annie," Sidney told him. "Luis brought her from Denver with promises of marrying her." Both men laughed wickedly.

"I inspected her good. She is a virgin," Luis told Jake. "I knew she would be worth much money, which is why I saved her until I got what I thought would be enough. And now you come along offering even more! This is a very good day."

Jake rose. "I'll go get the money, but you'd better be telling the truth. You don't want to see me angry, believe me."

"Ah, *señor*," Luis told Jake. "I know your reputation, but we are well guarded. And I must ask you, you were once a lawman. Surely you're not foolish enough to have come here to try to steal this girl. Another man already tried that, and he is very likely dead now from many bullet wounds. Perhaps someone hired you to come here and find this girl?"

Jake sobered, longing to bury his fist in the man's face. "Mister, I've never been a gun for hire. My job as a marshal was part of a prison sentence, and the minute I got that sentence set aside, I left that miserable job and headed for Colorado. I'm no fool." He lit another cigarette. "Do you want my money or not? I can always go someplace else. And I know a very beautiful whore up in Denver who will accommodate me any day of the week. So if you don't trust me, I can just leave."

"No! No!" Sidney objected, rising. "Luis, why have you insulted this man? We can double our money."

Luis frowned. "I just do not want to offend Don de Leon. He is very powerful. He might come after us if he is not pleased with this girl and realizes she is not a virgin."

"And we have our men in place," Sidney reminded Luis. "We will just promise to find him another virgin free of charge. And once he sets eyes on our beautiful Annie, he will not even care."

Luis looked up at Jake. "Try not to leave marks on her."

"Luis, I was raised in brothels. I know how to handle a woman, virgin or not."

Luis nodded. "Then show us your money. We will take you to our finest room and bring her to you."

And I can't wait to destroy that pretty face of yours with a bullet, Jake thought. *You'll never smile again when I'm done with you!*

"Just a last reminder that we are well guarded, Jake," Sidney warned. He looked up to the tops of the hacienda walls, indicating the men stationed there. "Even the great Jake Harkner can't get out of here if we don't want him to." The man's disturbingly pale eyes narrowed in his last-minute hint of trouble waiting.

We'll see about that. Jake headed out to his horse to get the money from his saddlebags. He'd never had such a hard time controlling his temper as he was having right now. What happened yesterday at his mother's grave didn't help his mood. *Think about the girl and getting her out of here,* he told himself. *One wrong move, and you've blown it. All that matters is the girl…and killing Sidney Wayland and that cocky sonofabitch Luis Estava!*

Forty-six

JAKE PACED...AND SMOKED. HE'D PLANNED ON BUYING Annie outright and taking her home, but he'd ended up having to buy her for just one night, which created a problem for tomorrow morning. Getting her out of the brothel would be more difficult than he'd planned. Thank God Don de Leon hadn't come for her yet.

The door finally opened, and someone shoved a young girl inside. She stumbled from being pushed. The door was slammed shut behind her. She stood there in a negligee so thin Jake could see right through it.

She was incredibly beautiful, more so than he'd expected. Now he understood why Sidney Wayland considered her worth a lot of money. Her long, blond hair was brushed out and hung in thick waves nearly to her waist. She was tall for her age, her legs slender, her breasts almost too full for a fifteen-year-old.

She folded her arms over those breasts and stood there, staring at Jake, her beautiful blue eyes as big as saucers. The look she gave him reminded him of how Randy had looked at him the first time she'd met him— and shot him—in that supply store back in Kansas. The story was a family joke now, because she'd later found him dying and had taken the bullet out, saving his life. *If she had been smart, she would have left that bullet inside of me*, Jake liked to tell others.

"Get away from the door," he told Annie.

She hung her head as she walked closer on unsteady bare feet. She shivered so badly Jake thought she might pass out. He walked to his gear and took out one of his shirts. "Look up here," he told her.

She raised tear-filled eyes. *My God, she looks just like a young Gretta.* "Put this on," he told her, handing her the shirt.

Her eyes remained wide and her lips quivered. She swallowed before answering. "Why?"

"Because I don't think you want me seeing right through that thing they put on you."

She looked down again. "Isn't that what you want?"

"No." Jake draped the shirt over her shoulder and walked to the door, noticing there was no lock. Most whorehouses didn't have locks on the bedrooms. That was so a pimp or a guard outside could burst in if it sounded like a woman was being beaten, although he knew some places that actually accepted extra money from men who preferred to beat a woman first.

He yanked the door open, revealing a local man wearing a gun. "Get the hell away from here!" he ordered.

"*Señor*, it is my job to—"

In the blink of an eye, Jake's gun was under his chin. "I paid three thousand dollars for that girl in there, and I'll have some privacy," he ordered. "I don't want anybody standing out here listening or trying to peek under the door or barging in on us. Got that?"

The man swallowed. "*Sí, señor.*"

The man left, and Jake slammed the door shut again. He shoved a rug under the bottom of it so no one could try looking inside, then propped the back of a chair against the doorknob so no one could barge in. When he turned, the girl had his shirt on. It was so big on her it came to her knees. Jake suddenly remembered little Sadie Mae. "I don't wanna be bare," she'd said when he'd taken her nightie off and given her his shirt. This girl had had the same devastated look on her face.

"You Annie?" he asked. He knew he had the right girl, but he wanted to hear it from her own lips.

She nodded. A tear slipped down her cheek. "You... paid three thousand dollars for me?"

"I sure did."

"Luis said...you were going to...rape me. He said I have to do whatever you say, but...I don't know about...those things." She backed away when he stepped closer. "I think I'm gonna be sick." She burst into tears. Jake grabbed her up and whisked her into an adjoining washroom, hanging on to her as she leaned over the bathtub and threw up. He grasped her hair and held it behind her neck.

"Annie, I'm not going to do anything to you. I'm here to help you." He hung on tightly as she threw up again, after which she couldn't stop the tears.

"Don't...tell Luis. He'll do something bad to me if he...thinks I disappointed you."

Jake turned on the water and cupped some in his hand, rinsing her face with it. "Rinse your mouth under the faucet, Annie. I have some peppermint candy that will make it taste better."

She jerked in a sob and rinsed her mouth. Jake hung on to her the whole time, then picked her up when she was through and carried her to the bed, laying her on it. She instantly curled into a ball and cried again. Jake took a handkerchief from his gear, along with the clothing Gretta had given him. All he could think of was what Gretta's uncle had done to her. He dearly wished he could have killed the man. He grabbed a stick of peppermint and brought it to the bed, laying the clothes on a nearby chair.

He crouched beside the bed and handed her the handkerchief. "You have to stop crying, Annie. Use this. And when you stop crying, suck on this peppermint." He laid the candy on the stand beside the bed, thinking about the peppermint he'd left with Randy. God, he missed her. He kept his voice low as he tried to explain. "I promise I'm not going to touch you, Annie. I bought you just to get a night alone with you so I can explain what's happening. I'm taking you home, understand?"

She took the handkerchief. "How do I know you're telling the truth?" she wept. She blew her nose and wiped at her eyes.

Jake remained crouched in front of her. "Look at me, Annie."

She remained curled up when she met his gaze. "I have a wife, Annie, a son and a daughter, a pack of grandchildren, and an adopted son. I own a big ranch up near Denver. Your—" He hesitated. She still thought Loretta was her mother. "Your mother hired me to come and find you. I'm taking you out of here in the morning. I have a friend along who will get you over the border while I hold off anyone who tries to stop us. His name is Cole. You can trust him."

She wiped at her eyes again. "I don't believe you."

Jake nodded toward the chair. "I brought those clothes for you. They'll probably be too big, but it's better than a man's shirt, and there is even some lady's underclothes there. Don't get dressed till morning, mind. If for some reason anyone knocks and wants to come in here, it has to look like we're doing what we're supposed to be doing, which means you can't be dressed."

She watched his eyes. Jake was in a killing mood, but he smiled for her. "Everything is going to be okay, Annie," he told her.

Annie noticed his guns. "Who are you?"

"My name is Jake. Your mother knows I'm good with these guns. I used to be a U.S. Marshal, so she figured I could get you out of here."

Her eyes filled with tears again. "Another man already tried. They shot him a whole bunch of times."

Jake smoothed her hair back from her face. She jumped at first when he touched her, then curled up even tighter. "It's okay, Annie. I'm not lying to you. As far as that other man, he wasn't experienced enough in these things. I know people like the ones who run this place. I'll get you out of here. That's a promise. You just have to do everything I tell you, without hesitation, understand? That's very important. Once we get out, you don't look back. You stay with Cole, and you ride hard for that border, understand?"

She reached for the peppermint and put it in her mouth, a gesture that reminded Jake of Sadie Mae and Tricia begging him for candy. And then there was Randy. Their reason for sharing peppermint sticks was something very different. He turned away and rose. Would they ever have the chance to eat another peppermint stick until their lips met?

He lit another cigarette, then moved the clothes to the bed and sat down in the chair next to it. He leaned his elbows on his knees and studied the flowered carpet on the floor. "I need to know if you're... Your mother will want to know if you're still a virgin, Annie. Do you know what I mean?"

She didn't answer right away.

Jake sighed, feeling like an ass. He drew on the cigarette before speaking again. "Your mother will need to know, Annie, so she knows how to help you when you get home. Nothing that has happened is your fault, understand? There's no shame in any of it."

Annie pulled a blanket over her face. "I don't know."

Jake frowned. "How can you not know?"

"I'm not sure," she wept. "Luis made men hold me down, and he...touched me." She started sobbing again.

Jake stood up and paced again, so full of rage he was sorely tempted to charge out of the room and start shooting people. He ran a hand through his hair. "Is that all he did?"

"He made me touch him."

Keeping the black rage away was giving Jake a headache. "Then you're still a virgin, Annie, unless there is anything else you aren't telling me."

"No. That's all." She shook under the blanket. "I think I'm gonna be sick again."

Jake set his cigarette in an ashtray and hurried to her side. He pulled away the blanket and picked her up in his arms to carry her to the bathtub once more, where she threw up. He helped her wash her face, his headache now more of a searing pain from a need to hit someone, shoot someone, scream out his rage. When Annie was through being sick, he kept hold of her and half collapsed to the floor, leaning against the wall and pulling Annie into his arms. He held her tight as she continued sobbing.

"Baby girl, you'll be all right," he again assured her.

"He said he loved me! He said he was rich and would marry me and I would live in a beautiful hacienda!"

"I know what he said. And I know your father died and you were all mixed up. You haven't done one thing wrong, Annie. I want you to believe that, because it's true." He stroked her hair. "Do you want to hear a funny story about one of my little granddaughters?"

"Please don't hurt me."

Jake sighed. "Am I hurting you now?"

"No."

"And I won't. I'm just holding you to help you feel safe."

She sniffed and wiped her tears with the sleeve of his shirt that she wore. "You can tell me the story."

Jake told her about the ranch where he lived, and about Sadie Mae and the chickens. He needed to think about happier things or go crazy. "I came out of that damn chicken coop with hen scratches on my face and feathers in my hair. And I told my wife I was never going in there after eggs again."

Annie actually laughed softly. "That's really funny. Did you keep Sadie Mae's secret?"

"I sure did. But she didn't. She told everybody about how I used a lot of bad words when I was inside that chicken coop."

Annie smiled. "If we really get out of here, can my mother and I come and see where you live?"

God, she was so innocent. She was reacting like the child she was. "Of course you can. My wife and children and all the grandchildren would love that."

Annie moved her arms around his neck. "Please don't be lying. I don't know who to trust."

"I have something to prove you can trust me. Let's go back into the other room. I have a couple of biscuits in my gear. Maybe you'll feel better if you eat something."

Annie wiped at tears again, then got up. Jake reached up for her. "I'm getting old, Annie. You have to help me up."

She smiled and reached out her hands. He grabbed them and grimaced with the pain in his hip as he rose. "It's hell getting old, Annie." He put an arm around her and led her back to the bed, then went to his gear and pulled out two biscuits and Evie's Bible. He brought them to Annie, setting the biscuits on the table beside the bed. "My daughter gave this to me and said to give it to you. She thought it might help you feel better, and show you that you can trust me." He handed her the Bible.

"She did?" Annie's beautiful blue eyes widened as she took the Bible and opened it. She sucked in her breath. "She even put my name in it!"

"See? How can I be lying when I already knew who you were when I left Colorado? And if I have a daughter who thinks of things like this, would I be such a bad man?" Jake sat down in the chair again, smiling inwardly at his own words. Little did Annie know just how "bad" he could be.

"I guess not." She met his gaze. "But you have kind of a mean look on your face."

Jake rubbed at his eyes. "That's because right now I very much want to kill Luis and Sidney. I'm very angry at what they did to you, and I intend to make sure they're dead before I leave here."

Annie glanced at his guns. "Are you a hired gunfighter?"

Jake smiled sadly. "I guess you could say that. But I'm not doing this for money, Annie. I'm doing it because I can't stand to see a young girl like you, or even a grown woman, abused." He glanced at the Bible. "You keep that with you all the way home, and you remember what a good person you are. You must remember that God doesn't blame you for one thing you've been through. Promise me."

"I promise."

Jake sighed and rubbed at his eyes again, still having trouble staying calm. "Annie, I have to make this look good. Someone will probably come around later to see if we want food in here. You'll need to stay under the covers when they do, and don't let them think for one minute I haven't…that you aren't afraid of me. They'll want to see the terrified look on your face, because men like that find enjoyment in hurting young girls. I'm going to have to be in my underwear, so don't be afraid when I undress. If they for one minute realize why I'm really here, I'm a dead man, understand? I'll have to crawl into that bed with you tonight, but I won't touch you.

"We'll get up and dressed before sunrise, and after that, you have to do everything I tell you, do you hear me? You can't waver for one minute. And don't be afraid of Cole. He's a little rough-looking, but he's a damn good man. He knows where to take you when you get out of here."

Annie picked up a biscuit. "But what about you?"

"I'll be with you if things go right. I'm just telling you that no matter what happens…no matter what…you keep going with Cole. I promised your mother I'd get you home, and I'll damn well do it. In four or five days you'll be back home in Denver."

She shook her head. "But what if they kill you like they did that other man?"

Jake smiled sadly. "Sweetheart, I've lived a long life. Things have happened to me that should have killed me a long time ago. Believe me, dying won't be such a bad thing."

"But you have to go home to Sadie Mae. She'll cry if you don't come home. And what about your wife?"

Jake closed his eyes and looked away. Randy. He'd promised her he'd make it back. "My wife has been through all those bad times right alongside of me, Annie. She knows I'm ready to meet the Good Lord, if that's how this ends up. She has my son and daughter and all those grandchildren to love her and take care of her. And she knows she and I will be together again, someplace better than anywhere here on earth. Of course, that depends on if God takes me in. He just might order me out of heaven."

Annie shook her head. "No, He won't. You're helping me. He'll remember that. He'll let you go home to your wife and to Sadie Mae."

Jake rose, wondering how he'd make it through this night without losing his mind. "I guess that's for Him to know and for us to find out, isn't it?"

"I guess." She ate a little more of the biscuit. "You really love your wife, don't you?"

Jake walked to a window that faced north. He carefully peeked through the curtains. Colorado seemed so far away. "Yeah, I really love my wife, Annie."

"I'm not scared of you anymore."

"Good." Jake watched one of the whores walking with Luis. He was laughing. Jake quickly closed the curtain and remained turned away. "Annie, I get really angry inside sometimes at men like Luis Estava, and sometimes it shows in my eyes. I don't want you to be afraid of that, okay? Sometimes I scare my own family when I get like this. Things have happened in my life that…It just brings out a rage in me, but never at good people, so don't be worried when I get that way." He started undressing, and Annie looked away as she ate the second biscuit.

"It's okay," she told him.

Such innocence. How did a man take advantage of something like that, like what his father did to Santana?

Jake stripped down to his underwear and hung his gun belt on the bedpost on his side of the bed. "If anybody comes to that door later, you scoot under the covers. Act like you're crying, make them think something went on in here. They can't think otherwise for one minute, understand? I can't stress that enough."

"Yes, sir."

Jake propped some pillows against the headboard and crawled into bed but remained sitting up against the pillows. "I don't intend to sleep much. I'm too worked up, and I don't trust those men outside the door."

Annie scooted back into bed and curled into a ball again, facing away from him. "You're a nice man, Mr. Harkner."

Jake snickered and lit yet another cigarette to help keep himself calm. "Call me Jake, and no, I'm not a nice man at all. Even my wife says that sometimes. I like to embarrass her, and when I do, she just frowns and says, 'Jake, you are a mean man.' Even my daughter says that sometimes. And my son has been known to call me a mean, stubborn sonofabitch."

"They don't really mean it, I'll bet."

Jake took a long drag on the cigarette. "Come morning,

you'll find out how *not* nice I can be, Annie. Speaking of which, I want to be sure you understand what will happen." He explained again what he intended to do, wanting to be damn sure she was ready for the morning. "I wanted to buy you outright, which would have made things easier," he told her, "but they already sold you to someone else. They will expect me to leave alone in the morning, but I'm not leaving here without you. And the worst thing you can do is hesitate, Annie. Hesitating could cost me my life and maybe Cole's as well, and leave you a prisoner here. I'm sending you out that window in the morning, and you're going to run to Cole, and he's leaving with you. We'll have the element of surprise on our side, as well as sleepy guards who won't be expecting what I have in mind. I'll stay here and create some havoc of my own to take their attention away."

Annie lay very still for a few minutes, then jerked in a sob. "What if you get killed and I never see you again?"

"You just keep that Bible. Think of me when you read it, and pray for me. God knows I'll need all the help I can get if I'm going to make it to heaven, Annie. I've never been very Christian in my ways or my words, but my daughter seems to think I have a good chance of reaching the Hereafter—the cool one—not the hot one."

Annie laughed through tears. "You tell funny stories."

Jake grinned. "I could tell you a lot of stories that aren't quite so funny."

Annie remained turned away. "Jake?"

"What?"

"What's she like? Your wife, I mean."

Jake laid his head back and closed his eyes. "She's beautiful. She was the most beautiful woman I ever saw when I met her, and she's still beautiful today. She's gone through years of hell with me, Annie. When we met, I was a wanted man and we lived on the run. I can't begin to tell you what she's been through because of me."

Annie turned onto her back and looked at him. "Then she must love you a whole lot."

Jake looked at her and noticed she was clinging to the Bible. "I guess she must."

"And you love her a whole lot."

Jake smiled. "Yeah. A whole lot."

Annie sat up, keeping the covers over her bare legs. "I'm scared about tomorrow. Can I sit up by you?"

Lord, help me. The girl had no idea what she was asking. It was a good thing he was sixty-two and not sixteen. "Sure."

Annie scooted against him, nestling her head on his shoulder, much like Randy did practically every night. *You come back to me, Jake.*

He'd damn well try. He had to smile, though, at the jabbing comments Randy would think of to tease him. If she only knew he was sitting in bed with a beautiful fifteen-year-old girl wearing nothing but *his* shirt, and snuggled up against him like he was a damn stuffed toy.

And I suppose that didn't faze you at all, he could hear her saying.

Of course not. She wasn't you.

Jake, I'll never be fifteen again.

Why would I want a girl-child when I have a beautiful, voluptuous, grateful woman in my bed?

Grateful?

Grateful for how I make her feel when I make love to her.

Could you be any more egotistically confident?

Isn't it true?

Randy would smile at that one. *Of course it's true…and you're too damn sure of yourself, Jake Harkner.*

I'm sure of how much I love you.

He leaned back and closed his eyes. He wished he were equally confident about getting Annie out of there come morning.

Forty-seven

JAKE HURRIEDLY DRESSED, BUTTONING HIS SHIRT AND pulling on his leather vest. He pulled on his boots and strapped on his guns, hoping he'd have time to get to his rifle and shotgun still on Outlaw. "Get dressed, and quick!" he told Annie when she came out of the wash-room. "I heard someone out in the hallway talking about making breakfast. They'll be coming to this door any minute. I want you out the window by then."

"Jake, I'm scared!"

"There's no time to be scared." Jake turned, and she had underpants on and was struggling with the camisole. He hurried over and quickly laced it up for her. "My wife is always fussing over these things." He helped her pull on the dress, and he buttoned up the back of it as fast as he could. "Sit down on the bed, and I'll help you button the shoes I brought. I hope they fit." He put one on, and she pulled on the other.

"They're kind of big."

"Better than barefoot in case you need to run over hard ground full of prickly plants."

She buttoned one shoe, and he buttoned the other.

"You go out that window…*now*! Walk casually through the courtyard out there. Hang your head like you've just been through the worst night of your life, and don't talk to any of those guards. Let them think it's okay for you to be walking outside. I can't be with you. I'll attract too much attention. Aim for the front gate. You'll see a man standing there with a packhorse and two that are saddled. You head for him. He'll put you on the packhorse, get on his own, and take off at a hard run. You hang on for dear life, you hear me?"

"Yes."

Jake met her gaze, and she threw her arms around his neck. "I'm scared for you."

"Just go. Like I told you, if you hesitate now, this will all be for nothing. I paid for a night with you, but they expect me to leave you behind for Don de Leon when I leave here. Once they realize I'm taking you with me, all hell will break loose, because they don't want to have to answer to de Leon, who's probably on his way here right now. If you don't want to end up in that man's bed, you do what I told you to do." He pulled her arms from around his neck, and she kissed him smack on the lips.

"Thank you." Tears forming in her eyes, she grabbed the Bible. "I don't want to leave you. I'll be scared without you."

"Cole will do just as good a job getting you out of here. There's no time for tears or arguing, Annie." He gave her a quick smile and kissed her forehead. "Go on. I'll be all right." He helped her climb through the window, then closed his eyes and said a quick prayer for her and Cole.

"Don't worry about my worthless hide, Lord. Just save those two." If not for Evie's constant preaching at him, he wouldn't pray at all. He waited, peeking through the curtains to see Annie making her way toward the gate. She suddenly bolted.

"Hey!" someone yelled.

"*La muchacha! Ella está escapando! Ella está escapando!*" one of the guards shouted.

Jake waited for the sound of horses galloping away, then charged out the bedroom door, not even taking his remaining supplies. Most of his valuables were with Cole anyway. He headed down the hallway. He needed to draw the attention of the guards away from Annie and Cole. And he was not about to leave without killing Sidney Wayland and Luis Estava.

"Sidney Wayland!" he roared. "Show yourself!"

Guards were running into the main living quarters as he got there.

"You!" one of them shouted to Jake. "You let that girl get away!" He pulled a gun. It had barely cleared its holster when Jake shot him in the heart.

Another came at him, and Jake fired again.

Sidney and Luis ran into the main room from two different doorways. Sidney had a gun, but Luis didn't.

"What's going on here?" Sidney demanded.

"You'll not kidnap any more innocent young girls, that's what!" Jake shouted the words and fired, then turned his gun on Luis.

"*Señor* Harkner! I am not armed!"

"You're a fucking rapist!" Jake shouted. "That's good enough for me!" He fired again, making sure his bullet hit Luis in the mouth and shattered those pretty teeth. Luis squirmed, blood pouring from his mouth. Jake walked up and fired again, putting a hole in the man's forehead.

"Oh, my God!" A woman screamed, and Jake whirled at the sound of men running down the hallway. A couple of whores stuck their heads out the doors of their rooms, then ducked back inside.

Men ran toward Jake, and he raised both .44s and fired three more times, killing another man with each bullet.

One gun empty. The other had five bullets. Jake moved into a dark alcove near the front door and quickly reloaded the empty gun. He charged for the doorway, guns blazing when two more guards tried to stop him.

"Get the horses!" someone shouted from the rooftop as Jake ran through the courtyard toward Outlaw. He had to stop and duck as more bullets whizzed past him.

"He is stealing one of the girls!" someone yelled. "Don de Leon's promised!"

"*Siguelo! El mato al Señor Wayland!*" another yelled.

"*Andale! Traigan los caballos!*" someone else yelled from inside the courtyard.

Jake mounted Outlaw and took off at a hard gallop. The last order was about getting horses. They would soon be on his heels. He could see Cole and Annie far ahead—they had a good head start. More bullets whizzed past him as he galloped for the border, a good two miles away. He didn't need to look to know that a small posse had quickly gathered and was after him. He turned and fired. One man went down, and that was a pure miracle, because he was firing at random. He kicked Outlaw into a faster run. His hat flew off. More bullets whizzed past him. Seconds seemed like minutes and minutes like hours.

He glanced back. He had a decent lead now, but he felt sorry for Outlaw. The horse was already wheezing and sweating. The temperature seemed too hot for early morning. Ahead of him, dust swirled from Cole and Annie's horses. *Get her across that border, Cole. Don't stop for anything!*

Ten minutes turned to fifteen, and then there it was. The Rio Grande! Cole and Annie were already splashing across the river and headed up the other side.

Then it happened. A bullet hit Outlaw. The horse screamed. His hooves slid for several yards before the horse went down hard, catching Jake's left leg under it. Jake cried out with the pain, knowing without even looking that his leg was broken. The horse whinnied wildly and struggled to get up, but it couldn't, and every time it tried, it smashed against Jake's leg again. Excruciating pain enveloped him. He tried to pull free but couldn't. It was then he noticed Cole riding back in his direction.

"Go back!" he screamed.

"Jake! Jake!" He could hear Annie screaming from somewhere.

Cole reached him. "Jake! Goddamn it!" He dismounted and tried to get Outlaw to move off Jake's leg, but the horse wouldn't budge.

"Shoot Outlaw and get the hell out of here!" Jake screamed at Cole. "I told you not to stop for anything. Get back across the river! They won't follow you into the States!"

Outlaw screamed and squirmed again. Jake cried out at the pain in his leg. Cole shot the horse in the head, then fired a few times at the oncoming riders to keep them at bay. "I can't leave you here, Jake!"

"You have to! Get back across that river and take her home, or they'll come for her! Goddamn it, Cole, *go*, or this is all for nothing!" Jake handed him his .44s. "Give these to Little Jake. I promised them to him! And tell Randy…I love her."

More bullets whizzed past as the riders came closer.

"Damn it, Cole. Go! Get the hell out of here! Hurry up! Annie's coming back across the river! Don't let her!"

"Fuck it, Jake, I can't leave you here for them!"

"You don't have any choice! Get over there before they kill you and force that child into a living hell. Don't make this all for nothing! Get the hell out of here!"

His eyes tearing, Cole stumbled backward. "Damn you, Jake!" He shoved Jake's guns into his belt, then mounted up and headed for the river, meeting Annie halfway across and grabbing the packhorse's bridle. "Get back across!" he roared at her.

"Jake! No! We can't leave him!"

"We have no choice!" Cole forced her horse back to the United States side of the river as more bullets flew past both of them. He charged both horses up the bank and behind huge boulders on the other side. They ducked behind the boulders as more bullets came at them.

Cole grabbed his rifle off his horse and began firing at the men who were circling around Jake. He managed to get two of them before three others began a volley of shots that pinged and sang against the rocks and kept him behind the boulders. When he looked again, men had tied ropes around Outlaw and dragged him off of Jake. He was surprised when Outlaw moved and whinnied. A shot was fired. Cole knew they'd just shot the horse again. Outlaw had been the best horse a man could own. He wanted to vomit then at the sound of Jake's chilling screams of pain.

"Jesus God, I think his leg's broke," he groaned.

"Oh, dear God, Cole, they're tying a rope around Jake! They're dragging him away! They'll kill him! They'll kill him," Annie wept. "Oh, my God, he did this for me!" She broke into uncontrollable sobbing. "Jake! Jake! God help him! God help him!"

Cole watched Jake being dragged off. He sank against the boulder and wept right along with Annie. She was right. Jake didn't have a chance. The worst part was hearing his screams as they dragged him off. How in hell was he going to tell Lloyd and Evie about this? And Randy. How could he tell Randy her husband wasn't coming back to her?

Annie wept uncontrollably. "He did this…for me," she sobbed. "Why?"

Cole pulled Jake's guns from his belt and stared at them. "Because he can't stand a woman abused. He's Jake Harkner, and I guess you could say he's America's last outlaw." *Damn you, Jake. Damn you! Why did you pick me for this?* He'd never wept over another man's death, but he couldn't help it this time. He broke down and shed his own tears, sure Jake's screams of pain as he was dragged off would haunt him the rest of his life.

Forty-eight

PETER WATCHED LITTLE JAKE STACK WOOD NEXT TO THE fireplace in the great room. The young man had remained very defensive during his visit, telling Peter early on that the big, red-leather chair beside the fireplace was his grandfather's and that no one except Randy could sit in it—Little Jake's way of telling Peter to stay out of that chair. It was sweet, and a bit comical. The rest of the family was kind and accepting and seemed to understand his visit was probably good for Randy...except, of course, Lloyd, who scowled at him almost as often as did Little Jake.

Three days had gone by since Peter had arrived. Since he'd gotten here, grandchildren and Ben were almost constantly underfoot whenever he visited Randy. He spent his nights at Evie's home, the always-genteel, gracious, kind Evie, who accepted his presence as good for her mother. But heaven forbid he should stay at Jake and Randy's house. And Ben and both older grandsons always stayed the night, as though they had been ordered to run interference in case Peter should decide to sneak over after dark and steal their grandmother away.

Every single family member seemed to watch out for Randy Harkner. She was the matriarch, the woman Jake Harkner loved, and woe to anyone who failed to keep her safe, warm, and cared for. He suspected there was more to it than that, however. They all were worried Jake wouldn't come home this time.

As soon as he'd arrived, Peter had noticed the difference in Randy. It tore at his guts to think about her ordeal, and he couldn't even imagine what that had done to Jake. Randy didn't mention it, and Peter didn't ask. In fact, she seemed to be living in a world removed from all of that, always cooking, always fussing, always asking if he was comfortable and had what he needed. And she talked about Jake almost constantly... *Jake usually helps Lloyd this time of year, cutting and threshing oats and other feed for winter storage... Jake loves my bread. I've been making it fresh every day in case this is the day he comes home.*

The man hadn't been gone long enough to even make it back yet, but she kept talking about the day he would. *He promised he'd make it back, and he always keeps his promises.*

Peter sat in a nearby chair, reading a several-days-old newspaper as Little Jake finished stacking the wood. The young man was a true offspring of Jake Harkner. The kid had sprouted several inches taller since Peter had seen the whole family in Denver last summer at Jake's hearing.

Still, it wasn't the height or even the dark eyes and thick, dark hair that showed Little Jake was Jake's grandson. It was his attitude, and those dark eyes had a look in them that said "don't mess with me or my grandma." Even now, he stacked the wood in a way that Peter could tell he was trying to show off how strong he was getting. When he finished, he turned and straightened, putting his shoulders back and puffing out his chest a little, as though to look as big as he possibly could. He looked at Peter with a sober face and folded his arms in front of his chest.

"Me and Stephen and Ben look after my grandma when Grandpa isn't here," he told Peter.

"Well, then, Randy is in *very* good hands," Peter answered. "I'm sure your grandfather has every confidence that she is safe and cared for when he's gone, Little Jake, or he wouldn't have asked you to watch out for her."

"I talked to my mom and Uncle Lloyd about my name," Little Jake told him then. "I think I should just be called Jake, 'cuz I'm not little anymore."

Randy was coming over to sit near Peter, and she heard the conversation. "Then how will you and your grandfather know which one we're speaking to when you're in the same room together?" Randy asked him.

Little Jake pursed his lips and thought about it. "You could call Grandpa Big Jake."

Randy and Peter laughed. "I never thought of that, Little Jake," Randy told him. "And I'm sorry, but you will have to give all of us time to get used to calling you just Jake. Come over here and give me a big hug like Big Jake would do."

Little Jake walked over and embraced her. The kid was already the same height as Randy. "Do you want me to stay, Grandma?"

"I'm fine," Randy told him. "Your mother must have chores for you to do, and I think it's reading time at your house."

"I hate reading. I'd rather go watch the men break horses."

"I'm sure you would, but in this day and age, a man also needs an education. You can't run a ranch just knowing how to corral a cow or break a horse, Jake. You need to be able to read and understand new laws, and you have to be able to count those cattle and keep track of your losses, but that's for Lloyd to teach you. Go on now. I certainly don't need any more wood until it gets colder out."

Little Jake glanced at Peter. "I'll be around if she needs me."

Peter grinned. "I'll remember that."

"She's scared for Grandpa, but he'll be back. How long will you be here?"

"Jake, be nice," Randy told him. "Peter is a dear

friend, and he's helped your grandfather in many ways. Mister Brown is welcome to stay as long as he wants."

"Randy, he asked a fair question," Peter told her, setting the newspaper aside and addressing Little Jake. "I'm going to stay until we're sure your grandfather is fine and is coming home," he told the boy. "Your grandmother says it shouldn't take more than two weeks, and I have to go home by then anyway. I'm just here to enjoy this beautiful ranch and the cool, clean air. And I care about your grandmother and grandfather *both*. Your grandfather is…well, he's the most interesting man I've ever known. I respect and admire him."

Little Jake nodded. "Ain't nobody like my grandpa."

Peter nodded. "That, son, is an understatement. I've had enough encounters with that man to know it's so."

Little Jake looked from Peter to Randy and back to Peter. "You'll be back at my house by dark, right?" he asked.

"Of course I will. And your mother is very gracious to give me a room there. And since it's *your* room, I thank you for letting me put you out."

"It's okay. When Grandpa is gone, I always sleep over here anyway… Me and Stephen and Ben all sleep over here, and there's always a man outside. When Grandpa is here, though, she doesn't need protecting. Nobody gets near my grandma when Grandpa is around."

"Oh, I have absolutely no doubt about that, Jake." Peter struggled not to burst out laughing. The statement couldn't be more true! "And I can help watch her, too, while I'm here. She'll be fine."

Little Jake studied him a moment longer before he very reluctantly left. The two little granddaughters scurried off to one of the bedrooms to play with their dolls.

"I'm sorry he gets a little rude, Peter," Randy laughed. "He wants so badly to be as big as Jake that he tries to make up for it in other ways."

"I understand. Someday that kid is going to be a man not so easy to contend with, just like someone else I know."

"I'm so glad you're here, Peter," Randy told him—something she'd repeated many times. "It's good to have a friend here, and one who understands and cares about Jake."

She glanced at Jake's chair, where she'd slept every night, holding his pillow. Peter saw the quick sign of terror in her eyes. She turned away. "Come back to the kitchen, and we'll have another cup of coffee," she told him.

Peter followed her to sit down at the huge table that often held the entire family for a meal. It was early morning, he'd just eaten the best homemade coffee cake he'd ever tasted, and Randy was already cutting him another piece. "I'd better go home soon. If I stay here too long, I'll be fat," he told her, trying to get her mind off Jake.

"Treena wouldn't like that," Randy answered. "I actually make the cake for myself because Jake wants me to gain weight. I'm trying hard, but he still thinks I'm too thin." She set the coffee cake in front of him and turned away to pour more coffee.

No matter how hard he tried to change the subject to something else, it always came back to Jake. He'd seen flashes of Randy's old strength and independence, but he also saw what Lloyd must have meant. She seemed to fluctuate between the old Randy and the child afraid to be alone.

She set two cups of coffee on the table and sat down near Peter. "Are you enjoying your visit, Peter?"

"Yes. Very much. Stephen took me out to the new barn yesterday. It's a beautiful building. And it's nice that one stall was left empty in memory of Pepper." He wanted to kick himself, realizing the mention of Pepper would bring back memories of the old barn fire...and what had happened after that.

Randy looked away. "Yes. Pepper was a good man. It's terrible what those men—" She caught herself and rose to walk over to a cupboard and put away a few more dishes. "Did Lloyd tell you?"

"Tell me what?"

"About the barn fire…how it happened."

"Yes, he did, Randy."

She remained quiet for several long seconds, her back to him. "We lost a lot of horses, but Jake saved Outlaw. And he…came for me. I knew he would. That's how I survived. I knew Jake would come, just like he saved my life after we first met. He tried to ride away, you know. I left to go west and find my brother, and Jake ended up coming after me. I was dying of snake bite, and I was in a…terrible place. Jake came and took me out of there, and that's when we knew we were in love."

"I know the story, Randy." Did she even hear him?

"That thing last winter…" Her back was still to him. "Jake can be so ruthless. You have no idea what he can do to a man. But they deserved it. They did…something terrible to me. But Jake can turn right around and be so incredibly kind…and gentle…and understanding. He has a way of making things better…a way of almost making the bad go away. I think it's because he's had to do that for himself…make the bad go away…the things he's been through."

She didn't mention shooting Brad Buckley herself, and like Lloyd and Evie, Peter wondered if she even remembered doing it. She was still turned away, but he could tell she was wiping at tears.

"Randy, it's okay. I shouldn't have mentioned Pepper. I apologize."

She sniffed and put away a few more dishes. "It's all right." She moved the coffee pot off the hot burner. "If this sits here too long, it will be bitter," she said. She wiped at her eyes again and came to sit down, then just stared at her coffee cup. "Jake has a way of making everything better," she repeated. "When he holds me, all the terrors of the world go away. And he has a way of making a woman feel like she's the most beautiful and perfect thing God ever created." She drank some coffee, then looked at her hands. "I *am* still too thin, aren't I? Jake says I need to fatten up. He says he's scared to hold me too tight or he might break a bone or something."

She suddenly burst into tears, covering her mouth as she wept. "Peter, something is wrong! Something is terribly wrong! I've felt it all morning! Jake needs me! He needs me!"

"Randy!" He reached out to touch her arm. "Should I go get Evie?"

She shook her head. "I need you to hold me, Peter. I haven't felt this way since...since I knew something terrible had happened back in Guthrie...when we found out those awful men took Evie and Little Jake!"

Peter rose and pulled her out of her chair, holding her close and letting her cry on his shoulder. Ben came in just then and looked at him questioningly.

"Go get Evie and Lloyd, Ben," Peter told him. "Something is wrong."

Ben left, and Peter kept his arms around Randy. "Honey, it will be all right. He'll make it back."

"He won't! Not this time. I feel it, Peter. Something has happened. Something really bad." She threw her arms around his neck and clung to him.

She needs holding sometimes, so I guess I'll have to let you do it. He remembered Jake's words back in Guthrie, when Jake had to leave on a mission as a marshal and Randy needed to go to a hospital for surgery. That was the first time he and Jake had faced off over the fact that Peter loved her too. There was no way Jake Harkner was going to let another man try to move in on his wife, but the man had somehow known that he could trust Peter for that very reason—that Peter loved her enough to take care of her without even considering anything more.

This was one of those moments when he figured Jake wouldn't care if he held her. The woman was falling to pieces. In two minutes, Lloyd and Evie were both at the house, followed by practically everybody in the family, including Brian, who came over and touched Randy's back.

"Randy, what is it?" he asked.

She continued to sob against Peter's shoulder until Lloyd grasped her arm. "Mom, what's going on?"

She turned and fell into Lloyd's arms. "It's Jake! It's Jake!" she carried on. "Something awful has happened. I feel it! I feel it!"

Evie turned away. "Daddy," she groaned.

Lloyd just held her, not sure what else to do. "Mom, let Brian give you something to help you sleep. I know you're not sleeping. The boys told me you're up pacing half the night."

"I don't want to sleep. I want Jake. He's in pain, Lloyd."

Lloyd led her to Jake's chair. "Mom, he knows how to take care of himself. And he has Cole with him."

She shook her head. "It's worse than anything before," she wept. She grasped Jake's pillow and curled into the chair, holding the pillow close. "Evie needs to pray for her father. He needs God's hand right now, Lloyd. He's got no one else. Cole isn't with him. I feel it. He's alone. He's alone and in pain."

Everyone just looked at one another. Lloyd's hands moved into fists. "I should have gone with him."

"Lloyd, you did the right thing," Evie reminded him. "It's what Daddy *wanted* you to do. We have to have faith. Mother is right. We need to pray Daddy out of whatever fix he's in. And maybe he's just fine."

"He's not! He's not!" Randy sobbed.

Peter suddenly felt like the odd man out. He walked

over to Randy and knelt in front of the chair. "Randy, do you want me to leave?"

"No! No, please stay." She reached out and grasped his hand. "I need you to stay till we know. I'm so sorry, Peter. I know you need to go home."

"I said I'd stay till Jake and Cole got back, remember? So I'll stay. But you aren't the woman I once knew, Randy. That woman was strong, and she believed in her husband's abilities and in his promises to always come back to her. And he always did, didn't he? Didn't Jake always come back?"

Her tears subsided a little. "Yes."

"And would he want you to give up on him like this?"

She straightened a little, still clinging to Peter's hand. "No."

"Then you need to keep the faith, Randy, for Jake's sake. You might be right. He might be alone, and he might be in pain, but you are what will help him through whatever has happened. Okay? He needs to feel you with him and remember you're waiting for him. If you're going to fall into a puddle of tears and give up on him, he'll feel that too, don't you think? Isn't he better off if you're strong and have faith that God will watch out for him?"

Randy sat all the way up. "You'll wait with us, won't you?"

Peter nodded. "I'll wait, but only if you stay strong. You know damn well how strong Evie's prayers are, so let's just all pray for Jake. And you remember what a tough man your husband is. The man can be leather and stone when he needs to be. Any little boy who can survive what Jake survived is even tougher as a man."

Lloyd looked at Evie. She could see how much he hated admitting Peter was good for his mother, but right now, Peter was the only one able to calm her down. He turned away, pacing. "Damn it," he growled. "Damn it, Pa, what have you gone and done?"

Evie walked up to her brother and touched his arm, feeling the hard anger running through him at the moment. "Daddy will be all right," she told him. "I just know it." She squeezed his arm and turned to the others. Little Jake stood near his grandmother, fighting his own tears.

"Let's all pray," Evie said.

They bowed their heads, and Randy squeezed Peter's hand so tightly that her knuckles went white. Evie managed to get through an intense prayer while struggling against her own need to break down and weep. She knew her mother's strong intuition when it came to her father. If the woman felt he was in pain, he probably was, and that tore at Evie's heart. Next to Jesus Christ, she worshipped her father as the strongest man on the face of the earth. Whatever was wrong, he could surely get through it.

Forty-nine

JAKE STRAINED AGAINST THE ROPES THAT HELD HIS wrists to two posts. He did all in his power to stand on just his good leg. The pain in his broken left leg was enough to beg God to let him die. Through a haze, he saw the fancy-dressed don approach him.

"By now you know that I am Don Jesus Ricardo de Leon," the man sneered, "and I know you are the famous gunman from America. Soon I will report you as *dead*, Jake Harkner! You stole the woman who was to be my virgin mistress. They say you paid big money to spend the night with her. You took her *virginity*, and then you tried to steal her away. You killed the men I paid to bring her to me. *No* one goes against Don de Leon! Especially no *American!*"

Jake grimaced with the ungodly pain as the man walked in a circle around him. He wore only his denim pants, and he knew the left leg of those pants was soaked with blood from his broken leg. He'd been stripped to the waist, and he knew what was coming. He refused to speak, and he refused to cry out. *God, if this man is going to kill me, just let it happen quickly!*

"I see that you have many scars on your back." The don walked around to stand in front of him again. "Scarred tissue does not heal well when it is reopened." He leaned closer. "And I am going to reopen your scars, Jake Harkner. And then I am going to feed you to the buzzards and let them finish you off. You will die feeling them pulling the meat off your back and your leg. You will die feeling them peck out your eyes." He stepped back, turning to someone. "Open up every scar on his back!" he ordered.

Jake had no idea where he was. Still somewhere in Mexico. That's all he knew. God willing, Cole had made off with Annie and was well on his way north. He knew the skin on his arms and chest and back was already torn from being dragged. He'd have been killed right then if Don de Leon hadn't ordered it to stop. He wanted Jake still alive so he could make him suffer even more.

Somewhere in the swirl of black pain, Jake knew what was coming. He gritted his teeth. He'd never once cried out when his father used the buckle end of a belt on him, and he wasn't going to cry out when de Leon's whip lashed into him.

That promise proved hard to keep. He knew that when the first horrible sting came. He heard the loud snap of the whip, and he forced his mind to fall deep into the world of blackness where nothing hurt and nothing mattered. He'd learned to do that as a boy, and he could do it again.

Time and the number of lashes faded into a shroud of smoky clouds around him. Randy. He had to think of Randy...another lash.

And his beloved son, Lloyd. Another lash.

And his angel of a daughter, Evie. She seemed to be full of his own mother's spirit. Another lash.

And his precious Little Jake keeping his guns. Another lash.

And the love in Ben's eyes for finding a man who loved him like a real father should. Another lash.

The adoration in Stephen's eyes. Another lash.

And little Tricia and Sadie Mae. Another lash. Sadie Mae. Another. Sadie Mae...her gorgeous, dimpled smile. Another. The chickens. Sadie Mae's giggle. Her big eyes that held secrets. Another. Sadie Mae crying over broken eggs and then laughing over her grandpa's wild cussing when he went into the chicken coop.

Another lash.

He heard a chicken cluck. Somehow in the hideous darkness and pain, he managed to open his eyes and see it. A chicken. While he was being whipped, a chicken strutted right in front of him. Another lash.

Clucking. Pecking at grass seed. Another lash.

He actually grinned through the awful pain. Somehow Sadie Mae was with him. That chicken was a sign. Another lash.

Sadie Mae's little hands were folded, and her saint of a mother was praying for him. Another lash.

Of course she was. Whose prayers had more power than Evie's? Maybe the Pope. Another lash.

Randy! Was that Randy walking toward him? Was she greeting him like she always had back in Guthrie? Yes! There she was! *I'm back, Randy. I can't wait to hold you again*.

That was his last thought before he passed out, unaware that his abuser continued to wield the whip until his back was completely raw.

Don de Leon smiled. "Cut him down and take him into the desert. Let the buzzards finish him," he ordered his men. "And before you leave him there, cut off his privates!"

The two men taking Jake away looked at each other with the same thought. How could they do such a thing to a man? De Leon had never requested such a dastardly punishment.

De Leon walked away. He would report to the authorities that the famous Jake Harkner was dead, at the hands of Don Jesus Ricardo de Leon. He'd dealt his own form of justice, and now he would be famous for killing an American legend. Mexican authorities would do nothing about it. He owned them all.

Fifty

LLOYD SAW HIM FIRST. ON THE HORIZON. A LONE MAN on a horse, and pulling a packhorse along. Lloyd was familiar enough with every single horse and man on the J&L to know it wasn't Jake, and it wasn't Outlaw. His stomach tightened. It was a roan gelding. Cole. *God, no!*

It had been seven days since his mother nearly collapsed over thinking something had happened to Jake. *Damn it, Cole, where's Outlaw?*

Terrel happened to ride past, and he shouted to Terrel to get down off his horse. "Go tell Peter to keep my mother in the house," he told Terrel.

"Yes, sir." Terrel looked toward where Cole was coming in. "Shit," he mumbled, hurrying to the house.

Lloyd mounted Terrel's horse and charged up the hill before Cole could come any closer. He rode in a circle around the man. "Where's my father?" he shouted.

Cole reined his horse to a halt, devastation written all over his haggard face. He just closed his eyes and shook his head.

"Goddamn it, Cole, where's my *father!*"

Cole removed his hat and rubbed his shirtsleeve across his forehead. "He ain't comin'."

"That's it?" Lloyd practically screamed. "*He ain't comin'?* That's all you have to say?"

Cole whirled his horse. "Yeah, Lloyd, that's it! He's as much as dead, and I couldn't do a damn thing about it! *Shoot* me if you want. I'd be *glad* if you did, because right now I'd just as soon be dead myself except for the fact I don't have the guts to put my own gun to my head and pull the trigger! Jake *chose* what happened, Lloyd! He did it to give me and Annie time to get away, and now he's *dead*!"

"You're *lying*!" Lloyd leapt right off his horse and into Cole, knocking him off his mount and to the ground. Cole covered his face as the much bigger Lloyd began pummeling him, calling him a fucking liar and a coward. "You left him!" he roared. "You left him behind, didn't you?"

In moments, several of the ranch hands surrounded them. It took six of them to get Lloyd off Cole, who got to his knees, then managed to stand up, his face cut and bleeding. Lloyd went for his gun, but Terrel grabbed it, and with the help of three other men, they managed to get it away from Lloyd.

"Jesus, Lloyd, that's *Cole*!" Terrel told him. "He'd never abandon Jake of his own accord, and you *know* it! And he ain't gonna fight you back. He knows you still ain't healed on the inside."

Lloyd glared at Cole as he jerked away from the men who held him. He grasped his middle and turned away. "Where's my father?" he groaned.

"I did every goddamn thing I could do, Lloyd. You gotta know that! It came down to a choice of me and him *both* dyin' and a Mexican don getting his hands on Annie… which would have defeated the entire purpose of Jake riskin' his life like that. Jake even gave me his guns to keep for Little Jake. I tried my best to save him, but I *couldn't*! Do you understand? I couldn't! If I could go back there and trade my life for your father's, I *would*, because my life ain't worth a *shit*. I'd die for any member of this family, and you goddamn well *know* it. You *know* there wasn't one damn thing I could do, or I would have *done* it!"

Lloyd stumbled away from them, then went to his knees. *Pa!* He heard his mother then, screaming for him. "Oh, my God," he moaned. After a moment, he managed to get to his feet and turned to see the men standing in a group, surrounding Cole as though they feared Lloyd would charge into him again. Blood streamed from a cut on Cole's cheek, mixed with silent tears that came from Cole's eyes. Cole, a man seemingly immune to softer feelings—a crusty cowboy as tough as nails, crying. Cole, a hardened ex-outlaw, much like Jake…the kind of man Jake would be if not for—

"Lloyd, where is Jake?"

Randy screamed the words as she headed up the hill. Lloyd hurried down to intercept her. A moment later, she screamed Jake's name loud enough for everyone around the homestead to hear.

"No! No! It's not true!"

Lloyd had to keep an arm around her to keep her from collapsing as he helped her back to the house.

Evie came running, then folded to her knees. Katie came out of her and Lloyd's house and ran to Lloyd. He put his other arm around his wife and herded her and his mother inside. Peter came out to help with Randy, and Brian ran to Evie, helping her up. She turned and collapsed against her husband, weeping.

Cole looked away and walked to his horse . He studied the vast expanse of the J&L spread out in all its glory beyond the hillside. "This place ain't never gonna be the same," he told the other men. "Not ever."

"What happened down there in Mexico, Cole?" Terrel asked.

It took Cole a moment to answer. "I think he just gave up." Cole swallowed and sniffed. "Jake Harkner has been fightin' his own demons his whole life, and he finally stopped tryin'. That's the only way I see it."

A couple of the other men turned away with tears in their eyes.

Terrel spoke up. "This will kill his wife. She won't survive this. Last winter was bad enough, but she only got through that because of Jake. She ain't gonna get through this."

Fifty-one

AFTER EVERYTHING HAD CALMED DOWN SOME, LLOYD had someone get Cole and bring him to the house. The whole family sat in stunned silence as Cole explained exactly what happened, fighting his tears as he did so.

"Poor little Annie is so devastated. She can't get over what he did for her. *He was so nice to me*, she kept sayin'. *He spent the whole night with me, and all he did was put his arm around me and tell me not to be scared*. She feels horrible about having to leave him behind."

Brian spoke up. "Then we need to have her come out here to the J&L. She needs to know none of this is her fault, and I think the family will feel better if they can meet her."

Cole nodded. "She's a beautiful, beautiful girl. Incredibly innocent for what she went through." He glanced at Randy. "She said as how Jake said how much he loved his wife. She couldn't get over the fact that he paid three thousand dollars for a night with her and then sat there and talked about his wife and grandchildren."

That brought a few smiles, a welcome break from the heartache they were suffering.

"Gretta's in a bad way too," Cole told them. "She's just flat-out destroyed. She said she's closin' up her place and turnin' it into a legitimate roomin' house, but right now I'm worried about her state of mind. She's so happy Annie is back. She just wants her daughter to have a normal life and fall in love and marry like a natural woman ought to do, but she's sick about Jake. She's so damn sorry to all of you, and she feels so guilty. I promised her nobody would blame her, but she's a mess."

"Then you need to go back to Denver, Cole," Evie told him. "We'll give you a letter to take to her."

Cole sighed, nodding toward the cloth bag he'd laid on the table. "There's Jake's guns," he told them. "He half threw them at me and said as how he'd promised them to Little Jake. I think he just didn't want them men who was after him to get hold of them, 'cuz they're famous and all. He wanted them to stay in the family."

Little Jake got up from his chair and stormed over to Cole and started hitting him with his fists. "I don't want 'em!" he cried. "I don't want Grandpa's guns! I want Grandpa! You let him die! You let him die!"

Brian pulled the boy off Cole and hung on to him as he kept kicking and flailing his fists. "Stop it, Jake!" he demanded.

"Jake, this is not Cole's fault," Evie told him as she joined Brian in trying to calm the boy down. "Your grandfather is probably with God now. He's in the best place he's ever been." She broke down herself, and turned away.

"Apologize to Cole!" Brian ordered his son. "He risked his life trying to get Jake out of there. You *know* Cole. He wouldn't leave your grandfather to die unless he had absolutely no other choice!"

Little Jake jerked in a sob, hanging his head. "I'm... sorry."

Cole grabbed one of his arms and squeezed. "Little Jake, as much pain as he was in, your grandfather thought to give me them guns. Just think what that means. He was thinkin' about you. You can honor him by taking damn good care of them guns and growin' up to be a strong, good man like your grandpa was. And don't use them guns for nothin' bad. Your grandpa wants you to learn the new ways and be a law-abidin' man. You've seen how your grandpa suffered because of his own past. He doesn't want that for any of you."

Little Jake straightened, wiping at his tears. He looked around the table. "Don't anybody call me Little Jake again," he told them. "You call me *Jake*! Just *Jake*!" He ran out the door, and they could hear his sobs as he kept running. Ben laid his head in his arms on the table and wept, and Stephen got up and walked into the great room to curl up in his grandfather's chair.

Lloyd stood near Katie, and she reached out to grasp his hand. "Lloyd, I don't know what to say to you. I'm so sorry for you," she wept.

Brian sighed and rubbed at his eyes. Evie sank back into her chair and covered her face, breaking into more tears. "Daddy," she cried.

"I should have gone with him," Lloyd lamented again. He squeezed Katie's hand, then let go and turned away. "Ever since the Outlaw Trail, we've been together through everything. We've had each other's backs for years, all those times in No Man's Land back in Oklahoma, going up against the worst of them, we always looked out for each other. And last summer, when I was shot, he stayed right there with me day and night for weeks and took care of me, and he almost got hanged for avenging what happened to me." His voice broke, and he wiped at his eyes. "Damn it! He can be such a stubborn...sonofabitch! I never should have let him talk me into staying. I should have been *with* him!"

"You probably would have *died* with him, Lloyd," Cole told him. "He didn't want you to take that risk. Look at that beautiful wife of yours, carryin' another one of your young 'uns. You couldn't risk leaving her to raise all them kids alone. And you have a big ranch to run. The welfare of the whole family depends on this place and on you. You gotta know this is what your father wanted...for you to be right here where you belong. He damn well knew you'd have risked your life for him in a second, but he didn't want that."

They remained silent for a few minutes, every one of them trying to get control of themselves. Peter took hold of Randy's hand and squeezed.

"Some of you…uh…aren't my biggest fans," he told them, "but"—his voice broke a little—"you have to know I liked the hell out of Jake…and I respected the man for the way he could…keep going in spite of the hard life he led. I saw his goodness, in spite of that gruff facade he had. Surely you know how much I cared about him, or I wouldn't have done so much for him. Yes, it was for your mother too, but I was proud to call Jake a friend. I wish I knew what to tell you now…how to find comforting words."

"You've been a good, good friend, Peter," Evie told him. She broke into tears again and couldn't finish.

"Did he find anything about his past in Brownsville?" Randy asked. She sat rigid, clinging to Peter's hand, but after her initial screams of devastation and nearly collapsing, strangely, she wasn't crying now.

"Yes, ma'am," Cole told her. "He…he found the house where he grew up."

Nearly all of them gasped.

"What did he do?" Evie asked.

Cole shook his head. "It was pretty bad. He took a sledgehammer to it. It was just stone walls…no roof and nothin' inside. He battered them walls till they was knocked into rubble. Then he showed me where his ma and brother was buried. He'd already gone to a mortician and ordered a headstone for it. He told me that if he didn't make it back, I should make sure the headstone was taken care of. I did."

"Jake…oh, Jake, I should have been with you for that," Randy said, closing her eyes.

"He did say…more than once, ma'am…*I need Randy.*

But he got through it, and if it's any comfort…I think it gave him some peace, bein' able to put a headstone on his ma's burial place."

"Oh, my God, that must have been awful for him," Lloyd groaned, finally sitting down beside Katie. Katie rubbed a hand across his back, and Lloyd put his head in his hands.

"I just sat and waited for him to do what he had to do," Cole told them. "He sat there by his ma's grave most of the day, not sayin' nothin'."

"Jesus, Cole, I'm sorry for attacking you," Lloyd told him. "You've been a damn good friend to me and Jake both. I just didn't want to believe…" He couldn't finish.

"I half expected it," Cole told him. "And you don't know how bad I wish it had been me them men made off with and not your father." He looked at Randy. "Randy, Jake's last words was to tell you…uh…tell you he loves you," Cole told her.

Randy looked around the table, then let go of Peter's hand and rose. "All of you listen to me."

They looked at her in surprise. Lloyd got up again and moved to stand behind her. He put his hands on her shoulders. "Mom—"

"It's okay, Lloyd." She thought a moment before speaking. "Lloyd called Jake a stubborn sonofabitch, and he damn well is. He's the toughest man I've ever known. And any boy who can survive what he survived can handle a lot more as a man. We already know what a fighter he is." She looked at Evie. "Jake is not dead, Evie. Your prayers are too strong for God to have let him die. And he said he'd come back to me."

"Mother, you have to face the truth."

Randy looked at Cole. "You said they dragged him off, but they didn't kill him."

"Ma'am, he had a broken leg, and then they dragged him. Ain't no man gonna survive that. And even if he did, them men ain't gonna let him live. There's no sense thinkin' otherwise."

Randy turned to Peter. "I should think we have a right to demand to see a body," she told him. "Don't we? Can't we send someone to Mexican authorities and explain what happened and demand to know just what happened to my husband after they took him away? It was Mexican *citizens* who took him, not the law."

If not for the gravity of the situation, Peter would have smiled. Randy was not going to give up on Jake Harkner. "I can see what we can do."

"You do that, Peter." She looked at the rest of them. "Until we have a body—some kind of real proof—I refuse to believe my husband is dead. Jake Harkner knows suffering, and he'll bear it if he sees any hope of making it back here to his family, to little Tricia and Sadie Mae, to Ben and to the grandsons he so treasures... and to *me*! He'll come back for *me*! He *always* does. He promised me he'd be back, and I choose to believe that he will. And you, Evie, need to pray that whatever your father is suffering now, God will bring him help and solace and take away his pain."

They looked at one another, trying to decide if Randy could be right or if she'd finally lost her mind. After all, how could Randy go on without the man who was her lover, her soul mate, her heartbeat?

"Ma'am, you shouldn't get your hopes up," Cole told her. "You don't know them men down there. They're bound to execute him. And they have a lot of power, even over the law."

Randy looked at Cole. "But when they took him away, he was still alive. Those men don't know my Jake. He is a mean sonofabitch," she repeated. "Lloyd always says so. Those men are going to make him very, very angry, and we all know what Jake is like when he's angry. Even I don't want to be around him when he's like that. And pain doesn't frighten him. I, for one, will never believe he's dead until I have proof."

"Mother, don't do this to yourself," Evie begged.

"Evie Harkner Stewart, what happened to your faith? You've prayed your father through prison and that leg wound back in Guthrie, and me through surgery, and it's your faith that helped you survive. You prayed your brother back to life last year, and you prayed for me when"—her voice wavered—"last winter. And your father and I found each other again, and our love has never been stronger. Now you need to believe your father is alive and pray that whatever he is suffering, God will help him through it and bring him back to us. And right now, I need to be strong. Jake would want that."

She turned to Lloyd. "He would want that for you too, Lloyd. You are damn well your father's son. You're an absolute replica of the man, right down to your very soul. You need to go on with life, running this ranch, being a wonderful father and husband and brother and son. Keep this ranch going like it always has, because when Jake gets back, he'll want to see that you've gone on just fine without him. He'd *want* that."

Who do you belong to?

Randy nearly gasped when the words hit her. It was as though Jake was standing right beside her and whispering the words into her ear. She put a hand to her chest and nearly doubled over.

Jake Harkner, she told him inside.

Every beautiful inch of you.

Randy put a hand to her quivering lips, new tears coming. "He's alive. I know it. He's alive. If he wasn't, I'd know it."

Fifty-two

THEY WAITED...AND WAITED. IT WAS ANOTHER MONTH, the end of August, when Peter showed up again at the J&L, this time with Jeff Truebridge. Once Jeff heard the story, he couldn't resist being part of the search for Jake in Mexico. Not only was the subject of Jake Harkner's possible demise a top nationwide story, but Jeff deeply cared. The whole family greeted him with hugs and handshakes, their tears mixed with Jeff's when he and Peter brought them the bad news.

"We got next to nothing as far as cooperation from Mexican authorities," Peter told them.

Jeff removed his ever-present wire-rimmed glasses and wiped them with a handkerchief, then wiped at his eyes. "It's pretty obvious the law in that area is run by this Don de Leon," he told them, "and he refused to talk to us. He sent some older man who worked for him to speak with us and the Mexican authorities. He told us..." Jeff hesitated, wiping at his eyes again.

"My God," he continued. "Jake's just about the toughest man I've ever known. Being his friend has been the best thing that ever happened to me. When I got to know him... I never dreamed he could be that good of a friend. Being able to say I rode with Jake Harkner is my proudest honor."

"What did that Mexican man tell you?" Lloyd asked, fearing the answer.

"He said—" He put his glasses back on. "I don't know how to tell you without just saying it flat out. The don accused Jake of stealing from him. We all know it was that girl, but he claimed it was horses, which he said gave him the right to kill Jake. He admitted Jake had a broken leg and was pretty battered from being dragged for a ways. They didn't do a thing to wrap or set his broken leg, and the don ordered him—" He removed his glasses again. "God help me get over this," he wept. "He ordered him…to be whipped until he passed out."

"Oh, my God, Jake!" Randy bent over in her chair, her head in her hands. "Jake! Jake!"

"It's a good thing we talked you into staying here and letting us go," Peter told Lloyd. "You're as bad as your father with that temper of yours, and you probably would have done something to get *yourself* in trouble too. You probably would have gone after that wealthy don and ended up missing, just like your father." He sighed. "According to the old man, some of de Leon's men took Jake into the desert to die a slow death," he finished, his own emotional pain obvious in his voice. "The don's words were to let the buzzards finish him off."

"Daddy!" Evie groaned. "How could God let this happen?"

"But we still don't have a body, do we?" Lloyd growled. He stood behind Katie, refusing to sit down or to cry. "Did anyone take you to where they left him to die?"

Peter reached over and touched Randy's shoulder. "Yes."

"And?" Lloyd looked ready to grab something and throw it.

"No body," Peter told him. "The old man swore that's where they left it, but they'd stripped him naked, so there were no clothes left to prove anything."

"Not even any bones?" Lloyd asked, feeling ill at having to put it so bluntly.

Peter shook his head.

"Then my mother might be right. It doesn't matter

if it was buzzards or ants or coyotes or anything else. I've seen enough animals with their bones picked bare to know there is always *something* left. Always *something*! The only way there would be nothing left is if the body got moved—or if he lived."

"Or was buried," Peter reminded him.

"Who would bother, out there in the desert?" Lloyd argued.

"But how can a man survive something like that?" Katie asked.

"Father is no ordinary man," Lloyd insisted. "Over time, I've come to think like Mom. She says she has felt Jake with her, and so have I."

Randy looked up at him. "Lloyd, what happened?"

Lloyd nervously began smoothing Katie's hair away from her face, his voice broken from the pain in his heart. "I heard his voice." He held his chin high, his jaw flexing from a struggle not to completely break down. "Last night. I was dead asleep, and someone called my name, clear as a bell. I actually grabbed my gun, because I thought someone was in the room. *I love you, son*, he said. I got up and turned on a light, but no one was there. Katie slept right through it."

Evie raised her head and looked at him. "I heard him too!" She wiped at tears. "I didn't say anything, because I was afraid you'd all think I was losing my mind—or letting prayer give me false hope." She turned and looked up at Brian, who stood behind her, grasping her shoulders. "Brian, I couldn't sleep. I went downstairs to heat some coffee, and I could swear he was standing right behind me. He whispered in my ear. *My angel*, he said." She jerked in a sob. "As God is my witness, someone spoke to me. I turned, and no one was there."

Jeff shook his head. "I'd like to think you're right, but from what we heard and what we saw where he was left...the condition he must have been in. There's no way he could have survived. Not on his own. It was obvious the don is a powerful and ruthless man. He would not have allowed Jake to live."

"I hate to say it," Brian told them, "but an untreated broken leg goes wrong terribly fast. He wouldn't have been able to walk on it, and lying out there in that kind of heat... Even if he somehow lived, he'd lose that leg to infection."

"I'm so sorry to say this," Peter said, "but hearing his voice—it could be his spirit talking. From someplace else. Evie, maybe you simply prayed him to heaven. We searched all the surrounding villages, and no one knew of him. Believe me, we did everything we could to try to find out what might have happened to him if he didn't die. But it would have been virtually impossible for any man to survive what was done to your father. And maybe"—he squeezed Randy's shoulder—"maybe coyotes or whatever did drag his bones away. Besides that, the desert sun can turn bones to dust."

Lloyd turned away. "Not right away," he insisted. "It takes years." He leaned against a doorjamb and held on to it. "Pa! It can't be this way! It can't be this way! He should be buried here on the J&L, up at that line shack, where Mom wants to be buried beside him. It can't end this way. Not for a man like Jake Harkner."

"I don't even know what to report to the newspapers," Jeff told them. He swallowed and sniffed. "The man made me famous. That book earned me a writing award. Little did I know how unfinished it was when I had it published. *Jake Harkner, The Legend and The Myth*. Now the legend is—what the hell really happened to the man?"

"All we can do is pray for his soul," Evie told them. "We have to behave as though Daddy were gone. He always said he'd have a hard time getting into heaven because of the life he led, but I've never feared for one minute that God would turn him away."

"We should have some kind of ceremony," Katie told them, rubbing at her now-growing belly. "And we need to remember that Jake Harkner isn't dead. He lives in Lloyd and Evie and all his wonderful grandchildren and the one I'm carrying now. Jake never thought he would end up with such a big, loving family, so he...he died a happy man. That's the only way we can face this and live with it."

Lloyd turned from the pantry doorway and looked at his mother. "Somehow, we have to put this to rest. We need to go on as a family."

Peter kept rubbing Randy's shoulders. "Jake was definitely one of a kind," he offered. "And he most certainly lives on. He's standing right in front of us over there in that pantry doorway."

Lloyd shook his head. "No. There's nobody like my pa." He turned and walked out. Katie quickly got up and ran after him.

Randy could hardly feel her own body. How was she going to go on? How? She'd never even slept in their bed in the loft since that last night they made love before Jake left for Mexico. *Jake! You promised you would come back! You promised!*

This wasn't real. It simply couldn't be. Her whole life had been centered around Jake Harkner. Who was Miranda Hayes Harkner? She'd melted into a man named Jake all those years ago in the back of a wagon, and she'd never emerged as just Randy since then. It had always been *Jake* and Randy.

Darkness engulfed her, a darkness that took away all reality.

Fifty-three

ANOTHER WEEK PASSED.

Nothing.

Late August moved into mid-September.

Nothing.

Peter drank some of the coffee Randy had just poured for him. He watched her stack some dishes and pump water into the kitchen sink.

Busy. Always busy. She was constantly cleaning or cooking or trimming her roses or sewing or reading to Tricia and Sadie Mae. He knew it was all a facade—stay busy, don't think about the very real possibility that Jake Harkner was never coming back. Don't allow herself to believe that for one minute, or she'd fall apart and never recover.

Ben left for chores, and Peter decided to take this rare moment alone with her to settle what needed settling. "Randy, sit down, will you?"

She stopped what she was doing and just stood at the sink a moment. "You're leaving."

"Honey, I *have* to. I have a wife and a lot of work waiting for me in Chicago. Jeff has to go too. His wife could deliver at any time, and he's praying he's not already too late. We've done all we can possibly do to find out…what happened."

"To find out if Jake is really dead," she said rather coldly.

Peter sighed and rose. He walked up to her and grasped her arm, turning her. "Randy, look at me."

She closed her eyes and shook her head. "Your eyes will tell me the truth, and I don't want to hear it."

"My darling Randy, I am not going to make you admit Jake isn't coming back. I just want you to prepare yourself...to face the fact that Jeff and I and most everyone else believe the worst, but I'm not saying you have to give up hope. Please look at me."

Randy finally looked up at him. He studied the gray-green eyes that had always fascinated him. Her exotic eyes were part of her beauty. He had no doubt they were part of the reason Jake had fallen for her. A man could get lost in those eyes. "Please tell me you'll write, and that you'll send for me or come to me in Chicago if you truly need me. I'll go crazy with worry over you."

"Peter, I have a whole great big family to fall back on."

He shook his head. "That's not the same, and you know it. Randy. I have big shoulders. You can cry on my shoulder any time you need to."

Randy put a hand on his chest. "You have a wife, Peter."

"And she knows all about our friendship—and that's what it is. God knows when I was still single I longed for much more, but I knew better than to consider such a thing. Even so, I intend to remain a damn good friend, and I will always care about you. There is no changing that, and Treena knows it. And if you reach a point where it might help you get over this, you come to Chicago. Treena will welcome you with open arms, and Lord knows she can take you to all the best places a woman would want to see—the best shopping, stage performances, museums, you name it."

Randy shook her head. "You truly are my best friend, Peter Brown, but it wouldn't do any good for me to leave this place that Jake and I love so. I could go away for a year, but when I came home, all the familiar things around me would just hit me even harder.

Leaving won't change anything, Peter. It won't take away the memories. It won't heal the hurt. Only time can do that, and I'm not sure what's left of my lifetime will be long enough."

He put a hand to the side of her face. "Then promise me you will take the comfort of your children and grandchildren and remember they need you. And not for my sake, but for Jake's, because he'd want that. He'd want you to eat right and take care of yourself. Promise me you will do that, if not for me, then for Jake, whether he ever comes back or not."

Randy grasped his hand and kissed his palm. "I promise." She withered a little, leaning forward to put her head on his shoulder. "Jake Harkner is the toughest, most resilient man I've ever known, and that's why I cling to the hope he's still alive. God knows what he's suffering right now, but one thing I'm sure of is that he'll do anything it takes to get home…to the J&L… to his children and grandchildren…and to me. He'll do everything in his power to keep his promise that he'd come back. That's all that keeps me going."

Peter wrapped her in his arms. "And how long will you cling to that hope before facing the truth?"

Her eyes teared. "As long as necessary…until I know I can handle the worst. Right now, I can't. And I feel him with me, Peter. I don't know how to explain it. I just feel him with me. And I actually think he wouldn't mind you holding me."

Peter grinned. "I'm not so sure about that, although he did tell me once, when I took you away for that surgery, that you needed holding. I think the permission he gave me was only for then. If he walked in here right now, it might be a whole different story."

Randy smiled through her tears. "Maybe. You know Jake."

"Oh, my dear, I know him all too well." He rocked

her in his arms. "And I want him to come back as badly as you do, because I know what this is doing to you, and your happiness is all that matters to me. If I thought for one minute that wild ex-outlaw ever once abused you, things might be different. But I know he's never treated you with anything but adoration. Anyone can see it in his eyes, and sometimes the look in those eyes can be pretty intimidating, but never when he looks at you."

Randy straightened and kissed his cheek. "Peter, you *are* a good friend, and I'm so glad you came when you did. God meant for you to be here for me. Having you to talk to has helped me so much. And thank you for the invitation to come to Chicago, but I wouldn't fit in there. As sweet and accommodating as I know Treena would be, I would still feel out of place. I've lived out here in the Wild West too long to feel comfortable in a big city. And it wouldn't be fair to Treena, no matter how accepting she might be." She pulled away but kept hold of his hand. "I'm sure she misses you terribly. You go home to her, Peter. I promise I'll be all right. And I promise to write and tell you every single thing that's happening. But I can't promise I'll ever accept that Jake isn't coming home."

But he hasn't written or sent any kind of message. Surely if he was still alive he'd let you know. Peter couldn't bring himself to say the words she didn't want to hear. If he *was* alive but hadn't written, he could be wounded so badly he would never recover, or maybe he was rotting away in prison. "Then I can only pray very, very hard that I'll get a letter telling me Jake came home," he told her, squeezing her hand reassuringly. "I have always wanted to hate the man but never could. I wouldn't have minded landing a fist into him a time or two, but God knows what I'd get in return would have put me in the hospital."

Randy smiled and shook her head. "No. He'd probably

just get up and say he deserved it. Jake is very fond of you. He respects you, and he appreciates the things you've done for him and this family."

Peter studied her lovingly. "No man could have fallen into better luck, considering his condition when he met you, than Jake Harkner did. You're a fine woman, Randy Harkner. Be proud of what you did for that man, and for the kind of mother and grandmother you are. If I had ever enjoyed the privilege of loving you as a wife, I would have considered it a great honor. But I know that even if Jake is no longer alive, it wouldn't matter. You will remain married to a memory and unable to love any other man that way. But I feel damn lucky to have been able to remain your friend. You remember that I'm here for you. Don't ever, ever hesitate to ask me for anything you need, understand?"

A tear slipped down Randy's cheek. "I do. And if things had worked out differently, I would have considered it an honor to *be* your wife. But that never once entered my mind, Peter. I couldn't let it. Since I was twenty years old, only one man has consumed my heart and soul, and if he never comes back, that won't change. Thank you for being so good to me...to *all* of us. You and my son-in-law Brian are two of the finest, most patient, most genteel men I have ever known. You're both honorable and truly good men." She let go of his hand. "You'd better go now. Come to supper tonight, will you? You and Jeff both."

"We will. And I think it's best we leave plenty early tomorrow."

Randy wiped at tears with a shaking hand. "Yes. Take some of my homemade biscuits with you. And do give Treena my love."

Peter struggled against his urge to cry. God, how he loved her! Yet there was nothing he wanted more now than to learn Jake Harkner was still alive...that he'd come home. As much as he loved this woman he could never have, he loved the thought of her true happiness even more, and there was only one thing that would give her that. He sighed deeply and turned, squeezing her hand once more before letting go. He walked to the door and hesitated. "This isn't goodbye, Randy. I hate goodbyes. I want to always stay in touch and maybe bring Treena out here again. She loved that last visit. Would that be all right?"

"Of course it would."

"I mean…even if Jake doesn't make it back?"

Randy wiped at more tears. "Yes. Even if he doesn't make it back. He would want that. He's never quite gotten over Treena calling him magnificent. We joke about it… I mean, we used to joke about it often. The men ribbed him something awful about that."

Peter grinned and nodded, then turned away again. "God bless you, Randy Harkner."

"And God bless *you*, Peter Brown."

He walked out. He could hear her crying, but he didn't dare go back inside. Damned if he didn't feel someone watching…someone big and tall and strong and intimidating and possessive. No one would ever touch Jake Harkner's woman. He owned her, even in death.

Fifty-four

SEPTEMBER SOON BECAME OCTOBER, AND THE ASPEN IN the surrounding foothills turned a bright gold, creating glorious color against the dark pine trees. An empty feeling prevailed over the ranch as November moved in. Even the aspen seemed to reflect the mood, becoming empty and bare as heavy snows blanketed the magnificent peaks in the higher mountains.

Ranch hands took on the chores of storing feed, and Lloyd was compelled to travel to Boulder to use some of the Pinkerton reward money to buy that extra feed. It was a long trip there and back, and heavy snow slowed them down, but he made it back to the ranch. Sometimes it felt as though something were eating up his insides. His soul felt as desolate as the winter winds and the lifeless terrain.

His third child with Katie was born late December, a son they named Jeffrey Peter, after the two men who'd become such an important part of the family's life. Family was his only reason for hanging on, and it was the same for Evie, whose husband remained her rock, along with her faith. By the time Jeffrey Peter was born, Evie was pregnant again. New babies helped them to understand that life goes on. Jake Harkner lived on, his blood running in the veins of the grandchildren.

But Randy was not quite the same and probably never would be. The hardest part of all was not even having a body to bury. She never slept upstairs again, and the line shack she and Jake had loved to visit sat unused.

The woman seemed a mere shell of herself. She seldom smiled, pressing on only for the sake of the grandchildren.

Christmas passed with only light gift-giving, and then only homemade dolls and clothing for the little girls. The older boys weren't in the mood for giving or getting gifts. They only brought in a small tree and didn't decorate it as heavily as normal. The family struggled to make it a merry Christmas for the smallest children, but none of the adults nor the older boys felt the normal Christmas joy.

January came and went. February brought spring snows that would melt with the sun and then return. Horse Creek began to swell from snowmelt higher in the Rockies, and it came time for searching the sprawling J&L rangeland for cattle that managed to survive the winter. Soon they would have a full roundup and start sorting and branding the calves.

Randy kept herself busy baking extra bread for the men to take with them as they scattered throughout the rangeland and camped for days at a time. Several loaves sat on the table the morning it happened. It was one of those Sundays when the whole family sat around the big kitchen table for breakfast. Randy was still in her stocking feet when she heard it.

The whistle.

She'd been ready to set a plate on the table.

She dropped it.

The plate crashed to the floor.

"Mother?" Evie rose. "What's wrong?"

"Jake! Did you hear it? That whistle?"

"Mom, the men are coming in and out all the time. Sometimes they shout and whistle."

There it was again! This time, Evie gasped. She remembered that whistle…the morning her father had come to rescue her at Dunc Hollow. It was the same whistle he used to give when he came into Guthrie with outlaws in tow, signaling Randy he was back home. She knew instantly she was safe. Jake had come.

Randy charged out the front door.

"Mom, you don't even have any shoes on!" Lloyd yelled, running after her.

"And no coat!" Evie hollered.

Too late. Randy was off and running in stockinged feet through snow a good eighteen inches deep.

Four of the men came charging down the hill toward the houses, all of them whistling and whooping and shouting and yipping until the sound filled the sky.

"Jake's back!"

"Mother!" Evie started after Randy.

Lloyd grabbed her arm. "Leave her be, sis."

By then the whole family was out on the veranda, even the littlest ones, no coats or boots and not feeling a thing. Sadie Mae jumped up and down. "Grampa! Grampa!"

There came more whistles and shouts when men came tearing out of the bunkhouse, some of them standing there in only their long johns.

Little Jake—whom everyone now called "just Jake"—moved beside his father and started crying. Brian put an arm around him. Evie looked up at Lloyd, and Lloyd pulled her into his arms.

"My God, he's alive," he wept into his sister's hair.

And Randy kept running. She fell twice. She didn't feel the cold snow at all. She just ran. Jake kicked his horse into a faster run and climbed off it before it even came to a halt.

"Evie, he's limping," Lloyd said.

Evie let go of him and watched. "But he's alive! Dear God in heaven, he's alive!"

Randy left all of them behind. She reached Jake, and there was nothing to say. He grabbed her up and turned with her, keeping her feet off the ground until he stepped wrong and they both fell into the snow.

"I have a bum leg, Randy," he told her.

"Jake, just hold me! Hold me! Hold me! Nothing else matters! I knew you were alive! I knew it!"

They rolled over and over in the snow, until they were covered in white.

Jake buried his face in her hair, breathing deeply of its rose scent, then buried his face against her neck. "My God, I can't believe you're in my arms. For a long time I was sure I'd never hold you again."

"Don't let go, Jake!"

"I sure as hell won't!" He breathed deeply of her familiar scent. "By God, you've been baking that bread, haven't you? The best goddamn bread in the whole country. I can smell it on you."

Randy couldn't talk for her tears. Jake found her lips, and her mouth had never tasted so sweet.

For Randy, his kiss had never been so precious. For several minutes, they just lay in the snow, holding, touching, kissing, unable to speak until Randy finally found her voice again.

"Jake, how? When?"

"It's a long story, *mi querida esposa*. An old Mexican man found me and took me to a cave where he lived. He was some kind of hermit, gave me food and water, a place to rest. But what really saved me was thinking about you…and my family…and little Sadie Mae and the chickens."

More kisses. More tears.

"Chickens? Jake, what on earth—"

"I don't want to talk about it now. I just want to look at you." His eyes were wet with tears as he kissed her hair, her eyes, her lips, her throat. "I was so scared you'd give up if you thought I was dead. My God, you look so good, baby." He wiped at tears, then used his thumbs to wipe away Randy's tears. "It's that promise I made that kept me going through the worst pain and blackness of my life. That promise that I'd come back." He looked down at her, just then coming to his senses and realizing she wore no coat. "Randy, you'll freeze to death!"

"I don't feel it. I saw you coming, and I just started running. Oh, Jake, we searched for you. The Mexican authorities kept telling us you were dead, but I wouldn't believe it. I wouldn't believe it!"

"Terrel rode in with me. He told me Cole made it back, and Annie is all right."

"Yes. Oh, Jake, Cole was so heartbroken. There is just so much to talk about. Little Jake won't let us call him that anymore. It's just Jake. And Katie had a baby—another boy. And Evie is pregnant again. And Cole has been visiting Gretta a lot. She closed her place and runs a rooming house now and—"

He cut her off with another kiss, a deep, long, warm kiss of a man hungry for much more. "We have so much catching up to do, so much to say. I found her, Randy. I found my mother's grave and—"

"Cole told us, Jake. I'm so, so sorry you went through that alone." They continued kissing over and over. Randy put her hands to his face. "Let me look at you."

Jake smiled as she ran her hands over his face and into his hair. "Jake, you look the same, but you're so much thinner."

"That bread and your homemade pies will fatten me up soon enough." He pushed some of the hair off her face. "Tell me you didn't starve yourself like last winter. You look thin, baby, but not as bad as then."

"I've been eating as best I can. The children made me eat."

Jake sobered. "They whipped me, Randy, as bad as a man can be whipped. My back is worse than before. Scar tissue doesn't heal easily. It took weeks for the skin to close up. And the pain... I forced myself to think about you. I saw your face. I heard your voice. I saw you walking to greet me, like you used to do back in Guthrie."

"Oh, Jake, I heard your voice. And I felt you with me. I felt it when you were in pain. I can't imagine how awful it must have been for you."

"And I broke my leg. Outlaw fell on it. They refused to set the bone. The old Mexican man wanted to cut it off, but I wouldn't let him. I have a limp, Randy—"

"Jake, it's all right. You're alive, and you're back home on the J&L. Brian can help you." She grasped his face in her hands again and lay still to look at him. "And you still have that smile that melts my heart." She shivered with new tears. "And just look at you! You're still my handsome Jake. I'll feed you and nurse you and you'll heal even more, Jake. We'll get you completely well and—"

"Do you even know how beautiful you are?" he interrupted her. "In all our years together, you've never looked more beautiful." He ran his hands over her body, as though to prove to himself she was really in his arms. Again he showered her with kisses. "There were moments when I feared I'd never get to touch you again, hear your voice, hold you in my arms."

"It was the same for me, Jake." She hugged him around the neck again.

Jake kissed her neck again, her lips. "Let's get you out of this snow." He sat up and removed his wool jacket and put it around her. Yes, he was thinner, but still solid and strong...the same broad shoulders and the same solid arms, the same dark eyes and that smile...that smile...

"I want to spend about a month with you up at the line shack," he told her. "Just you and me and the wolves and the bears and the wind and—" His voice broke.

"My darling, Jake, I want the same. But first you need to rest...truly rest...for as long as it takes to get all your strength back. I'll fatten you up again on that bread. And right now there is a big, beautiful family waiting for you down at the house. I want to hog you all to myself, but they've all been so devastated. You need to go down there and let them see it's really you and that their father and grandfather is alive."

He pressed her close. "Tell me that peppermint stick is still on the nightstand."

"It is. I never moved it."

"You have no idea how badly I want to sleep in our own bed tonight. It will be like heaven."

"And it will be heaven for me just having you there beside me."

"Baby, I can't stand on my leg for too long at a time yet."

"It's okay, Jake."

"I don't want to let go of you."

"I don't want to let go either, but we have to get you someplace warm, and Lloyd and Evie and all the grandkids are waiting to see you, Jake."

Another long, delicious kiss. Jake managed to get to his feet. He helped Randy onto her horse, then grimaced as he mounted up behind her to ride down the hill to the homestead. Ben and the four bigger of his seven grandchildren literally tackled Jake when he dismounted, screaming and laughing but also crying. Jake fell back into the snow, and Brian and Randy helped pull them off.

"Hold up there! We don't know if your grandpa is still hurting," Brian warned them.

"I'm all right, Brian."

Brian could see the man most certainly was *not* all right. Without even examining him or asking what had happened, he could tell Jake was in pain. God only knew what had happened to him, but he most certainly needed to get inside and get some rest. He couldn't even get to his feet on his own. Brian reached out for him, and Jake grimaced a little as he got to his feet.

In the next second, Lloyd grabbed his father close. Father and son held each other for several long seconds. "Damn it, Pa, I should have been with you."

"It's okay, Lloyd. I'm damn glad you *weren't*. You would have insisted on staying to help me, and you might have been killed. I'm damn lucky to be alive."

"We heard you, Pa," Lloyd told him, his voice wavering as he continued to embrace Jake. "Me and Evie and Mom—we all heard you talk to us. We never fully believed you were dead."

"God, I missed you, son. I missed all of you. I thought about giving up, but I couldn't stand the thought of never seeing any of you again, or never holding your mother in my arms again."

Jake finally let go of Lloyd. Both men had tears on their cheeks. Jake turned to Evie, crushing her close as she wept. "You did this, Evie. I knew you'd be praying for this worthless old man."

"Oh, Daddy, God knows what a good man you are. That's why He brought you back to us. You're so loved, Daddy."

Jake made the rounds, hugging every grandchild again, wiping at more tears, hugging Katie and the new baby. "By God, Katie, I think you get more beautiful with each new baby you have. At this rate, you'll have fifteen more, because you just keep getting prettier."

Katie blushed as Jake was herded into the house and peppered with questions while every family member cried and laughed and cried and laughed. Jake kept telling them it had been a long, tiring trip home, and he'd tell them everything after a good night's sleep.

Cole rode in before Jake could make his way upstairs. He dismounted and charged into the house and up to Jake, embracing him.

"Jake, you tough sonofabitch," he joked through tears. "Randy insisted you weren't dead, but after what

I saw them bastards do to you…" He pulled away for a moment, grasping Jake's shoulders. "Don't you ever, ever ask me to go with you for somethin' like that again! Your son beat the hell out of me when I got home for showin' up without you. I was wishin' he'd just shoot me and get it over with."

"My God, Cole, you did what you had to do. I never would have forgiven you if they'd got their hands on that girl. You did right, Cole."

"Gretta and Annie are goin' to be so happy to find out you made it home. They were devastated over this. Poor little Annie couldn't get over what you did for her."

Jake embraced the man again, slapping him on the back. "Go on out there and get drunk with the other men. I don't think Lloyd will mind if you end up having to sleep it off tomorrow."

Cole grinned and wiped at his eyes before looking Jake over. "Damned if you don't look good, Jake. When I saw them drag you off—" He sniffed and wiped at his nose with his coat sleeve. "Goddamn, I felt like somebody was rippin' my heart right out of my chest. You're a sight for sore eyes." He raised his chin a little, obviously embarrassed at his tears. "You can explain to me and the boys later. You need to be with your family." He grasped Jake's hand and squeezed it. "Welcome home, boss." He nodded to the rest of the family and left.

Little Jake walked up to Jake and hugged him all over again. Jake stepped back a little and looked him over. "By God, you've grown!"

Little Jake straightened to as tall as he could make himself. "Yup. And they call me Jake now—just Jake. From now on I am Jake, and you are *Big* Jake." The boy threw his arms around his grandfather once more.

"Calling me Big Jake is just fine with me." Jake gave him another hug, then turned to Stephen and Ben. Stephen was taller than Katie, and Ben looked like he was pushing eighteen. "Look at the three of you. The future of the J&L is looking damn good!"

The three boys had red, puffy eyes from crying. "We love you, Grandpa," Little Jake told him. "We talked a lot about how we didn't believe you died on account of you're too tough to die. I told everybody that."

"Well, we all die eventually, son, but I had a talk with God, and He decided it wasn't my time yet."

The three boys smiled through tears and straightened to stand as tall as they could. Jake kept hold of Randy's hand and limped over to sit down in his favorite chair. He noticed a blanket and pillow.

"That's where I've been sleeping," Randy told him. "I couldn't bring myself to sleep alone in that big bed upstairs."

He leaned down and kissed her. "Well, you sure as hell won't be sleeping up there alone tonight." He sat down in the chair and pulled her onto his lap. She kept his coat pulled tight around herself, and she curled her still-wet feet under the skirt of her dress to warm them. She rested her head on Jake's shoulder, and he wrapped his arms around her. "You feel so good in my arms."

"And your arms feel so good around me," Randy answered.

"Randy, I have a lot of healing to do yet. And I'm tired to my bones. I can't—"

"Jake, all that matters is you're here and alive and I can lie next to you tonight. We have plenty of time for everything else. We'll go to the line shack as soon as you feel up to it."

The rest of the family got some food ready, and all was sweet bedlam again. It was music to Jake's ears. He studied Randy's face as he smoothed back her hair and leaned down to kiss her again. "*Lo nuestro será eterno, Randy. Tu y yo estaremos unidos eternamente.*"

You and I are forever.

She was safe now. Jake was home.

Fifty-five

RANDY HELPED JAKE BATHE, HER HEART SICK AT THE sight of more scars on his back. There was barely a half inch of his original skin left there. She gently washed his back, almost afraid to touch it.

"It's okay," he told her. "There is no feeling to scar tissue."

Her eyes teared. "My God, Jake, how you must have suffered." Her voice broke as she rinsed his hair and back.

He reached behind him and touched her hand. "Don't cry, Randy. I'll be all right." He sighed. "Obviously, Don de Leon wasn't too happy that I stole his virgin from him."

"But you didn't even touch her."

"It wouldn't have mattered, and I didn't bother explaining. It was worth every lash, because it helped me cope with what my father did to Santana. I couldn't save her, but I did save Annie. At least this was something I could stop, and I'm glad as hell Cole got Annie back to Denver."

"We've seen her, Jake. She is so beautiful...and so deeply saddened by thinking you gave up your life for her. She and Gretta will be so incredibly happy to find out you're alive and home." She held out a towel for him, closing her eyes at the sight of the bump on the front of his left leg from the poorly healed break. "Jake, I know you're in pain. Please let Brian give you some laudanum."

He wrapped the towel around himself and limped over to where clean underwear lay. "No. You know how I feel about laudanum. It's nothing more than enhanced whiskey. You know I don't drink if I can help it."

"But, Jake—"

"Randy, I've lived with pain all my life. Brian said the bone just healed crooked, so my body produced more bone to fill in the gap. That's all it is. It will get stronger and stronger, and eventually the pain will lessen. It's one hell of a lot better than having the damn thing cut off. I would never have come home to you like that. Never. I can ride a horse, and I can walk on it." He pulled on the long johns and faced her, studying her lovingly. "I'll just have an old man's limp, I guess." He smiled sadly.

Randy walked closer, running her hands over his muscled arms and still-firm chest and flat belly. "You are no old man, Jake. You're amazing—the strongest man anyone could know." She moved her arms around his middle and kissed his chest. "And you're here and alive, and you know damn well I'd love you the same if you *did* come home with half a leg."

He sighed and wrapped her into his arms. "Well, I have a good one for you. Don de Leon told the men who dragged me into the desert to cut off my privates before they left me—just payment for taking his virgin, I guess."

Randy gasped. "My God, Jake!"

He leaned down and kissed her forehead. "Apparently, they chickened out. Maybe they even felt sorry for me. I don't know. All I know is when I came to, I still had my equipment, much to my great relief." He grinned and gave her a squeeze. "What if I'd come home without *that*?"

Randy laughed lightly and looked up at him. "That, Mr. Harkner, would have been something to give a lot of thought to. I suppose we would have had to reinvent how to have sex." Jake laughed too, and Randy drank in the sound with relish.

"I'm not even going to comment on that, Mrs. Harkner," he told her. He grasped her face and leaned down to kiss her softly. "And right now, I'd love to make sure this thing is still in working order, but I'm so goddamn tired and in so much pain, that's going to have to wait."

She reached up around his neck. "Oh, Jake, surely you don't think that matters. This is your first night home, and you've been to hell and back. Just being able to touch you, hear your voice and your laughter, and to know that tonight I can sleep in your arms are the most wonderful gifts God could have brought me. We have weeks, months, years to make up for this. As soon as you're fattened up a little and well rested, we'll go to the line shack, and we'll make up for lost time."

He gave her his best smile. "Sounds damn good to me." He kissed her hair. "Get undressed, woman. We might not be able to make love yet, but by God, I intend to feel your naked body against mine tonight. That's all I've thought about ever since I was able to think straight. That old Mexican told me I lay in a near coma for about a month. It was two more months before I could get up and walk around, but I was still in incredible pain and so weak I could only take a few steps. An old woman was there—his wife, I guess. He never said. She kept putting some kind of salve on my back that helped, and she rubbed my leg and kept bending it and making me move it so it wouldn't seize up on me. I don't know where they came from, other than God Himself must have sent them. I suspect one more day of lying naked and wounded in that desert would have done me in for good."

"This whole family was praying for you." Randy took his hand and led him to the bed. Jake gladly climbed into it.

"This feels so good I could cry," he told her as he settled into the quilts.

Randy smiled and undressed. "That bed will feel good to me too, because I haven't slept in it since you left. That peppermint stick is still lying there on the nightstand."

Jake rolled over and grabbed the candy. Randy climbed naked into bed, and he studied every curve, every slender line, the flow of her hair, the fullness of her breasts. He threw the covers over them and pulled her close. "My God, Randy, this is the longest we've been apart since I went to prison for four years." He put the peppermint stick into her mouth and kept the other end in his. They licked it until their lips met. Through it all, he moved his hand over her breasts, her soft belly, her hip bones, her sweet bottom, her slender legs, drifting his fingers past the blond hairs of her love nest, up to her neck. They finished the candy together, kissed deeply, settled against each other…and fell asleep in each other's arms for the first time in months.

Deep in the night, Jake ignored his pain. Bad memories woke him: the whip lashes, the desert, his broken leg, the boiling sun burning up his naked body. When he roused to consciousness, it took a few seconds to realize where he was…and that his beloved Randy was lying right beside him. She'd saved him from the darkness of hell over and over again. She lay here now in the flesh, not his imagination—naked and beautiful—still the woman he loved beyond measure, the woman who'd given up so much for him. He had to know this was real. It had simply been too long.

"Randy," he groaned. "*Tu eres mi vida, mi querida esposa.* I need to be inside of you."

She turned, rubbing at her eyes by the soft light of a low-lit lamp in the washroom. "I want that more than anything," she answered softly. "I just wanted you to be rested." She threw her arms around his neck. "I haven't even slept yet, Jake. I was just lying here enjoying the feel of your strong arm around me."

He moved on top of her, and she gladly opened herself to him.

"I don't want to hurt you. It's been such a long time, Randy."

"It doesn't matter." She helped guide his hard shaft into her depths, drawing in her breath at the feel of him, the realization that he really was here and all in one piece and making love to her. Usually he took his time with foreplay, but right now, they both needed this...just this...anxiously, desperately. She smiled at how glad she was that those men who took Jake into the desert hadn't cut off what gave her so much pleasure now.

He grasped her arms and moved them over her head. He moaned as he buried himself hard and deep, nuzzled her neck, and kissed her ear. "Who do you belong to?" he asked.

"Jake Harkner," she answered.

"Every last inch of you."

Epilogue

July 1898

IT WAS THE GRANDEST COOKOUT THE J&L HAD EVER held. The whole family was there, of course, Katie holding six-month-old Jeffrey in her lap and Sadie Mae pushing around a pram that held Evie and Brian's new baby, just two weeks old—a son named Cole, for the man who'd been such a good friend to their father. Sadie Mae beamed with pride over mothering her new baby brother.

Most of the ranch hands were there. Teresa, Katie, Evie, and Randy had been cooking and baking for days. Tables made of sawhorses and planks of wood were covered with checkered tablecloths. An entire steer was roasted over an open fire. A few neighbors came. The guest list was long, and included Peter and Treena, Jeff and his wife and two children. Loretta and Annie came, and so did Gretta and Sam. Annie knew the truth now and understood her real mother's sacrifice. Cole rode in for the affair, and he and Gretta announced they were getting married, which brought rousing cheers from everyone.

Randy started out of the house with another pie in her hands just as Jake came from the upstairs bedroom. He walked up to her and grabbed her from behind before she could get out the door, making her let out a little scream. With the pie in her hands, she couldn't stop him from moving his hands over the square-cut bodice of her dress.

"Jake Harkner, do you know how many people are out there? Get your hands off my breasts."

"But I love these babies."

"And between three weeks at that line shack and what just went on upstairs this morning, you should be able to keep your hands off of me long enough to welcome everyone and sit down and eat."

"You taste better than any of the food."

Randy turned her head and looked up at him. He met her mouth in a deep kiss, gently squeezing her breasts at the same time. Randy grinned and wiggled away from him. "Stop!"

"Hell, you shouldn't have worn yellow. You know how I like that dress on you. And look at you—all filled out again in all the right places. It's nice to hold a woman with some flesh on her bones and all kinds of soft things to grab hold of."

Randy whirled around in a teasing dance move. "You'll have to save the grabbing for later." She hurried through the screen door just as Gretta was coming up the steps to get more pies. She stopped in front of Jake.

"You know, big guy, that if the light is just right, a person can see right through that screen door. It appears you've healed well."

Jake grinned. "Damn right." He leaned down and kissed her cheek. "A man just needs the right motive to get well."

"Mmm–hmm. And your wife seems very happy."

"I aim to please."

"I'm sure you do." Gretta laughed and walked past him to retrieve more pies. Jake walked out onto the veranda and limped down the steps to join the others.

Everyone sat at the huge length of tables, sixteen different conversations going on at the same time. Even Katie's parents were there, having moved from Oklahoma to take up residence and help out on the J&L.

It was a great relief for Lloyd and Katie, who needed their help with the children. Jake considered Katie's parents two of the nicest, most unselfish people he'd ever known. He had the men build a cabin for them and liked to joke that if any more people came to live on the J&L, they would simply create their own little town right here. *Harkner Acres, we'll call it*, he told everyone.

He still could not quite get over the fact that all of this was because he'd fallen in love with a woman from Kansas almost thirty-three years ago and bedded her one wild night in a covered wagon. His life had never been the same since.

Evie prayed and sang Amazing Grace, everyone's favorite hymn. They ate…and laughed…and ate… and laughed…and Jake enjoyed teasing Katie into deep blushes, one of his favorite pastimes.

By then, Jake had made all the headlines. *Jake Harkner, America's Last Outlaw, Escapes the Hands of Death!* Articles explained how he was saved by an old Mexican healer, a man he would probably never be able to find again if he tried…a man Jake personally believed was sent by God in answer to Evie's prayers.

Randy sat down next to Jake, and they held hands—often. They kissed—often. They shared looks of desire—often. Not long after he first returned, they'd spent over three weeks at the line shack, making love and making love and making love, some of it quite disrespectful.

Jake's leg had healed more, becoming a bit less painful, but he feared the pain would never truly go away, and he would always have a limp.

Before dessert was served, Sadie Mae came to sit on Jake's lap. She showed him an egg she'd snuck out of the chicken coop, but in the next instant, Outlaw appeared between Jake's legs and snatched the egg right out of her fingers, then ran off.

"Sadie Mae, what just happened?" Jake asked her with a frown.

She whispered in his ear. "I gave the egg to Outlaw. Don't tell, 'cuz Mommy said I'm not s'posed to feed him chicken eggs." She covered her mouth and giggled.

"You sure do like secrets, Sadie Mae."

She nodded her head vigorously.

"I have a secret too," Jake told her. He whispered in her ear. "When some bad men were hurting Grandpa, I saw a chicken right in front of me. And I said, *Jake, that chicken must be little Sadie Mae, come to help you and make you feel better.* So you were right there, Sadie Mae, and you helped Grandpa feel better."

Sadie Mae hugged him around the neck and kissed his cheek. "I'm glad, Grampa. I don't want you to hurt."

A buggy appeared over the rise, and Terrel rode in.

"There's a woman comin'," he told Jake. "Calls herself Dixie, and damned if she don't look like a… You know, one of them women."

"Dixie?" Jake grinned and glanced at Lloyd. "Dixie James is here!" He looked at Randy. "How in hell did Dixie know about this?"

Randy grinned. "Because I wrote to her and invited her."

Jake rose and handed Sadie Mae to Randy, leaning down to kiss Randy when he did so. "That was damn good of you."

"Yes, well, just remember who you belong to. We have two prostitutes here who are both crazy about you."

Jake laughed. "Woman, I've always known who I belong to."

Lloyd grinned and rose to watch the buggy come in as Jake walked out to greet Dixie before she reached the house.

"Who's Dixie James?" Gretta asked.

"Let's just say you and Dixie have a lot in common,"

Lloyd answered with a grin. "She's from our lawman days back in Guthrie. You know Pa. He has a natural gravitation."

Gretta let out one of her loud guffaws. "I think it's the other way around," she joked. "The *women* gravitate toward your *father*."

Jake limped to the buggy, and in the next moment, a buxom, blond woman in a pink dress was in his arms.

"Dixie! My God, you came all the way from Guthrie?"

"They do have trains now, love." She laughed as Jake whirled her around. "I wanted to see for myself that Jake Harkner really did still live and breathe," she told him. "Besides that, I always wanted to see this ranch I've heard so much about and see my favorite outlaw and that gorgeous son of yours."

Jake set her on her feet. "You're as beautiful as ever."

"Me? How about you? My God, don't you ever age?" Dixie asked. "It's been years. Hell, I thought I'd come here and find a crippled old man."

"I *am* a crippled old man!"

"Not from what I'm looking at." Dixie ran her hands over his chest and arms. "You haven't changed one bit. And here I was feeling sorry for you."

"Don't be feeling sorry for the likes of me," Jake laughed. "I have a bad right hip and a bum left leg, but I'm alive and here with my family and friends." Jake grabbed her close to plant a kiss smack on her lips. "Come and meet Gretta MacBain. You two have a lot in common."

"I'll bet we do!" Dixie kept an arm around his waist and let Jake lean on her shoulders a little as they walked to the tables, where some just stared and shook their heads as Jake introduced Dixie and Gretta.

"Good God, Dixie's damn right," Lloyd said, shaking his head. "He *hasn't* changed one bit. Not even a little."

Randy stood up with Sadie Mae in her arms. "The

man hasn't changed, Lloyd," she answered, smiling as Jake introduced Dixie to the men. "It's the boy inside that has changed. That boy is happier now. That dark place down deep inside is gone."

They all enjoyed a long afternoon of eating and visiting and celebrating.

Inside the house, Jake's guns again hung where they always had—over the front door...just in case.

Author's Note

This is supposed be the last book in my Outlaw series, but never say never. Jake's legacy will go on…in Lloyd… and in Little Jake. Maybe someday I'll write a fifth book about Jake. I truly don't want to leave this man or his family, and I have thoroughly enjoyed writing every one of these stories and watching Jake grow from an abused little boy turned outlaw turned lawman, and finally, a settled rancher and family man. What's more, this deeply troubled man learned how to give and accept love…and how to finally be free of his past. And one woman led him through all of it. There is nothing better or more fulfilling than to read—or to write—a great love story. This has been one of my very favorites. The Harkners have lived in my heart for years, and I will never be able to truly let go of these characters. I hope it's the same for my readers. As a finishing touch to this story, be sure to read my Christmas story about the Harkners in "A Chick-A-Dee Christmas," coming October 2017 in the anthology *Christmas in a Cowboy's Arms*.

About the Author

Award-winning novelist Rosanne Bittner is highly acclaimed for her thrilling love stories and historical authenticity. Her epic romances span the West—from Canada to Mexico, Missouri to California—and are often based on personal visits to each setting. She lives in Michigan with her husband, Larry, and near her two sons, Brock and Brian, and three grandsons, Brennan, Connor, and Blake. You can learn much more about Rosanne and her books through her website at rosannebittner.com and her blog at http://rosannebittner.blogspot.com. Be sure to visit Rosanne on Facebook and Twitter!